THE FANG OF BONFIRE CROSSING

THE FANG OF BONFIRE CROSSING

LEGENDS OF THE LOST CAUSES

BOOK 2

BRAD MCLELLAND & LOUIS SYLVESTER

SQUARE
FISH

HENRY HOLT AND COMPANY

NEW YORK

▛▜
SQUARE
FISH

An imprint of Macmillan Publishing Group, LLC
120 Broadway, New York, NY 10271
mackids.com

Our books may be purchased in bulk for promotional, educational, or business use. Please
contact your local bookseller or the Macmillan Corporate and Premium Sales Department
at (800) 221-7945 ext. 5442 or by email at MacmillanSpecialMarkets@macmillan.com.

Library of Congress Cataloging-in-Publication Data

Names: McLelland, Brad, author. | Sylvester, Louis, author.
Title: The fang of Bonfire Crossing / Brad McLelland & Louis Sylvester.
Description: New York : Henry Holt and Company, [2019] | Series: Legends of the Lost
    Causes ; book 2 | Summary: In a 1850s Wild West filled with supernatural beasts and
    magic-wielding outlaws, Keech and his band of fellow orphans, seeking revenge for their
    killed families, search for Bonfire Crossing, the mysterious land that holds clues to the
    whereabouts of the all-powerful Char Stone.
Identifiers: LCCN 2018019647 | ISBN 978-1-250-23360-8 (paperback) |
    ISBN 978-1-250-12435-7 (ebook)
Subjects: | CYAC: Adventure and adventurers—Fiction. | Magic—Fiction. | Supernatural—
    Fiction. | Robbers and outlaws—Fiction. | Orphans—Fiction. | Revenge—Fiction. |
    West (U.S.)—History—1848–1860—Fiction.
Classification: LCC PZ7.1.M4628 Fan 2019 | DDC [Fic]—dc23
LC record available at https://lccn.loc.gov/2018019647

Originally published in the United States by Henry Holt and Company
First Square Fish edition, 2020
Book designed by Liz Dresner
Square Fish logo designed by Filomena Tuosto

10 9 8 7 6 5 4 3 2 1

FOREWORD

We would like to express our heartfelt gratitude to the *Wah-Zha-Zhi* Cultural Center and Language Department in Pawhuska, Oklahoma. Without the continued guidance of our Osage partners, who have so generously offered their time and counsel since the beginning of this project, this series would not exist.

Friends, we thank you for your patience and your insights as we tell the story of Keech and his Lost Causes. We will always work hard to honor your culture.

—B & L

PART 1

INTO BLEEDING KANSAS

NOVEMBER 1855

PROLOGUE

Big Ben Loving gazed across the frozen bog and checked his compass.

Heavy days on the saddle through Missouri had brought him to the eastern edge of Kansas Territory, a lonesome track of rolling prairie that teemed with giant foxtail weeds. The late-evening sky churned with deepening shades of purple and gray. A blustery wind drove across the hushed plains, battering his cheeks.

Returning his compass to his coat, Big Ben spurred his bay mare and tramped across the bog to the western bank of a slow-moving stream. He dismounted and stretched a thorny ache out of his back. He glanced around the low sandstone hills, sensing his attendant was near, but nothing stirred on the prairie except the brown grass.

Big Ben estimated fifty more miles to ride before he reached the garrison. He desired a short rest before traveling on. He searched the area for a suitable campsite, a place near the stream where a fire wouldn't be visible. A sprinkle of snow fell from the purple clouds, an unnatural shift in the weather that brought a smile to his face. The flakes gathered on the flat brim of his hat, and when he turned his head, the snow shook free and salted his red beard.

He found a clear spot beside a mulberry tree, a good place to settle the horse and prepare her protection. The creature who traveled behind him did his bidding, but its bloodlust couldn't be trusted in the dead of night. Big Ben had woken before to a slaughtered horse.

He tied the mare's reins to a drooping limb, then retrieved the large pigskin pouch of bloodroot from his saddlebag. Out of habit, he let his fingers graze the other pouches nestled inside the bag. He rarely needed to open those pouches, but Big Ben yearned for the day when he could use each of his conjurings, particularly the Marsh Bane, a concoction he had brewed to be especially wicked. It was the stuff of nightmares for those unsuspecting men who were foolish enough to cross rivers infested with the brew.

Big Ben dipped his hand inside the pigskin pouch, scooped out a handful of red powder, and proceeded to spread the bloodroot in a broad circle around his bay and the mulberry tree. The horse looked on, accustomed to the routine.

The day's light disappeared over the horizon, and the plum sky turned the color of spilled ink. His small campfire blazing, Big Ben placed his saddle on the ground, leaned back against the seat, and hummed a cowboy tune.

He sniffed the air. Something gamy rode the wind, the barest scent of rotten meat. Near the mulberry tree, his horse nickered in fear.

His attendant had arrived.

Big Ben called out to the darkness. "Come closer."

Silence returned his command. A sense of reluctance tugged at his mind.

"Obey me, beast." Big Ben peeled off his gloves. He pressed a finger to the spiral mark that had been charred upon his other palm. The Reverend's Prime stirred within his hand, his arm, his entire body, then gripped the mind of the thing waiting in the dark. There was a wounded cry.

Big Ben said, "I've a job for you."

A jagged claw scraped across a nearby tree—*skritch scratch*—and the creature approached the cold fringe of the camp.

Big Ben searched the dark but saw only the mulberries and the delicate profile of the sandstone hills. Yet over the crackling campfire and murmuring wind, he could hear the hellish rasp of his companion's breath.

"The Reverend has sent us a task, and we shall not fail him."

A low grumble vibrated the night. After years of commanding the creature, Big Ben knew the beast understood his words well enough to obey its master's orders.

"An enemy is moving west. Five children," Big Ben said.

The grumbling grew louder as the creature stalked closer.

"There is a boy among them. An important boy. Bring him to me." Big Ben pulled a piece of brown wool cloth from his overcoat and tossed it over the protective barrier. "This rag carries the scent you need. Kill the other lambs if you wish, but bring the boy to me alive and unspoiled."

The figure slipped through the shadows and sniffed at the rag.

"Now go."

A guttural growl followed the sound of soft padding, as if a wolf had suddenly run past him and dashed away into the frozen night.

Big Ben Loving finished humming his tune and settled in for the night's rest. Tomorrow, Coward was expecting him at the garrison.

There was much work to do.

CHAPTER 1
THE TRACKER

Keech Blackwood knelt beside a plump cottonwood tree, inspecting two small dips in the frozen soil. They were shaped like bowls and sat a few inches apart, each covered in leaves and brittle twigs. One hollow was larger than the other, and when Keech ran his palm over the dirt cavities, he realized a short tunnel connected the two dips below the ground.

He grinned in admiration.

The November day was standoffish with cold. Pockets of light snow and ice dappled the Kansas forest—a decline in the weather that felt too early for these parts. A heavy mist clung to the hills, turning the region ghost-pale.

Tethered to the cottonwood, Keech's pony, Felix, blustered at the cold. Keech pointed to the ground with a smile. "Felix, do you know what these holes make? A Dakota pit."

The pony gazed off into the woods, unimpressed.

"I haven't seen one of these in a long time."

Keech poked his finger down into the dirt and felt the void of the little tunnel. *Read the earth*, his foster father, Pa Abner, used to say. *Let it tell you its story.* The history here was blurry, but one tell-tale sign was clear: Whoever had filled these holes had done it willy-nilly, sliding the dirt back in with the side of one foot.

"Something interrupted you," Keech murmured, envisioning the traveler standing here. "You didn't want to leave your camp, but you had no choice."

He peered around the campsite for signs of quick passage. There were none, not even horse tracks. Disappointed, he returned his scrutiny to the indentations.

"You were sloppy to fill the holes too quick, but smart enough to erase your prints. And crafty enough to build a Dakota pit in the first place."

Those who knew of Dakota fire pits understood they had two purposes. They concealed the traveler's firelight below the ground, and their tunnel-and-vent design left no rising smoke for enemies to see. Keech had learned to build one five years ago, when he was only eight. His orphan brother Sam had been seven. Pa Abner had taken them on a two-week hunting trip up to Nodaway country. The first week, Pa had taught them how to build the fire pit and how to cook small game. The following Sunday, he instructed them to leave no sign of their camps, then left them alone for five days in the wilderness to practice. The excursion had pushed Keech and Sam to their limits, but after the week was done, Pa rewarded them with a sackful of Granny's homemade peanut brittle and a special campfire recitation of Edgar Allan Poe's "The Raven," one of Sam's favorite poems.

The memory warmed Keech's heart. It was nice to see Sam's face in his mind again. The past few days he'd been trying to remember every little tidbit about Sam—as well as Granny Nell and the others,

Robby, Little Eugena, Patrick. He'd also been trying to cherish all the memories he could of Pa Abner, whose real name, whose Enforcer name, had been Isaiah Raines. Forgetting the family that Bad Whiskey Nelson had murdered would be easier than suffering alone in their haunting memories, but Keech knew he could no more forget their faces than stop breathing.

A fierce breeze rustled around the cottonwood, fluttering Keech's dark bangs. He tucked the hair back into his bowler hat and returned his focus to the buried camp.

"Could be the Kickapoo," he said to Felix. The Kickapoo tribe resided on lands not far from here, and they would be careful not to build fires that the harsh Kansas winds could sweep across the hills and plains.

Widening his sweep of the ground, Keech realized it wasn't the Kickapoo. Whoever had built this fire pit had slipped up, leaving a clue: a heel print at the base of the cottonwood. The heel was from a large boot, not a moccasin.

"Maybe this print belongs to Red Jeffreys," Keech said.

Red Jeffreys was the Enforcer who had apparently stolen the Char Stone from the grave of his mother, Erin Blackwood, in Bone Ridge Cemetery. In the Stone's place, the thief had left a peculiar trinket in Keech's mother's hands—a child's figurine with a carved wooden head, a doll Keech now carried in his coat pocket.

Before dying, Pa Abner had told Keech that a devilish fiend known as the Reverend Rose had now set his dark sights on this Jeffreys and that Rose wouldn't stop hunting till his gang of killers found the man and retrieved the Stone.

What Rose wanted with the Char Stone was still a mystery, but Bad Whiskey had claimed it would thwart damnation itself. *The*

Reverend took my soul, the one-eyed scoundrel had said. *He brought me back, but left me empty. The Char Stone's the only thing that can save me.* All Keech knew was that the Stone was cursed and should never be touched. Pa Abner had been clear about that.

"Blackwood, get over here! You need to see this!"

Keech peered through the woods to where his new friend Cutter was crouching beside a maple tree. John Wesley hunkered behind him. Both boys were intently studying the ground.

Keech moseyed over to his trailmates. As he moved toward John Wesley's chubby gelding, Lightnin', the horse pinned his ears back and released an angry snort. "Hey now, take it easy," Keech said under his breath. "Be a good boy." They were not on the best of terms, he and Lightnin'. Whenever Keech approached the horse, the ornery beast would spin his behind toward him, as though aiming to kick his head off. This time, Keech made sure to walk an extra foot away.

Neither boy looked up when he approached. Cutter had scored a large circle in the frozen mud with his bone-handled knife, the blade he liked to claim was magic. His palomino mare, Chantico, waited nearby, watching her master work while she chomped on stiff grass.

"About time, Lost Cause." The dusty clothes Cutter wore made him look bronze, almost statuesque, in the midday light. He would have blended almost perfectly with the Kansas forest if it weren't for his light blue neck bandana and the red silk sash tied around his waist. Though his real name was Miguel Herrera, he preferred to be called Cutter on account of his wicked blade.

"I was occupied. I found a strange campsite."

"Hang your campsite." John Wesley jabbed his finger at the

knife circle in the mud. He was a heavyset boy, nearly six feet tall, and one of the unluckiest people Keech had ever met. If a piece of a plan went off-kilter, John Wesley usually bore the brunt of the mishap, such as the time in Missouri when he almost drowned in the Little Wild Boy River. "Tell us what you make of *that*."

Inside Cutter's knife circle lay a large paw print, strange and deformed. There was only one print where Cutter had drawn his boundary, but when Keech glanced ahead, he spotted a second marking, emblazoned in a thin patch of snow. "There's another."

"We saw it," Cutter said.

Keech knelt beside his companions to get a closer look. "This track isn't natural."

A less experienced tracker might have assumed the print belonged to a coyote, or perhaps a large red fox. In a sprint, both animals left a four-print pattern, with visible claw marks on the front two toes. This was no fox or coyote paw print. It was far too large.

"I've never seen anything like it," Keech said. "The footpads have the markings of a canine, but the toes split up the middle, like a deer's hoof."

Cutter and John Wesley scowled at the print. Both were superstitious boys, prone to anxiety about midnight ghosts and boogermen. After all the young riders had witnessed in Missouri—dead men rising from their graves, Bad Whiskey speaking through the mouths of his thralls—Keech reckoned they were entitled to their fears.

Cutter frowned. "Maybe an oversized wolf got caught in a trap." But he didn't sound convinced.

"A mangled paw would leave traces of blood and fur." Keech glanced around the forest floor, hoping for more tracks. Sure enough, a little beyond the second track lay another run of prints where the animal had apparently dropped to lope on all four limbs.

Then, *nada*.

"This doesn't make sense."

"Nothing's made sense since we met you," John Wesley said.

Keech straightened and balanced on his left foot. "It's like the animal stopped here and rose to one paw," he said, reenacting the image he saw in his mind. "Then leaped to the other paw, like this"— he hopped toward the second track and landed on his right foot— "then dropped to all fours. But where did it go afterward?"

"I think I know," Cutter said, and pointed up at the forest canopy.

"The trees," Keech said. "It jumped into the trees." The cottonwoods and maples were dense in this area, forming white spiderwebs of icy boughs and branches.

Cutter and John Wesley backed away from the track. "*Shifter,*" Cutter whispered, and crossed himself with his blade. Keech shivered deeply at the sound of the word. He hadn't heard mention of Shifters in a long time, not since Pa Abner's campfire tales from years back. Whenever Pa spoke about them, he would do so with a hushed tone of respect. *There are things in this world we sometimes won't understand, but that doesn't mean we shouldn't appreciate them*, Pa said. *Revere all creatures, because each holds a vital place in the world.*

Cutter heaved a nervous sigh. "When I was a kid, *mi mamá* used to tell me stories at bedtime. The tales that scared me the most were about the Shifters from another world, the monsters that could turn into dogs and wolves and roam about in the moonlight."

"That don't sound like a bad life," said John Wesley. "Think of all the chickens you could eat!" He bumped Keech on the arm and chuckled.

Cutter's face remained deadly serious as he stared at the mangled print. "The thing is, I don't think they were just stories. I saw something like this before, when I was a boy."

"Tracks like this?" Keech asked.

Cutter nodded uncertainly.

"What did you mean 'from another world'?" John Wesley asked.

Keech had never heard tales of Shifters from other worlds; the notion was disquieting, yet intriguing.

Cutter glanced around the forest, then shook his head. "I don't want to speak of Shifters in the woods. Let's get back to camp. We shouldn't be in this forest when night falls."

"I agree. Nothing good comes from the dark these days," said Keech, and he headed back to Felix with extra speed in his step.

CHAPTER 2
SUNRISE ALBERT

The Kansas wind crackled through the icy woodland, turning the trees into angry brutes. Keech pondered the sky with concern. A fierce norther looked to be brewing, driving fresh bundles of snow and ice clouds over the tepid afternoon sunlight.

As the trio rode back to camp, they came upon a deep ravine. The ground fell away at a steep angle, the deep bottom full of dead limbs and mammoth red stones. Felix skirted the chasm with confidence, but Chantico and Lightnin' balked at the sight of it.

"A river must have cut this ravine," Keech said, leaning over his saddle to inspect the chasm's floor. The dried-up gorge appeared to run south for a spell, then veer east. "I bet if we followed it a day or two, we'd reach the Kansas River."

"Ravines are nice, but I'd like to get out of these woods," John Wesley said. Since saving all their lives at Bone Ridge, John seemed to be in loftier spirits. He still refused to speak about his mother's killer, but at least he was riding a little taller in his saddle and joking with the gang. Sometimes, though, Keech sensed that John was feeling more and more apprehensive the deeper they rode into Kansas.

Truth be told, Kansas was getting under the whole group's skin. Since leaving Missouri, Cutter didn't spit the fire and vinegar he usually did, and Nat, the usually unflappable rancher, had taken to constant glances over his shoulder. But it was Nat's young sister, Duck, who concerned Keech the most. She was the kindest, fiercest person he'd ever met, other than Sam, but sometimes in the night, she would wake by the campfire, hugging herself into a tight ball, the corners of her blanket tucked into her mouth to hold a scream at bay. *It's just bad dreams. Everybody gets those,* she said once. *Don't you worry about me. We got bigger fish to fret over.*

Keech understood the foreboding. This whole territory had a foul temper about it, like a rotten child with a toothache. His travels with Pa Abner had never taken him into Kansas, but Pa had sometimes spoken of it as a dangerous place, a harsh region of wildfires and tornadoes and open spaces that could rob a lonely horseman of his sanity.

The trio approached a dense wall of twisted brush and thistle. A narrow fox run meandered through the tangle, and Keech suggested they use it as a shortcut back to camp.

As they plodded in single file down the critter path, Keech's mind couldn't help spiraling to thoughts of Bonfire Crossing, the Osage encampment where Pa Abner and his Enforcer chums had taken the Oath of Memory, the mysterious ritual that had caused them to forget the Char Stone's hiding place. Pa's clues on how to find this Crossing had been rather vague—*Ride west,* he had said, *follow the rivers, the bending trees*—but there were dozens of rivers in Kansas Territory, and Keech had never seen a "bending tree" in his life.

"Blackwood, we got company!"

Every rambling thought fell away at Cutter's voice, and Keech snapped to attention.

A Morgan horse with a black mane stood in the distance. A brown hairy monster sat on its saddle. The beast and the horse lingered on a short hill thinly covered in snow.

"What in blue tarnation?" John Wesley muttered.

Cutter clenched his reins. "Am I seeing things, or is a *bear* riding that horse?"

Keech squinted at the terrible rider. It was no monster; the figure on the hill wore a heavy coat made from the pelts of a brown bear. The bear's open maw wrapped around the rider's head, its fangs encircling the stranger's face.

"Stay ready," Keech said, sizing up the clearing, the forest, their potential escape. "If he pulls a gun, split east and west."

The stranger rode forward a few steps, revealing himself to be a middle-aged man. He raised a large gloved hand in greeting. Keech returned the gesture, keeping a sharp eye on the fellow's other hand.

"We shouldn't stop," John Wesley mumbled.

"We best learn his purpose. We don't want a stranger to our backs if he has ill intentions."

"You're the leader, Lost Cause," Cutter said. "You talk to him."

"Who said I'm the leader?" Keech asked. Nat Embry was the top dog in their crew, and Keech wanted to keep it that way. He had already gotten his brother Sam killed; he didn't want to carry the responsibility of any more lives.

From across the distance, the stranger announced, "Pleasant day, boys!"

Frowning, Keech called back, "Good day, sir."

"A rabble of young fellers in the deep woods," the horseman mused. "Musta run away from yer chores, eh?"

"We're just out hunting."

"Ride closer!" the stranger called. "A life of shootin' prairie hens done spoilt my ears."

"He's baiting us," Cutter said.

"Yeah, he wants a look at our getup," John Wesley added.

"I know." But Keech prodded Felix forward a few steps anyway and said to the man, "Okay, we're closer. Now kindly state your purpose, mister."

The grizzled horseman grinned, revealing chipped teeth. He wore a heavy brown beard that matched his bear pelt, and his eyelids drooped lazily in the sunlight. One of his hands gripped a yellow paper, rolled into a loose tube. He didn't appear to be armed—though he could have been hiding any manner of weapon inside his barbaric pelt.

"I'm a hunter, young feller. Go by the name of Sunrise Albert, on account that I rise like the sun and spread my joy 'cross the world." The man chortled. "You've heard of me, I'm sure."

"Sorry, Sunrise, we never have," Keech said.

The horseman grunted his disappointment. "That baffles me. I'm well known in these parts."

"I'm sure that's true," Keech said. "What brings you out today?"

"Just collectin' for a feller named Friendly. Surely you've heard of Friendly Williams."

"No, sir."

"You ain't never heard of him, neither? He oversees the trade affairs from Atchison all the way down to Wisdom."

Keech nearly reeled when he heard the name of the town. Wisdom was the place that Sheriff Bose Turner told them might hold clues to Bonfire Crossing's whereabouts. Turner had said the lawman there, a fellow by the name of Strahan, knew the Osage folks in the region and might be able to help guide them in the right direction. "This town, Wisdom. How far is it?"

"About a day's ride southwest, as the crow flies. 'Course, the crows in these parts been actin' mighty peculiar the past few days."

The stranger was surely referring to the Reverend Rose's unnatural messenger crows, those dark agents of the sky that had followed the young riders all over Missouri. Since entering Kansas Territory a week ago, the gang hadn't seen any trace of the crows. Yet Keech felt sure they were somewhere up there, watching from a safe distance. Spying for the Reverend.

Keech's fingers crept to his chest, seeking the familiar crescent of metal through the fabric of his coat. Tucked inside his shirt rested Pa's silver pendant, the quarter-moon object that Pa had called "sacred." The magical amulets killed thralls and kept the monster crows at bay.

Keech called to the stranger. "What exactly are you out collecting?"

Merrily, the tracker unrolled the yellow paper. The boys leaned forward in their saddles to read the contents. When Keech realized what he was seeing, a mixture of anger and sorrow squeezed his heart.

The paper was a government poster. A drawing at the top depicted what appeared to be a boy, silhouetted as if he were a mere shadow, running with a bindle over his shoulder. The proclamation printed below the image read:

$300 REWARD!

FOR 1 RUNAWAY

ANSWERS TO OSCAR

HEIGHT: 5 FEET 2 INCHES

WEIGHT: 95 POUNDS

13 YEARS OF AGE, SLENDER BUILD

LAST SEEN WEARING A BROWN SHIRT,

GRAY PANTS, BLACK HAT, AND BLUE SACK COAT

STOLE:

1 FOOD BASKET, 1 PAIR OF BOOTS

DELIVER TO

FRIENDLY WILLIAMS

WISDOM, KS

Sunrise Albert was hunting a person.

Keech wanted to rip the paper to pieces. He glanced at his trailmates. Cutter's face twisted in disgust, while John Wesley hung his head.

Pa Abner had not spoken often about slavery, but when he did, he would shake with rage. He had settled the Home for Lost Causes near Big Timber because the folks in that area held to a higher belief, namely that all people were equal in the eyes of their maker, regardless of skin color. Big Timber even boasted a sign at the outskirts of the settlement that declared A FREE TOWN FOR ONE AND ALL. SLAVERS NOT WELCOME! The people there weren't perfect, but at least they refused to allow hateful men to live among them.

A malicious grin spread across Sunrise Albert's face, giving Keech the impression that a bear was smiling at him. "Y'all should notice that the reward is three hun'ert dollars. That's Friendly's generosity. I'd split it fifty-fifty if'n you kids helped me."

"No one's crossed our path," said John Wesley.

With a tug of the reins, Keech edged Felix toward the western trees, a route that would skirt around the clearing past Sunrise.

The tracker tapped the poster. "Y'all certain ya can't help?"

"We're certain," Keech said. He considered adding that they would never turn over another human being to a hunter, no matter the price. He wanted to cuss the man out, but they weren't equipped for a gunfight, which such words would surely earn them.

"That's a shame," Sunrise said, stuffing the yellow poster back under his bear pelt. The approaching north wind picked up and rustled the coat's dingy fur.

"*Amigos*, we better go," Cutter said.

The boys started toward the western trees.

They didn't get far before Sunrise called out, "Stop right there!"

Keech's breath hitched when he saw a pistol in the tracker's hand. Sunrise must have pulled the sidearm when he tucked away the poster. A foolish oversight, to miss such an obvious draw. Pa Abner had always taught Keech that clever movement of the hands could dupe careless eyes.

"I believe we got unfinished business."

Keech swiveled Felix back around. Cutter drew his long blade as he turned his own mount. Fifty paces lay between them and Sunrise, far enough that a pistol shot was no sure success. But the man could still hit a pony without the need for much accuracy.

"Mister, we're only hunting squirrels," Keech insisted.

"A storyteller, I see."

"We're just riding through," John Wesley said. "Let us pass."

John's words fell away when Sunrise thumbed back the side hammer of his pistol. "Or what? Tell me somethin' useful, boys, or I'll fling a lead ball."

"Mister, don't get your back up," Keech said. "We're telling the truth."

"Nah, I been watchin' you boys. Yer huntin' somethin'. My gut tells me it's my bounty. Or maybe you want to hide the boy and whisk him off to—"

Before Sunrise could finish, a deep crack thundered across the forest.

The tracker's gun hand whipped sideways, and the pistol sprang from his grip. His Morgan reared in surprise, and Sunrise yelped, blood pouring from his gloved hand.

Spinning on their saddles, the boys tracked the source of the gunshot.

Forty yards to the east, a dirty gray hat bobbed over a gooseberry bush. The long black barrel of a plains rifle poked out from the center of the shrub. At first, it appeared the gooseberry bush was wearing the hat and holding the rifle, but then a tall figure pulled the barrel from the shrub and stepped out from his cover.

Nat Embry tipped his hat to the boys, then dropped to one knee to reload his Hawken.

CHAPTER 3
THE BENDING TREE

"You no-good bushwhackers!" Sunrise bellowed, cradling his wounded hand. "I'm a law-abidin' tracker! I got a certified right to my bounty!"

"Shut up, you low-down snake," Keech said.

Sunrise used his uninjured hand to seize his horse's reins. Fighting the spooked animal, he whipped around to the south. He made reckless tracks through the woods, his bearskin coat flapping in the hectic wind. "You'll pay for this!" He disappeared into the thicket.

Next to Nat, Duck emerged from the trees on Irving, her buckskin Fox Trotter. She was leading her brother's matching horse, Sally. The girl's thick woolen coat made her look almost as wide as she was tall.

"We're sure glad to see you!" John Wesley shouted as Nat and Duck joined them in the clearing. "That was a mighty fine shot. Took the hide right off his knuckles."

"Thanks," Nat said, looking proud.

"What brought you out from camp?" Keech asked.

"A spot of trouble," said Duck. "Three cowpokes in yellow face paint. They was asking after a fugitive boy."

Nat rested the Hawken over his shoulder. "They thought we was hiding him in one of our tents. They drew on us. Held us at gunpoint while they kicked down the camp."

"They woulda stole Nat's rifle," Duck added, "but he'd tucked it under some shrubs before they got to us."

Nat turned to John Wesley. "Sorry, John, but they threw your tent and blankets into the fire. I gave them as much mean talk as I could, but the more I spat, the more stuff they burned."

John Wesley loosed a loud huff of anger. "Why *my* tent? What'd I ever do?"

Cutter frowned at his friend. "Don't worry, *hermano*. Tonight you can squat with me."

"How'd you get rid of them?" Keech asked.

"They lit out after they was satisfied we weren't hiding nobody," Duck said. "Rode off west, and we worried they'd find you three."

"I reckon one of them did." Keech hooked a thumb back to where Sunrise had fled.

Freezing wind hissed across his face. Keech shivered and glanced up at the sky. The norther was advancing fast, choking out the day. In less than an hour they would find themselves in a heavy storm. He searched the brewing clouds for signs of the Reverend's crows, but the varmints were nowhere in sight.

Nat said, "We best get a move on. Wisdom ain't getting any closer."

"I vote we find shelter," Duck said. "The sky's awful dark, and that wind's kicking up."

"The longer we take finding Sheriff Strahan, the more chances we got of running into trouble," Nat told his sister. "I don't like the idea of waiting around for those ruffians to come back for revenge."

"We won't find Strahan at *all* if we freeze like a bunch of icicles," Duck said.

"Maybe if we head for the Kansas River, we'll spot a place to hole up," Keech said.

"What about that?" John Wesley pointed through a thin spread of icy woodland to the west. "Looks like maybe there's a barn down yonder."

Although dusk was falling quickly and the wind stung his eyes, Keech could make out a dark blockhouse with a triangular roof standing alone in the wilderness. The building jutted like the prow of a sunken ghost ship against the unpromising sky.

"I don't think we oughta hole up so near those paw prints," Cutter said. "I say we ride at least a few miles."

"What paw prints?" asked Nat.

"A weird critter looks to be prowlin' the area," said John Wesley. "Cutter thinks it's a Shifter from another world."

Nat looked confused.

"You know, a *Shifter*." John grinned. "A man who turns into a bulldog at night and stalks chicken houses."

"That ain't what I said!" Cutter barked.

"Fellas, pay attention," Duck said, snapping her fingers. "That storm's coming fast. Let's just go fetch a peek." She pointed across the distance at the lone building. "If we don't like the look of it, we'll move on."

Nat scratched his cheek. "I reckon it wouldn't hurt. If that barn looks safe, we'll let the storm pass, then head to Wisdom."

"What a bully idea." Duck smirked, rather sarcastically. "Glad you thought of it."

By the time they reached the dirt path that led to the structure, just a few minutes of scant light remained of dusk. Holding on to Felix's cantle, Keech felt a speck of ice tap the tip of his nose. He glanced up at the peevish sky, which had turned the darkest indigo and churned with the oncoming storm. They would awaken the next morning to an ice-covered territory.

"I've never seen weather turn this quick in early November," Keech said.

"The old-timers in Sainte Genevieve always say that when the crows fly low, you best brace for a hard winter," Nat said.

"Makes sense," said John Wesley. "We saw plenty of crows."

Duck held out her hand, palm up to the sky, and a flake of ice drifted down and landed on her finger. "We're outfitted for cold weather, but we ain't dressed for a blizzard. Let's hope we can get into that building."

As the group traveled, Keech kept glancing over his shoulder, expecting Sunrise Albert and his men to sneak up on the Lost Causes and ambush them. They weren't out of the clear just yet.

But all thought of Sunrise left his mind when his eyes fell upon a meadow to their left. A strange growth stood in the center, a short distance off the path. At first glance, it looked like two solid trees standing alone in the field, but when he looked closer, he saw it was actually a single white oak tree with a trunk that split at the base. One thick arm stretched straight into the darkening sky. The other ran away from the base for a few feet, then curved sharply upward, forming a distinct shape, like an upside-down letter h.

John Wesley chuckled. "Look at that twisted, old tree. I wonder what happened to make it grow bent like that."

Hearing that word—*bent*—made a lightning bolt of excitement snap through Keech. "Everyone stop!"

Duck yanked on Irving's reins. "What are you going on about?"

"It's a bending tree! I'd wager a thousand dollars."

Nat hauled Sally around in a semicircle. "You mean like your pa said we should find?"

"It has to be," Keech said, his breath catching into a lump.

"Let's check it out, but hurry. I don't feel cozy dawdling in the open," Nat said.

The horses wheezed bitterly as the young riders directed them off the road and into the meadow. The tall grasses and the sedge were bent sideways here, pushed nearly horizontal by heavy winds and frozen in place by the weather. As the band approached the curious tree, Keech noticed that four white stones surrounded the roots, as if someone had purposely marked off the tree, setting the oak apart from the wilderness. The stones looked smooth and perfectly round, and ice had glazed them.

This is it, Pa, Keech thought. *We found it. We found your bending tree.* Sliding off Felix, he hurried over to examine the twisted oak. "It looks like the bent arm is pointing to the south."

Cutter shrugged. "Does that mean we head that way?"

"Maybe so." Keech reached one of the white stones set a couple of feet from the tree's base. Each stone was no larger than a kitchen saucer, and two of them had cracked in the middle like eggshells. Nature could not have produced such flawlessly rounded, consistently spaced markers. They had surely been designed to sit around the tree like the points of a compass.

The tree itself lingered over him like an old, leaning man with a warped cane. Now that he was standing here, Keech felt shivers tingle his nerves.

He had no idea how this crooked, old growth was meant to guide them, but he felt that if he crossed into the circular space marked off by the stones, his mind would open up and he would understand how to find Bonfire Crossing.

He took a step over the first glossy marker.

No ideas, no understanding. Keech frowned. There had to be a message here, something more than a simple bough aimed to the south. He reached out and touched a finger to the tree's wet bark.

Duck said, "Well?"

"Nothing. I don't get it."

"Well, there ain't no time to figure it out," Nat said. "We're losing light, and like Duck said, we'll freeze to death if we don't go to ground."

As if to prove his point, a few more flakes of icy rain pelted Keech's cheeks. A brilliant shaft of lightning blazed across the sky, illuminating the heavy clouds. A violent crash of thunder rolled across the hillside.

"Keech, we have to go," John Wesley said.

Disappointed, Keech turned away from the bending tree and stepped toward Felix. They were back to where they had started. Except, when he threw a final glance over his shoulder, he thought for one second he saw movement inside the crook of the oak's south-facing bough. A scurrying patch of darkness, unnatural yet somehow familiar.

Somehow, the tree's shadow had *twisted*. Like a snake springing to life.

Keech's eyes must have been fooled by another lightning flash. He mounted Felix and popped the reins. Duck glanced back at him as they all headed back to the path. "Sorry, Keech. It was worth a shot."

He forced the girl a quick smile. "We'll figure this out. Pa wouldn't have sent us on a wild-goose chase."

The young riders veered back onto the road and continued toward the structure, where Keech hoped they could find a little rest and perhaps some peace of mind.

CHAPTER 4

MERCY MISSION

The blockhouse in the wild was not a barn but some kind of abandoned stone church with a wedge-shaped roof. Keech suspected the building's tall oak door hadn't been opened in years.

"Whaddaya know, it's a mission," Nat said.

A dilapidated sign stood on two stilts in the church's weed-choked plot. As the young riders crossed the desolate yard, Keech gazed at the words carved on the wooden slab:

MISIÓN DE LA
MISERICORDIA
EST. 1820
SOBRE ESTA PIEDRA
EDIFICARÉ MI IGLESIA

"My Spanish ain't so good," Nat said. "Cutter?"

Cutter trotted Chantico closer to scrutinize the sign. "First couple lines say, 'Mercy Mission.' The last part's from the Bible. It says, 'Upon this rock, I will build my church.'"

"Not another Bible verse," John Wesley groaned.

"It's from the book of Matthew!" Duck said.

Keech understood Duck's excitement and John Wesley's despair. Back in Missouri, Pa Abner and Noah Embry, Nat and Duck's father, had scattered clues from the book of Matthew all over the countryside. The young riders had discovered one of the verses in Floodwood forest, as well as another engraved on the tombstone of Granny Nell's husband, Abraham. But this was no clue to the Char Stone. This was simply coincidence.

More flecks of ice walloped Keech's face. A moment later, the impatient clouds released a torrent of stabbing needles. Thick pellets of ice bounced off the brims of their hats.

Nat bounded off Sally, ran to the mission's arched doorway, and pushed against its long iron handle. The door didn't budge. He pushed again. There was a jangle as the top of his hat bumped a brass bell dangling over the arch.

"Someone help me!"

Dismounting, John Wesley sprinted over and threw his weight against the door.

"On the count of three," Nat said. "One, two, THREE!"

The two large boys shoved.

With a boisterous squeal, the swollen door scraped inward, revealing a dusty gloom that reminded Keech of the Floodwood bear's cave, deep and dark and full of menace.

Furious bundles of ice pummeled them, followed by a gust of wind so powerful, it made the horses stagger.

"Everyone inside!" Nat yelled.

"What about the ponies?" Duck asked.

"Bring 'em!"

Once the gang had led the horses inside, Nat shoved the heavy door. As he strained, the storm wrenched the oak out of his grip. "I can't close it!"

Keech darted to the rancher's aid and pushed with his shoulder. There was a cavernous *slam!* as the oak met its frame, and the howls of the norther diminished to a low moan. Cold darkness encased the young riders.

For the moment, they were safe.

Still holding fast at the entrance, Nat called to John Wesley in the dark. "John, fetch us a little light, would ya? We need to find a way to bar this door."

"What for?" asked John.

"In case those bounty hunters come this way. If they decide to come looking for us, at least we can make it hard for them to get in."

When John Wesley lit a match from his saddlebag, the tiny orange light didn't do much to reveal Mercy Mission's true size, but Keech could tell its stone walls reached back a good distance. Long, narrow church pews filled most of the room, but otherwise the big chamber looked empty of furnishings. He did spot a tall metallic object standing in a nearby corner. It was an old brass candelabrum, its five points draped with cobwebs. "Hey, that should work," he said.

Duck grabbed the candlestick and handed it to Nat as John Wesley's flame died and darkness refilled the chamber.

Keech heard a loud *clunk* as Nat shoved the five points of the candle tree against the door's iron handle. A second later, the foot of the candelabrum scraped against stone as Nat angled the base down onto the floor, creating a sturdy wedge that locked the main entrance.

"There," Nat said. "Now let's find something we can use for permanent light."

The young riders spread out, searching along the walls. Keech scared up an old lantern sitting on the floor by a church pew. To his delight, the globe still contained kerosene.

After John Wesley lit the lamp, the steady light revealed the mission's true size. Its walls stretched back almost a hundred feet, and above them, cobwebbed rafters pointed up like arrowheads to a shadowy peak. On the opposite end of the chamber sat a raised wooden platform where ministers or teachers had once given their lessons.

"They built their church upon the rock but forgot to build a town for the worshippers," Duck observed.

Despite the chill in the air, Nat's face gleamed with sweat. "Let's take inventory."

The young riders spent a few moments checking their saddlebags. Not much remained of the rations that Sheriff Turner had given them except for a meager loaf of rock-hard bread, bags of salt and pepper, and a couple of sacks of salted peanuts, which they passed around.

Luckily, they still had their most important accessories: the amulet shards.

As Duck placed her crescent charm on the floor in front of her, Keech took Pa Abner's pendant from his own shirt and gazed at the strange markings in the silver. Pa's dying words murmured through his mind: *The amulets are sacred. They can hold the Reverend's power at bay. I shattered the original piece into five. The other Enforcers have the other fragments. Find the shards, Keech, and unite them.*

"All right, here's the situation," said Nat as they all joined together on the floor in a tight circle around the lantern. "I'm low on powder for the Hawken, and our rations are near gone. I can shoot plenty of food for a day or two, but we ought to fetch a supply for the gun pronto."

"How, though?" asked John Wesley. "It ain't like we can just mosey into a store. We're as poor as a buncha toothless coyotes."

"Yeah, Blackwood spent all his pennies in Floodwood," Cutter said with a chuckle.

The kids had taken off their hats and placed them on their laps, and Keech thought they looked like apparitions in the soft light. Maybe they were. Maybe Keech was, too. Maybe they had all died in Bone Ridge Cemetery and Sheriff Turner had sent a posse of spirits off to Wisdom, Kansas, unaware that he had deputized five dead kids.

Keech shrugged off the foolish idea. Ghosts didn't bleed and get hungry. Ghosts got along much easier than the living.

Nat's breath chilled in a white fog around his face. He had placed the Hawken rifle close beside him, prepared for battle should the bounty hunters come knocking. "We'll have to figure something out. If we don't, we're likely to starve."

A deep hush fell over them as the banshee wind raged outside and the sleet banged on the roof. The brass bell on the other side of the door clanged and rattled a hectic melody.

"We won't starve," Keech said. "As long as Cutter's got his blade, I know a thousand ways to fetch us food without a gun. I can make bows and spears."

"Let's hope it don't come to that," Nat said, then rubbed his weary-looking face. "Now, I reckon we should get some shut-eye—"

A loud thudding noise from somewhere in the back of the

church jarred Keech's ears. Every kid sat up straight. Nat's hand dropped to the Hawken and gripped the stock. Duck seized the lantern's handle and swooped the light around the cold darkness.

"What was that?" Cutter hissed.

"Sounded like a boot banged a piece of wood," Duck said.

Nat stood and swung the Hawken's barrel toward the direction of the noise. The gang listened, no one stirring or breathing, but the sound didn't repeat. Keech could hear only the furious whistle of the norther outside and the *jing-jing-jing* of the bell at the mission door.

Cutter pointed to the southern end of Mercy Mission, where the cobweb-shrouded platform stood before the rows of church pews. "It came from that stage. I'm sure of it."

"Let's go take a look," Nat said.

The young riders hurried down the center aisle with the lantern. Going first, Nat kept his Hawken aimed in front of him; Cutter drew his long blade. Keech had scooped up his and Duck's amulet shards off the floor. Neither charm had sparked any sort of unnatural cold.

Standing at the edge of the platform, Duck shone the lantern over the raised wooden floor. The lamplight revealed a tall cross made of dark cedar, fastened to a pair of wooden feet. Next to the cross stood a pulpit, the place where the ministers would have issued their sermons, resting on a wide foundation of pine. Duck flashed the lamplight on the pulpit, exposing a familiar etching on its face:

SOBRE ESTA PIEDRA
EDIFICARÉ MI IGLESIA

"'Upon this rock, I will build my church,'" Nat said. "Same as the sign in the yard."

Duck hopped onto the stage and swept the lantern light around the floor. Handing her amulet back to her, Keech tucked his own into his coat pocket, then searched the platform for clues to the strange noise's source.

"I'd swear it came from right around here," Duck said.

Keech's eyes fell on a couple of long, shallow scratches in the floor, two small channels that resembled claw marks. "Duck, take a gander at this." When she brought the light over, Keech dropped to his haunches and ran a finger over the score marks. "Looks like something got dragged away from here and made these scratches."

Duck followed the cut trails. The path took her to the minister's pulpit. She shone the light down on the bottom, then tilted the lectern away from her, revealing the pointy ends of two rust-red nails protruding from the square foot. "Somebody dragged this pedestal across the floor, but I reckon they didn't realize there was nails on the bottom."

Keech knocked a boot heel three times against the pine. The noise that returned was deeper and more hollow than it should have been, and the sound of it renewed his dread. "John, help me move this pulpit, would ya?"

Working together, Keech and John Wesley slid the pulpit a few feet across the stage, the rusty nails in the base scoring two new tracks in the floor. Beneath the place where the pulpit had stood was a small metal ring fastened to the pine. The ring had been put there, from all appearances, to raise a panel.

"It's a trapdoor!" Keech said.

Nat turned to Cutter. "Stand ready." He aimed the Hawken's

barrel down on the pine door. Cutter positioned himself in a similar fashion, his blade pointed toward the false floor. Duck held the light steady.

"Open it," Nat said.

Keech put his finger through the ring. A bump and a crash echoed up from below them. "Someone's on the move down there." He heaved on the ring. The wooden panel opened, presenting a square of damp darkness. Keech motioned for Duck to lower the light.

The trapdoor had been hiding a stone staircase. The stairs descended at least fifteen feet below the mission.

Steeling himself, Keech planted a foot on the first stone.

A voice bellowed up at him from below: "Hold it right there! Take another step down, I'll make you regret it!"

CHAPTER 5
QUINN REVELS

Keech dropped into a fighter's stance as a figure emerged from the shadows at the base of the stairs—a dark-skinned boy with a lean, rawboned face. He moved with purpose, wasting no time in meeting the young riders head-on. He clambered up a few steps, his teeth clenched, but when his wide eyes caught the glint of Duck's lantern, they blinked in surprise. He stopped, his chest heaving.

Nat stood at the lip of the opening, pointing his Hawken down the stairs. "Don't move a muscle!"

The boy in the darkness dropped back a step, away from Duck's light and the Hawken. "Don't y'all come any closer!" he shouted, but his voice quivered with doubt. His hands were tucked down in the gloom, possibly hiding a weapon.

For Keech, the moment froze like a winter sky as he recalled the bounty poster that Sunrise Albert had shown them. "Are you Oscar, the kid who escaped Wisdom?"

Panic and uncertainty and other emotions Keech would never

understand crossed the face of the boy below. "That ain't my name no more," he said.

"Well, what's your name?"

The boy ignored the question. "I just wanted to sneak a peek. I heard kids' voices and got curious. I didn't mean to scare y'all. I just want to be left alone."

Keech didn't know what to think or how to react. For close to a decade, Pa Abner had trained Keech's body and mind to respond to situations with calculation and control, but now neither his body nor his mind could establish his best move.

His memories slipped back to a cold December afternoon, a few days before his tenth birthday. Pa had taken him and Sam into Big Timber to purchase a Christmas ham from Greely's General Goods. Keech's birthday was the same day as Christmas Eve, so he had been doubly excited for the coming festivities at the Home—till he saw a bearded roughrider stroll into Big Timber on a rugged, slab-sided Appaloosa.

The man steered his speckled mount down the center of Main, rambling at a leisurely pace, but he was not alone on the street. Another person walked a few feet behind the horse, a gaunt man with striking, dark skin and threadbare clothes unsuitable for December. The walking man's shoes were an embarrassment of tatters, and his hands were bound to a pair of rusted iron chains that stretched to a couple of rings on the Appaloosa's saddle.

Keech and Sam watched the procession in horrified silence.

As the bearded horseman passed Greely's, he doffed his hat with a dingy smile. Keech didn't smile back. Instead, he locked eyes with the dark-skinned man in the chains and filthy rags. The fellow trembled in the cold and stumbled a bit. The horseman yanked at the chains, pulling the fellow along. The walker returned his attention to the street, but Keech had seen that his reddened eyes were hollow, full of misery, empty of hope.

A couple of townsmen had stepped out of the Big Timber Drugstore and halted the horseman in the center of the street. *You ain't wanted here*, one of the men told the rider. *Didn't you see the sign? No slavers!*

Apologies, the horseman said, spitting on the ground. *I thought this was a free country, where a man could go where he pleased.* Then the rider led his desolate footman away, disappearing into the wilderness beyond Big Timber.

Back at the Home, Keech and Sam pressed Pa Abner for some kind of explanation. *Those men told the rider to leave town, but they didn't say nothing about helping the man in chains*, Sam said.

Pa Abner looked down at the sitting room floor. *Sometimes you have to pick the best way to stand your ground. The men of the town did what they thought was best for our folk.*

Keech remembered his pa's words now—an answer that had never stuck well in his heart or soul—as the boy on the stairs faced down Nat's Hawken.

Keech backed away from the trapdoor. The jumble in his mind untangled a smidge as he moved, keeping his gaze on the stranger. "Nat, lower the gun."

"We are deputies of the Law. Show us those hands, nice and slow," Nat said.

The kid ignored the command. "You don't look like no deputies I ever saw." He had a pleasant voice that sounded shrewd, though a touch of rasp enveloped the words, no doubt from the wintry bite in the air.

"We're not going to hurt you. You've got my word." Keech raised his hands, palms out, to show them empty. "Nat, put the gun down."

Nat shook his head. "We don't know this kid."

Keech started to repeat his demand, but suddenly a large hand seized the barrel of the Hawken and tugged upward. Keech braced himself for the fierce blast of the gun, but instead of firing, the rifle slipped completely from Nat's grip. Keech and Nat wheeled about, stunned.

John Wesley stood between them, clutching the Hawken. "He said he just wants to be left alone."

"Give me the gun," Nat said.

John Wesley stepped back, out of reach. "Go suck an egg, Embry."

Duck touched her brother's hand. "Nathaniel, calm down."

Nat's face turned a furious shade of red, as though he might explode and lash out with fists, but when his eyes dropped to meet Duck's, he swiveled and walked away a few steps.

Turning back to the kid on the stairs, John Wesley said, "We ain't gonna hurt you, friend. We swear it."

"We're the good guys!" Duck called out.

"Yeah, that's what they always say." The stranger's eyes flicked to Cutter's knife.

"Put that thing away," Keech hissed.

Cutter flipped the long blade through his fingers—a show-off trick he liked to do for new folks he met—and then stuffed the knife back into its sheath.

Keech looked again at the kid in hiding. "My name's Keech Blackwood. My partners and I call ourselves the Lost Causes."

The boy remained frozen on the stairway. Duck's lamplight

revealed a black forage cap on his head, the kind of covering that US Army soldiers wore as part of their uniforms. The stranger frowned. "Lost Causes? What kinda name is that?"

"It's from Saint Jude," Duck said.

"It's the name you take when you're on a deadly mission that's sure to get you killed," Keech added. "We're after a gang of ruffians who murdered our families."

The kid pursed his lips. "I suppose y'all don't look like bounty hunters."

"Heavens no." Duck laughed. "In fact, we scuffled with a rotten hunter just today. A fella who called himself Sunrise. Wore a big bear pelt, all dirtied up and ugly."

"That's the snake who's been tracking me!"

"We were told you ran from Wisdom," Keech said to the kid. "That's where we're trying to get to. There's a person we have to see there. The sheriff. He goes by the name of—"

"Tom Strahan," the boy answered for him, and his eyes lit up. "I know him. He's a friend."

"No way. You gotta be jokin'." John Wesley turned back to Keech, his round face warming. "This can't be coincidence, can it?"

After meeting the others who had been in pursuit of the same outlaw as Keech, he could not believe that mere coincidence was guiding them. Now, finding this young stranger in the wilds of Kansas Territory—a boy who had escaped the very town they were trying to find, a boy who claimed to know the lawman they were trying to reach—sealed the deal for Keech.

Granny Nell had always called matters of good fortune and chance *providence*—as in "Providence wills that you and Sam will be doing dishes today," or "It's pure providence, Keech Blackwood, that you know how to paint window shutters so well"—but Keech knew a much better word for what they were all experiencing: *fate*.

Outside, the Kansas norther raged against Mercy Mission's roof. The brass bell at the front door clattered so furiously that Keech thought it would rip free from the arch.

After a moment, the kid said, "All right, if y'all step on back, I'll come up."

Once the entire troop had retreated, the boy climbed the remaining stairs, then stepped out onto the platform. The light of the lantern illuminated his getup. He wore a pair of muddy gray trousers, a torn brown shirt, and a ragged blue sack coat. His boots were too big for his feet. A man's boots. About the right size to make a heel print near a Dakota pit, Keech figured.

The kid took a few seconds to peer into the dark corners of the mission. Keech liked how he checked his surroundings, peeked into the shadows. He was clearly a survivor. "Y'all have horses?"

"We do," said Duck.

The kid's left arm had been tucked behind his back, but now he brought it forward, revealing a thick wooden rod, a stick as big around as the neck yoke on a wagon. He held the rod out like a club. "If y'all try anything, I promise to put up a mean scrap."

"We won't make any sudden moves," John Wesley said.

"In that case, I'll introduce myself." The boy raised himself taller. "My true name is Quinn Revels. I *spit* on the name 'Oscar,' shackled on me by terrible men. I am the son of George and Hettie Revels, who died in the cornfields of Tennessee. My mama died birthing me, my papa died while hiding me from slavers, and Auntie Ruth helped me escape out west to be a free man. I got a free body,

I got a free soul, and I won't ever wear chains again. Anybody tries to lock me up, I'll kill them dead or die fighting."

After a moment of silent contemplation, Duck stood. "No need to fight, Quinn Revels. You're with friends." The girl smiled. "Now come and sit with us."

CHAPTER 6

THE STASH IN THE CELLAR

The cold air of Mercy Mission made them all shiver, so Keech suggested they build a small campfire in the aisle. "It'll have to be a tiny one," he warned. "We don't want the church to fill up with too much smoke."

"I can help with that," Quinn Revels said. "I'm good at building campfires."

The gang worked together to clear a large enough space to sit in the aisle. They gathered boards from a broken church pew and Quinn built the fire, a perfect construction of kindling and planks that smoldered with very little smoke. After he was done, Quinn sat on his knees before the crackling fire, keeping the wooden rod right next to him.

"All right, so y'all know my name. It's high time you tell me yours," he said.

The young riders went around the circle introducing themselves. Cutter didn't give his real name, Miguel Herrera, but he did mention to Quinn that "Cutter" was a nickname given to him by his deceased friend, Frank Bishop. The gang followed their introductions with a quick recap of the Bad Whiskey situation and the battle at Bone Ridge Cemetery.

Quinn raised his hand as if in a schoolroom. "Y'all mentioned you was deputies of the Law, but you're only kids like me. Were y'all just playing around, or are you truly the Law?"

"We truly are," said Duck, grinning. "A sheriff by the name of Bose Turner deputized us back in Missouri. We don't carry the stars yet, but he promised to give them to us when we returned."

"I ain't sure we're Law in Kansas, though," said John Wesley. "Jurisdiction and borders and such, but I'd have to consult a book on it."

"You've never consulted a book in your life," said Cutter, chortling.

"Well, I believe we *are* the Law," said Duck.

"So do I," Nat replied. "And we'll carry ourselves as such. That may be the only thing we've got to get us through this mission."

"What mission?" said Quinn.

Nat tossed a sudden glance at Keech, his frown suggesting he didn't wish to speak openly about their undertaking.

Keech waved an unconcerned hand back at him. "Let's just say our first objective is to find Sheriff Strahan in Wisdom. That's what we're focused on right now."

"Well, I could point you to Wisdom, at least," Quinn said.

The kid started to mention something else, a thought that had puckered his face in concern, but Duck interrupted him. "You'd go back there, even after escaping?"

Quinn loosed a long sigh. "I *have* to head back. Auntie Ruth's still there."

"You mentioned her before," Keech said.

"Four nights ago, me and Auntie Ruth tried to escape Wisdom together," Quinn said. "We ran a good mile from the burg, but Friendly Williams and his men caught up to us and hauled her up on a horse. She hollered for me to keep running. I wanted to stop right there and give myself up, but I didn't. I kept going till I couldn't breathe no more. By the time I was done, Friendly's men was nowhere to be seen. But that didn't make me feel no better." At this, Quinn slipped off his US Army forage cap. "Auntie Ruth is all I got, you see. She raised me as her own in Tennessee after Mama and Papa died and taught me everything she knows. How to stitch, how to swim, how to read the alphabet, how to mend shoes out of buckskin. I've got to get her back, no matter what."

"But ain't Kansas a neutral territory?" asked John Wesley. "Why're you running from bounty hunters in the first place?"

"Don't ever think this territory's neutral," Quinn explained. "This whole place is a dried-up hay bale waiting for a lit match. You said terrible things happened in Missouri?" He paused to look at each of them. "Well, welcome to Kansas."

Keech let a small silence fill the space before he said, "Maybe we can help each other, Mr. Revels. Since we're headed the same way and all."

Nat looked irritated at the suggestion. "We can't just uproot our mission to help a fugitive."

"But it wouldn't slow us any," Keech protested.

"No, Keech. I can't allow it."

John Wesley gave Nat a hard look. "Hang your permission! We're going the same direction. It only makes sense."

Duck quickly changed the subject. "What happened after you ran, Quinn? How'd you end up here at the mission?"

Quinn gazed into the fire. "After I got separated from Auntie Ruth, I spent a couple nights in the woods. I kept on the move since the bounty hunters were about. I knew if I stopped for too long, I'd be a goner. I built a campfire not too far from here when, about two days ago, a mountain man stepped out of nowheres and grabbed me."

"A mountain man," Duck repeated. "In Kansas?"

"Well, I say mountain man 'cause he wears leathers over his clothes and such. He's actually a Texas Ranger."

Keech smiled in surprise. Pa Abner used to tell stories about Texas Rangers and their deeds at the Battle of Monterrey. To think a Ranger was in the territory made Keech's skin tingle with excitement.

"What do you mean, he stepped out of nowhere?" Cutter asked Quinn.

"One minute I'm all alone in my camp, the next I'm in this rugged fella's grip and his hand's over my mouth. I thought he was one of Friendly's trackers, but the man hushed me. Said the Chamelia was near. I'd never heard that word before, but I was sure scared, so I stopped fussing."

The word sent spidery shivers down Keech's neck.

"Then what happened?" Duck asked.

"The fella made a few weird-sounding noises, like some kind of chant," Quinn continued. "We sat there, still as a couple of trees. Then something showed up."

The gang exchanged uneasy glances.

"Tell us what you saw," said Nat.

"It looked—I dunno—like a messed-up bull or buck, but that was only at first. It crept on past not ten feet away, sniffing at the air and flicking its pink tongue. I figured we'd be its supper, but then it stood up like a man and *changed*. It took on the shape of a giant coyote or wolf. Then it jumped into the trees and disappeared."

"I *told* y'all those prints belonged to a Shifter!" Cutter exclaimed. Rising quickly, he began to pace in a nervous semicircle around the fire.

Quinn looked confused. "The Ranger called it a Chamelia, not a Shifter. He said it came from a different place, not our world."

Cutter pointed at John Wesley. "See? I told ya."

John Wesley shrugged. "Whatever it's called, we saw the weird tracks it left. We couldn't figure out what kind of animal had made them."

"Truth is, it didn't look like no proper animal," Quinn said. "More like a demon sent by the Devil himself."

"We shouldn't be talking like this," Cutter said. "We'll invite evil right down on us." Crossing himself, he stomped away from the group to visit the ponies. John Wesley squirmed to his feet and chased after him.

"Don't mind Cutter," Duck said. "He don't like talk of the Devil, is all."

The old rafters of Mercy Mission groaned under the norther's assault, and they all looked up. "That storm's gonna tear the roof off," Nat said.

Quinn rose to his ungainly boots and brushed off his trousers, a fool's errand since the old pants were caked in grime. "It's safer down in the cellar. C'mon. I'll show y'all something."

Duck reached for the lantern, but Quinn stopped her. "You can leave that for your friends. I got another one downstairs."

Keech and Nat followed the boy to the trapdoor on the stage, and Duck brought up the rear. As he led the way down the stone steps, Quinn explained, "After the Chamelia left, the man in leathers brought me to this mission. He told me to hide down here till he came back."

"So he's the one who slid the pulpit over the trapdoor," Duck said.

"He said to lay low, but when I heard your voices, I had to peek and see who it was. I just forgot the pulpit was sitting over me, and it near toppled when I sneaked a look."

"This friend of yours, the Texas Ranger. Where is he now?" Nat asked.

"He's out searching for his trail partner, a fella named Warren Lynch. I gathered he went missing a while back. Mind your noggins. The ceiling's low here."

When they reached the bottom of the stairs, the darkness of Quinn's secret room was almost as complete as the Floodwood cave. Through the murk, Keech detected a strange odor. Oily and somewhat sweet, like a bundle of fruit.

"What's that smell?" asked Duck.

Quinn didn't answer. Instead, he slipped into the frosty gloom of the cellar and fell silent for a moment. Then Keech heard the strike of a safety match, and dull yellow light lit up the hidden chamber.

The cellar was smaller than Keech thought it would be, supported by a low ceiling of wooden beams cluttered with ancient dirt. A disheveled cot sat up against a nearby wall, and beside the cot, a stack of folded blankets and ponchos. A few burlap sacks of horse feed had been heaped on the stone floor, and three flat wooden crates were stacked in the far corner, unmarked. Keech also noticed a large barrel of drinking water sitting by the stairs, and standing in the middle of the room was a clumsy-looking table stocked with sacks of corn and salted beef.

"Glad to see you're well supplied down here," Keech said.

Quinn surveyed the room with a proud face. "The food was here when the Ranger hid me. Some folks in these parts like to help people on the run. They keep the room stocked so anyone can hole up till the trackers have moved on."

"'Upon this rock, I will build my church,'" Duck quoted, clearly impressed at the secret chamber. "Maybe that's why this mission was built in the middle of nowhere, because they had protection in mind when they put it here."

"I suppose so," Quinn said. "I plan to bring Auntie Ruth here when I get her out of Wisdom. We'll rest up before we leave Kansas."

"Where will you go?" Keech asked.

The dull lamplight captured Quinn's buoyant, hopeful eyes. "To the Free States, of course. I want to go to Boston, Massachusetts. Maybe Auntie Ruth could start her very own sewing shop." When he glanced back at Keech, his face went abruptly grave. "Let me show y'all why I brought you down here. C'mon."

He led them across the room to the stack of flat wooden crates and lifted the lid off the topmost box, revealing piles of brownish hay used for packing.

"What's in there?" Nat asked.

Quinn looked at each of them. "I know you don't rightly trust me yet, and I ain't got a reason to ask you to believe what I'm saying. But if we go to Wisdom together, I may be able to help your team more than you think."

"How?"

"Wisdom ain't what you're expecting. It used to be a nice place, but it's changed. You won't be able to stroll into Wisdom and find Sheriff Strahan. He's been arrested. Friendly Williams hauled him into custody not long before I ran."

Keech felt his teeth grind painfully at the bad luck. He had hoped their Kansas operation would be a snap, that the young riders could find Strahan in a matter of days, question him about Bonfire Crossing, then move on to the next plan. But now they had a slaving fiend named Friendly Williams standing in their path.

"So what's your proposition?" Nat asked.

Reaching inside the flat box, Quinn withdrew a black sphere the size of a large onion from the packed hay. The ball sat perfectly in his palm, the surface shiny, as though it had been dipped in oil and hadn't quite dried, but no liquid rubbed off on his hand.

The crate held a few more of the peculiar orbs. The oily, fruity smell was coming from the objects.

"The man who saved me calls these whistle bombs," Quinn said.

"Bombs?" Duck took a cautious step back from the crates. "But they don't have a wick to light."

"I suppose a fire could set them off without a wick, but the Ranger told me when you squeeze them, the insides mix up and you hear a big whistle, then *boom*. Apparently, these here boxes got too wet to be relied on, but he warned if I happened to squeeze one, or get a flame too close, it could still go off. He said if I hear a whistle, I best run for my life."

Sudden clarity struck Keech concerning Quinn's thoughts. "You plan to use these whistle bombs on Wisdom."

Quinn smiled, though his face looked severe. "I'm gonna head back to Wisdom and free Auntie Ruth, then I'm gonna use these whistle bombs, at least the ones that still work, to blow that whole wicked town to kingdom come. You Lost Causes can come with me. I'll take care of my auntie, but I want your help getting Sheriff Strahan out before the fire comes down."

Keech glanced at Nat and Duck, who both looked skeptical.

Nat leaned forward to inspect the contents of the crate. "Your friend, the man in leathers. Does he have a name?"

"He goes by the name of Edgar Doyle. I call him *Ranger* Doyle."

The sound of a heavy thump upstairs jarred their attention.

"What in blazes was that?" Duck said.

Nat dashed back to the stairwell and peered up. "Sounded like a knock."

Suddenly, Keech heard Cutter and John Wesley rush across the platform.

"Y'all need to get up here pronto!" came Cutter's frantic voice.

"Somebody just banged on the front door!" John Wesley added.

They all hurried up the stairs and sprinted to the north end of Mercy Mission. Thunder cracked outside, again and again, a constant pounding that rattled the church's heavy oak door: *thud thud thud.*

Duck grabbed the lantern they had found earlier. "Could it be the storm? Maybe a tree limb banging against the door?"

Keech plucked the amulet shard out of his coat, but the shard failed to register any hints of strange cold or unnatural light. "Whatever's out there, I don't think it's a thrall or a crow."

Duck pulled out her own shard. "Mine's quiet, too."

"Everyone, listen!" Nat said.

The swirling high winds shrieked around the church. Beyond the door, the brass bell jangled wildly under the arch.

The sound at the front entrance came again: *thud thud thud*. The brass candelabrum that Nat had wedged against the entry rattled a bit but remained firmly secured.

Duck held her lantern toward the door. The dull orange light gave Mercy Mission the appearance of a catacomb. "Maybe someone's trying to get out of the storm."

"I bet it's that Sunrise Albert out looking for revenge!" John Wesley said.

"We oughta set an ambush," Cutter said. "Open the door and surprise whoever's out there." He made a long slashing motion with his blade.

Quinn had retrieved his wooden rod during their sprint across the mission and now gripped it like a warrior's club. "Don't y'all open that door," Quinn said. "Just let whoever's out there move on. Ain't no way I'm letting those slavers capture me."

The frantic knocking abruptly ceased. The bell jangled one more time, then a loud ripping noise sounded behind the door, as if the person outside had grown tired of the bell and yanked it straight out of the arch.

"What happened?" Duck asked.

The pounding kicked up again—*thudthudthud*. This time, the door rattled so hard that the candelabrum slid an inch or two across the floor. Nat moved to secure the barricade—but a second later, the portal stopped shaking. Silence overtook the mission.

"Maybe he gave up," Cutter suggested.

"Shhh!" hissed Nat.

The group listened.

Something slammed against the roof of Mercy Mission above

their heads. Dust rained down on their hats as savage knuckles smashed against the building's clay tiles, opening a jagged hole in the roof. An icy torrent of sleet rained down into the chamber.

Through the wound in the rooftop, the leering face of a scaly creature stared down at them. Ranks of cruel, dripping fangs filled its wolf-like maw, and long ears jutted from each side of its head.

"It's the monster!" Quinn screamed.

The hole in Mercy Mission's roof splintered and gave way, and the Chamelia dropped into their midst.

CHAPTER 7
THE RAMPAGE

The creature was unlike any animal Keech had ever seen. It was as large as a man, yet it hunkered on all fours like one of the ugly hyenas pictured in Pa's nature books. Across its shoulders and back, sharp porcupine barbs coated the beast's hide, while scales enveloped its stomach and neck. The beast's long snout and limbs looked hairy with thin spikes.

Keech spotted a seared mark in the exact center of the monster's forehead. It was the same spiral-like brand that Bad Whiskey's stallion had worn beneath its forelock.

The Devil's mark.

"Rose's spawn," Keech muttered, but oddly, no supernatural cold flared from Pa Abner's pendant. Back in Missouri, Bad Whiskey had only to take a step and Pa's charm would wildly spark and stab Keech's heart with ice. Yet now, for some reason, it lay quiet on his palm.

Rearing on its muscled hind legs, the monster rose to a terrifying height of more than six feet. The beast straightened its spiny back. A long shudder ran down its body, and white sleet shook off its head. Crimson eyes that promised death glared at Keech and each of the kids. Its snout sniffed in the direction of John Wesley and Cutter, who were backing toward the horses. The creature's pink tongue wriggled out and sampled the mission's cold air. Then it roared.

"Everyone, steady," Nat murmured.

Panicked, all five ponies bolted from the wall and raced across the mission, battering church pews out of their way as they galloped for distance from the creature. Quinn lifted his oak rod.

"It's a demon!" Cutter turned and scampered after the mounts. John Wesley followed close on his heels.

Snorting and licking the air, the Chamelia pivoted after the two boys. As it whirled, Keech thought he saw the creature's scaly flesh *ripple*, the quills along its spine and shoulder blades ruffling and loosening to become a wild mane of impossible hair.

"What should we do?" Duck called out.

Nat dropped to his knee and set to priming the Hawken. "I just need a few seconds."

Keech considered a mad dash to slam into the creature, but Pa Abner's voice sounded in his mind. *See your opponent clearly.* Keech blinked, followed the turn of the beast's shoulders, and saw viper-quick speed in the creature's movements. Every attack he could imagine would be like trying to wrestle a mountain lion—sure to get him killed.

Let your team contribute to your strength.

Keech saw the lantern in Duck's hand. "Duck, the flame!"

She understood at once and tossed the lamp. It shattered against the Chamelia's shoulder, splashing kerosene and flames down its bristled back. The sulfurous smell of singed flesh filled the chamber. The beast howled. It tumbled to the floor, but flames continued to roll madly across its spikes.

Keech held his shard in front of him like a small shield. Encountering this devil hadn't turned his fragment cold, but he prayed it might work its magic if the silver touched flesh.

Rising on all fours, the creature shook itself like a wet dog, throwing a shower of embers up into the air. The ribbons of flame lashing its hide were a powerful distraction but not enough to stop the beast. Its scarlet eyes locked on Duck, and a deep growl rumbled from its throat.

Nat yelled, "I'm firing!"

But before he could fire the Hawken, Quinn Revels spoiled his aim by charging the creature with his wooden rod. The boy screamed, "Take this, you mangy dog!"

The beast's jaws snapped down on the club in midswipe, shattering the rod into splinters. Flames continued to dance across the Chamelia's shoulders, casting frantic shadows across Mercy Mission's walls.

Sputtering fragments of wood, the Chamelia swiped the back of a hand across Quinn's shoulder. The kid tumbled over a pew and landed hard on the stone floor.

Gunfire thundered through the mission, and a cloud of blue smoke coughed out of Nat's Hawken. The rifle's lead ball slammed the creature squarely in its scaled hide.

The beast barely flinched.

"Duck, toss your shard!" Keech shouted, and he whipped his own pendant at the beast, letting the quarter-moon fragment sail. Duck timed the toss of her pendant perfectly with his. Her shard crashed into the Chamelia's chest, while Keech's struck its forehead, the exact place where the Reverend Rose's brand had charred its flesh.

Both bounced off with no effect.

The smoldering creature hesitated, as if realizing what Keech and Duck had just attempted, and glanced down at the amulet shards on the floor. Amid the smoldering flames, the creature took a tottering step backward. Lantern flames rolled across the Chamelia's back and flared brightly up its neck. A horrible howl escaped its maw, and the beast rattled its head, grinding its fangs.

A battle cry sounded from across the chamber. Keech caught a glimpse of a red sash as Cutter sprang from one of the church pews, leaping at the Chamelia's burning back. His long blade gleamed orange in the flames.

The Chamelia spun to mark Cutter's scream, just as the boy landed and slashed his knife across the creature's back. The beast reared up on its hind legs again and clobbered Cutter's shoulder, sending him spinning toward the eastern wall. Cutter slammed into the stone and collapsed. His knife skittered across the dark floor.

Nearby, John Wesley had plucked up a flaming board from the makeshift campfire. He stepped toward the Chamelia, waving the hot stick back and forth. His legs weren't set well for balance, and his pale face brimmed panic, but the boy held his ground.

"Careful, John!" Keech called. He doubted the boy could frighten the beast, which had endured being on fire for almost a full minute and had shrugged off a lead ball to the gut.

Nat bellowed, "Keech! Over here!"

The rancher had dropped his Hawken and was running with his sister toward the mission's barricaded entrance. "We're sitting ducks in here. We have to get this door open."

The siblings pulled at the five-pointed candelabrum braced against the door, but the pole refused to budge. "It's wedged in," Nat grunted.

"We need help!" Duck cried.

Keech darted over to assist. He grabbed the candlestick, and the trio worked together to tug it loose. The pole's brass foot screeched as it grated across the floor and ripped free.

Nat reached for the door and tried to pull it open.

The candlestick still in hand, Keech turned back to John Wesley just in time to see the creature spring for the boy. John whipped the flaming plank at the thing's head, but the burning Chamelia lunged and knocked him backward. The back of John's head smacked against stone, and he shook his head in a daze.

A turmoil of hoofbeats reached Keech's ears. The ponies were crowding the far corner of the western wall, kicking at the stones in wild fear. Felix was shuffling back and forth in front of the others, darting left and right, as though giving them cover.

Another great roar thundered from the Chamelia.

John Wesley backtracked on his elbows, his face contorted in terror, but the creature had cornered him as a coyote might trap a hen. It reached for him with long claws, grabbing for his leg but seizing a handful of trousers instead. The beast pulled him closer. John Wesley lunged aside. When he did, the claws of the creature raked down John Wesley's hip. A spray of blood splashed across the mission floor, and the boy wailed in frenzied agony.

Keech's stomach twisted. "John!"

Quinn Revels emerged from the secret cellar. Keech was shocked the kid was standing again after taking the Chamelia's blow, but now he clutched two of the black whistle bombs, one in each hand.

Behind him, Duck cried, "We can't budge the door!"

"Get into the cellar!" Keech yelled at Nat and Duck. He spun the candelabrum so that the five-pointed head faced the creature. He touched two fingers to his lips and whistled.

The Chamelia turned away from the bleeding John Wesley and loosed a violent hiss. Embers showered from its shoulders, making it look as if it were dripping fire.

"Over here, you mangy mongrel!" Keech hollered.

As Nat and Duck hurried toward the back end of the mission, Cutter stumbled toward the cellar to meet them, his knife retrieved and back in his scabbard.

The Chamelia leaped for Keech, its dagger claws leading the way. Keech jammed the bottom end of the candlestick against the seat of a pew, anchoring it with the head aimed upward like a pike, then tucked himself low. The creature smashed into the prongs, the metallic points puncturing the thick hide of its chest, and it released a pained bark.

Keech rolled aside as the beast dropped sideways, the metal rod still pinned to its torso. On his feet in a flash, he dashed forward, catching up to Cutter. He threw an arm around the boy's shoulder. "C'mon." They stumbled toward the cellar door.

Just ahead, Nat and Duck hurried down into the underground room. Keech and Cutter passed Quinn, who squatted next to John Wesley. Setting down one of the whistle bombs, Quinn reached for the boy with his free hand. "Get up!"

"I'm *trying*," John Wesley said, struggling to crawl.

Cutter stumbled just as Keech made the platform. "Almost there, Cut. A couple more steps."

"Help John," Cutter said, then staggered a few more feet to the trapdoor, where Nat and Duck waited to help him down.

Keech glanced at John Wesley's hip. Dark crimson had stained his torn trousers. "Can you stand?"

"I-I don't think so."

A ravenous howl echoed through the mission.

Keech looked desperately at Quinn. "If you're gonna squeeze your whistle bombs, now would be a good time."

"I *tried* to squeeze them, but they're broke! So I tossed them *there* instead." Quinn gestured behind him to the place where their small campfire crackled. He had rolled his bombs across the floor, and now they rested in the heart of the flames.

"Oh boy," Keech muttered.

Working fast, they reached under John Wesley's arms and tried to haul him to his feet, but as they lifted, the boy shrieked. "I can't!" John said. "It hurts!"

Two high-pitched whistles suddenly ripped across the mission, sending white-hot spikes through Keech's ears. They sounded slightly different in pitch, like two manic wood thrushes competing to see who could screech the loudest, till both reached the same unbearable timbre.

"You two go first," John Wesley said. "Help me down."

Quinn started down the steps.

Releasing John Wesley, Keech began to descend. "Hurry, John. C'mon."

John Wesley gripped the edge of the hole and stretched his arms down so Keech could grab them. Keech gripped his friend's hands and hauled John headfirst, leading him down the stairwell as he tugged. Standing alongside him, Quinn grabbed the rope handle on the pine door and pulled it over so it could close as soon as John's body cleared.

"You're almost there, *amigo*!" Cutter called up from the cellar. The frenzied trilling of the bombs almost drowned out his words.

John Wesley gripped a step and dragged himself forward. "I made it!" His yellow straw hat sagged on his head.

Suddenly, John stopped moving, as if he had forgotten how to crawl. His jaw unhinged in a look of terror.

Two clawed hands had wrapped around John Wesley's booted ankles.

"No!" Keech yelled. Leaping for John, he pulled as hard as he could, but the boy's arm dragged through his palms.

The Chamelia yanked John Wesley away from the hole. There was a loud squeal of surprise, then the pine trapdoor slammed shut over their heads. John's hat tumbled down the steps.

Cutter launched himself forward, trying to shove past Keech. "John! No! John!" He struggled on the stairs, trying to crawl back out of the cellar, but Keech held him fast.

From the other side of the closed door, the sound of a terrified scream mounted over the furious whistling and tore through Keech's soul.

Then two explosions boomed through Mercy Mission.

CHAPTER 8
THE BROKEN GUN

The Lost Causes sat breathlessly in the dark cellar, staring up at the trapdoor.

For a time, no one spoke. To Keech, the explosive clamor had sounded like an entire mountain had dropped on the platform. He wondered if they had been buried alive beneath timber and stone.

Duck's small voice broke the silence. "Do you think it's dead?"

"I'd be surprised if it weren't crushed," Nat said. "Nothing could've survived that."

A low sob hitched out of Cutter, like an unexpected hiccup. Keech heard him try to muffle any further sounds with his hand, but Cut couldn't hold them back. He began to mumble in Spanish. Keech reached out blindly in the dark, found Cutter's shoulder pressed against a wall, and squeezed. Soon the boy's body took to shaking, the way Keech had trembled when he realized he had sent Sam to his doom inside the burning Home.

At last, Cutter moaned, "We never should've come here! I told y'all we should've kept going. I told you we needed to put miles between us and the Shifter."

The gang looked at one another, but no one responded.

Quinn revived his lantern, and a yellow glow illuminated the chamber. They were all coated in thick dust, their faces gray and dreary. Wiping his eyes, Cutter pushed away from the wall and made his way to the bottom of the stairs, where John Wesley's straw hat sat in the grime. He picked it up and brushed off the brim, then he stuffed it inside his coat.

"We can't just sit here forever," Nat said after a moment. He climbed the steps and pushed at the trapdoor. It lifted a foot before hitting some obstruction. "I think I can fit," he said, then shimmied through the breach. Once he was outside, he said with a low voice, "Half the mission's collapsed. I don't see the ponies. I'm gonna scout. Wait for my knock."

Through the gap, Keech watched Nat's boots climb a pile of wet rubble and disappear. Then Keech lowered the trapdoor. He looked at the others and read devastation on their faces. He wanted to offer reassurances about John Wesley—perhaps he'd survived, perhaps Nat would return in a minute with good news—but he held his tongue. Not long before, Keech had been reveling in the idea that fate was guiding them toward victory. But the haggard look on Cutter's face could no longer abide such optimism. Even Duck, usually the first to offer a sunny outlook, kept quiet.

Quinn finally spoke. "I can't believe I blew it up."

"What do you mean?" Duck asked.

"This mission. It was the only sanctuary for miles." Quinn clutched his forage cap in one hand. "I was gonna bring Auntie Ruth here. But I blew it up."

Keech pulled off his bowler hat and turned it around in his hands, searching for comforting words. "Sanctuaries can be rebuilt," he said, immediately feeling foolish for his feeble attempt at consolation.

"I suppose," Quinn said, but he didn't sound convinced in the least. He slipped his cap back on and looked at each of them with tired eyes. "I'm awful sorry about your friend. Here I am, going on about a building, when your trailmate just died."

"Maybe John got away," Keech said. "We shouldn't lose hope."

A swift triple knock on the pine door above made him almost leap out of his boots. Recognizing Nat's signal, Keech scuttled up the stairwell and raised the panel. Nat's dusty face appeared in front of him.

"It's clear. Everyone out."

"What about John Wesley?" Keech asked. "Any sign of him?"

The rancher looked distraught in the lamplight. "No trace."

Immediate and terrible silence overtook the cellar. Keech glanced down at the others. Cutter brought a pair of knuckles up to his eyes and made those small hiccuping sounds again. "You're sure?" asked Keech.

"I couldn't lift all the rubble," Nat said, "but I gave it the best search I could. He ain't there."

"What about the ponies?" asked Duck.

"Looks like they scattered after the walls collapsed. Powerful lucky they huddled in that back corner, otherwise they would've been crushed. We'll have to round 'em up."

As the gang crawled out of the secret room, freezing air blasted Keech's face, and thick snow tumbled onto their hats and shoulders. He looked around in shock as Quinn swept his lantern around the church. Mercy Mission stood intact on the north and south ends, but the center of the building had been gutted, as if a giant bite had been taken out of it. The high rafters had disintegrated, and the walls had crumbled, creating a mound of wreckage that the young riders had to help one another scale.

There was no sign of the Chamelia or John Wesley.

"The monster must've run off with John's body," Duck said, grimacing.

Keech didn't want to think too deeply about the creature's grotesque reason for doing such a thing. All he knew was that their trailmate deserved a proper burial.

"The norther's died down a bit, but the snow ain't letting up," Nat murmured. "We best round up the ponies." He turned to Keech. "Why don't you and Quinn stay and look for my Hawken. I dropped it after that devil attacked. And fetch a few blankets from the cellar. We'll freeze if we don't cover up proper."

"Be careful. Keep your eyes open." Keech didn't like the notion of the group separating, especially with the Chamelia still on the loose, but Nat didn't need the whole gang to gather the ponies.

Wrapped up in ponchos and blankets from the cellar, Nat, Duck, and Cutter set out into the wilderness to round up the horses, leaving Keech and Quinn to search through the rubble.

Bundled tightly in his own blanket, Keech followed Quinn's lantern light and dug through Mercy Mission's ice-covered wreckage. Through the snow, he spotted a glint of silver and soon uncovered both amulet shards. He slipped Pa Abner's fragment over his neck and tucked it down his coat. He placed Duck's shard into his coat pocket.

"What are those?" Quinn asked.

"Long story. But the quick answer is *magic*. They're magical shards we've used to fight the creatures that have been after us. Didn't work against the Chamelia, though."

"Monsters and magic," Quinn mused. "I feel like I'm living in a strange dream."

They continued to kick through the rubble. Quinn pushed back a mantle of fresh snow with his oversized boot and pointed to a long, broken object lying under a stone. "There's Nat's rifle."

Keech felt his heart drop as he lifted the Hawken from the icy debris. The collapse of the eastern wall had smashed the walnut stock to pieces. A large chunk of stone had also bent the barrel near sideways. The rifle was useless.

"Oh no," Keech said.

"Maybe if Ranger Doyle catches up, he can outfit us with another gun," Quinn suggested, his breath a solid white fog in the lamplight.

Outfit us. Keech smiled at the notion that Quinn Revels would ride on with the Lost Causes, even if only till they reached Wisdom and he rejoined his aunt Ruth. The kid was smart. Most important, the team could use a guide who knew the lay of the land.

"I want you to know, all that stuff that Nat said before—"

"About me being untrustworthy? He meant every word, and you know it," Quinn snapped.

The reply momentarily jolted Keech. "I was gonna say that you're in no danger with us. The gang you need to beware is the Reverend Rose's brood."

As soon as he spoke the name of that mysterious, malignant man, Quinn's features twisted. "You mean the Big Snake gang?"

"Big Snake," Keech said, pondering. That was what Bad Whiskey had called Rose's cursed militia. He had said he was the

Gita-Skog, the Big Snake that consumes all. Whiskey had tried to hide behind the Abenaki word, but Keech hated to use that name because they intended it as a word to be feared. Calling them rotten snakes felt far more accurate.

"So you're telling me *you* know about Rose's killers?" Keech asked.

Quinn made a low whistling noise. "Boy, do I. Not long after me and Auntie Ruth got to Wisdom and settled in, that low-down Friendly showed up with his hunters. He locked me and Auntie Ruth back in chains on account of our skin, locked up anybody else who dared to stand against him, and then he tossed poor Mr. Strahan inside one of his own jail cells. We didn't imagine life could get worse, but a few weeks later, things got downright terrible when the Big Snake showed up."

"I won't call them by that name anymore. They don't deserve to be feared."

"You got no complaint from me," Quinn said.

"Good. Now tell me more. When did they first come?"

Quinn shivered at the cold. "They rode in sometime in late September and took over Friendly's operations. I never saw who led them, but a strange pack of men came along with them, men who shuffled 'round and never talked. Friendly told us he worked for them. They put everybody in chains to work around the town."

A mountain of anger dropped on Keech's soul. The Reverend Rose's murderers had infiltrated Wisdom. "Are they still there?" he asked. The Lost Causes were counting on tracking down Sheriff Strahan—he was their best hope to find Bonfire Crossing. If Rose's outlaws were still in town, that would complicate matters.

"Sure are. They set up shop and started working on something big."

Keech felt his hands bundle into fists. "Did you ever see a big man in a tan coat, with a red beard parted up the middle? That's Big Ben, the fella who killed Nat and Duck's folks."

Quinn pondered the description. "I don't recollect a man like that, but as I said, I never saw the leaders, only the men who followed."

The familiar song of a warbler echoed across the dark landscape, and Keech and Quinn glanced out across the chilled forest. Nat, Duck, and Cutter came riding up astride their ponies. Felix and Lightnin' followed along at the ends of two lead ropes held by Cutter.

Reaching down from Chantico, Cutter handed Felix's lead rope to Keech.

"Thanks," Keech said, putting a hand on the pony's neck. Felix returned the gesture by leaning his head into Keech's shoulder. "Good boy. You're okay now."

Cutter glanced at the rope attached to Lightnin'. "I don't know what to do with John's horse," he told the gang, staring blankly at the braid.

The Embry siblings kept their eyes trained on their saddle horns.

"I reckon we could sell him," Nat said.

"That don't seem right," Duck replied.

"We can't just turn him loose," Nat said. "John Wesley would hate for us to do that."

Cutter said, "I know what to do," and he held the rope down to Quinn.

"Me?" said Quinn, blinking in surprise.

For a second, Keech thought he saw tears bubble up in both boys' eyes. "He needs a good *jinete*. Someone strong," Cutter said.

Quinn seemed at a loss for words, so he simply took the line. John Wesley's gelding balked a little when the boy drew him closer, but the horse settled down when Quinn whispered a few nice words into his twitching ear.

Keech turned to Nat and lifted the piece of walnut stock he was holding. "I hate to break more bad news to you, Nat, but I'm afraid you're gonna need a new gun."

Nat regarded the broken walnut rifle the way a fellow might look upon a beloved pet who'd just perished. Shirking off his blanket, he dismounted Sally and took the busted walnut from Keech and gazed at it. "My pa gave me this gun." He looked up at Duck, but she kept silent. "He told me, 'As long as you carry this rifle, you'll feel me near, protecting you.' I've kept this Hawken near for almost ten years."

"I'm sure sorry," Quinn offered.

Nat pitched the broken pieces back into the rubble. "It don't matter. Nothing matters." He wiped at the corner of his eye.

Keech tried to change the subject. "Good news, though. Quinn's gonna guide us on down to Wisdom."

The rancher only grunted. "I ain't sure we should even keep on."

The bitter sound of defeat coming from Nat surprised Keech. He looked up at Cutter and Duck, but they, too, were speechless.

"I thought we could do it," Nat continued. "We stopped Bad Whiskey. Sheriff Turner deputized us. Even your pa gave us his blessing. Everything was possible. I thought I could lead us on to stop the Reverend Rose. But now John Wesley's gone, and it's all my fault."

"How was this your fault?" Keech asked.

"I led us to this mission and locked us into a trap. It was a foolish move. And at the end, I was so focused on getting me and Duck to safety, I forgot the rest of the team. I wasn't there to save John."

Spitting a loud Spanish curse, Cutter swiped at an errant tear on his cheek. "No, Embry. You don't get to quit. We keep on to Wisdom, no matter what. We need to find Strahan and get to Bonfire Crossing. Keech's pa said we could face Rose's *bandidos* if we got there. That's what we're gonna do. Get our justice for John Wesley, for your folks, for everybody who fell on their path. Make them answer in *blood*."

Nat threw his hands up, frustration shaking his entire frame. "I reckon you didn't hear the news, Cut. Our sheriff is in jail. If we keep on to Wisdom, we'll be placing ourselves in the hands of an outlaw named Friendly Williams and his bounty hunters."

Keech grimaced when he spoke the next few words. "I don't mean to bear more bad news, but Quinn's told me something you're not gonna like. Apparently, the Reverend's gang has moved into Wisdom. From the sound of it, they run the town now."

"I'm afraid it's true," Quinn added.

Nat hauled back and laughed in surrender. It was, perhaps, an even more haunting sound than the Chamelia's howl, for it told Keech that Nathaniel Embry had lost his critical edge. More than ever, the Lost Causes needed their leader, and Nat was unraveling before their eyes. "The jig is up then. Riding on to Wisdom would be hopeless now that we've lost everything."

"Not everything's a loss," Quinn said. He pointed to a bulge in the pocket of his tattered blue sack coat. "I snatched a couple more of those whistle bombs. Maybe we could use them on Rose's killers. You know, if they try to cross us while we look for my auntie and free Mr. Strahan."

"It's a fool's mission," Nat said.

Gloomy silence overtook the group—till Duck stepped down from Irving and pushed up close to her brother, her nostrils huffing fog. She slipped the thick arms of her coat around his middle and squeezed. Nat's stomach pushed against her wide-brimmed hat and shoved it backward on her head, but she didn't stop hugging. As she pressed her face into his shirt, her words came back to Keech as a muffled whisper. "Remember what Ma and Pa used to tell us whenever we got down? 'A person whose chin drags the ground never sees the sunset.' Let's make our folks proud, Nathaniel. Let's find the sunset. It's right there for us; we've just got to look up."

Nat's dismal face became a world of emotion.

"Let's get on to Wisdom and find Strahan," Keech said. "Let's go for John Wesley."

"I'm ready," said Cutter. He yanked his coverings close around his arms. "*Vámonos.*"

Keech fished Duck's amulet shard out of his pocket. "You probably want this," he said to her. Duck slipped the pendant back around her neck and smiled.

Nat wiped his eyes with a trembling hand. "Okay, Lost Causes, let's ride. For John Wesley. We'll travel through the forest, avoid open roads, and be on the lookout for the Shifter. There may be more trackers on the hunt, too." He glanced at Quinn as he spoke the last part. "We'll need to be ready."

A brilliant kind of light appeared in Quinn's eyes. Keech couldn't help recalling the tattered man in chains who had been dragged down the Big Timber street years ago, the man whose eyes had spoken of hopelessness and sorrow. There was pain in Quinn's gaze, no doubt about it. But even more, there was fire and determination.

CHAPTER 9

ABOARD THE *LIBERATOR*

Numbing winds churned from the north and snowflakes drifted across the black sky as the Lost Causes plodded toward Wisdom, Kansas. Thick layers of snow and ice had covered the logging road, but Quinn read the forest well enough to point them south into the wilderness on a furtive route toward the Kansas River. Keech pulled his blanket and poncho close to his body and prayed for a warmer morning.

Before departing what was left of Mercy Mission, the young riders had stocked their saddlebags with the salted beef and corn from the cellar. Duck suggested they prepare a few torches for the next leg of the journey. "Fire was the only thing that slowed the Chamelia down," she reminded them.

"I want a torch for myself," Cutter said. "My magic knife never works, so I want something that does a little damage at least."

Keech grabbed a jar of kerosene from the cellar and worked with Duck to wrap cotton rags around two splintered wooden shafts. They fashioned a pair of passable torches for Cutter and Nat, then soaked the rags in kerosene.

As the young riders started south, Quinn rode John Wesley's gelding. He sat tall on the saddle, his face turned down against the wind. The boy had a calming effect on Lightnin'; the pony rode softly and without a single fuss.

"You're good with John's nag," Keech said, impressed. "He took right to you."

Quinn smiled bashfully. "I never got to touch a saddle back in Tennessee, but after me and Auntie Ruth lit out, I learned on the move. Picked up most of what I know from kind strangers who helped us."

"I'd sure call you a natural," Nat said, tipping the boy a nod.

The torchlight turned the territory's snowy darkness into brilliant portraits of golden trees, gilded leaves, and dancing shadows as the group traveled. In a way, the silence of the deep night was all too perfect for their collective mood, giving the young riders a proper respite to think of the mission ahead and reflect on John's loss. It also gave Keech time to think about the Chamelia.

He rode up to Cutter. "Okay, Cut, I think it's high time you tell us what you know. Back when you first saw the tracks, you knew something."

"Nothing that can help John," Cutter said. He turned away quickly and coughed, but Keech had seen his bottom lip trembling.

"Tell us anyway. You said you saw something as a boy."

"Yeah," said Duck. "Any information can help."

Cutter took a long, shuddering breath. "Back in Culpa, my old village, *mi mamá* used to tell me stories of monsters that roamed the Territories. Things not of our world, she said, but *demonios* that somehow slipped into our lands long ago."

Quinn's eyes widened. "That's what Ranger Doyle said about the Chamelia! 'From a different place,' he said. Your mama must've seen the same thing."

Cutter didn't look comforted. "Maybe. As *mi mamá* told it, the monsters could mimic animals, sometimes even people, and they would sneak into towns and villages at night and leave strange signs that they were watching."

"Did you ever see one for yourself?" Nat asked.

"No, but I saw strange tracks one day," Cutter said, shuddering anew. "They were all around our sunflower garden. After I saw them, I couldn't sleep for weeks."

Cutter's story was deeply unsettling, but another terrible disquiet scratched at Keech's mind. Not once had he felt the amulet's chill when the creature attacked, and the silver hadn't sparked an ounce of light when it struck the thing's hide. He turned to Duck. "Did you feel any sort of cold from your shard when the creature was near?"

Duck shook her head. "Nothing. What do you think that means?"

"I think it means this monster plays by different rules." Keech paused to consider something else, something Duck had said back in Missouri. "Do you remember the first few hours after we met? You told me a story about a monster that ransacked your ranch. A monster that came with the man who killed your folks, Big Ben, and tore down one of your barns?"

"How could I forget." Duck tossed a grim look to her brother, then back to Keech. "But we only heard the thing, we never saw it. Do you think this is connected?"

"Well, I don't reckon it's a coincidence that thing attacked us.

You saw the black mark of the Reverend Rose on its forehead. Just like the brand on Bad Whiskey's horse."

"We shouldn't speak of these evil things," Cutter croaked. His hand had crept back to the handle of his knife and gripped the carved bone.

Quinn gestured to the blade. "You shouldn't be worried if that knife is magic as you claim."

Nat chortled. "That pigsticker did no more good than those silver charms."

"This knife *is* magic," said Cutter. "My *amigo*, Bishop, told me a prophet spoke about it."

"A prophet?" Keech said. "You never mentioned that back in Missouri. You just said it would kill *El Ojo*."

"And it didn't," finished Nat.

Cutter opened his mouth to keep speaking, but then he closed it, as though he was holding something back, opting to glower instead. The hand gripping the bone handle returned to his reins.

The company fell into another dreary silence as it continued through the frigid night.

As Keech watched the flickers of light on the frosty oaks, his eyelids began to grow heavy. To keep his eyes open, he asked Quinn to tell them more about his aunt Ruth and how they'd come to know Tom Strahan. The rest of the riders steered their ponies closer to listen.

"I was nine years old when she took me out of Tennessee," Quinn began.

"Nine?" Cutter said. "How long does it take to travel across a couple of states?"

"Long time when you're on foot. Near four years all told. But

Auntie Ruth's the smartest person on Earth and kept us hid the whole time. Not only did she get me to Kansas, she also taught me all the skills I'd need to make it on my own."

"Four years is a long time to run," Keech mused.

"Thing is, I never noticed the time. Took us two years to get across Arkansas—for a while we kept house with a good family, even spent months holed up in some abandoned shack—but to me it felt like the blink of an eye. Auntie Ruth made the whole thing feel like a big adventure. She'd tell me the story of the *Odyssey*, how the Greek hero in that old yarn took a full ten years just to get back to his island."

"Our ma used to read us that story," Duck said happily. "Did you ever read the first one, about Helen of Troy?"

"Naw. But me and Auntie Ruth did sing parts of the *Odyssey* back and forth to each other." On this, Quinn began to sing in a lilting voice that Keech considered angelic:

> "*Tell me, O muse, of that ingenious hero*
> *Who traveled far and wide*
> *After he sacked the famous town of Troy.*"

Quinn stopped singing and chortled. "That probably ain't how the Greeks used to tell it. We just made up that tune for fun."

Keech smiled. "I used to sing to my orphan brother, Sam. He liked my cowboy songs. He would tell me stories from the Bible; I'd sing him tunes about cattle drives and outlaws."

"Mr. Strahan knows a cowboy song or two," Quinn said.

"How'd you meet him?"

"He found us down the Kansas River, running from a mean

pack of border ruffians. Auntie Ruth was sick with a bad fever. He took us on to Wisdom and nursed her back to health. Put us up in his own house for a spell. One day he moved us to our own cottage. Auntie Ruth made curtains for the windows, and Mr. Strahan would come to visit and cook us supper. 'Course, this all happened before Friendly Williams and Rose's gang."

Cutter said, "Those *bandidos* do have a bad habit of ruining a good time."

Nat huffed. "You sure said it."

"But the likes of them won't stop us from reaching Bonfire Crossing," Duck piped in.

Quinn fell silent for a moment. Finally, he said with a curious tone, "Bonfire Crossing. I've heard of it before."

Keech and Nat pulled rein so quickly, their horses' hooves skidded a few inches over the ice and snow. Keech looked at Quinn, whose face glowed a vivid amber in the torchlight. "How'd you hear of Bonfire Crossing?"

"From Mr. Strahan. I heard him talk with another man about it once. He mentioned Bonfire Crossing by name. 'If I could take you right to it, I would,' he told this fella. 'But I can't find it no more.' Then he said something about a bent-over tree."

"A bending tree!" Duck exclaimed.

"That's right," Quinn said, his face turning more curious by the second.

"We saw a strange bent tree just before we got to the mission," Keech said. "It was standing by itself in a field with four white stones around the roots. Did you ever see it?"

"No. It was dark the day I got to the mission," Quinn answered.

Sally's hooves crunched through snow and ice as Nat hauled the mare a few steps closer. "Quinn, it's important you tell us every-thing you can remember."

"Well, I only overheard the talk. I didn't even see the man Mr. Strahan was talking to. I was standing outside, and I just heard voices."

"What else did Strahan say?" Keech asked.

"There was talk about a fang. It didn't make sense."

"A fang from the Chamelia?" Duck asked.

"I ain't sure. The fella in Mr. Strahan's house must've been look-ing for it, 'cause Mr. Strahan said, 'If this fang is so important, I do hope you find it.' And the other fella said, 'I *have* to. It can't fall into the wrong hands.'"

Keech mulled over the story. "It must be some kind of weapon."

"Maybe so," Nat said. "What do you think, sis? Did you ever hear Pa mention a fang?"

But Duck didn't answer. She stepped off Irving and slogged her way toward a nearby thicket, a narrow stretch of dogwood that looked almost terra-cotta in the yellow torchlight.

Keech hopped off Felix. "Nat, borrow the torchlight for a sec?"

Nat handed his torch down, and Keech followed Duck to the brush. The warm glow of the flame cast long shadows over the white forest. Just ahead, Duck knelt to examine a bare dogwood limb. When Keech caught up to her, he noticed that a few of the branches had been snapped.

Cutter's voice called to them from the horses. "What are y'all doing over there? Hunting rabbits?"

"A big animal came through here," Duck shouted back.

Keech leaned in closer with the torch and noticed something dark on the broken offshoots. A quick sniff sang coppery in his nostrils and told him the liquid was blood. He swept Nat's torch around the area.

"Do you think it was the Chamelia?" came Quinn's voice, just behind them now.

"Ain't sure," Duck said.

After nothing obvious turned up in the torchlight, Keech stopped straining for clues and allowed the land to speak. The recent snowfall had covered the ground, but a subtle divot in the way the icy blanket lay revealed that something had been dragged through the area a short time earlier.

A few careful steps to the south brought Keech to the base of a blue ash. All four of the others had fallen in behind him, but he squeezed them out of his vision and focused on the tree. He noticed a narrow smear of blood, darker than ink and still moist but freezing quickly to the bark. Just above this smudge, a series of ragged holes punctured deep into the wood, as though a carpenter had scaled the tree some six or seven feet and driven in clumsy nail pits.

He handed Nat's torch back to him so he could point with both hands. "I think the Chamelia dragged John Wesley's body through *here*." Keech indicated the path. "What's mighty peculiar is, I think it pulled him *up this tree*." He gestured over his head to the blood streaks. "The holes in the bark tell me the Chamelia had one hand on John, the other on the tree, clinging to it with its claws. The back feet dug in here, and here, see?" He motioned to the rough progression of holes.

"You mean that thing's up in the *limbs*?" Quinn backed away.

"I doubt it," Keech said. "These tracks are half an hour old, at least. I bet it's long gone."

"Why would it carry John Wesley up a tree?" Cutter asked.

"Maybe it spotted something it didn't like and skedaddled into the branches for cover," Duck said.

"It looks to me like this thing's on a clear path to the river," Keech said, then got a sudden, terrible thought. "Do we really want to be tracking it without proper weapons?"

"Least this way, we know its general where'bouts," Duck said. "Better than losing sight of the beast and having it ambush us."

"Good point." Nat glanced back at the ponies. "Let's get going. It'll be light soon."

They rode for another half hour through driving snow, till the purple glow of dawn kindled on the eastern horizon and pushed back some of the white haze. The young riders crested a broad hill, and before them appeared a flat, open valley blanketed with snow and ice. A large brown river cut through the midst of the valley.

"Look, Felix, there's the Kansas," Keech said to his pony.

Felix replied by smacking his mouth against his bits, a gesture that Keech knew meant, *Let's just get a move on already*.

The Chamelia's tracks cut sharply down the hill to the river's edge. Keech noticed a sizable ferryboat anchored to a sturdy wooden post on the northern shoreline a few dozen yards away from the beast's trail.

Four dark mounds lay scattered across the beach near the boat. Keech knew instantly what he was looking at.

"*Dios mío*," Cutter said. "Those are bodies!"

"That's the old Uniontown trade crossing," Quinn said. "The ferry connects the logging road that runs past Mercy Mission to the Sherman Trading Post about a mile upriver. The traders use the ferry to barter with the Potawatomi Indians. Maybe those are the ferrymen."

"I best go find out. Y'all wait here." Nat clicked at Sally and started down.

When he returned a moment later, his face looked sick. Even Sally's demeanor wasn't at peace. "I reckon our old pal Sunrise and his men rode to the wrong place at the wrong time."

Quinn looked stunned. "That's the bounty hunter?"

Nat nodded. "The other three are the fellas who ransacked our camp. The Shifter must've got them before they could cross the river. When we go down, I advise everyone to look the other way. They're torn up something awful."

Quinn exhaled grimly. "I wish they'd been good men. I wish they led decent lives, instead of wasted them on bad deeds. Now it's too late."

The gang approached the white beach, giving the macabre lumps that were Sunrise Albert and his fallen hunters a wide berth. Near the river's edge, Keech drew rein on Felix and slid off, resisting a powerful urge to glance back where the trackers lay.

After studying the area for a moment, he pointed. "The Chamelia entered the river here. Swam for the opposite shore. And notice these drag marks." With an easy gesture, he traced two thin channels in the snow left by a pair of boots. "It pulled a body along."

"One of the bounty hunters?" asked Duck.

Keech shook his head gloomily. "No, I'm afraid it's John Wesley." Everyone looked shocked.

"You can't know that," said Cutter.

"There's a clear boot print there, see?" Keech gestured to a single impression on the bank, the place where the boot in question had pressed flatly into the ground. "After traipsing all over Flood-wood with y'all, I know your boot prints like the back of my hand, and that one belongs to John."

Cutter mumbled a bleak-sounding curse. "That's it then. Any chance John was alive is gone. If he somehow lived to this point, the river either drowned him or froze him."

Keech felt new waves of despair crash into him. Though his sensible mind had told him that his new friend had died in the explosion, some kind of desperate hope had lingered that John Wesley was still alive. But as he gazed across the Kansas River, he finally knew that John was gone forever.

The torches had at last burned out. Tossing the useless wood to the ground, Nat suggested they all dismount and discuss their next steps.

His eyes swelling, Cutter gestured to the ferry. "We should take the boat across."

"That is the only way over the Kansas for miles," Quinn noted.

Where the abandoned ferry was docked nearby, heavy ice frosted the shoreline, freezing the sand so that the day-old tracks left behind there held their shape. Keech inspected the area. "I count at least three sets of boot prints and maybe five horses. It looks like the ferrymen lit off west down that trail." He pointed out the path.

"I can't figure why they'd leave the ferry deserted," Quinn said. "Maybe Sunrise and his men scared them off."

"Last night's norther was something fierce," Duck said. "A storm that wild likely drove them off to shelter."

"Or maybe they caught a glimpse of the Shifter," Nat suggested.

"Well, I don't aim to wait for them to wander back." Cutter bounded off Chantico and led her to the boat. "Let's get going."

The ferry was a curious-looking vessel; it appeared to be a giant raft with two covered horse stalls on the deck, one standing on the starboard side, the other on the port side. Keech had never seen a watercraft like it. Nailed to the ferry's anchor post on the shore was a small wooden sign bearing a message:

UNIONTOWN CROSSING
1 Man 1 Horse 40 cents
Single person 20 cents
Horses 30 cents each
Loaded Wagon & Team $4
Empty Wagon & Team $2

Keech considered their options. "I don't think we should just steal this ferry. Seems wrong."

Quinn cleared his throat. "I realize y'all are used to working inside the Law, but if the ferrymen come back and get a look at me, we don't know if they'll help us or turn us over to hunters. If you're gonna ride alongside me, you'll have to get used to keeping out of sight." On that note, he trudged Lightnin' across the white beach and hopped on board.

"Maybe we can pay the ferrymen back after we've stopped Rose," Duck said.

From the deck of the boat, Quinn added, "Wisdom ain't far. You Lost Causes can debate your plan for the rest of the year, but not me. I'm gonna sail this river with or without y'all and go free Auntie

Ruth." He paused to glance down at the iced-over boards under his feet. "In fact, I dub this here boat the *Liberator*. Now, who's with me and who's staying?"

"I'm with you," Cutter said. He led Chantico onto the ferry.

Keech guided Felix to the platform next. Letting out a sigh, Duck followed.

Nat looked at everyone else aboard Quinn's *Liberator*, then glanced up and down the shoreline as though entertaining a second thought. For one moment, Keech thought the rancher would refuse to join them. Then Nat announced, "Okay. We've got a mission to accomplish. Let's get this boat sailing."

There was no cable or rope stretched across the river that a ferryman could pull, so at first it was a mystery how to propel the big boat across the channel. After a quick study of the ferry's mechanisms, Keech realized that the horse stalls on each wing of the vessel were long treadmills.

He whistled in amazement. "This ferry's run by horsepower."

"What's that mean?" Cutter asked.

Before Keech could explain, Nat and Duck walked their Fox Trotters toward the two stalls. Nat directed Sally into the starboard compartment, while Duck led Irving into the port side box. The horses faced opposite directions, north and south, and each pony was soon harnessed up to a sturdy iron bar inside their stalls. Nat pointed back at the hemp rope attached to the bank post. "Cutter, toss that anchor. Me and Duck will show you fellas how this contraption works."

With the rope released, Nat and Duck nudged their ponies to walk in place on the treadmills. Two big paddle wheels on each side of the boat commenced to churn the slushy water. The ferry lurched forward on the channel, and the gang was off.

"I never saw a more ridiculous boat," Cutter said.

Tucking his bowler hat against the cold, Keech gripped the rail as the *Liberator* drifted gently toward the southern bank, its curved bow driving through the ever-tumbling snow.

CHAPTER 10

Attack of the Marsh Bane

The young riders had traveled more than halfway over the Uniontown crossing when a shadow suddenly slid across the misty brown water. Keech glanced up to mark the source and saw it was a massive, malformed crow. It was too high to spark his amulet but was quickly diving.

"Lost Causes, we got company!" he said. The gang looked up and watched as the malevolent fowl circled down closer to get a better look at the *Liberator*.

"I'd hoped we had lost those rascals for good," Nat said.

"Rose knows exactly where we are now," Cutter groaned.

Keech recalled the first time he laid eyes on one of the Reverend's emissaries: in Missouri, just before Bad Whiskey rode up to the Home to confront Pa. "Those things always follow Rose's men. We should keep a lookout."

Suddenly, Duck pointed to the southern shoreline.

"It's him! It's Big Ben!"

Sitting on the low bank atop a bay horse was a hulking man in a tan coat. The man wore a massive red beard split right up the middle and braided to tapers at each end. It resembled a diabolical, upside-down fork. A dark, flat-brimmed hat perched on the short red curls of his hair. The killer sat on his horse in the wafting snow and watched them.

Swift movement on Big Ben's left shifted Keech's gaze. Two more of the Reverend's crows perched nearby on the branches of thick bushes. They rustled darkly against the backdrop of forest. One bird released a thunderous *Ack!*

"What do we do?" Quinn said. "We can't just float over to him."

Nat didn't take his eyes off the killer. "Turn this thing around. We'll seek cover back in the forest."

"No, Nat, we have to take him down," Duck insisted. "Now's our chance."

"I'm with Duck," Cutter said. "We've got the amulets. The crows will keep their distance, and if Big Ben's anything like *El Ojo*, the silver charms can drop him dead."

Through the snowy haze, Big Ben dismounted and shuffled down to the river's edge.

"He's moving into the water," Duck said.

Stopping to tuck the tails of his riding coat into his waistband, the brute pushed back a thick wall of reeds and waded knee-deep into the river. He held something in one hand. Not a pistol, but a small brown pouch.

Keech studied the man's movements. "What's he up to?"

The others gathered at the snow-dusted rail and stared across the water.

"This is reckless," Nat said, his teeth clenched. "I want justice on Big Ben like everybody else. Probably more. But if he pulls a pistol, we're sitting ducks. We ain't equipped for a fight."

Keech fumbled down the neck of his coat and drew his amulet shard. "I believe we are."

Big Ben's burgundy whiskers parted into a smile, but the grin contained nothing of the devilish joy that Bad Whiskey had displayed when hurting others. He reached inside his pouch and scooped out a small grayish mound onto his palm.

The desperado tossed the material across the water. Most of it fanned out over the sludge a few feet in front of him, but the cold wind swept some of it into the air and carried it farther offshore to mingle with the snowflakes drifting into the river.

Big Ben gave the young riders a two-fingered salute. He then wheeled about and returned to his horse. The bay jolted at the kick to her sides and Big Ben was gone in a flash, galloping into the shadowy forest that hemmed the southern bank. The brace of crows perched on the branches leaped into the sky and followed him, heavy black wings battering the snow.

"What just happened?" Duck asked. "Where'd he go?"

"No idea," Keech said, "but I don't like it none." He kept his eyes on the places in the river where the grayish material had fallen, but he saw nothing but brown water.

"This is a trap. Turn the ferry around! That's an order," Nat said, but instead of waiting for someone else to fulfill his command, he hurried over to the starboard driving stall, where Sally trotted on her clacking treadmill.

A strange movement on the water caught Keech's eye—a large green bubble had gurgled up to the river's surface a few yards in front of the ferry. However, the bulbous contour was not a water bubble at all but a grotesque, fish-like head the color of a moldy lime.

A sharp, serrated fin sprouted up from the creature's crown. A moment later, a dozen of the spiked greenish heads popped up.

Quinn backed away from the rail. "Looks like a bunch of walleye fish!"

"Those ain't fish," Duck murmured. "They look like *people*."

Unsheathing his blade, Cutter said, "We need to help Nat turn around. Quick."

The spiked heads started swimming straight for the *Liberator*.

Whatever nasty ingredient Big Ben had scattered across the river, the stuff was germinating into humanoid figures, complete with slimy green arms and backs and wart-covered torsos. A dozen emerged ahead of the boat, bobbing like corks in the brown water. Fangs like ice picks chattered in the brown wash, raising a terrible clatter that reminded Keech of a thousand wagon wheels rattling on a pebble road. The frenzy of oily bodies churned the river. Their eel-like mouths gibbered above the surface as they paddled the currents.

"They're getting closer!" Cutter hollered.

As if to prove the boy's point, the amulet shard in Keech's hand sparked cold. "Duck, fetch your shard!"

The girl had already pulled out her fragment and was coiling its leather cord around her hand.

Standing next to her, Quinn reached into his own coat and drew out one of the oily whistle bombs he carried. "Let's see if *this* can slow them down." He lifted the bomb and squeezed it, but the orb crumbled in his hand like an ebony egg. The shell cracked into pieces, and a creamy paste seeped between his fingers. The kid shook his hand, dropping the goo into the river.

"Guess that one was rotten," Cutter said. "Looks like we're gonna be facing these things *mano a mano*."

The *Liberator* rocked to a stop as the creatures crowded the hull, causing Keech to tumble to one knee. Slimy tentacles gripped at the raft, and the creatures started crawling under the rails and onto the deck. Their chattering, fang-lined mouths were as wide as supper plates, and peeking from their foreheads were three walnut-shaped eyes, blacker than beads of oil.

Keech raced toward the clambering pack, his amulet shard raised, and slammed the flat surface of the metal against one creature's shoulder. The silver's magic sparked. The creature shuddered, then its chattering head exploded like a burst grape. A putrid stench of rotten fish filled the air, and the abomination's body vanished in a cloud of dull fish scales.

Keech bellowed, "Duck, the shards work!"

He wasted no time glancing back to see if the girl had heard. Instead, he swung his charm to the left and right, invigorated, and with each touch of the shard, he destroyed another unnatural thing crawling toward him on the deck.

Pivoting, Keech caught a glimpse of Nat booting a creature off the rail and back into the water. Quinn had picked up a wooden pole and was swinging it into the head of a slimy monster attempting to climb Sally's driving stall. A few feet over, Duck leaned over the starboard railing, and with a bold sweep of her amulet shard, she rendered one of the atrocities back into gray powder.

"Blackwood, help!"

Keech spun toward the voice. Cutter was working to hold back a fish creature. The boy had driven his blade into the thing's soft body, but the writhing fiend continued to lurch. "Stupid *cuchillo*, work for once!" Cutter cried at the knife.

Suddenly, the boat pitched sideways, throwing Keech off

balance. To his horror, the amulet shard skittered out of his grip. He glanced around wildly to mark where it landed.

"These critters are trying to capsize us!" Duck yelled.

Scurrying on his hands and knees, Keech reached for the shard. As he moved, a slimy green deformity rose out of the river and lunged for him, its fishbone nails swiping at his boots. He yanked his legs away to avoid the attack, then caught a sudden flicker of brown fur beside him. There was a loud bray, then one of Felix's back hooves kicked out and crunched against the monster's head. The fish thing flew back into the Kansas, squealing in surprise.

"Good boy!" Keech said—but he felt his blood freeze when momentum from Felix's attack sent the pony toward the raft's edge. Felix's thick body flopped and twisted, but the port edge of the *Liberator* pitched down too suddenly, sending Felix and Keech in a wild slide toward the river.

"Felix!" Keech screamed, but before he could find a hold, he skated boots first over the edge into the freezing wash. Felix toppled in beside him, an almost human-like cry issuing from the horse's throat.

Churning water entombed Keech. A muffled shriek escaped his mouth, a cry that turned into frantic bubbles around his face. He pinwheeled his arms, an attempt to roll his body horizontal in the water and look for Felix, but his boots felt like millstones and he began to sink.

A repulsive green face with three black eyes swam directly toward him. Hundreds of needle-sharp teeth chomped inches from his nose.

Keech seized the monster's neck, hoping to strangle the disgusting life out of it. The flesh under his fingers felt spongy, like touching frog eggs on a lily pad. The creature seized Keech's wrists with its tentacled grip and dragged him down. As he sank, he caught a glimpse of Felix a few feet away, and another river-choked scream rumbled out of him.

More than a dozen of the green horrors were swarming the pony.

Keech kicked desperately at the creature clutching him, hoping to escape and save poor Felix from a terrible death, but he couldn't break free of the tentacles. A bleak thought entered his mind as the monster pulled him deeper: *This is it, Sam. Felix and I will be joining you now.* And for one second, all he wanted was to quit everything and see his orphan brother again. The inviting thought warmed the icy river and enveloped him like one of Granny Nell's homespun quilts.

Then the creature holding his wrists evaporated into mist.

Keech blinked in surprise, but there was no time to ponder what had just happened. His lungs blazed for air. He spun in the abyss, hoping to find a way to the surface, and saw Quinn Revels swimming next to him.

The kid grabbed his shoulder and hauled him toward the *Liberator.* As they drifted upward, the edges of Keech's vision began to dim. He felt seconds away from drowning. The churning water obscured his vision, but he could see movement all around, a dark swirling mass of death, as more of Big Ben's creatures approached.

A strong hand gripped his coat and tugged him out of the river. Keech found himself spread-eagled on the deck of the ferry, staring up at the clouded Kansas sky. Nat knelt beside him, his face hectic with fear and exhaustion.

"Breathe, Keech, breathe." The rancher's large hands pushed against his chest, and Keech managed to suck in fresh air.

"Felix!" he shouted when his throat could form words. "Someone has to save him!"

Nat muttered, "It's too late, Keech. He's gone." He glanced back down at the river. "Hang on." Dipping his arms back into the water, Nat grabbed Quinn's hand and hauled the kid out of the water. As soon as Quinn's body smacked against the icy floor, he arched up onto all fours and grabbed his own lungfuls of air. "Much obliged," the boy said, his teeth chattering.

"Thank me later. The fight ain't over." Without a glance back, Nat was on his feet and dashing across the ferry to where Duck and Cutter were battling a fresh wave of monstrosities.

Keech felt desperate. "I'm going back in. I have to try to save Felix!"

"No! It's too dangerous." Quinn started crawling across the floorboards. "Scoot back a few feet."

"How come?"

"My other whistle bomb. I squeezed it back in the river."

Keech's breath barely had time to freeze before a mammoth tremor shook the ferry, and a geyser of water erupted from the Kansas. Brown water mixed with slimy green chunks rained down across the raft, coating the young riders in a foul spray.

"What in blazes!" shouted Duck nearby.

Keech felt his heart clench as the boat tottered beneath his feet, then rocked back to rest. All he could think about was poor Felix, trapped under the water.

"That bomb worked like a charm," Quinn said, shaking slime off his arms. He held up Pa's amulet shard with a quivering hand. "Here. You dropped this."

Keech took the silver charm in a daze. He shook his head to

focus, his mind refusing to accept that he had just lost Felix, when he noticed that Quinn's eyes had suddenly veered off to look over his shoulder.

"Heaven have mercy!" Quinn exclaimed.

Keech wheeled around to look. Even after witnessing the risen dead, Devil crows, a bloodthirsty Shifter, and now an army of slimy abominations, what he now saw stole his breath.

A large black steed galloped across the surface of the Kansas River and toward the *Liberator*. The horse paid no mind to the fact that it sprinted on top of deep water; its broad hooves clopped down on the wash without so much as a splash or a sinking shoe.

Atop this water-walking horse sat a man, a heavyset fellow bundled in wool garments, draped and wrapped in brown deerskins. He raised his gloveless palms high, as though offering surrender, but the gesture had an altogether different meaning.

A great rushing noise filled Keech's ears, like a heavy wind invading the rafters of a barn, and suddenly a massive spray of river water exploded into the air a few yards away from the *Liberator*, as if yet another whistle bomb had detonated. Screaming winds kicked up all around, and Keech squinted as the spray twisted into a swirling funnel that danced on the river.

As the black steed galloped closer to the *Liberator*, the rider flicked his fingers in the direction of the monstrosities. The rumbling tornado obeyed his command. It thundered over the surface of the Kansas, lapping up river water as it moved, and fell upon the slimy horde.

The violent gale ripped around the stunned young riders but did nothing to them, barely even ruffling Keech's collar.

The impossible cyclone scooped up the devils and lifted them off the sides of the boat and into its raging swirl, shredding them to pieces. Their howling pandemonium turned deafening.

The twister moved away from the raft and carried what was left of the creatures down the river. Only a solitary monster remained, trying to board the boat, its tentacle-fingers grasping for Duck's boot. The girl reached down with her amulet shard and slapped the monster's head. The thing crumbled into dry scales.

Keech hugged himself for warmth as the cyclone spun down the Kansas, the clamor of wind easing back, the funnel gradually losing its force. The gang huddled near one another on the ravaged deck of the *Liberator*. Keech's drenched clothes numbed his entire body, but worse, he felt numb inside. His breath hitched as if a thick stone had lodged in his throat.

Aside from a few cuts and bruises, the young riders appeared undamaged. They were looking at the black horse riding across the Kansas. The large steed shook its midnight-colored mane and wet snowflakes sprinkled the air. The horseman's thick frame stood out against the winter-white backdrop like a dark sculpture.

Quinn said, "Ranger Doyle. I'm sure glad to see you."

"Hello, Quinn." The man's gruff voice carried the hint of a smile.

"These are my new friends."

The stranger gazed at each of them. He wore no sidearm on his hip, and there appeared to be no weapons on his range saddle.

"My name is Edgar Doyle, and we should make haste," he said. "Linger out here and you're all likely to die."

PART 2

WISDOM

BIG BEN AND THE PRISONER

A light snow drifted down around Big Ben Loving as he pushed his mare through a thinning woodland of ice and mud.

Back to the north where the Kansas River cut its east-west line, he could hear the bedlam on the water, the faintest din of shouting. From the sound of things, the Marsh Bane he'd scattered at the riverbank was accomplishing the Reverend's orders to finish the children. He smiled.

High above the leafless canopy, a small number of the Master's harbingers circled below the whirling clouds. The crows had warned Big Ben to ride without delay. Danger was approaching from the north, an enemy of great power on his trail, and Big Ben's connection to the Prime was too weak to protect him at the moment. He needed to rest and stretch his aching back. But he wondered how much rest the Reverend Rose would afford him. Because he was a Harvester of the most powerful chaos magics on Earth, Big Ben had vast energy at his fingertips and, therefore, the Reverend would not tolerate talk of discomfort and malaise.

The Reverend's missions of late were growing difficult for Big Ben. Periodic rations of the Prime restored pieces of his vitality, but every new assignment, every pursuit, cumbered his aging body like anchors on his bones. Terrible twinges had set up in his fingers and back, turning even mundane tasks into feats of pain and frustration. The folks in these parts believed that if you put a teaspoonful of salt in your boot, the creaks in your bones would soften. But that business was nonsense. Only the Prime restored vigor, but each time the Reverend gifted him with more power, Big Ben felt his mind harden and grow callous.

There was always a dark trade involved with dark magic.

Big Ben slowed his horse when he spotted a stand of bluish boulders, a stone jumble that marred the gentle rise of the landscape. A curious scent rode on the wind there, a mix of copper and pain. The smell of blood.

Disquieted by the odor, Big Ben's mount grunted nervously.

As he walked the mare around the boulders, the snowy forest on the other side revealed a slender beast bristling with a coat of spear-sharp spines. Its breath rattled from its snout in a dense mist. The animal hunkered on two clawed feet over a large boy lying on his back in the snow. When it saw Big Ben, the creature dropped to all fours and bowed its head in deference.

Big Ben drew rein and met the fierce gaze of his pet, a member of the ancient Shifter pack known as the Chamelia. Stories had it they were the first creatures to slip through the Dead Rift in the First Age of Man. Unfettered from the Underworld itself, they had scattered over the countrysides, mingling their forms with the animals of the desert and forest.

"The boy looks sick."

A vicious bark escaped the Shifter, a noise of both fear and intimidation.

Big Ben lifted his palm, revealing the Reverend's charred symbol, a warning that he would use the brand to make the creature suffer. "I'll abide no back talk from you."

The Chamelia loped off a short distance to lurk in a stand of brush. The barbs along its back fluttered and sank inward, its flesh turning into murky scales. Big Ben chortled at the change; he knew the creature too well. When it felt threatened or surprised, the Chamelia tended to shift serpentine, a more cold-blooded demeanor, to cover its mammalian shame and despair.

His back burning with discomfort, Big Ben dismounted and stomped through the mantle of snow till he stood over the boy's body. Shadow painted the kid in a bluish pallor, making him look like a corpse.

The tips of the boy's fingers were black with frostbite. Ice caked the lad's clothing. Not only had the Chamelia dragged him through snow, it had also crossed the Kansas River with the boy in tow. It was impossible the youth still lived.

Yet he continued to breathe.

Big Ben then noticed a pool of crimson beneath the kid's body. "You scratched him, didn't you?" He lifted the boy's leg with a boot to get a better look. A dark ragged bloodstain across the lad's hip made the answer obvious enough. "You foolish thing. The Reverend said unspoiled. I should take your head."

Big Ben took a second to study the boy's fingers and realized he wasn't looking at frostbite after all. "Look at what you did! You infected him." He put a finger to the kid's top lip and pushed upward, exposing a gum line full of protruding ridges.

"I suppose it don't matter. We can still set the trap even if he is infected." He would have to slow the change. Doing so wouldn't help the ache of Big Ben's own exhausted body, but there was no choice. If he still wanted to deliver a normal boy to Wisdom, he would have to expend the energy.

Big Ben jogged back to his horse, retrieved one of the pigskin conjure pouches stowed inside his saddlebag, and dug his fingers into a white powder. The pungent scent of rotten cabbage mixed with floral hints of jasmine crinkled his nose.

Under his breath, Big Ben began a steady chant, words from the Black Verse that were meant to focus his mind, expand his inner senses, and activate the powers of the white medicine. He allowed the itch in the back of his throat to grow.

The primordial energy that Big Ben knew only as the Prime stirred within him. Sprouting from a pea-size glow in the center of his head, the power sent electricity down his aching spine and wrapped around his veins, till the energy infested his entire being.

Only after each of his muscles purred with the Prime did Big Ben cease the chant of the Black Verse. He opened his eyes and clapped his hands together. When he drew his palms apart, the grains had altered their form. Strands of glowing white threads stretched between his fingers, like a spiderweb woven from lightning.

Big Ben lowered his hands to the infected boy.

The webbing dripped light onto the lad's chest and face. As the substance touched the kid, it gathered into pools, a pattern of glowing puddles that spread across his cheeks, his neck, his forehead.

Once the last of the white webbing had dripped free, Big Ben clapped again, and the noise activated the material. The white pools moved, a living liquid that skittered across the boy's skin toward his eyes and mouth, diving into the openings, disappearing under the flesh.

Big Ben rose to his feet. The energy would hold the boy on the verge, a lock impeding his physical change. For now, at least.

Perched on the branch of a nearby oak, one of the crows screeched. Big Ben approached the tree, his arthritic back screaming in pain. The creature flapped down and landed in the snow before him. The Reverend liked to call these things the *P'mola*, but they had nothing to do with the Abenaki lore of old. Rather, they were the Master's creations, perverse beings spawned from the Reverend's own blood.

Big Ben knelt to one knee slowly and bowed his head.

"I have the boy, Reverend."

You've done well, Ben. Hurry him to Wisdom.

"Yes, Master."

Once there, gather your strength and be ready. Coward is waiting to set the trap, but he will need you at your strongest.

Big Ben hesitated to speak about the pain in his body—but there was no need to voice the concern anyway, for the Reverend could read the thought as easily as Big Ben could read a Kansas map.

You will have more of the Prime soon.

Big Ben said, "What of my Chamelia?"

The crow made a chattering noise, as though laughing at the question. *Keep the beast close. There will be need for it again soon.*

With an *Ack!*, the crow took to the air and sailed into the cold morning to join its brethren.

Big Ben whistled to the Shifter. A boggy stench reached him

before he caught sight of the thing, hunkered low between two crooked pin oaks not far away.

The Chamelia slunk forward. Along the way, it shifted again, abandoning the scales and bulky length to become smaller, hairier. The beast that now approached was closer in size and appearance to a coyote.

Big Ben scowled. "Go, beast. Be alone if you wish. Stay in the shadows and remain close enough to hear my call."

The Chamelia turned and leaped into the canopy of a nearby oak. It sprang from branch to branch, the bare limbs swaying under its sleek weight.

Big Ben returned to the unconscious boy. Stooping, he slid an arm beneath the lad's back and lifted him off the ground, wincing as he did. He carried the slumbering boy to his horse and heaved his body over the mare's croup.

Big Ben paused as his prize groaned. A whispered word escaped the kid's lips.

"Papa?"

Big Ben punched the boy. The knock caused the youth to slump across the horse.

"Back to sleep, boy. I need you alive, but I prefer you stay silent."

Without another word, Big Ben Loving mounted his bay and rode south toward Wisdom.

CHAPTER 11
EDGAR DOYLE

Pa Abner stirs a crackling campfire as Keech and Sam rest for the evening, their boots kicked off in the low grass, their backs against their unfastened saddles.

"Now, boys, recite the rules of alliance," Pa says. He lifts a finger to start them. "One."

"Know your friend, know your enemy," the boys recite, their voices echoing faintly across the crisp Missouri wilderness.

"Two."

"To learn a man's heart, watch his actions."

"Good." Pa walks a few steps away to retrieve a fresh log, then returns to their tight circle. He points at Sam. "How can you know if an enemy is pretending to be your friend?"

Sam struggles with the answer, so Keech speaks it for him. "His intent will be made clear through his actions."

"Exactly so. Sam, make sure you learn the words proper."

"Yes, Pa."

"Look at this log, boys. On the outside the wood appears to be dry enough, like all the others in the pile. And we desire warmth, so we might be tempted *to accept any fuel that promises a good heat. But how do we know the truth of the log? We place it in the fire, test its intent. If the log is our friend, the wood burns clean and gives us heat. If the log is our enemy, moisture hidden inside the wood stifles the burning and fills our eyes with smoke."*

Keech marvels at how Pa Abner could take difficult concepts and make them simple.

"Vigilance will tell you if a man is true," Pa continues. "Learn his heart . . ."

". . . watch his actions," Keech recited below his breath as the rawhider known as Edgar Doyle rode his magical steed across the surface of the Kansas River.

The leather-clad stranger trotted his horse along the length of the *Liberator.* The vessel was drifting downriver. Doyle extracted a coil of long rope from his range saddle. Keech caught a glimpse of two other backup lariats hanging from his tack. The steed carried the man around the boat's corner to the bow, where he flung the rope over the front railing. "Someone tie this off. I'll tow you to shore."

Nat and Cutter volunteered to help Doyle tether off to the railing. After they had secured a clove hitch to the front board, the Ranger slung his rope over one hefty shoulder and gripped the taut edge of the cord near his chest. "Steady now, kids," he hollered. He spurred his horse with a loud "Giyahh!" and the *Liberator* pitched forward. Doyle guided the boat while his steed lumbered over the channel, its broad hooves stamping the river's surface.

Despite the dreadful panic and sorrow of losing Felix, Keech couldn't help watching the extraordinary way the man's enchanted horse strolled on water.

Nearby, Nat shook his head. "How in purple tarnation is he doing all this?"

Quinn beamed. "I told y'all he was something. After he hid me from the Chamelia with his special chant, I knew he had talents, but I never saw business of *this* sort."

"And you're sure he can be trusted?" Cutter asked.

"Ranger Doyle saved my life. And yours, if we're keeping count."

Duck slung a dry blanket over Quinn's shivering form. As she tossed a second one around Keech's shoulders, reaching up to touch his face in a gesture of sympathy, he whispered to her, "Duck, when the Ranger rode up, did you feel anything strange with your charm?"

"I don't think so. Did you?"

"Nothing." Keech peeked into his shirt and saw no glow on the metal. "I think we're safe." He gazed beyond the bow of the ferry, where the Ranger and his magical horse were tugging the *Liberator* to shore. "I reckon there's no reason to get up a fuss. I got a good look at his horse. No Devil's mark on the forehead or anywhere else. And the man doesn't look to be packing iron."

"What kind of Texas Ranger doesn't wear a sidearm?" Duck asked.

"Maybe the better question is how can a man control the wind and walk his horse over open water?" There was a gentle splash ahead. Then Keech rocked back a little on his boots as the *Liberator*'s nose nudged onto the snowy shore.

"Everyone out," Doyle urged, his steed stepping up the bank.

The young riders marched ashore, leading their ponies. Keech kept his eyes trained on the bank ahead, refusing to look back at the river; there was simply no use. When they had cleared the water, the Ranger said, "You kids still wearing dry clothes head into the forest and gather some wood. We need to get these two in front of a fire pronto."

Nat, Duck, and Cutter scattered into the surrounding grove to grab logs and kindling. When they returned, Doyle built a fire for Keech and Quinn in a small clearing. As the man worked, he hummed a strange, lonely tune and occasionally scanned the morning sky. The Ranger's monotonous hum gave Keech the willies.

The boys opened their blankets to allow the heat to thaw them. They laid their soggy socks and coats over a log near the flames for drying. The driving snow had stopped for the moment, leaving a pearly calm over the land.

As the others joined them, Keech's eyes drifted to the ponies. Tethered to branches nearby, the four animals looked about nervously, as if searching for their missing companion, and Keech suddenly couldn't hold up his head to keep watching them.

Felix had been his partner for years. Keech had learned every reining maneuver, every gallop, every gait from atop the gelding's saddle. When Pa Abner had given Minerva to Sam, the boys took their ponies on a long ride past Low Hill. On the trail, they happened upon a coiled rattler. Felix jumped in front of Minerva and stomped the snake to death. The pony had possessed the heart of a hero and had given his life to save his master.

After losing his family and facing down dangers that would shake any man, Keech had started to believe himself beyond overwhelming sorrow. At least he expected to be better at coping with loss, but losing Felix to the monsters in the river was too much to bear. He felt as if he were standing over the ruins of the Home for Lost Causes all over again, choked with such grief that he couldn't even speak a proper eulogy.

"Sorry about your horse," Quinn said through chattering teeth. "It's powerful unfair."

Keech tried to offer some sort of proper response, but the words caught in his throat. He simply hung his head and wiped at his eyes.

Rubbing his palms together over the fire, Nat turned to the stranger. "I'm sure you realize we got a few questions. Our new friend Revels here has told us you're a Texas Ranger seeking your lost partner."

Doyle scratched at the heavy stubble on his face. "That's right."

"Yet you happen to show up on the Kansas River while we're crossing. Have you been following us?"

Before the man could respond, Duck added, "And why don't your horse sink in water?"

"And what about that whirlwind? How did you do that?" Cutter asked.

Doyle raised his hand to pause the barrage. "I understand. You've witnessed some curious happenings and want to know how they came to pass." Again, the man looked up and scoured the heavens. "Problem is, I don't have time to sit around in the woods telling tales to a bunch of ragamuffin kids."

"I ain't no kid," Cutter grunted.

This time, Doyle barked laughter—a sound that reminded Keech of Pa Abner's guffaws after Granny Nell told a joke. "Son, in my experience, if you have to tell someone you ain't a kid, then you're still a kid."

"You won't answer any of our questions?" Duck asked.

"I will. But not here." Knocking mud off his rugged deerskin moccasins, Doyle stepped over to his black steed and dug through his saddlebag. He produced a handful of squirmy things—beetles and grub worms, from the look—and much to Keech's surprise, fed them to the horse. The animal chomped on the critters as gleefully as oats. "If you're up to riding a pace, I know of a homestead farther south where we could bunk for a spell. Once there, you could eat some grub and grab a nap. You all look like you could use it. While we're there, we can talk."

Nat said, "Listen, Mr. Doyle, we appreciate your help on the river, we surely do. But we can't just follow a strange man to a strange house without knowing more."

The fellow considered, then shrugged. "You don't have to trust me, but I think I proved I'm on your side. I know where you can get dry and rested, but maybe you have another way."

To learn a man's heart, watch his actions, Keech thought. So far, Doyle's actions had been noble. Keech understood there were plenty of risks involved in trusting an outsider in the wilderness—not long ago, they had encountered a scoundrel in Sunrise Albert—but shelter would offer some small protection against spying crows and lurking beasts. Maybe they could actually rest up a little, regroup, and make plans before reaching Wisdom.

"*I'll* come with you, Ranger Doyle." Quinn tested the moisture in his wool socks, found them still too damp for comfort, and pulled his oversized boots onto his bare feet. "If these others won't tag along, I may need a ride."

"No, I think we should follow," Keech said, glancing at the others. The pity in their eyes stirred anger in his gut—he didn't need their pity; he needed Felix. "Let's hear him out. He saved our lives."

Duck turned to her brother. "Nathaniel, I think they're right. We should go. I don't know about you, but I'd like to eat a proper meal."

"I could use a long *siesta*," Cutter joined in.

Nat pondered for a moment. "Fine. We'll ride to the homestead. But after meals and naps, we head out for Wisdom."

Doyle's head suddenly tilted. "Wisdom, you say?"

"You know it?" asked Nat.

"I do. And if you plan to go there, you'll want to listen to what I have to say."

Keech glanced at Nat. "Like I said, we best hear him out."

After dousing the fire, the Ranger climbed up on his horse. "We'll be skirting the Potawatomis and heading through Shawnee land. The Indians there will allow us untroubled passage." Pushing his brown hat low, he clicked at the horse, and the creature hurried toward the southern woods, a white forest full of pin oaks and deep shadows.

The young riders trotted after the man. On Quinn's insistence, Keech rode double with him on Lightnin', sitting just behind the saddle on the gelding's wide rump. The pony didn't care for the arrangement at first, shuffling about with the clear hopes of shaking Keech right off, but Keech held tight to Quinn's wet coat. In time, the animal consented. To Keech, riding another pony felt like a strange kind of betrayal, but he had no choice.

The morning snow had started up again, tumbling in fat flakes, but the forest beyond the Kansas River was thick enough to screen most of the drift from their faces. After half an hour of frigid riding, the gang clambered up a lofty hill. Doyle pulled back on his reins when he reached the crest and held up two fingers to halt them.

"Why're we stopping?" asked Duck.

Keech looked down the hill and spotted a company of Native horsemen passing in a tight cluster, moving toward a heavy thicket to the west. Four of them wore draping buffalo pelts. The other two men rode in sawtooth robes that reminded Keech of the traded blankets that Pa Abner had kept inside his study.

Doyle watched the six horsemen with interest.

"Potawatomi?" asked Quinn.

"No, they're Osage." The Ranger smiled. "I believe I've seen this team before, farther south on the prairies."

Cutter wiggled a finger at Keech. "You're Osage, right, Blackwood? You can speak to them for us."

Keech shook his head in disappointment. "Pa Abner taught the orphans what he could—a few handy words and phrases, how to respect all the people and traditions around us—but he didn't know everything. There's a whole heap I don't know."

He wanted to say more on the subject—that ever since Pa Abner had divulged who his real father was, Keech had been feeling a lonely disconnect from his place in the world—but he was cut off when Doyle called down to the riders with a loud "*Hah-weh!*"

The horsemen glanced up the hill.

Keech had been wrong about the band's number. There were seven of them, but the seventh member—a young Osage girl on a short brown pony—rode inside their crowded assembly, nearly invisible in the cluster till one of the men nudged his horse aside. Like her four companions in buffalo robes, the girl wore a shaggy pelt draped over her shoulders, a billowing bison hide that blended her almost perfectly with her mount and the brushwood. Keech imagined that if she wanted to, the girl *and* the horse could pass completely unseen in a thick forest.

Doyle started down the hillside. "I need to speak to those men, if they'll permit. It's a matter of some urgency, so follow quick."

When the horsemen saw them coming, one of the men in buffalo hides galloped out in front of the group. He spoke something in Osage, and the other riders kicked up their pace. Keech caught a glimpse of ornaments and eagle feathers tied into the leader's hair, denoting war honors and the man's bravery in battles, a distinguished headdress of an Osage warrior.

Doyle pushed his steed faster, forcing Quinn to goose the stubborn Lightnin' to keep up, but by the time everyone had reached the bottom of the hill, the Osage riders had slipped into the dense brush.

The Ranger continued his pursuit, driving his horse into the thicket.

"I don't like this one bit," Nat said, but he led the young riders onward in single file through the compact woods till they caught up to Doyle. It took a few moments to negotiate the brake, and the shadows inside were menacing, but before long a powder-white meadow opened up before them.

"Would you look at that!" Keech said when he saw what stood in the clearing.

The Osage riders were nowhere to be seen, but standing in the meadow was another bending tree, much like the one near Mercy Mission. It had the furrowed bark of a sugar maple, and the thick base had grown into a deep split, forming a twisted Y. Both trunks bent away from each other, then curved up before fracturing into a thousand slender branches. One thick arm pointed back toward the Kansas River; the other bent to the south.

"Is that what I think it is?" Cutter asked.

Steering his horse closer to the maple, Doyle answered, "It's a marker tree. The tribes in these parts have cultivated them from saplings to guide others to water or safe passages."

"The Osage must've known it was here," Duck said.

"They rode off lickety-split, like they weren't too tickled to find you near it," Nat added.

"Or near *them*," said Duck.

Disregarding the comments, Doyle dismounted and stepped toward the tree. Though the growth bore a slightly different shape than the white oak farther north, four white stones surrounded the maple, one at each point of the compass, exactly like the ones around the first tree. A thin layer of snow coated the ground, covering the stone circles, but Keech could still see their faint outlines.

Doyle moved to the stone nearest him, dusting off the snow with his moccasin. Then he placed the same foot on its smooth center and held it there. For a time, he stared between the Y of the tree, tilting his head as if struggling to see something just out of focus. A moment later, he shook his head with something like frustration. Reaching into his coat pocket, he drew out a small leatherbound journal and a stubby pencil. He opened to a cluttered-looking page and began to scribble a note.

The journal and pencil went back into his pocket, and out came a cherry-colored pipe and a small leather bag of tobacco. After emptying the dottle and packing in a fresh plug, he took his foot off the white stone and turned back to Keech.

"I gather you've seen a marker tree before. Most folks pass them right up. Think they're just part of the normal landscape. They would never imagine these trees keep old secrets."

"What kinds of secrets?" Keech asked.

Doyle glanced at the bending tree's branches. He rested a finger on the puckered bark and slowly grazed the wood. "All kinds, son." A thick cloud of blue pipe smoke wafted from the side of his mouth. "Let's get back on the trail. I've dallied long enough. The house ain't far from here. Less than a mile or so."

As the young riders followed Doyle back into the forest, Nat reined Sally a little closer to Keech and Quinn. "Maybe this is good luck after all, Keech. Especially if the Ranger knows a connection to these trees and Bonfire Crossing. All the same, keep your eyes peeled. There's something odd about this fella."

"I'm telling you, ain't nothing to worry about," said Quinn.

A baffling notion suddenly occurred to Keech. The sight of the bending tree had startled him so he hadn't recognized an obvious detail about the meadow itself.

The snow on the far side of the tree had been undisturbed. The Osage travelers had ridden into the clearing but had left no tracks when they departed.

CHAPTER 12

THE MOSS FARM

On the distant side of a rolling lea, Keech spotted the rooftop of a two-story farmhouse nestled inside a ring of redbud trees. Edgar Doyle drove straight toward the property and called back to the gang, "This is it."

"Have you ever seen this place?" Keech asked Quinn.

"No. But I suspect Ranger Doyle knows all sorts of places to hole up."

The group approached the gate of a broken split-rail fence. The low barrier divided the meadow and the farm's front yard and zig-zagged around the entire property. A tall red barn stood off to the right, its tapered roof smothered in ice. The whole place looked deserted.

"Everyone wait here. Let me check out the situation, put down some protection." Doyle clicked his tongue and rode through the gate. A moment later, he disappeared around the back of the house.

"What does 'put down some protection' mean?" Duck asked.

Before anyone could guess, Doyle reappeared at the far side of the house, moving swiftly on foot, his horse strolling beside him. The Ranger held a large leather pouch and busied himself sprinkling some kind of dark red substance around the property. After completing this mysterious task, he called to them.

Nat led the young riders into the yard. As they dismounted, Doyle held up a cautioning hand. "Don't disturb this barrier even in the slightest."

Keech took a closer look at the powder Doyle had scattered on the snow. It resembled flecks of rust grated off a piece of old tin. "What is that stuff?"

"*Sanguinaria canadensis.* Bloodroot. Indian tribes use it for sores and cramps and whatnot, but in this case, it'll protect us."

"From what?" Duck asked.

The Ranger's tone darkened. "The Man Slayer at work in the region. A Shifter beast from a dark place, a creature that crawled up into our world long ago."

"The Chamelia," Quinn said.

"It's been roaming these parts for a few days now. I know it attacked your troop at the mission." Doyle glanced at Quinn. "That's what I was doing north of the Kansas. I was checking on *you*, Mr. Revels. I saw the rubble and the bodies the Man Slayer left at the river. I also saw peculiar tracks. Looked to be dragging something, maybe a person."

Cutter spoke up, his voice bleak. "It killed our friend John and took his body."

Doyle looked down at his moccasins. "I'm sorry for your loss. A beast like that is a tough critter. Near impossible to kill. Once it has your scent, it won't stop coming. You kids have defensible ground here, at least. The Chamelia can't get you inside the bloodroot."

"You're saying a line of red powder can stop that thing when bullets can't?" Nat asked.

"The bloodroot will keep it out, not stop it." The Ranger slipped off his brown hat, revealing a head of curly, dark blond hair, and rubbed his forehead. "Let's stable the horses and get inside. I'll cook some grub, and we'll talk more."

Sleet kicked up while the riders stowed and fed their ponies in the barn. Ice pellets tinked and jangled on the rooftop, reminding Keech of the Chamelia's nails scratching at the clay tiles of Mercy Mission.

The Ranger took a moment to sprinkle more bloodroot where the sleet had disturbed the circle. "You can never be too careful," he explained, then they followed him up to the farmhouse.

The home was spacious but timeworn. A narrow staircase ran up to the second floor, and a short hallway led back to a large kitchen. While Keech glanced around, wondering who the house might belong to, Doyle built a roaring fire in the stone hearth. The group crowded around the fireplace and sat on a moth-eaten rug. Keech and Quinn hung their damp coats and socks near the flames to finish drying.

"I'd forgot what proper warmth feels like," said Cutter. "I may never leave."

The Ranger moved to a long table next to the sitting room, pulled out a cobweb-covered chair, and sat. He scattered a pouch full of nuts and dried figs on the table. "Come get a nibble. It'll ease your hunger till I can cook up something proper."

Keech joined the others around the table. As he chomped on a handful of pecans, he took a moment to further examine Edgar Doyle, who had paused a moment to fuss with his red pipe.

Underneath his curly locks, Doyle's deep walnut-brown eyes refused to linger on any one thing. They roved about the room, delving into the dusty corners. They teemed with a wild energy, a sort of manic intensity that left Keech feeling both curious and wary.

After lighting a new plug in his pipe, Doyle inspected the food left on the table and chortled. "You kids are like a pack of hungry wolves. I best get to cooking lest one of you gnaws an arm off." Before excusing himself to the kitchen, he gave Quinn's battered clothes a fretful once-over. "Mr. Revels, remind me to fetch you better garments before we light out."

While they grazed, Keech turned his attention to the house's dim stairwell. A frightening unease suddenly creased his heart when he saw the pulsing darkness of the second story, a crawling murkiness that seemed to seep down the stairs. He snapped his eyes away and tossed a few more pecans into his mouth. They tasted curiously stale now. He wondered if the others were feeling anything unusual, but they were happily munching.

Doyle returned with a lit lantern and a handful of deer jerky. "I've set some beans on the stove. Till they're ready, we can talk."

Keech accepted a strand of the jerky. "I'll start," he said, and swept his gaze around the house. "Whose place is this?"

"This house belonged to the Moss family, Elijah and Abigail. A few weeks ago, I found the place empty. A traveling farmer informed me that the Mosses had died while in St. Louis, so I've used the house to rest during my investigations." The Ranger shifted his weight to lean against the wall. His deerskin coat fanned back, revealing a sheath for a knife and three or four small, bulging pouches tied to his belt.

"We appreciate the house and the grub, but I just want to know one thing," Duck said.

"How my horse walks on water?" Doyle chuckled. "He's called Saint Peter. An unusual name for a horse, I know, but he answers to it. He's named after Peter the disciple, who climbed from his boat and walked on the water with Jesus."

"A name don't make a horse magic," Cutter said. "I named my mare Chantico after the Aztec goddess of volcanoes, but you don't see her spittin' lava."

The Ranger's flickering eyes lit up. "Saint Peter's a Kelpie. A Scottish spirit in the shape of a horse. I acquired him for a goodly sum while traveling through East Jersey. Some believe the Kelpie to be a demon who preys on men, but Saint Peter won't even bite a pear without looking to me first."

"What about the water funnel?" Nat asked. "How does a lawman control the wind?"

"Ah, yes. That, my friend, is a feat I can't explain in simple conversation. What I can tell you is that I work for a special division of the Texas Rangers. We investigate unusual circumstances. Our work has uncovered teachings that have expanded our arsenal. The funnel is just such a trick. In fact, I may have a few more stunts hidden up my sleeve." He winked.

Nat said, "The horse is a powerful sight, Mr. Doyle, and your water funnel saved our lives. But we want to know what you're doing in Kansas. Revels tells us you're out looking for your partner, a man called Warren Lynch. But what led you here in the first place?"

Doyle's light smile slipped away. "Warren and I came to this territory to investigate a gang of outlaws, a depraved company of scoundrels who've been terrorizing the Southern regions for some time now."

"The Big Snake," Cutter said.

Doyle's tone grew sober. "You've heard of them?"

"We've run across their ilk," Nat said.

"Then I'm surprised you kids are still alive. Many skilled Rangers have gone up against those fiends only to perish. Now Warren's gone missing. Perhaps he cashed in on the trail, but I got a feeling they rattlesnaked him. Till I know he's alive or dead, I aim to keep looking. My next stop is the town of Wisdom."

"I had a feeling," Nat said.

Doyle puffed on his pipe, letting the smoke drift around his face. "I've been studying the outskirts of that place. Unusual storms and a terrible darkness surround the area. They're up to something. I plan to search the town and hopefully locate Warren."

"Don't forget Auntie Ruth," added Quinn.

"Yes, your aunt Ruth as well," Doyle said.

"Ranger, there's another man in the town, a fella by the name of Strahan," Duck said. "He's the sheriff in the region, but Quinn told us he got taken, too. Do you know him?"

"I know his reputation. He's said to be a good man, kind and fair, but forceful when it comes to the Law."

"We need to find him," said Duck.

"Like I said, I've been devising a plan," Doyle replied.

"There's just one problem." Quinn's eyes dropped to the table. "The whistle bombs I wanted to use, I lost them back on the Kansas."

Doyle waved away his concern. "I told you those bombs in the mission were next to worthless. Warren's got the good supply. I'd venture a hefty sum he's tucked away a few crates somewhere in

Wisdom. If I find him, I'm certain he'll help you get all the whistle bombs you desire." Using his hands, he mimed an explosion.

"You know about Quinn's plan to blow up the town?" Duck asked.

"That ain't very Texas Ranger of you," Cutter quipped.

"Destroying the hornet's nest will take care of the hornets," Doyle said, then gestured to the kitchen. "How about you kids help spoon up the beans?"

The young riders followed Doyle to the kitchen, where they served up bowls of red beans. Doyle surprised them with a wedge of hard cheese. He pulled a short knife with a curved horn handle out of his rawhide sheath. Spinning it on his palm, he winked at Cutter. "Mine's not as big as yours, but it cuts cheese just fine."

Back at the dining table, Keech considered what they had discussed with Doyle. He understood the desire to liberate a partner, but something was poking at the back of his mind. The bending tree in the nearby meadow. Doyle had wanted to follow the seven Osage travelers there. *Most folks pass them right up*, he'd said. *Think they're just part of the normal landscape. They would never imagine these trees keep old secrets.*

Pa Abner's dying words were more important now than ever. The young riders were close to finding Bonfire Crossing. Keech felt it down in his heart. "Ranger, is all this bending-tree business somehow related to your friend, Mr. Lynch?"

Doyle's spoonful of beans hovered just in front of his lips. "Yes, I figured you'd have more questions about the trees. Back in the glade, I saw the looks on your faces when I stopped at the maple. They mean something to your team. The trees are important to me as well. There's a kind of code to them I'm trying to crack. Thing is, I can't."

"But Warren Lynch can," Keech guessed.

"Without my partner's knowledge, I can't figure out the path."

"The path?" Duck repeated, but Doyle offered nothing more.

Keech turned to Quinn, who was busy devouring a small hunk of cheese. "Back at the mission, you said you overheard Mr. Strahan talking to a man. Do you suppose that man was Mr. Lynch?"

Quinn shrugged. "Maybe so. Maybe they swapped notes on what they knew before they got captured."

Doyle said, "My partner and I rode separate so that we'd cover more ground. He's been working secret in this quarter for some time. He would've established a contact with the sheriff, since Strahan knows this part of Kansas like the back of his hand."

"Ranger, you should know we're determined to go along to Wisdom," Keech said. "We promised Quinn we'd help him find his aunt and rescue Sheriff Strahan if we can. Maybe if we work together, we could help one another." *And track down Bonfire Crossing in the process*, he thought.

Doyle put down his spoon. "It'll be awful dangerous. One wrong move could spell violence. I can't lead a bunch of kids into peril."

"You won't be leading anyone," Cutter said. "We help you find your *compañero*, you help us find Strahan. We'll call it a temporary team-up."

The Ranger held up his hands in surrender. "If you say so, kid."

"I do say so. And I ain't no kid."

Doyle grinned. "Then we'll travel together." Standing, he gestured to the empty bowls. "Now, how about you kids clean these dishes, then get some shut-eye. I'd like to leave for Wisdom before nightfall."

Doyle shoved his pipe into his mouth, left his empty dish on the table, and headed upstairs.

After the man disappeared, Nat held his hands up to the young riders. "I think we ought to reconsider. I don't like the notion of nestling up to a stranger, no matter what he did to help us. I vote we leave while he's asleep."

"I'll be going with the Ranger," Quinn said promptly. "No offense, but he's my best chance of finding Auntie Ruth and getting her out."

"You can take the path you want, Revels. What about you, Cut?"

Cutter ticked his fingers against his knife's bone handle. "I say we tag along, but only for now. He could distract all the bad men while we go about our business."

Nat sighed. "So you vote to ride with him. What about you, sis?"

Duck pinched her lips in thought. "He does know an awful lot, but he ain't too quick to volunteer answers. I vote we ride but keep our eyes wide open."

Nat turned to Keech. "What about you, Blackwood? Do you trust him?"

Keech gazed up at the ominous second-floor landing, where Doyle had vanished for his nap. That bleak, stony feeling returned to squeeze at his heart. "I think Doyle could be a real help finding Strahan. We're on the right path. I feel certain about that. Pa wants us to find Bonfire Crossing, so we should do whatever best gets us there. Even if it means riding for a spell with this fella."

Nat waved his hands. "All right then. The posse's spoken. We stay vigilant, but we ride with the Ranger."

CHAPTER 13

SHADOW OF THE BUFFALO

Keech dreamed he met his father—his *real* father, Black Wood.

They passed through a great stone cavern together, a vast chamber filled with impossible light. On the black stone walls were thousands of primitive engravings, a millennium's worth of ancient etchings depicting gruesome creatures and human sacrifices. As Keech approached the carvings, he realized the figures on the walls were not static; they *moved*, crawling over one another, seeking places to peel away, as if alive and breathing. Disturbed, Keech looked up to tell his father they had to leave.

He couldn't see the man's face, only a smeared darkness.

The Reverend, his father's shadow face murmured. Rough hands seized Keech's shoulders and yanked him toward the source of the fearsome light. A terrible heat baked his face, and the stench of death filled his nostrils. *The Reverend has woken in the Palace....*

Keech's eyes snapped open. He sat up, his heart pounding, and rubbed sweat off his face. Then, mostly out of habit, he clutched at the crescent charm inside his shirt.

The young riders were still asleep by the fireplace, Nat and Quinn unleashing loud snores that could awaken Bone Ridge all over again. The fire had died down, but a couple of logs were still glowing on the hearth. Gray afternoon light continued to suffuse the common room.

Nearby, Cutter napped in a curled-up position, clutching a flimsy yellow object to his chest. With a pang of sorrow, Keech realized it was John Wesley's straw hat. Cutter had stuffed it into his coat before leaving Mercy Mission.

Tiptoeing over the sleeping bodies, Keech grabbed his dry socks and his bowler hat off the mantel. The fire had dried his clothes, but he didn't expect the dreary Kansas weather to let them stay that way. If his journey thus far had taught him anything, it was to expect to get wet.

As he slipped back into his socks and coat and poncho, echoes of the strange dream—*The Reverend has woken in the Palace*—tugged at his thoughts. He pushed away the terrible images of the writhing figures on the chamber walls, but they wriggled back to the foreground, refusing to disappear.

A small cry startled Keech. The noise had come from Duck. She appeared to be trying to awaken from her own bad dream but couldn't. Keech crouched beside the girl. "Duck, wake up."

A dismal sob escaped her throat.

Keech placed a hand on the girl's shoulder and shook her. "Wake up. You're dreaming."

Duck came awake like a young deer shot in the woods. She

sat bolt upright, tears springing from her eyes, and her knuckles flew to her mouth to stifle a scream.

"Hey, it's okay." Keech kept his voice low to avoid stirring the whole house. "You're awake now."

The terrified look on Duck's face suggested she might punch him square in the nose. Instead, she surprised him by reaching out and hugging him so tightly, Keech thought he might choke. He returned the embrace. She whispered in a tearful, gurgling voice, "It was awful. I never want to dream that again."

Keech patted her shoulder. It saddened him beyond words that she should suffer so many dream terrors. "Come take a walk, and you can tell me about it."

"Okay," she said.

He moved out to the front porch, where the cold afternoon wind rustled a wooden chime that hung near the front door. He sat on a porch step while Duck dressed inside. Off in the barn, the ponies made occasional chuffing sounds, perhaps wondering about the strange black horse that had taken Felix's place in the fold.

As he waited in the chill, Keech reached into his coat pocket and pulled out the wooden-headed doll, the one taken from his mother's grave. He sat it upon his palm. He wanted to feel calm when he held the figurine, but the doll still didn't stop the thought of monsters from invading his mind. He recalled Bad Whiskey standing over his mother's grave, screaming *A doll!* when he realized the trinket had replaced the Char Stone.

Then Keech envisioned *another* man, this one mysterious and faceless, removing the Stone sometime before and placing the doll in his mother's skeletal embrace.

Red Jeffreys.

Duck stepped out onto the porch and sat next to him. Shuddering from the cold, she glanced down at the figurine. "You know, I used to have a doll that looked just like that, only it had yellow britches and a blue hat." She lifted it from Keech's palm and tinkered with its tiny plaid dress and red bonnet. "I called her Clementine. She was a present from Nat. I played with her in the mud holes out behind the house." Chortling lightly, she handed it back.

Keech turned the doll's tattered frame over in his hand. "I don't like it much."

"Why don't you throw it away then?"

"I don't know. I reckon it helps me feel closer to my ma."

As Keech stuffed the figurine back into his coat, Duck put a hand on his arm. "I'm awful sorry about Felix, Keech. I still can't believe he's gone."

Keech wanted to assure her that he would be fine. He wanted to remind her that he had managed to remain focused on their mission even after losing his family. But suddenly a sound like a ragged cough spilled out, and he found himself weeping. He turned his face away, not wanting her to witness such a spectacle, but when he did, Duck simply shifted on the step to where she could see him. He wiped at his nose, and his hand came away shiny with snot. He felt his face burn red-hot with embarrassment.

"No shame at all crying over your pony," Duck said. "I lost a pet rabbit once. Charley Dickens. Nat's mean little hound dog Rascal attacked him. I cried for a whole year. I know how it feels."

Dabbing his nose with his coat sleeve, Keech muttered, "Thanks." He appreciated her words—and couldn't fathom such courage and wisdom in a soul so young, especially given Duck's recent night terrors—but he couldn't stand the thought of someone seeing him so messy.

After a time, he felt hollowed out, as if there were absolutely no more tears left in that mysterious well from which they sprang. Smearing his face clean, he took a few burning breaths. His ears and nose were freezing, so he turned his coat collar up to the wind. "C'mon. Let's take a quick walk."

As they started across the yard, Duck asked, "Where're we going?"

He took a breath to compose himself. "You'll see. It's not too far. About a mile or so."

"But what about the Ranger's protection line? We ain't supposed to cross it. What if the Chamelia comes around?"

No sooner did she finish speaking than they approached the red border that Doyle had scattered around the property. Fresh snow and bits of sleet had damaged or covered the protection in places, but not enough to break the perimeter. Keech looked at the bloodroot with interest, then he bent and scooped up a small amount. The powder was wet and cold on his palm. He smeared a little on Duck's cheeks, then rubbed the rest over his own face.

"There. If the Chamelia tries to get us, we'll be safe."

"I don't know if I believe that."

"We'll be quick. I promise."

They didn't have to walk too far from the Moss farm for Duck to realize where he was leading her. "We're headed for the bending tree, aren't we?"

"I need to look at it again. I can't figure things out with everyone gabbing around me."

Their boots crunched in the snow as they backtracked over the rolling lea the gang had crossed that morning. "Tell me about your dream," Keech said as they trudged over the alabaster ground. "It must've packed a wallop."

After a moment's hesitation, Duck said, "I was walking with my pa, and we were in a giant cave. There was wretched movement all around us, like thousands of wriggling bats or snakes on the walls. I was so scared, I couldn't breathe. I told my pa I wanted to leave, but he wouldn't let me. We walked toward this big light. 'We have to get closer,' he told me. When I tried to pull back, Pa dragged me along. The light got so bright, I couldn't see Pa's face anymore, just a pile of shadows. Then the light grew hot, like Pa and I was standing near the mouth of a big furnace. I tried to scream again, but Pa said, 'Hush, girl. The Reverend has—'"

"—woken in the Palace," Keech finished, feeling his legs almost give under him.

Startled, Duck froze in her tracks. "How do you know what Pa said?"

"Because I had the same dream. It woke me, too."

Duck's face turned skeptical. "You did not! Folks can't have the same dreams. It's impossible."

"I'm telling you, I dreamed about the cave and the bright light, and my pa was there, too, only it was my *real* pa. His face was all shadows. He said, 'The Reverend has woken in the Palace.' I swear it, Duck. On Pa Abner's grave."

Duck's face turned as pale as the snow. "How can that be?"

Keech searched for the proper answer. "I don't know, but whatever the Reverend Rose is up to, I think his plans are heating up. I reckon we need to find Bonfire Crossing pronto."

As they walked across the lea, Duck kept flipping her gaze to the left and right—most likely worried about the Chamelia. Keech was more concerned about the crows. He probed the skies for the Reverend's emissaries, but not one was in sight.

The feeble sunlight had dipped a bit lower when they reached the bending tree. Keech approached the maple, his eyes taking in every detail of the curious growth. Duck followed close behind.

The dim afternoon light did nothing to improve the eerie nature of the tree. Its mangled Y formation cast a crooked shadow over the snow like a pair of cupped hands straining toward the clouds with splayed fingers. He circled the tree once, then again, and examined the four snow-covered stones that encompassed the roots.

"What are we looking for?" Duck asked.

Keech squatted to brush the powder off the stones. "I don't rightly know, but I think these strange circles give us our strongest clue. When Doyle first brought us here, he put his foot on one. Maybe to push it down."

"What for?"

"Perhaps the stones open up something, like the log in Floodwood opened up the cave when we used Pa's charm as a key."

Duck knelt near a neighboring circle and flattened a hand on the stone. Keech did the same, and they pushed down in unison on their respective stones. The surface under his palm felt as smooth as new leather, and the cut of the circle looked so perfect, it almost confounded his mind. But the stone didn't budge.

"Mine didn't sink down any." Duck felt along the edges of her stone. "Hey, do you know what I think this rock is? Moss opal."

"What's that?"

"It's a precious stone. Some folks think it holds supernatural power and helps you talk to nature spirits. When I read about the Middle Ages, I learned that some folks wrapped their moss opals in bay leaves so they could become invisible."

Keech chuckled. "Bay leaves and nature spirits? You've studied some mighty weird subjects."

"Pa taught me Latin and old medieval stories since I was a baby. I reckon that might be weird, but I always enjoyed learning such things. And maybe he knew one day all that knowledge would come in handy. Anyway, we just saw a horse walk on water and a man summon a tornado to kill river monsters, so what I study ain't so weird by comparison."

"Good point." He turned his focus back to the stones. "I suppose whoever buried these circles chose moss opal for a reason."

"But the stones don't do anything."

Keech stood, wiped the moisture off his hands, and planted both boots on the stone he'd been testing. The notion of *keys* sprang to his mind again, and he suddenly remembered their conversation with Quinn Revels about Bonfire Crossing.

"Duck, do you recall what Quinn said about a *fang*?"

"He said he overheard a fella tell Sheriff Strahan he wanted to find it."

"Right. We thought he might be talking about a weapon. But what if it isn't? What if this fang is some kind of key? What if we need it to open up Bonfire Crossing?"

Duck considered the idea. "Could be. But we don't have it. Which means we're back to where we started."

Keech slumped on the stone his boots were inhabiting. "Let's take a gander at the limbs. We have to be missing something." He faced north on the circle, the same direction that one of the two main boughs aimed. "This limb here directs you back to the Kansas River."

Duck placed both feet firmly on her marker, mimicking Keech, and glanced up at the tree. "The other limb points down south. I reckon to another river?"

"Or maybe toward the Santa Fe Trail," he guessed. "Pa Abner taught me about the trail several years ago. He had a big plan to travel it for adventure when the orphans got older. The Santa Fe crosses south of here and cuts a path clear across Kansas. It used to be a buffalo path for hunters. 'Course, that don't help us find the Crossing." Keech gritted his teeth in frustration. He was about to lift his boots off the stone marker when a flash of movement captured his eye. The tree's shadow—the pair of cupped hands on the ground—had begun to *gather*.

Keech's body went rigid at the sight. "What in blazes?" He blinked and looked again. It was not a trick of the sunlight. The shadow was *squirming* on the ground, the fingers cast by the maple's limbs and branches rumpling closer together like some kind of ghostly flower closing up for the night.

"What's wrong?" Duck asked.

"The shadow! Look at the tree's shadow."

"Looks like the snout of a buffalo to me," Duck said in amazement.

Her words surprised him, but Keech dared not glance away from the crumpling dark form. He was struck with a vivid memory of the Mercy Mission tree. He recalled how the crooked oak's shadow had, for a brief moment, *slithered* away.

"It looks like a pair of hands to me," Keech said—except now he could see it. The side view of a buffalo head. "What's going on?"

Duck suddenly gasped. "It's moving! Like the head is turning."

Keech's heart galloped across his chest when he saw the bison-like shadow swivel left and right on the ground, as though peering at the landscape. "I saw movement like this at the first tree. I thought it might just be the lightning, but the shadow of that tree *slithered* like a snake."

A moment later, the phenomenon on the ground stopped. It didn't just cease movement; it disappeared completely, leaving behind the normal, cupped-hand shadow cast by the tree's two boughs.

"It's gone," Duck said.

Keech twisted his head and rubbed his eyes, but nothing he did reawakened the phantom buffalo. He recalled how Ranger Doyle had stared between the Y of the tree and shaken his head in frustration. "He was looking for the shadow," Keech said. "Doyle was hunting for the buffalo this morning, but he couldn't find it. *That's* the code he's trying to crack. The shadows are the secret, and he knows it."

They watched the ground till Duck said, "We ought to get on back. If Nat wakes up and I'm gone, he'll get his dander up."

Keech agreed. "We'll just have to keep our eyes peeled for other bending trees. I think we're on the right track. But we best not say anything about this in front of the Ranger, not till we ask him a few more questions."

They tramped their way back across the snowy field side by side, leaning against the frigid wind. Keech glanced back one last time at the mysterious maple, hoping to spy a hint of the buffalo mirage, but the bending tree stood still, its thin shadow unmoving.

CHAPTER 14

LESSONS ON THE PRAIRIE

I cy rain drizzled as Keech and Duck returned to the Moss farm. They passed through the gate and stepped over the bloodroot barrier. The property was still, the wooden chime on the front porch the only thing stirring.

"Looks like everybody's still asleep," Duck said. They sat again on the porch steps and cleaned the bloodroot smears off their faces.

Not long after, the front door squeaked open, and Edgar Doyle stepped out onto the porch, followed by Quinn, who carried a bundle of scarves. The Ranger lugged a bulging knapsack over his shoulder. His stubbly face looked tired and pale, as if he hadn't rested a second. Nat and Cutter appeared after them, dozy-eyed, their hair in disarray. Cutter's own face was red and swollen, full of a sadness that no sleep could drown.

Freshly clad in a cotton shirt and boots that fit him snugly, Quinn tipped his forage cap to Keech and Duck. "Mr. Moss had a dandy wardrobe. I found a cabinet full of these." He tossed them a woolen scarf. "They smell a tad moldy, but they'll come in handy on the prairie."

Doyle marched toward the barn with his knapsack. "We move out in ten minutes. Get your ponies ready to ride."

After the gang had saddled up and Keech took his cantle seat behind Quinn, Doyle trotted Saint Peter into the yard and gave all the young riders a grave look. He had secured his bulky knapsack with two or three ropes to the Kelpie's cantle. "Listen up. From here we veer west. Be aware, you'll see strange sights when we near the town."

"Stranger than this *loco* weather?" Cutter asked.

"You'll see darkness. And soldiers that ain't rightly men no more."

"Thralls," Nat said, scowling.

"So you've heard of them," Doyle said.

"We faced them back in Missouri," Duck said. "A fella named Bad Whiskey raised a whole cemetery full."

The Ranger's expression turned both puzzled and circumspect. "Good. Then you won't freeze up at the sight of them. I reckon you know that regular weapons won't help, so stay out of their way and don't draw attention."

"We'll stay out of their way, but not because we can't stop them." Duck reached into her coat and pulled out her amulet shard. "We can take thralls down with these."

Though Keech hadn't wanted to unveil the shards in front of Doyle, he reluctantly drew out his own, and they held the silver fragments up to the dull afternoon light. Doyle's eyes narrowed when he saw them.

"Yes, I saw you wield one back at the river," he said. "It took down one of those fish monsters. Good trinkets to have. But no conflict if we can avoid it. Let's keep the mission nice and quiet."

The young riders followed Doyle back into the white forest. They passed through a narrow gap in the low thickets and soon veered upon a deer trail that switched back and forth through lanky hickories and twisted red mulberries. The high branches swayed above them as the winds whined down from the north. After a time, they nudged their ponies out of the thickest part of the woods and started up a long slope.

Keech thought about the shared nightmare of the cavern and the strange excursion to the bending tree. The buffalo phantom he and Duck had seen on the ground haunted him. Perhaps the Ranger might be willing to help them figure out what they had witnessed—but first the gang needed to know more about the man. As the troop proceeded through more brushwood, Keech said, "Ranger, I need to ask you something."

"Fire at will."

"What are you hoping to find at the end of the bending trees?"

When Doyle turned to look at him, his gaze penetrated into the very core of Keech's mind. "I suspect you already know the answer, seeing how your troop is headed to the same place."

"Bonfire Crossing," Keech said. He *had* suspected the answer, of course, but he wanted the Ranger to confirm.

"Your company fascinates me, Mr. Blackwood. I'd like to know why you're seeking such a secret place."

The others had urged their ponies alongside Lightnin' and Saint Peter and were listening intently to the conversation. Nat looked worried but held his tongue.

"We don't rightly know," Keech answered. "We were told we'd learn something there in order to find and destroy a monster named Rose. Have you ever heard that name?"

Doyle's expression turned darker. "I have heard it, yes."

Quinn glanced around at the gang. "So you're all chasing after the same place—this Bonfire Crossing. But why? What do y'all expect to find?"

"Something of great worth to the Texas Rangers," Doyle said.

"It's the fang, isn't it?" said Duck. "You're looking for the fang."

Doyle gave the girl a surprised look. "I suppose I am. And I have to warn you kids, when I find it, I'm taking it. The Fang of Barachiel isn't some toy."

"'Barachiel,'" Duck said, rubbing her cheek. "Sounds like a name you'd find in the Bible."

"Sounds like a mean liquor to me," Cutter scoffed.

"I have no idea what it means," Doyle said. "I'm only charged with securing it."

Puzzle pieces tumbled into place as Keech considered the Ranger's words. Some time ago, Sheriff Strahan and another fellow—most likely Doyle's partner, Warren Lynch—had discussed the hidden path to Bonfire Crossing, and Quinn Revels happened upon their conversation and heard mention of the Fang. Then Friendly Williams and Rose's gang showed up, and both men went missing, likely imprisoned somewhere in Wisdom. Competing forces were aligning to find the secret Osage encampment and seize what lay inside: the Fang of Barachiel.

These realizations brought up another vital question. "Ranger, what *is* the Fang? A weapon of some sort?"

"It's top secret government property."

Nat asked, "Then what's it doing in a hidden Osage camp?"

Doyle sighed heavily. "I understand you want answers. But

when it comes to matters of the Law, I cannot discuss top secret information."

"But we *are* the Law," Cutter mumbled. "We got deputized."

Doyle chuckled, as if he didn't quite believe Cutter's assertion.

For the next few miles, the company fell into an uncomfortable silence—except for the Ranger, who set to humming a peculiar tune, a refrain of notes as dreary as the weather. It was the same lonely tune that Doyle had purred after they first met him.

The dull melody grew so bothersome, Keech tried to shift his ears to more comforting noises: the steadfast wheeze of the wind, the tromping of hooves on frozen ground. He noticed, with no small curiosity, that Saint Peter's steps were utterly silent, neither crunching on the ice nor leaving a single hoofprint in the snow. Doyle's story about the horse being a Kelpie spirit seemed ridiculous, but Keech had to believe his own ears and eyes.

Before long, the group crested another broad hill, and rolling white prairie unfolded before them. The sight filled Keech with both melancholy and wonder. The abundant range bristled with clusters of snow-covered foxtail and reclusive trees, each one shorn bald and helpless by the constant wind. Occasional ridges punctuated the lowland, a series of cliff-like escarpments that gave Keech a feeling of constant motion, as though they were riding over the surface of a vast ocean.

A startling crack of thunder made him glance farther west.

"Looks like another storm," said Quinn.

Saint Peter suddenly came to a stop. Doyle held up his fist, a signal for the gang to rein back, and the young riders halted their ponies. Keech watched as the Ranger jiggled his head, like someone trying to jar himself from a bitter daydream.

Concern twisted Quinn's face. "Ranger?"

"No one move," Doyle barked. "Listen."

The man resumed his monotonous tune, this time placing a string of words on the melody. They sounded empty of meaning, like the irritating gibberish that Little Eugena and Patrick used to mumble to each other while playing. The noise slipped under Keech's skin and crawled over his nerves. He inspected the quiet prairie, hoping to see what concerned the Ranger, but save for the occasional set of rabbit prints, he saw nothing of note. He lifted his eyes to search the clouds.

Farther west, a narrow smear on the sky hovered like a dismal bookmark above the land, as if a powerful storm had gathered inside a single, mighty cloud. Keech remembered the Ranger's warning that they would see *darkness* and wondered if the terrible smear was what he had meant.

A too-familiar *Ack!* yanked Keech from his thoughts.

Doyle didn't stop chanting. Instead, his bothersome song grew louder. The frightful call came again, more urgent this time: *Ack! Ack!*

A quick movement near Keech's right flank made him spin. Not far away, a large black shape had perched on a thick sycamore limb. Keech's breath hitched. He expected the shard to suddenly ignite cold under his shirt, but it did nothing. Next to him, Duck grabbed at her own amulet, her face showing the same confusion Keech was feeling.

The monstrous crow on the sycamore had a rounded torso, bulging and lumpish, and giant wings. The talons that held the creature on the bough resembled the curved spikes of a deer's antlers, and the crow's long beak could have passed for a cutting froe. A pair of bloodred eyes scanned the prairie.

The creature looked straight at the young riders, but it was confused, as though a rock had just smacked it across the head.

Abruptly, Doyle's song ceased, and he whistled loudly at the crow, as if mocking it.

"Quiet, Ranger!" Duck hissed.

"Don't fret. I've made sure this one sees and hears nothing of us."

The Ranger spun his mount and strolled up to the sycamore tree, stopping a few feet from the crow. "Think of the crows as extensions of a main body, like the teeth of a crocodile. When the teeth strike, they can kill. But if the crocodile is blind, the teeth can't find their prey."

Keech considered for a moment. "Your humming. It's made us invisible somehow."

The Ranger smiled. "Put a blindfold on the croc, and he can't strike very well, can he?"

"I wish you would teach us to hum like that," Keech said.

"It's not the humming, son. It's the focus the tune provides." Doyle grunted. "Anyway, children should learn numbers and history, not enchantment."

"We're on a dangerous trail, not at home reading lessons," said Duck.

"It sure would come in handy," Keech said.

The Ranger thought for a moment, then sighed. "I suppose it wouldn't hurt to share a few concepts." He cleared his throat. "Energies exist inside everything you can see and smell, taste and touch. Some energies are shallow, like the bubbles that rise to the surface of a pond. They're the easiest to tap. Others lie deeper and are more challenging to find. The first step to connecting with these buried energies is to clear your mind of distractions."

"How?" Keech asked.

"Different methods work for different folks. I begin by listening to the songs of the scurryin' rodents, the whisper of the breeze, the crack of ice as the sun shines on the snow. When I discover the tune of the world, my focus sparks within. That's the secret: *focus*."

"'The tune of the world.'" Keech took a moment to listen to the prairie.

"Our method of focusing will be special to each of us, won't it?" Quinn asked.

"Indeed, Mr. Revels. Each person must find his own way to connect." The Ranger closed his eyes and drew in a steady breath. "Now, let's learn a more important lesson."

"Which is?" said Duck.

The Ranger pointed his gloved finger at the crow. "Breaking the crocodile's teeth."

The massive bird squawked but remained unaware of the group.

"*Bang*," Doyle said.

The crow exploded into a grisly ball of black feathers and muck. The remains of the monster drifted to the ground.

Keech gawked in surprise, unable to speak.

Gravely, Doyle looked at the young riders. "Your first lesson is complete. Now let's get back to the trail." Snapping Saint Peter's reins, the Ranger forged on.

CHAPTER 15

THE TOWN OF PERPETUAL NIGHT

For a time, Keech lost himself in the image of the rupturing crow till the prairie folded back up into another forest and the land dipped to a shallow gully. Following Doyle, the young riders entered the gulch and soon emerged into a network of cottonwood trees, their heavy crowns iced over and dusted with snow.

Doyle said, "It's time we find a place to hide the horses. Wisdom is only two miles away, through these woods. We'll want to travel the last bit on foot."

Keech felt his nerves pulse with dread—but he also felt excited to finally reach Wisdom. As Quinn steered them onward, he braced himself for the mission and began to practice the Ranger's doleful tune.

Doyle guided the company to a narrow ravine and reined Saint Peter to a halt. He gazed around at the surroundings. "Sufficient cover, concealed from various points, easy access and escape. Let's use this for our rallying point."

Keech agreed with the Ranger's evaluation of the ravine. Pa Abner had taught him and Sam the best strategies for regrouping in combat. The clearing would make a fitting rendezvous and was close enough to the prairie that a swift retreat across the lowlands would be feasible.

After dismounting and tying off, the young riders gathered close as Doyle encircled the horses with his bloodroot. A frigid breeze swept down the ravine, blowing the curls of dark blond hair that peeked beneath the Ranger's brown hat.

The protections set, the Ranger patted the big knapsack and shook his head. He leaned toward Saint Peter and whispered into the Kelpie's ear, then he gently scratched the creature's broad muzzle. The black steed grunted back. "I've asked Saint Peter to help us protect our things. Your horses will be safe here. Now let's make haste. We have a lot to get done."

Nat hesitated, pulling off his hat. "Before we go, I need a word with my team. Alone."

Doyle shrugged. "Make it quick." He twisted toward the woods and strolled away.

Once the fellow looked out of earshot, Nat took to one knee in the snow.

The young riders huddled on their knees, and Nat put his arms around Quinn's and Cutter's necks. Keech followed suit, settling his arms over Cutter and Duck. Nat's eyes were heavy with doubt. "I just want you to know I'm doggone proud of every single one of you. That includes you, Mr. Revels. I didn't want to trust you at first, and for that I apologize. I was wrong to be so close-minded. You've shown true grit since taking up with the team. Thank you."

Quinn looked embarrassed. "I just want to find Auntie Ruth."

"We will. We'll get Sheriff Strahan out, too, and he'll guide us to Bonfire Crossing. We'll accomplish our mission down to the penny." Nat glanced at Keech and Cutter next. "I know you've both suffered loss and that you're grieving over it. Are you fellas gonna be okay in there?"

"I'll be dandy." Cutter tried to look proud, despite the heartache inside his eyes.

"And you, Keech?"

"I'm ready, too. Let's get moving."

Nat slapped their shoulders. "I just want to make sure your heads are clear." He then addressed the entire circle. "Before we go, let's remember one thing. No matter what happens in that town, we'll watch each other's backs. Agreed?"

"Agreed," said Duck. "Now let's go already."

Keech looked at his new friends with appreciation. After losing Sam, he couldn't have asked for better trailmates to help him chase Bonfire Crossing. "Agreed."

"Okay, that's all. Let's go get this done," Nat said, and the young riders moved swiftly to catch up to the Texas Ranger.

The trail to Wisdom slithered through heavy cottonwood country. The young riders tucked in close behind their guide, bending low and keeping to cover. There were no signs of roving bandits, but Doyle warned against letting down their guard for even a second.

Stark branches cut off most of the sky, but through the tangled thatch, a baffling stain of darkness appeared ahead, engulfing the trees. Keech thought of the way morning fogs would sometimes enclose the Home for Lost Causes and settle around Low Hill beyond Pa's property. Yet this fog was a wall of eclipse, engulfing them in terrible twilight, as if the hands of a clock had spun forward several hours.

With each step deeper into the darkness, the temperature

dropped and the air turned soupy on Keech's skin. He was reminded of the pressure and buzz of Floodwood. He set his teeth before they started chattering.

"*Dios mío*, it's night already," Cutter said.

"How'd this happen?" Quinn asked.

Doyle frowned at the sky. "A powerful curse, Mr. Revels. The work of a Spaniard named Ignatio. He can manipulate shadows, mold darkness, and raise the dead, and some who've encountered him suspect he can alter the weather, too. He laid this curse the day after you fled. The town of Wisdom will sit under this eternal night till Ignatio chooses to break it or till he perishes."

Under his breath, Quinn whispered, "Sorry, Auntie Ruth. I didn't mean to leave you in this nightmare."

The company approached the foot of a steep embankment, a slope covered with a skin of frozen sumac. Doyle studied the incline, then muttered, "On your bellies."

Following the Ranger's lead, the young riders hunkered in the sumac and slogged up the embankment. At the top, they saw a faint orange flicker—something like torchlight—down in the distance. A dingy settlement sprawled before them, situated between a narrow creek to the west and a run of white boulders to the east. Dirt streets and alleyways ran this way and that, like a topsy-turvy maze, and numerous torches and streetlamps lit up a tightly clumped collection of buildings in the center of the burg. Squat huts, large canvas tents, warehouses, and tall barns surrounded the downtown area.

Standing around the town was a craggy wall of oak and cottonwood logs. Rickety watchtowers perched at the four corners of the border. A shallow moat filled with icy mud ran around the front of the perimeter, half-finished, then abandoned. Perhaps once the town of Wisdom had looked alive and inviting, but from their hiding spot atop the hill, it seemed only a miserable settlement.

Eagle-eyed as always, Nat whispered, "One man on each tower. Two at the gate. I count four guards patrolling the perimeter."

Keech spotted the watchmen at the towers and the group wandering the outside of the wall, skirting the muddy moat. They carried musket rifles. The patrolling guards took lurching steps in the dirty snow, a stiff motion that Keech recognized all too well. "Thralls," he whispered to Doyle.

"Indeed," the Ranger said. "Ignatio must've raised this batch."

Keech instantly recognized a problem—one that Nat must have realized as well, for the rancher glanced at Keech and Duck and said, "The second you two go down there, the thralls will know. We need to hide the amulets."

Doyle gave the young riders a reassuring look. "Relax. My chant will quiet the charms enough to keep us hid."

"We can't trust that," Nat said.

"Yeah, how do we know you won't just leave us all exposed?" asked Cutter.

Quinn answered for the man. "Y'all don't recollect that he hid me from the Chamelia? And hid us from the crow back on the prairie? And saved our lives on the river? I think it's high time y'all trust the Ranger's word."

Nat glanced at Doyle with burning eyes. "Swear you won't let us down."

"You've got my word," Doyle said. "The chant will work. But

be aware that while you're under the tune, you won't feel any magics, either."

Keech didn't like the sound of that—the muscle of Pa's amulet and Bennett Coal's charm was often the only thing that kept the Lost Causes kicking back in Missouri.

"That's why our shards didn't turn cold or shine when we saw the crow back yonder," Duck said. "Am I right? Your tune was blinding the crow but stifling the silver, too."

Doyle shrugged. "Apologies. I don't make the rules. But don't fret. The silver will still work on the dead men, if needed. I'm only concealing you, not stopping the energies."

The group turned its attention back to the towers and the thrall guards.

"I know a way under the wall, a place the guards probably wouldn't check." Quinn pointed to the slender creek on the west side of the perimeter. "But we'll get dirty."

Cutter flashed a grin. "A secret way in? What are we waiting for?" He shuffled to get up, but Nat stopped him and motioned toward the rugged entrance to the town.

"The gates are opening."

Grumbling, Cutter settled back on his belly.

The Wisdom gate swiveled open, dragging through mud and snow, and a strange child with a bald spot on his head stepped out into the clearing, hands on his hips. The child took a wide stance and looked out toward the black hills.

Except it wasn't a child at all but a rather short man in a frock coat. The jacket looked too long for his stubby torso, as did the curved sword sheathed on his hip.

The small man muttered something to the pair of thralls

standing guard and pointed back at Wisdom. The two dead men shambled into the town, leaving the child-like man alone at the gate.

"*Coward.*" Doyle hissed the word through teeth gritted so tight that Keech thought they might shatter in his mouth.

Cutter's face contorted with something like terror. He squeezed Keech's arm.

"Cutter? What's wrong?"

"Not a sound!" the Ranger mumbled. "Don't even move."

Closing his eyes, Doyle began his low hum. The melody slithered into Keech's ear and burrowed into his mind. The lullaby dulled the sound of the Kansas wind and somehow robbed the forest of any scent.

The Ranger was hiding them again.

Down at the gate, the short fellow scanned the hills. His eyes slid right over Keech, but they didn't stop. The man's face turned up, and he sniffed deeply at the air like a mongrel dog.

Keech held his breath.

After a time, the small man scratched his bare crown and stepped back through the gate. The two thrall guards emerged and resumed their weary watch.

Doyle gestured for the group to crawl back down the embankment. Once the town had dropped back out of sight, Keech turned to Cutter. "What in tarnation's wrong with you?"

Cutter's eyes refused to meet Keech's. "Forget it."

"If you know something about that man, we need to hear it."

"Drop it, Lost Cause."

Nat shoved in closer to the boy. "No, Cut. You've seen that fella before. It makes no sense to keep secrets from your trailmates. Spill the beans."

Cutter's face turned to stone, except for his eyes. They twitched side to side—the look of a kid planning a swift getaway. But instead of escaping, he said, "I don't care none for your pushing, Embry."

"We have to know what's waiting for us down there."

Cutter crossed himself with a shaky thumb, as if requesting courage from on high. "I ran across him back in Arkansas when I rode with my friend, Bishop. We met some real snakes."

"Like Bad Whiskey?" Keech asked, remembering Whiskey's claim that he had encountered Cutter in a previous life.

"That fella's way worse than *El Ojo*. He ain't a fighter. He's something meaner. When he talks, his words rattle your brain. They stick to your soul like tar."

"He goes by Coward," Doyle explained. "No other name fits him, and it's a name he wears with pride. The Rangers have a bad history with that scoundrel."

"He looked like he was *sniffing* the air," Duck said.

Doyle appeared to shudder. "He's got a . . . let's call it *unique* sense of smell. He can track a man over a hundred miles. If not for my incantations, he would have sniffed us up here on the hill."

"You mean he's like a bloodhound?" Quinn asked.

"If a bloodhound had the Devil's purpose."

"We should stay out of his way," Cutter said.

"I agree. We should all do our best to avoid Coward," Doyle said. "But we still have a mission to attend. Now, I think it's high time you show us the way into town, Mr. Revels."

Quinn pointed to a spot beyond the northwest watchtower, where the Wisdom wall curved along the creek bed. "It's just there. If we can find a way to slip past that guard tower, the rest of the way there should be clear."

Keech peered across the distance. The ramshackle watchtower stood at least twenty feet high, and a dead man in an army uniform leaned against the tower's railing, looking out. A torch burned on a post inside the thrall's lookout, puffing black smoke into the forest.

"Leave that to me." The Ranger looked at the young riders with a steely gaze. "Silence from here on out, kids. Stay close and keep low."

The Ranger gestured for Quinn to lead the way, and the boy slipped down the hill, keeping his steps soft and measured on the snowy ground. Keech and the others followed, and the company moved closer to Wisdom under cover of sinister night.

CHAPTER 16
UNDER THE WALL

Quinn led them down through heavy thickets toward the northwest corner of the wall. As they drew closer to the tower lookout, Doyle motioned for them to gather into a close huddle behind a column of tall thistle.

Reaching into one of the pouches tied to his belt, the Ranger drew forth a pinch of black dust. He mumbled a few indistinct words, another one of his mystical chants, then poured the dust into his mouth. After swirling the dark powder around in his mouth for a moment, he extended his tongue, which was now an inky black, and curled it as if preparing to hawk a mighty gob. Instead of spitting, he puffed, like a child blowing out birthday candles.

Keech watched in fascination as a murky fog snaked out of the Ranger's lungs and swirled through the air, winding upward. The vapor coiled around the watchtower, deepening the night shadows, and obscured any view of the thrall standing guard.

When the black haze finally broke from his lips, Doyle dabbed his mouth with a sleeve. "We've only a few minutes before the smoke thins. Let's move." He gestured at Quinn to lead on, then started back on his unnatural humming.

The young riders quickened their pace till they reached the moat that ran parallel to the north wall. The ditch had been dug in a haphazard manner, broad in some places, pitifully narrow in others. Quinn hopped across. The others followed close behind, moving as silently as possible beneath Doyle's smoky veil.

Keech glanced up as they scooted around the watchtower. Again, no supernatural cold sparked upon his chest. He figured that, as Doyle had claimed, his incantation was concealing the shard's energy.

The group skirted the log wall in single file. Keech moved with the quiet precision taught to him by Pa Abner, and the other kids' footfalls were so discreet that not even a nervous deer would have noticed. But Edgar Doyle was the very definition of stealth. Much like his Kelpie horse, the Ranger's moccasins made no sound.

Somewhere inside Wisdom, laughter filled the night, rattling to the croon of a badly tuned piano. The melody sounded to Keech like "Camptown Races," a song that Little Eugena always tried to play on her bugle. The goons inside the town were apparently enjoying a party. Keech shivered at the thought of Big Ben nestled up on a bar stool beside that unsettling man, Coward, drinking rotgut whiskey while discussing the Reverend Rose's wicked schemes.

As the company neared the narrow creek, Quinn whispered, "This is it."

"What are we looking for?" asked Doyle.

Quinn beckoned for them to gather closer to the wall. "A few days before me and Auntie Ruth ran, one of Friendly's men loaded me up with buckets of fish fins and guts and told me to pour them out near the wall. I carried the buckets behind a big warehouse. Right about here." He pointed to the log barrier. "My feet sank in the ground all the way up to my knees. I thought I might get swallowed whole, but I managed to dig myself out. I realized the creek had washed out the dirt along this entire stretch. There's a gap here to crawl under."

"Big enough for somebody my size?" Nat asked.

"If you don't mind getting muddy up to your eyeballs."

"I'll go first, make sure the way's clear on the other side," Cutter said. He skulked to the wall, pulled off his tan hat, and stuffed it into his coat. Dropping onto his belly, he pushed deep into the black murk.

Once he had passed beneath the logs, Cutter peeked back under the gap, his cheeks covered in dark sludge. "That was powerful gross. Your turn, Duck."

Duck coasted as easily as a grass snake through the furrow, and when she made it to the other side, her grinning, mud-stained face reappeared in the gap. "C'mon, fellas, stop loafing."

Keech and the other kids followed soon after, spitting dirt and mumbling curses.

Finally, the Ranger himself pushed up from the wall's base, stood, and pulled a kerchief from his deerskin coat. After wiping his face, he grumbled, "That was unpleasant."

They were behind the warehouse Quinn had mentioned, a rectangular storeroom with a series of mismatched canvas swatches nailed up to make walls. A threadbare tarp had been thrown over the wooden supports to create a sagging tent roof. Keech peeled back one of the cloth walls and peered inside. The makeshift warehouse was full of horse equipment and range saddles. Yellow crates, some stacked as high as the floppy ceiling, filled half the room. The entire west side of the depository was open to the night.

A kerosene lamppost stood on the sidewalk of the nearby street, illuminating the interior of the tented building with dull light. A pair of figures, likely a thrall patrol, wandered away down the street. They didn't glance back and soon disappeared around a corner.

"Why is there so much horse tackle?" Keech asked.

"All this stuff wasn't in here before," Quinn noted.

Keech stole inside the warehouse and held the flap open for the others. Doyle checked one of the crate lids and found it open. He slid the lid off, and the gang peeked inside and saw folded clothing.

"What are they?" Quinn asked.

The Ranger gazed around at the dozens of crates around them. "Soldier uniforms."

"But Wisdom ain't a military base, is it?" wondered Nat.

"No. The closest garrison from here is Fort Riley up by the Kansas River," Doyle said. "The outlaws are up to something bad here. They've turned a regular town into a fortress."

A terrible thought rattled Keech. He wondered if the Reverend Rose was building a legion of thralls to attack every state and territory in the country. The more victims Rose's brood piled up, the more troops they could raise up for their militia. Death spawned life for the Reverend and his followers. With enough gear and supplies, there would be no stopping them.

"Over here," Duck murmured. "I found something."

The group stepped over to a dark corner where Duck squatted

next to a bundle of horse blankets. She was holding up the corner of the cloth, revealing a box filled with straw and four oily black spheres.

Nat hunkered closer. "Whistle bombs?"

Quinn answered, "Sure looks like it."

Doyle carefully scooped up two of the bombs. "This is good news. Means we have a powerful defense should something go skew-whiff."

"How did these get here?" Cutter asked.

"As I suspected, my partner hid stashes around the town." The Ranger slipped the shiny dark orbs into his coat. "Looks like he intended to blow up these supplies."

Duck lifted a bomb out of the hay and held it in front of her. Her face screwed up in disgust. "They feel like butter. Should we take these with us?"

Doyle mulled over the question. "Normally, I'd say children should keep far away from such deadly devices. But you ain't quite normal kids, and these are far from normal times. Have at it, but be careful."

Quinn took the fourth ball from the crate and slipped it into his pocket. When the others looked at him with surprise, he said, "I planned to blow up this town all along, if you recall."

Duck slid the bomb she was holding into her coat, but Nat grabbed her wrist. "No. I don't want you carrying one. Give it to Keech if he wants it."

"But I can handle it."

"I know you can handle plenty, but if something happened—if you tripped and that thing went off—I'd never be able to face another day."

Duck handed the bomb to Keech.

Keech smiled nervously. "Thanks. I think." He tucked the black orb into his coat pocket. He didn't relish the idea of carrying raw ordnance in his jacket, but he said nothing more.

"We should move," Nat said.

"Not just yet," Doyle replied, and glanced at Quinn. "Mr. Revels, give us the layout of this cursed place."

Quinn closed his eyes. "There are three big buildings where they held all the townsfolk prisoners down to the south. To the east, you'll find stockyards and pens where they keep all the livestock, and the place where Friendly built a run of holding cells for folks who fussed. If Auntie Ruth and the others you're looking for ain't in the south quarters, I'd say Friendly would've took them to the cells, as punishment for my escape."

"The holding cells," Doyle said. "Are they the only ones in town?"

"There's a jail on Main Street inside the sheriff's office. But Friendly boarded that place up, like they didn't want it used no more."

Doyle's dark eyes narrowed. "From here on, I suggest we split up."

"No, sir, I don't like that idea none," Nat said.

Doyle smiled, but the look that attended it was more stern than friendly. "I understand your hesitation, son, but this town's too large for the group to move together. Your aim is to find the sheriff. Mr. Revels aims to rescue his aunt. My own mission is to find my partner, Lynch, and get him to safety. We cannot accomplish all these things if we stay clustered together. When stealth is involved, large numbers invite sloppiness. We'll set a time to meet up at the ravine."

Keech couldn't believe how much the Texas Ranger sounded like Pa Abner. The tactical manner in which Doyle discussed teamwork and stealth all suggested a mastery of training.

Keech shrugged at Nat. "He's right, I'm afraid. Chances are good we'll be spotted if we clump together. A pair can hug to shadows easier than half a dozen. I propose Nat, Duck, and myself scout for the sheriff at the town jail. Quinn, Cutter, you two could head to the south quarters and look for Quinn's aunt."

"And I'll search for the holding cells east," Doyle finished.

Cutter held up a muddy hand. "Now hang on, *amigos*. If we split up, we should split the amulets, too. Doyle said they would still kill the dead men. I don't fancy sneaking about this foul place without proper defense. I ain't carrying no bomb, and my knife don't work on thralls."

Duck pulled the silver fragment from her coat. "Take this one. Keech can protect me and Nat with his."

Cutter looked surprised by the girl's offer, but he hung the fragment around his neck anyway. "I'll take good care of it. I swear."

"Once you've accomplished your mission, don't linger," Doyle said. "Retreat outside the walls and get Miss Ruth and Sheriff Strahan to the rally point."

"What's our cutoff?" Nat asked.

Doyle reached inside one of his pockets and extracted a watch. He looked at the time and said, "Let's say one hour. If we can't locate our friends within that time, regroup at the ravine and we'll design another strategy." Doyle wished them good luck, then slipped out of the warehouse, disappearing behind a stand of low buildings.

Nat studied each of the young riders, his stark blue eyes looking fretful. "All right, Lost Causes, we have our marching orders.

Quinn, Cutter, be danged careful. Watch for crows and thralls, and run like scalded dogs if you spot the Chamelia."

Cutter scowled. "You just had to go and say that, didn't ya?"

"Quinn, find your aunt Ruth and hurry her out of this god-forsaken town."

"You can count on it." Quinn gingerly tapped on his coat pocket, where he'd stowed the whistle bomb. "And I'll leave Friendly a little something to remember Quinn Revels by."

"Wait, I almost forgot," Keech said. "How do we recognize Strahan?"

"He'll be a fella with gray whiskers," Quinn replied. "But you'll know him 'cause he's missing his right hand. It got pinched off a while back in a wagon pileup."

"One-handed. Gray whiskers. Got it."

Watching Cutter and their new friend creep off to the south, Keech tried to calm the beating of his nervous heart. He had agreed to Doyle's plan of splitting the group, but as he watched them slip away, he began to second-guess his own reasoning.

The night Bad Whiskey had attacked the Home for Lost Causes, Keech told Sam they should split up. *I have a plan*, he told his little brother. *Find Granny Nell and the others and lead them out to safety*. Sam had done just as he was told. He ran into the burning house to rescue the family, only to be overwhelmed by flames.

CHAPTER 17
THE GRIM CIRCUS

Wisdom was a haphazard sprawl of shoddy buildings and lean-to shanties. With its bewildering checkerboard of streets and footpaths, the town had no general order to its layout. It was as if some mad farmer had tossed a handful of seeds into the wind, and tangles of shops and cabins had sprouted up from the mud.

Drunken laughter and piano music continued to plague the air as Keech and the siblings crept across the settlement. At one point, Nat held up a fist to halt them, and the trio melted deeper into the shadows. A solitary thrall wearing a shabby blue-and-white uniform shuffled past them. It stopped for a second, slanting its head. With a sudden panic, Keech wondered if it might be sensing the shard, but then the dead soldier muttered something and resumed its walk. Kicking at a pebble, it turned a corner and disappeared from sight.

"Doyle's incantation," Keech murmured, relieved. "Looks like it's still working."

Duck pointed ahead of them. "Let's head toward Main Street."

Their circuit sent them down an alleyway that turned into a

skinny footpath. They followed in single file till it spat them onto a tiny plot of land, a square parcel just wide enough for a small log cabin, a stable house, and a putrid-smelling pigpen. Icicles dangled from the stable house roof, and snowy rime covered the pen's wooden fence. Following the Embrys, Keech sidled along the fence line, careful not to slip in the half-frozen mud puddles.

A mammoth dark shape squealed inside the pen, then bolted straight for him and slammed into the fence rails, shuddering the wood. Keech wheeled backward, struggling to keep his balance. He put a hand over his coat pocket to secure the whistle bomb.

The thing that had charged him was a giant black boar.

The animal raked its curled yellow tusks across the fence. Its dark eyes reflected nearby lamplight, glimmering a feral kind of savagery.

"Filthy animal," Keech grumbled.

Suddenly, he was yanked through the open door of the stable house. He spun around and realized that Nat was pulling at his coat. The rancher shoved him down onto the stable's hay-scattered floor, next to a vacant horse stall, and threw a finger up to his lips: *Shhh*.

Duck pointed out the door to the log cabin. Lantern light flickered within. "I think we woke up somebody," she whispered.

A lanky cowpuncher stepped out, wearing grubby long underwear and a pair of muddy boots. He held a kerosene lantern. The boar in the pigpen loosed another screech, and the man shambled across the yard. "Henrietta? What's got you worked up, m'lovely?"

From the darkness at the back of the stable, a rowdy huff startled Keech. The skinny cowpoke trudged closer to the stable, tugging at his underwear. "Hector, you hush it up in there, you miserable brute!"

The trio pressed themselves deeper into the shadows, holding as still as marble statues.

As the scrawny man paused at the stable doorway, Keech made out a dark spiral shape on the side of his neck: the brand of the Reverend Rose. The fellow raised his lantern toward the aisle. "Don't you be spookin' Henrietta with your huffin' and puffin'!" he shouted. "I've a mind to feed you to her!"

The man lumbered back to his cabin and slammed the door. A minute later, the light winked out. The nervous trio waited till a loud snore sounded from the cabin.

"That was close," Keech muttered.

"Henrietta?" Duck shook her head. "That fella don't even realize his pig's a boy."

"Did y'all see the brand on his neck?" Nat asked.

Duck wondered, "Why would Rose have a *person* branded?"

"I don't know, but I sure don't like it none," Nat answered.

A loud huff sounded again from the back of the stable. Curiosity itched at Keech. He slipped down the aisle.

A massive stallion was crowded into the far compartment, watching him. The horse stood at least eighteen hands high from the floor to the top of his withers. His mane and tail were as white as dove feathers, and his fur was a beautiful cream shade, the color of freshly churned butter. Keech gestured at Nat and Duck, and they joined him to get a closer look.

"That's the prettiest horse I ever saw," Duck said.

Nat smiled. "A cremello stud. Rare in these parts."

"That man talked like he hates him," Duck added. "I bet this pony's been rustled."

Keech reached over the gate. He expected the animal to

withdraw, but the horse nosed his fingers instead, then licked his palm. A memory of Felix nudging his hand in Pa Abner's barn nearly overwhelmed his heart.

"I wish I had an apple for you, Hector. That's your name, right? Like the Trojan warrior?"

The white horse snorted, flashing eyes as blue as Nat's and Duck's.

Nat tapped Keech's shoulder. "He's a swell horse, but we have to go."

"You don't belong in this horrible place," Keech whispered to the stallion. "I'll come back for you."

The trio hurried out of the stable house. On their way past the pen, Henrietta charged the fence again, rattling the wood and gouging the air.

Duck patted Keech on the back. "That critter hates you something fierce."

"Trust me, the feeling's mutual."

After sprinting down another alley, they paused for a breath in front of a brown stucco building. The windows of the place had been boarded over, the front door sealed shut by planks. Shattered chairs had been piled in the yard, as if someone had built a pyre but forgot to light it. A streetlamp stood just beyond the clutter, revealing a snow-dusted street.

Keech glanced at the front of the stucco building. A dingy sign hung by two chains from the overhang:

SHERIFF'S OFFICE

CITY JAIL

OBEY THE LAW!

Peering through a narrow gap in one of the boarded-up windows, Keech could see a small room of holding cells, their iron-bar doors wide open. The building had been abandoned, the lockup empty. If Sheriff Strahan were still alive, he was being held elsewhere.

"What now?" asked Duck.

Nat pointed to the snowy street. "Since this is the sheriff's office, I'm guessing that's Main Street. Let's cut back south, closer to the town center. Look for signs of another lockup. If we don't find Strahan there, we'll need to head back to the ravine. I bet Doyle's hour is nearly up."

They scurried toward the heart of town, keeping to the shadows of tightly clustered storefronts. They passed a blacksmith shop, a mercantile store, and a barbershop. The businesses were all vacant, their windows and doors planked up like the sheriff's office. Just ahead, the street veered east, forming a sharp left turn in front of a massive three-story building, a whitewashed edifice that blocked any view of the rest of the town.

The building was a hotel with a long balcony on the second story that looked out over the dismal street corner. It appeared to be the sole place in town that was awake. The amateur piano playing and raucous laughter that Keech had been hearing for the last hour rolled out of the hotel's batwing doors. Muffled light shone out of the portal. Smoky shadows moved beyond the curtained windows in the rooms above and below.

Hanging from the hotel's balustrade was a large yellow sign that read WISDOM SALOON, only someone had scratched out the town's name and painted BIG SNAKE over it.

"Let's move closer," Keech whispered.

The trio stopped at the front porch of a telegraph office. They hunkered in the cold darkness and stared down the street at the Big Snake Saloon.

"That place sure is spooky," Duck said.

Keech studied the hotel's windows and balcony. The sounds and movement within reminded him of a grim circus—relentless swirls of bleak music and clownish cackles. "Maybe they're holding Strahan in there."

"That'd be my guess, too." Duck took a step forward.

"Wait." Nat reached out to stop her, his voice sharper than a knife. "Do y'all notice anything?"

Keech peered around the empty street, but everything was buttoned up.

From the ground floor of the Big Snake Saloon, the twisted sound of the piano called out a refrain that Keech recognized as the *Moonlight Sonata*. It drifted like snowfall down the street and mingled with the shadows trapped along the sidewalks.

Granny Nell used to hum that piece to him when he would awaken in the night from horrible dreams. *Hush now*, Granny would tell him as he cried to the sound of her humming. *Listen to the moonlight and fret no more.*

It dawned on Keech what Nat had seen—or rather, what he *hadn't* seen.

Duck voiced his thought: "No activity, no movement."

"Right." Nat raised an eyebrow. "The street's wide open. The saloon looks busy enough, but the town's quiet. I ain't seen a thrall guard on patrol for a good while."

Suddenly, a hard chill sparked inside Keech's coat. He grabbed for the amulet.

"Keech, what's wrong?" Duck asked.

"Doyle's spell! I don't think it's working anymore!"

No sooner had he said the words than he glanced over his shoulder and saw a nightmare vision.

A massive man with a split red beard stood behind the Embrys, as though he had just materialized out of the November wind.

"Behind you!" Keech yelled.

"Hello, little lambs," Big Ben said.

The outlaw caught the siblings by the sides of their heads and slammed them together. Keech heard a dull *clonk*, and Nat and Duck crumpled to the filthy snow at the man's feet.

Big Ben looked down at their unmoving forms with a smirk. "The children of Bennett Coal." His baritone voice rumbled like a cattle stampede. He rolled his wide shoulders and stretched his back, as if he needed to work out a kink.

"No!" Keech started toward the man, but rough hands seized his coat collar from behind and wrenched him backward. Yanked off his feet, he dropped flat onto his back.

The hideous face of a rotting thrall emerged over him. It wore a blue-and-white uniform the same as the other thrall they'd seen, and its horrible mouth drooled a dark ooze.

Keech reached for the shard, but the dead patrolman shoved both of his hands to the ground. "Don't even think about it," the thrall muttered.

Stepping over the bodies of Nat and Duck, Big Ben plodded toward Keech. The wind kicked up and ruffled the killer's long tan coat, giving him the appearance of a drifting mountain. His boots crunched on the packed snow.

"You're the little orphan lamb the Reverend has spoken of. The son of Screamin' Bill." Big Ben squatted beside him. "Your troop survived my Chamelia. Impressive. Raines trained you well. But not well enough."

Keech strained against the thrall's grip, but the dead man pushed his wrists down as Big Ben dug thick fingers into Keech's coat, found the silver shard, and pulled the charm free. The man licked his lips. "You were wrong to think a protective spell on your shard could hide you. I can reach past your tricks." He slid a bare finger across the fragment, then stuffed the amulet into his own coat. When his hand came out, he grunted, squeezed his fingers into a tight fist, then cracked his knuckles. Keech didn't think the shard had just caused the man pain. Faulty bones, perhaps, but not the silver.

Then Big Ben rifled again through Keech's pockets. "What else have you hid in there?" The killer's eyes went large when he pulled out the whistle bomb and examined it. "Now where did you find this? Young kids shouldn't play with explosives."

Keech shouted out to Nat and Duck, but the siblings didn't budge. Big Ben lifted a threatening hand to silence him. An intricate dark circle scarred his flesh. The Devil's mark. "The Reverend will be thrilled to learn you kids walked right into our hands. We've been preparing for another visitor, but you three are a special treat."

Keech looked up at the sky and saw dozens of crows lining the rooftops of Wisdom's downtown buildings. They would have been invisible but for the glow of Main Street's lamplights illuminating their silhouettes. The creatures didn't move or make a sound; they simply watched from the eaves, like spectators at the grim circus.

Big Ben planted a boot on each side of Keech, straddling him.

"Good night, little lamb," he said, and brought down a massive fist.

CHAPTER 18
THE FOURTH PRISONER

Keech has sunk to the bottom of a dark ocean.

He's never seen a real ocean, but he knows he's fallen into one. He feels the icy water press against his flesh, pushing him down as if a giant has stepped on his back and is grinding him into the sandy floor. He wants to open his eyes, but he can't pry his eyelids open. His lungs scream for breath. His ears detect a clanging, the pounding of hammers against anvils.

"It's okay, Keech." The voice is gentle, free of all troubles. The voice belongs to Sam, the Rabbit.

Though his eyelids refuse to open, Keech can see his brother's face, the wry smile, the blond shock of hair. He wants to reach out for the boy, but his body is paralyzed. A polar fear has flooded his veins, his bones, every muscle in his body.

"Remember what Pa taught us about fear," Sam says.

Pa Abner's lesson runs through Keech's mind: Fear is a tool. Use it to guide caution in dangerous times. Never allow fear to use you.

"Who are you, my brother?" Sam asks.

"I am the Wolf."

The resistance Keech feels drains away. If now is his time, then so be it. Death only means he will join his family. There is nothing to fear.

He welcomes the water in.

Keech sucked in a deep breath, and stale air filled his lungs. His eyes fluttered open, and dim light flickered across his vision. The chill of ocean water from his dream was replaced by a cold dirt floor pressed against his cheek. A terrible ache screamed across the side of his face.

After a short time, he dared to roll over and look around.

He was lying in the corner of a dank cellar. A candle set on the floor burned near a flight of wooden stairs that led up to a closed trapdoor. Flat boards covered the walls, and cobwebs dusted the shadowy recesses. The muffled moaning of cattle touched his ears.

"Keech," a small voice called out.

In the corner farthest from the stairs, Duck hunched against the wall. The left side of her grimy face was moist with blood. The girl held her knees close to her chest, as if she were trying to squeeze herself into the smallest space possible, but her eyes were focused and keen. Iron manacles bound her bare feet, and a heavy chain locked her to the wall. Her boots, socks, poncho, and hat had been tossed across the chamber into a sloppy pile, right alongside Keech's belongings.

Keech sat up, hearing the clank of metal as he did. Shackles clamped around his wrists and chains bound him to the wall. He lifted a hand to his tender cheek and winced at the touch.

"You're awake. Good." The faint voice belonged to Nat. The

rancher stood nearby, tethered to the wall in a pair of rusted handcuffs. He had also been stripped of his gear.

Keech breathed a sigh of relief. "Are you okay?"

"Been better," Nat said, bleary-faced. The chains binding him to the wall were too short to allow for sitting, so the rancher slumped on his feet. "I think we're in one of the holding cells Quinn mentioned."

That explained the cattle noises Keech heard. Quinn had told them the holding cells were built to the east of the town, where the stockyards were located. "Big Ben took my shard." Keech tried not to sound too defeated. "The whistle bomb, too."

Nat jangled his chains. "What a disaster. I hope the others are doing better."

Duck tugged against her leg bindings. She lifted her small face to the filthy ceiling and screamed to the unseen Big Ben, "You killed our ma and pa! I'm gonna make you pay!"

Nat's face sagged in the flickering shadows. "Save your strength, sis."

Across the room, an unmoving lump lay stretched out on a bed of dirty hay, the body of a fourth prisoner. The fellow had been rolled toward the wall, and his breathing sounded raspy and hollow.

Keech called out to the man. "Hello? Mister?"

"We've tried to get his attention, but it's no use." Duck sat crosslegged and began rubbing her bound ankles.

"Do you reckon that's Sheriff Strahan?" Keech asked.

"I can't tell if he's missing a hand," Nat said.

A terrible ruckus clanged against the trapdoor at the top of the chamber stairs. The hatch flipped open, and torchlight shone down.

A slender fellow descended. He wore a spotless white shirt with frilly trimmings around the cuffs and a pair of perfectly starched trousers. The man had long white hair that nearly matched the color of his shirt, and his Adam's apple was so big, it looked like a bullfrog was wedged inside his throat. In one hand he held a torch, which sent devilish light dancing across his bony cheeks. His other hand clutched a fat mutton shank that he gnawed with yellow teeth.

"The name's Friendly Williams. Welcome to my prison." He pointed the greasy chop at each of them. The man's neck bore the blackened brand of the Reverend Rose, just like the skinny cowpuncher. "I've been hearing about you rotten little trespassers. Children of Enforcers, eh? To tell the truth, I don't know what Enforcers are, but you seem to be a big deal to my associates."

"Your *associates*," Duck spat. "You mean Rose's disciples, the so-called Big Snake."

"A bunch of no-good killers," Nat added.

Friendly smiled. "Maybe so. But they've shown me *worlds*, things I couldn't have possibly imagined." The man rubbed the back of one hand over the Devil's mark as if the brand brought him a perverse pleasure.

"You've sold your soul to Rose," Keech said, disgusted.

"You're a passel of ignorant kids. I wouldn't expect you to understand."

Friendly stripped one last chunk off the mutton chop, then dropped the gristle-ridden bone to the dirt floor. "There's still some meat on there if yer hungry." With a laugh, he kicked the greasy thing in Keech's direction. "Eat up, then get some sleep. You'll wanna be rested."

Keech couldn't resist the bait. "For what?"

"We're gonna put on a show tomorrow. The Reverend wants to see you at the gallows." The slender man's Adam's apple bobbed up and down as he cackled in delight.

Keech exchanged a distressed glance with Nat and Duck.

"Best I be off now. The boss will want to know you're awake. He'd like a chat."

Grinning, Friendly turned back to the wooden stairs, but Keech stopped him. "Your bounty hunter, Sunrise Albert . . ."

"Ah, yes, my friend Sunrise! One of my best trackers. Did he ever find that rotten runaway, Oscar?"

"He's buzzard food. One of Rose's monsters killed him. They'll do the same to you when you've served their purpose."

Friendly's grin faltered, and his eyes dulled with uncertainty. "Scorn all ya want, sparrow. You'll meet your maker either way." Then he stomped up the stairs, kicking dust into the air. Once he had disappeared above, he slammed the trapdoor shut.

The room sat in silence as the quivering candle flame caused shadows to dance across the cell walls.

Then the silent body across the room shifted.

"Look," Duck said. "He's awake."

The prisoner on the bed of hay rolled over onto his back, revealing a grizzled face that smiled feebly at them. He was a lean fellow with a thin black mustache and terrible bruises all over his angular face. Perhaps the man had once been handsome, but he had suffered such a severe beating that his face was a mangled mess. His bare feet were muddy, and the flesh of his ankles was rubbed raw from a pair of heavy manacles that chained him to the wall.

Keech felt a heavy blow of disappointment. This wasn't Strahan. Both of the man's hands were intact. "You ain't the sheriff, are you?"

Rising on one elbow, the bruised captive coughed into his fist. "No, I'm not Strahan."

"But you know of him?" Keech asked.

"I knew him well. He was a good friend."

Nat spoke urgently. "We're looking for him, sir. We're deputies of the Law, and we've been sent by Sheriff Bose Turner of Big Timber, Missouri. If you have information—"

"I'm afraid you won't find him," the stranger interrupted. He struggled up to a sitting position. "Tom Strahan is dead. They killed him two days ago, just before the wagon trains lit out west with all the townsfolk."

The prisoner's news about Strahan's death drenched Keech in pure despair. But that wasn't the only bad part. If all the townsfolk were gone, that would mean Quinn's aunt Ruth was no longer in Wisdom.

The trio fell into a black silence. Keech's hope of finding Bonfire Crossing sank like a stone tossed into a deep lake.

"Are you sure he's dead?" asked Duck.

"I'm sure, kid. I saw it happen. But listen, I must know something—" Now the captive spoke with a sharp edge of desperation. "The slaver, Friendly Williams. He mentioned you were the children of Enforcers. Is that true?"

Nat answered, "We are. My name's Nat Embry, and that's Duck. Our father was Noah. He was better known by his Enforcer name, Bennett Coal."

"I can see the resemblance. You're both the spittin' image of Rowdy Bennett."

"Rowdy Bennett?" said Duck.

The stranger chuckled, then looked at Keech. "And who are you?"

Keech recalled Sheriff Turner's advice to be wary using real names on the trail, but the chained fellow looked utterly incapable of harm.

"I'm Keech Blackwood," he said, his lips trembling.

"Well, I'll be! The son of Screamin' Bill," the man said. "I thought I sensed the approach of allies in the area."

The response stunned Keech. "Mister, who the heck are you?"

The prisoner sidled closer to them, as near as his chains would allow. "My name is Milos Horner, and I, too, came to Wisdom to find Tom Strahan."

"Milos Horner." Keech had heard that name spoken recently. Before dying, Pa Abner had mentioned the name Horner when telling his story of how the Enforcers had hidden the Char Stone and taken the Oath of Memory. Bad Whiskey had also uttered the name at the Home. *Give me the Stone now, or tell me the name of the Enforcer who's got it. Does Horner have it? O'Brien?* "My pa talked about you. You're an Enforcer."

The prisoner tried to smile again, but there was no life in it. "I was once. I rode with both of your fathers a long time ago. But to Tom Strahan, I was known by a different name. Folks in these parts know me as Warren Lynch."

Duck gasped. "You're Edgar Doyle's partner!"

Mention of the Ranger's name flustered the man. He gazed at

the hay-strewn floor. After a moment, he grumbled to clear his throat. "I'm afraid you kids have been deceived."

Keech didn't like the sound of those words. "What d'you mean?"

"Nobody's been deceived," Nat argued. "Edgar Doyle's in Wisdom now. He's come with us to save you."

"I am not Edgar Doyle's partner, boy, and he is not who you think he is."

A cold draft whistled into the holding cell, fluttering Milos Horner's black hair and sending goose bumps across the back of Keech's neck.

"Like me, he rode with your fathers," the man said. "His real name is Red Jeffreys."

CHAPTER 19
SAMSON

Once Keech heard the prisoner's revelation, his mind traveled at once to Bone Ridge Cemetery. The angelic statue, the weeds over his mother's and father's graves, loosened before the young riders had gotten there—he saw everything as if he were still standing there. The fury of the Reverend Rose, riding inside Bad Whiskey's mind and body, yelling to the night that Red Jeffreys had stolen his Char Stone.

Edgar Doyle had broken into Erin Blackwood's coffin. He had replaced the Stone with the doll Keech now carried and had fled west into Kansas Territory, apparently with his sights next on the Fang of Barachiel.

To think they had ridden alongside the man.

Keech had trusted him with their secret mission, had sized him up and vouched for his sincerity. And all along, Doyle had been concealing his true identity. Worse, he'd been carrying the Char Stone and never said a word. Keech's entire body shook. The Ranger must have placed the Stone in his bulky knapsack. That would explain his concern about Saint Peter protecting their gear back in the ravine.

"Tell us what you know about him," Keech said to Horner. "What's his plan?"

The broken Enforcer dropped his head, his dingy hair falling over his eyes. "I'm sorry, but I don't know."

Nat leaned closer to the man, his arms straining against the chains. "Any idea why he'd claim you're his partner?"

"I don't know that, either. But if he says he's here to rescue me, then I presume he's trying to obtain answers from me."

Duck glanced at her brother. "Three guesses what he's trying to find out."

"The location of Bonfire Crossing," Nat answered.

"You kids know a surprising amount of secret business."

"You don't know the half," Duck said.

"He stopped at a bending tree earlier this morning," Nat went on. "Tried to figure out something there but failed. He told us he couldn't find 'the path' without his partner's help. What path is he talking about? Does he need a map of some sort?"

"It's a bit more complicated than a map," Horner replied. "I'm afraid I don't know the answer, either. I only have a piece of something."

Keech felt as if he were listening to their discussion from the bottom of a well. Every thought was distracted by the image of the knapsack tied to Saint Peter's back. "Mr. Horner, Doyle's got the Char Stone."

Waves of bleary emotions tumbled over the prisoner's face. He took a few deep breaths, as if to calm himself. The man muttered into his fist, "Dear Lord. The Stone is revealed again."

"Please, talk to us," Keech said. "We need information."

After another long breath, Horner grew more composed. "The

Char Stone is an artifact from the ancient world, perhaps as old as Earth itself. Some say it came from the Tower of Babel; others believe it to be the stone that Cain used to murder his brother, Abel. Some claim that the Stone can bridge this world to the beyond and grant life eternal, but the truth is, no person can wield it without the most dire of consequences."

"What does it do?" asked Nat.

"It weakens the walls of reality, allowing things from other worlds to touch our own. Understand, the Char Stone *wants* to lure people into darkness. Just being near it can weaken a man's sanity with its call to aberrant power."

"But if the Stone is so wicked and dangerous, then why would Doyle—I mean Jeffreys—dig it up?" Keech asked.

"I don't know. All I can say for sure is that no one should ever attempt to use the Char Stone for any purpose. If you can take it from Jeffreys, *do not touch it.* Bury it, and never let it be found again."

"When we take it, we're gonna destroy it," Nat said.

Horner shook his head. "Folks have tried. And they've failed."

"We'll find a way."

Another smile softened Horner's damaged face. "If you kids are the children of Enforcers, I'm certain you will." He looked at Keech with warm eyes. "You should know that your father, Bill, was a good man, as was Isaiah. Sometimes good men can be led astray, but the true test of a person's heart is how you find your way back to the good."

"Bad Whiskey called him 'Terror of the West,'" Keech said, hearing the sadness in his own voice.

"Yes, but only because Bill was strong," Horner replied. "Weak men find terror in someone else's strength, especially strength they don't understand. Just know that in the end, your father found his way back to the good."

Keech wanted to learn more about his father, if only to fill the strange growing disconnect in his heart and soul, but a series of muffled thumps pounded down from the chamber above. Crumbles of dirt sprinkled from the wooden ceiling.

"Someone's coming!" Duck said.

Horner sat up straight, then spoke swiftly. "Listen to me. The fiends holding us know about Bonfire Crossing. Word reached them that Strahan knew something about it, so they put Wisdom in their sights. Since then, they've enslaved the townsfolk and shipped them out west, and I suspect they must also know about Jeffreys, which means they'll most likely set a trap for him to get the Stone. If you make it out of here, secure the Stone, then find Bonfire Crossing."

"To fetch the Fang of Barachiel," Duck finished. "Can you tell us what it is? Is it cursed like the Char Stone?"

A metal clanking above struck Keech's ears. Likely the sound of an iron latch on the trapdoor being unlocked. Rose's fiends were coming.

Keech spoke briskly. "Never mind the Fang. How do we find the Crossing?"

"Strahan spoke a strange riddle to me. He said it showed the path to the Crossing." Horner then recited something that sounded like a poorly written poem:

> "Follow the rivers and bending trees
> to the den of the moon stalker.
> Gather the pack and speak his name
> before the noontide shift."

The Enforcer glanced up at the sound of the rattling lock. "Those were his words. I don't know what they mean."

Keech felt as if his gut had been kicked by a mule. When Pa Abner had told him to "follow the rivers and bending trees," he had assumed the instructions were simple advice to guide the young riders through the rough lands of Kansas. He had never considered that Pa had been too weak to finish a *coded message*.

"Did he say anything else?" Nat asked.

"He said, 'When the shadows speak, listen,' but I can't figure how a shadow can talk."

Keech glanced at Duck. Just that afternoon they had seen the shadow of the bending tree near the Moss farm twist into a buffalo head, but they had not heard any sort of voice.

The latch on the trapdoor clattered, and Keech grimaced. "What do we do to figure out the riddle?"

The answer came in a single, rushed breath. "There is a bending tree twenty miles southwest of Wisdom, just down the hill from a stand of round boulders. Start there." Horner's eyes fixed on the opening trapdoor. His voice sounded desperate as he added, "If you manage to obtain the artifacts, head down the Santa Fe Trail to Hook's Fort and look for the trapper McCarty. And avoid the lure of the Char Stone at all costs!"

Their time was up. The tiny man they had seen at the town gates stepped down through the trapdoor and descended into the chamber, followed closely by Friendly Williams.

Horner sneered. "Coward."

"Hello, Milos." One hand rested on the hilt of the sword hanging from the man's thigh. His face was as white as bleached bone, and his nose was large and thick. He wore a sloppy, dark beard, and the top of his head had a large bald spot like a monk's tonsure.

Keech noticed one more infuriating detail: Pa Abner's amulet shard had been slung over the ornate knuckle guard of Coward's sword, and the silver crescent dangled against the blade's sheath. The shard glowed a brilliant orange.

Coward sniffed the air as if inhaling the scent of a delicate flower. He turned back to glare at Friendly. "Mr. Williams, you've told too many secrets, I'm afraid."

Friendly looked confused. "But I didn't say nothing."

"I sent you down to make sure the kids were awake, not tell my old friend, Mr. Horner, that they were children of Enforcers."

"I never told him that, boss!"

"I'll deal with you later. Now hush. I need to concentrate." He closed his eyes and again smelled the air.

"What do you want with us?" Nat growled.

Coward continued to inhale—till his eyes popped open. "Red Jeffreys has arrived! His scent lingers on each of you."

"What's a Red Jeffreys?" Friendly asked.

"He's the prey, Mr. Williams. And for prey, we require bait, don't we?" He thrust a stubby finger toward Milos Horner. "Take him to the saloon. We want to make sure to catch Jeffreys's attention. I'll return presently."

Handing the torch to Coward, Friendly shuffled over obediently and unlocked Horner's shackles. With swift cruelty, he drove a fist into the prisoner's gut. Horner doubled over with a loud wheeze. Friendly gripped the poor man by his shoulders and manhandled him to his feet. "Let's go, you dog."

The two climbed the stairwell. Before Horner disappeared, he glanced back down at Keech. Their eyes locked just long enough for Keech to read his sheer desperation: *Don't fail.*

Once they were gone, Coward swiveled the torchlight on Nat, then Duck, then Keech. His bald pate glistened under the flame. "So you're the famous troop that took down Bad Whiskey Nelson. Kudos! I disliked that man. Always grinning like a fool and calling folks *pilgrim.*"

"We'll take you down just like we did Bad Whiskey," Nat snarled.

"Such pluck! Reminds me of your papa," Coward said. He sniffed in Nat's direction, moving slowly across the room. The closer the foul man stepped, the deeper he inhaled.

Nat lunged for him, but his shackles stopped him short.

Coward continued to smell. He closed his eyes. "Yes, I see." When he opened them again, he grinned. "Tell me what you know about *Miguel Herrera.*"

Keech and Nat swapped unsettled glances.

"I don't know who that is," Nat said.

"No need to lie, Mr. Embry. Or rather, Mr. *Coal.* I know you've been riding with Miguel. I can smell him all over you, just like I smell your rotten father. Where is he? I've got unfinished business with that boy."

"If I knew a Miguel, I wouldn't give him away to the likes of you."

"Even if I told you his *real* purpose for riding with you and little sis?" Coward glanced back to steal a gander at Duck. When he winked at her, Duck lurched against her bindings like a mad dog.

Nat scowled. "What real purpose?"

Coward chuckled. "*Atonement*, of course. He seeks redemption for the sins he committed against your family."

Nat's face scrunched in surprise. "I don't know what you're talking about."

Coward's small gloved hand waved Nat's stubbornness away. "Never mind. I'll let Miguel tell his own stories. Or should I call him *Cutter*? I suppose he gave himself that alias because of the knife he carries. I'm curious to see that blade. More curious to smell it."

"Take your nose somewhere else," Nat growled.

"Don't mind if I do." Spinning on his boot heel, Coward walked a few steps in Keech's direction. He sniffed vigorously. "My, you contain some fragrant secrets."

The closer Coward got, the harder it was for Keech to concentrate. He felt as if smoke were pouring into his head, swirling his thoughts, opening wide his whole identity.

"You found something buried at the Sullied Place. Bone Ridge. Whiskey thought he'd uncovered the Char Stone, but he found only a toy. A *doll*." Coward chuckled, then opened his eyes. "Am I right, Mr. Blackwood?" He pointed. "The doll is in your pocket."

Keech squeezed his eyes shut, feeling Coward's nose probe deeper. In a matter of seconds, the man would glimpse the ravine, the knapsack, the riddle of Bonfire Crossing that Horner had just given. Keech loosed a small cry, struggling to build a mental barrier.

"Enough!" Duck shouted. "We want to speak to Big Ben."

Coward slipped toward her, and Keech felt the tugging at his mind depart. He sagged to the floor, exhausted but relieved.

"Stay away from her, you fiend!"

"Nathaniel, hush," Duck said, then turned her steely gaze on

Coward. "Fetch Big Ben. We've got a right to confront him. He killed our ma and pa."

"Yes, I know what he did. Big Ben's indisposed at the moment, but never you fear, he'll be happy to listen to your curses while he preps your noose."

Nat rattled his chains ferociously. "You're all gonna pay! I'm gonna break out of here and send you back to whatever grimy hole you slithered out of. Then I'm gonna find your damned Reverend Rose and make him wish he'd never crossed two kids named Embry."

Coward pondered Nat for a moment. "More of that Bennett Coal pluck. I like it." He shuffled back to the stairwell. Keech's glowing amulet shard clanked against his sword as he ascended the steps. "The gallows await!" he called down, then disappeared from sight.

"You sure told him," Duck said.

Nat slumped. "Maybe I bought us some time."

"We have to break out of here." Keech glanced around, searching for any weakness in the chamber. He lifted a leg and thrust his foot against the wall, but nothing happened. "I don't have any leverage."

Duck yanked at her ankle bindings. "I can't budge these, either."

Nat studied the places in the wall where his chains were attached to thick metal rings. "This room is pretty damp. The walls might be soft. It's worth a try. Both of you, move as far away as you can."

"What are you gonna do?" Keech asked, sliding back.

"I'm getting us out of here. No matter what."

Nat wrapped his chains around his wrists, securing a firm grip. He lifted one foot behind him and pressed his sole flat against the wall. With a mighty grunt, he pushed against the wood. His face turned as red as an apple, but the bindings didn't budge. He put his foot down momentarily, sucked in a breath, and stretched his shoulders. "No matter what," he mumbled, his chest rising and falling. "No matter what."

Shoving his foot back against the wall, Nat began pulling again, thrusting his shoulders as far as they would reach. He cried out through clenched teeth, "No matter what!"

The tendons in the rancher's neck stood out like iron bars. He lifted his other leg and placed his foot against the wall, so that his entire weight was now pulling, driving him outward.

To Keech's surprise, a whine of distressed wood brushed his ears, followed by a sharp crack. He suddenly recalled images of Samson from the Bible, the great Israelite judge who had been one of Sam's favorite characters. Imbued with the strength of God, Samson had knocked down the columns of the Philistine temple, destroying his enemies. *Samson pulled those pillars down like they was made of pine kindling*, Sam had said once, during one of their bedtime stories. *He was the strongest man who ever lived. Maybe except for Pa.*

Nat released a ferocious wail, and the wood splintered around the iron rings. Blood broke through his ravaged wrists. His muscles were surely on the verge of tearing, and yet the rancher refused to stop.

"No! Matter! What!" he repeated through clamped teeth.

With a shattering snap, the iron rings popped loose and flew off the wall. Nat crashed to the ground, his chains flinging forward, whipping dangerously close to Keech's head.

"You did it!" Duck cried.

Nat rose to his knees, his chest heaving. Friendly's chains dangled from his bloodied wrists. When he stood, his legs wobbled. He shuffled over to his sister and tumbled back to his knees in front of her. She flung herself on him, and they embraced.

Keech heard Nat mumble into her ear. "I'll make sure you're safe. Nobody's going to the gallows today." Nat hopped to his feet.

Another knock rattled above, raining more dust on their heads.

"They're back! What do we do?" Duck said.

As the trapdoor began to clatter, Nat gathered the chains in his hands and began to swing the iron rings in a cross pattern. "First rascal down those stairs, I'm gonna smash him."

Keech readied himself for a scuffle. He hated that he couldn't properly join the fight, but maybe Nat would knock someone close enough that he could stomp on them.

The trapdoor swung open with a crash. Nat twirled his chains, ready to catch his first victim.

CHAPTER 20

THE BAIT

A draft of warm air fluttered down through the opening, and Cutter peeked down through the hole. "Never fear, *amigos*. I'm here to rescue you!" He descended a few steps and crouched upon a rung.

"Cut! You're sure a welcome sight," Nat said, lowering his chains.

"First time anybody's told me that," Cutter jested.

Duck jangled her leg irons. "We need out of these chains."

A large brass key ring tumbled down the steps and landed at Nat's feet. "Maybe something like that would help."

Snatching up the ring, Nat located the right key, released his own manacles, then freed his sister and Keech.

As they slipped into their boots and other duds, Keech glanced at the angry red scores and beads of blood on Nat's wrists. "I've never seen anything like that. I would've sworn you were gonna yank your arms clean off."

Nat rubbed at his shoulders. "At first, I thought I might, but then something weird came over me. I felt like I could tear open a mountain."

Cutter's voice muttered from the trapdoor. "Hurry up down there."

Keech climbed the rickety stairs, his bruised face throbbing. When Cutter stretched a hand down to help him, Duck's amulet shard dangled from his wrist. Cut's other hand clutched his long blade, and Keech recollected a spark of something Coward had said: *I'm curious to see that blade. More curious to smell it.*

"Coward was just here. How on earth did you get past him?" Keech asked.

Cutter scowled at the small man's name. "The Ranger's been humming his weird tune. We walked straight through town and didn't turn a single head. Craziest thing I ever saw."

"Doyle's with you?" Keech felt his heart hiccup.

"Revels, too. They're checking a few cabins up the street. I told them I wanted to scout out this hut." Cutter glanced around. "Did you find the lawdog?"

"Afraid there's bad news on that front. Strahan's dead."

Cutter frowned. "Oh."

Keech peered around. They stood in a candlelit shack. A small desk sat in the corner, untidy with papers, and a thick rug covered most of the floor. Spare shackles and chains drooped on hooks along the walls. Across the room, a narrow door stood open to Wisdom's charcoal darkness, inviting a breeze that smelled of a cow herd.

Two bodies were sprawled across the rug, their pale hands fastened around pistols and knives. Cutter held up the amulet shard. "This silver's something else. Made short work of this pair of thrall guards."

"I'm awful glad you had it."

Duck emerged from the holding cell, followed by Nat.

Upon seeing her, Cutter handed over the pendant. "*Gracias, amiga.*"

Duck placed the fragment back around her neck. "We heard what you told Keech. How'd you end up over here?"

Cutter explained that he and Quinn had gone from cabin to cabin in the town's south quarters, peeking through every door and window, but they never saw any sign of Ruth or the other townsfolk. "This place is a graveyard," he said.

"We know. Those devils are up to something big." Nat turned to Keech and Duck. "Let's hunt around for a weapon or two."

They ransacked the hut while Cutter continued his tale. "When Doyle's hour was up, I told Revels we had to head back. He got upset about leaving without his aunt and started kicking down doors, making a terrible *ruido*. That's when the Ranger found us. He told us he found another whistle-bomb stash. Revels got desperate to fetch them. So we headed back to the east, and that's when we spotted thrall movement around a bunch of huts. We hunkered down to watch them pass, and I saw . . ." He broke off, his face grave.

Keech finished the sentence for him. "You saw Coward."

"Yeah."

"He wanted to know about you, Cut. He even said your real name."

The pasty jitters Keech had witnessed outside the town returned to vex Cutter's face. "That don't matter one lick," he said tartly, and waved his hand as though shooing any further talk of the short man. "Let's get back to the others. They'll be happy to see I sprung ya." Clenching his knife, he started toward the open door when Nat stopped him. "Wait. We discovered something about Edgar Doyle you'll want to hear."

"Like what?"

"Like he ain't who he says he is," Duck answered. She told him how they had learned of Doyle's true identity, and Keech added his suspicion that the Char Stone was in the knapsack tied to Saint Peter.

Cutter looked thunderstruck. "Who told you all this?"

"A prisoner named Milos Horner," Duck said, "but he also calls himself Warren Lynch."

"The Ranger's *compañero*?"

Before one of them could respond, a gruff voice murmured, "Where is he?"

Edgar Doyle appeared in the doorway of the hut, stooping low so his hat would clear the jamb. Quinn stood just behind the Ranger, looking downcast.

Keech charged across the room and pointed at Doyle's face. "You lied to us!" He shook with anger. "You're Red Jeffreys!"

The Ranger seized Keech by the shoulders and scooted him sternly back into the center of the hut. Keech felt his boot heels drag the floor. He readied a fist to defend himself, for all the good it would do against the Ranger—or whatever he truly was.

"Lower your voice. We're still in the nest of the enemy." Doyle's hands were like vises on Keech's muscles.

The other young riders moved to circle the Ranger.

Doyle released Keech and stepped back. He held up a fist, and a flurry of cold air whooshed around the room, rattling the chains on the walls. "Stand down," he ordered. "There's no need to fight. I'm your friend."

"What in heck's going on?" Quinn asked at the doorway. His grimace of despair had turned to bewilderment.

"Your Ranger's an old Enforcer who stole the Char Stone," Nat said. "He's been playing us for fools the whole time so he can get what he wants."

"You have no idea what I want," Doyle snapped.

Quinn shuffled in closer to the group. "Is it true, Ranger? Did you lie?"

"I've done nothing but protect you."

Keech's shoulders ached where the Ranger had grabbed him. "We know you're only hunting Horner to get to Bonfire Crossing and the Fang."

"No. I'm hunting Milos because he's my friend, and if I don't save him, they'll kill him. Now tell me where he is."

"Friendly Williams dragged him to the saloon not ten minutes ago," Duck said. "Coward called you *prey* and said they was setting a trap."

Doyle's teeth clenched. "They're using him as bait."

"And Auntie Ruth?" Quinn asked the gang. "Any word about her?"

Keech frowned. "I'm afraid you won't like this, Quinn. She's been shipped out west on a wagon train. Apparently, Rose's outlaws sent the entire town. We don't know why."

Quinn ripped off his forage cap and pushed out a quick breath, like someone trying to expel a small bone. His arms dropped heavily to his sides. He turned back to the open door and stood peering out at the darkness, the cold night wind lightly whistling around his gaunt body.

Doyle put a hand on the boy's shoulder. "Take heart, Mr. Revels. We'll find her yet." Then he turned back to contemplate the young riders. For a moment, Keech expected a sharp reprimand, but when he spoke again, Doyle's voice was mild. "You kids are right. I lied to you. I am Red Jeffreys. But I don't go by that name no more, and I am not your enemy. I'm just on a mission, and right now my next step is saving Milos. During the Enforcer days, he saved my life aplenty. I can't allow Big Ben and Coward to hurt him." He looked around the room, meeting their eyes. "I could use your help, as deputies of the Law."

Nat looked skeptical. "What sort of help could we give?"

"The whistle bombs. A well-timed distraction to let me reach Milos. Once I have him, we break for the ravine. Big Ben will most likely give chase, but I can conceal us once we're out in the wild."

Quinn swung around. "Count me in. I still got the whistle bomb I nabbed at the warehouse. I'll fetch a few more from the stash you found up the block."

Nat glanced at the others. "What do y'all think?"

Keech pondered the dangers. They could help the man, but he worried they couldn't fully trust his word. Then again, Pa Abner had never taught the orphans to abandon allies. Horner was in trouble, and perhaps they could help.

A noble thought, but one of Pa Abner's rules of survival sparked in Keech's mind. *Always make a backup plan. Never leave the first option the only one.*

Keech realized what must be done. If Doyle didn't live up to the bargain, they would head to the ravine without him. They would take Horner's clues and leave the man to fight his own battle.

"I'm in, but this won't be easy," Keech said. "A whole rabble of the Reverend's crows are in town keeping watch on the rooftops."

"I'll continue to hide us," Doyle said.

"But what if I go to fetch more whistle bombs?" Quinn asked. "Your protection won't cover me, will it?"

"Maybe. The incantation works like the black smoke you saw at the tower. It shields over a good distance, but it thins if you get too far."

"Big Ben said he could get past the trick," Keech warned.

Doyle grunted. "Only if he's searching in the right place. We'll keep to the shadows and take our chances. I figure we can get close enough."

Cutter sheathed his knife. "I'll go with you, Revels. You can snag a few more of those *pelotas* while I keep watch."

Quinn smiled, though his face looked a bit sheepish. "Thanks." From inside his coat, he pulled out the whistle bomb he'd pocketed from Horner's hidden crate at the warehouse. He offered it to Nat. "Here. Use this one to get the rumble started."

Nat accepted the orb. "All right. A distraction." He eyed the Ranger. "But once we're clear, we expect some straight answers, *Jeffreys*."

Doyle shook his head. "Once we're clear, I'll tell you whatever you want to hear. And call me Doyle. I told you I don't go by that name no more. Now let's move. Keep your eyes open and your heads down."

"One more thing," Nat said. "How will we know when you need the distraction?"

The Ranger considered. "I'll speak a signal. When I tell the desperados to hand over my partner, you toss a whistler. That'll hopefully draw their attention and give me time to fetch him. Be careful about the timing. Let the ball whistle a second or two, then lob it as far away from Milos as you can."

"'Hand over my partner.' Got it," Nat said.

With a bold clap of his gloves, Doyle hurried out of the make-shift jailhouse. Keech heard the mysterious hum begin as soon as the fellow's moccasins touched the street.

The group slipped out of the shack and followed the man. The young riders made their way down a snow-covered lane, and at the first intersection of cabins, Quinn and Cutter broke off.

"Be careful!" Duck murmured.

"Y'all too," Quinn replied.

Before the boys could slip away, Nat stopped Cutter with a quiet whistle. He moved closer to speak. "When all this is said and done, you and me need to talk."

"'Bout what?"

"About a few things Coward told us. No more secrets, Cut. You know something about my family, and I want to know what."

Cutter frowned. "Whatever you say, *jefe*."

Then he and Quinn jaunted off to the east. Before the boys disappeared, Keech thought he heard Quinn murmuring a song—it sounded like the tune about the *Odyssey*, the ditty that Quinn and his aunt Ruth had sung while fleeing to Kansas.

There were no lamps in the area, and the cursed night sky looked empty of stars. Yet Keech's eyes had adjusted enough that he could make out the general passageways. He scurried alongside Nat, noticing that the rancher had taken Duck's hand. The siblings' boots moved in lockstep as they hurried down the frozen dirt lane. Keech tucked his head to the cold, letting the brim of his bowler hat slice the wind. He closed his eyes for a second to feel the exhilaration of the night. The strange poem that Horner had spoken echoed down through his memory like a dark reminder:

Follow the rivers and bending trees
to the den of the moon stalker.
Gather the pack and speak his name
before the noontide shift.

"And listen to the shadows," Keech added with a whisper. When he opened his eyes, he saw that Doyle had quickened his pace to a lively run and that Nat and Duck were struggling to keep up. Keech couldn't believe the Ranger's vitality and speed.

Doyle disappeared around a boarded-up building that appeared to have been a chapel in a former life. As the trio approached the old sanctuary, Keech spotted the Big Snake Saloon two blocks away. They stopped in the shadows of the church to catch a breath.

"Main Street looks empty, but it's hard to tell from here," Keech said. From the lamplights burning inside the hotel, the snowy northern stretch of the avenue looked a ghostly saffron. There appeared to be no movement on the street, not even from the Ranger. "We'll have to get closer. Watch out for crows."

They were almost to the southeastern corner of the hotel when a thunderous call echoed through the night, making them skid to another halt.

"Red Jeffreys!"

The voice rumbled across the entire settlement. It was Big Ben, bellowing to the heavens.

"The jig is up, Enforcer! Come out!"

A fat wooden barrel stood at the corner of the hotel. Keech scuttled for it and peeked over the top, catching a clear view of Main Street and a decent sliver of the Big Snake Saloon's front porch. Nat and Duck fell in behind him, crouching low.

Keech could almost feel Nat and Duck's fury when the massive outlaw stepped out of the Big Snake and onto the mouth of Main Street. He was holding his hands high above his head, as if offering praise to the blackened sky. He called out, "We have your old chum!"

Thralls in military uniforms shambled out of the saloon, holding muskets. A few other dead men armed with pitchforks and clubs emerged from side alleys and mingled along the shadowed sidewalks. The ragtag army awaited Big Ben's command.

Squatting behind Keech, Duck said, "My charm's getting cold! Doyle must've quit his spell."

"Steady," Nat whispered.

Big Ben pointed back toward the Big Snake Saloon. "I've got him, Jeffreys! Surrender now, or we kill him!"

Keech followed the gesture and saw a pair of slender figures stumble out of the saloon and onto the front porch, one behind the other. The man in front was Milos Horner; the second was Friendly Williams. He was holding a pistol to the bound and beaten Enforcer. Horner's black hair shrouded his face, and as Friendly shoved him across the porch, the prisoner took awkward steps on his bare feet to keep from losing his balance. Keech heard Horner mumble defiantly, "Kill me or no, you'll never get what you want from Red."

"I'm sure Big Ben will show us otherwise," Friendly returned.

Keech glanced back at Nat, who reached inside the pocket of his coat and pulled out the whistle bomb. The deadly orb captured glints of lamplight from the Big Snake's porch and gleamed like the body of a black widow. Nat gestured: *Wait*.

"You have ten seconds to surrender!" Big Ben shouted to the empty street. When nothing but silence returned, he began to count down.

CHAPTER 21
SHOWDOWN AT THE BIG SNAKE SALOON

When the desperado reached *four*, movement caught Keech's eye farther north on Main Street. Edgar Doyle emerged from the darkness and strolled into the illumination cast by torches and lamplight.

"I'm here!" the Ranger hollered.

From their hiding spot behind the barrel, Nat whispered, "Listen for the signal."

Doyle shuffled up the center of Main, approaching Big Ben with long strides. When Keech could discern more of the Ranger's features, he saw that the man's face held no hint of fear. Doyle continued walking, glancing to his left and right at the army of thralls that stood in the shadows, lining the avenue. Keech glanced at a few of the rooftops along the street, but he couldn't see if the crows were still there.

Doyle assumed a defiant stance. One hand gripped his small knife; the other was tightened into a fist. He clenched his pipe between his lips, a curl of thick smoke pouring out of his nostrils.

"Big Ben Loving," Doyle said with unmistakable malice. "You've aged quite poorly since we last met."

"Where is the Char Stone, *Enforcer*?" The outlaw sneered. "We know you uncovered it in Missouri. The Reverend wants it back. While you're at it, give us the coordinates to Bonfire Crossing. Do what I say, or suffer the Reverend's wrath."

Behind Keech, Nat muttered, "I ain't in a good position to throw the bomb. The second I squeeze it, the whistling will give us away. I need to move. You two stay here and keep low. Duck, hold that amulet ready."

"I'll be fine with Keech," Duck whispered back. She tugged the pendant from her coat, slipped it off her neck, and held it out to her brother. The metal faintly glowed orange. "Take it in case you run into a thrall."

Still grasping the whistle bomb, Nat lifted his other hand and let Duck wrap the charm's cord snugly around his palm. He murmured, "I'm proud of you," then turned and scurried into the shadows.

Keech returned his attention to the men on the street.

Big Ben Loving was chuckling. "I used to think you Enforcers had no weaknesses. You could slip any trap, build any weapon, tap any energy. But you do have a weakness: *loyalty*. Coward said you'd never resist saving your old friend. He was right. Now, surrender the Stone and the Crossing's location."

"Don't do it, Red!" cried Milos Horner from the porch. "Forget about me! Leave this forsaken place and bury the Stone!"

Friendly Williams struck the Enforcer's ear with his pistol. "Behave."

"I'm gonna tell you just once," Doyle said to Big Ben. "Hand over my partner."

Duck's eyes widened. "That's the signal."

Like clockwork, Nat emerged from a side alley not too far from the hotel, appearing for a mere second. Neither Big Ben nor Friendly noticed the boy. A high-pitched whistle chirruped across the night. Nat tossed the black ball in a high arc over Main Street and toward a cluster of thralls on the opposite sidewalk.

Keech tracked the orb's journey to the ground, then glanced back to gauge Nat's position, but he had already returned to the shadows.

Big Ben swiveled toward the shrieking sound. "You've brought allies! Good. I'll kill them, too."

Keech crouched lower to the ground. "Better stay down," he told Duck.

When the blast came, the night itself quivered. A giant blossom of flame erupted into the air. The fire shredded the clutch of dead men on the sidewalk and engulfed a stock wagon. The more fortunate thralls nearby scuttled away from the devouring heat.

The force of the explosion rocked the barrel that Keech and Duck were nestled behind and sent Big Ben tumbling backward on his rump. Keech felt a wave of heat attack the air. He saw Doyle spit his pipe onto the street, then stomp on it with a boot heel, cracking the wood. The Ranger rushed forward as spry as a fox.

"Take him down!" Big Ben thundered from the ground.

The remaining horde of thralls raised a chorus of anger and lifted their weapons. Muskets fired into the street. Multiple blasts filled the roadway with a thick cloud of smoke.

"They're gonna kill him!" Duck cried.

"No," Keech said. "Look."

Doyle emerged from the haze, somehow unscathed. The Ranger became a whirlwind of brutality. As a pack of dead men shambled onto the street, he spun the knife in his hand, grabbing it by the tip. He flung the blade, and it sank into a thrall's chest. His other fist opened to reveal yellow light glowing in the center of his palm, a shine that Keech recognized as a piece of the amulet. His hand slapped the cheek of a nearby creature, and the thrall convulsed and dropped at his feet.

"He's got one of the five shards!" Duck said.

Keech looked at the luminous fragment with awe. Pa Abner had been very clear about what to do: *Find the shards, and unite them.* Duck held her father's, and Keech's own charm was in the possession of Coward. And there, in the Ranger's grip, was a third piece.

"Maybe Doyle will work with us to find the other two," Keech whispered. "Right now we have to help him."

"But we don't have weapons."

Keech rummaged through his mind for possibilities. They could attack Big Ben directly, surprising him from behind, but Friendly would spot them from the porch and shoot them dead. A wilder option occurred to him. "I'm thinking about a pigpen."

"What do you mean?" Duck asked.

On Main Street, Doyle tucked into a roll and landed beside another thrall. He stilled the figure with a simple tap to the dead man's hand. In a fluid motion, the Enforcer yanked the monster's musket from his limp fingers and used the rifle's butt to smash the nose of yet another.

During this onslaught, Big Ben had been struggling to regain his feet. The outlaw grimaced as he pushed up from the snow-covered ground, one hand clutching the small of his back.

"You've gotten slow in your old age," Doyle taunted as he destroyed the last thrall in his path. The Ranger was no more than thirty feet from the outlaw, but he stopped when Big Ben Loving pointed back to the Big Snake and exclaimed, "Shoot Horner!"

"Wait!" Doyle shouted.

Milos Horner smiled with busted teeth. "It was a noble attempt, Red, but I'm afraid you've gotten slow, too." The prisoner's face then pivoted back to Friendly Williams. As his eyes moved, he appeared to notice Keech looking from the shadowy corner. Horner's grin widened.

To Keech, the look was oddly one of hope.

"The Enforcers live on," Horner said to Friendly. "Death is coming for you all." He raised his head high and laughed.

Friendly Williams pulled the trigger on his pistol.

The gunshot echoed from the porch, and Milos Horner dropped, limp as a rag doll. His body pitched over the edge of the deck and tumbled onto the street.

The scream that rattled from Doyle's lungs was the loneliest of all sounds, full of anguish and loss.

"I warned you," Big Ben said.

Standing amid a scatter of thrall bodies, Doyle raised one arm and muttered a few strange syllables. A shrieking twister kicked to life in the middle of the street, just as another batch of rotting monsters shambled from the side alleys. He pointed his finger at a nearby horse trough, and the twister went to work, sweeping the water-filled vessel off the ground. The trough tumbled end over end, sloshing water in chaotic sprays, and smashed into a snarling trio of thralls.

"At last, a real show of power!" Big Ben reached into a leather pouch on his hip, and a terrible song cascaded from his lips as he threw some sort of powder into the air. Grit accumulated in front of the outlaw, creating a wind of its own, then whipped into a violent funnel. The tornadoes collided into each other, tearing at the town, ripping boards off the faces of buildings.

Keech turned to Duck, who looked stunned by the display of dark magic. "I have an idea." He raised his voice to be heard over the squalls. "But we'll have to move fast."

"I ain't sure we ought to run into the middle of that."

"We won't have to. We'll go around."

"What are you planning, Keech?"

He looked at the pandemonium taking place on the street. "Doyle could use another distraction. We're gonna fetch the last thing Big Ben will ever see coming. A mean, smelly pig."

They hurried down the side wall of the Big Snake Saloon, away from Main Street, and cut a hard right at the building's edge. Keech found himself looking at the hotel's back alley. Down the way, a couple of dark figures dressed in uniforms scurried toward the battle on Main Street. After waiting in the shadows for the soldiers to pass, Keech and Duck shuffled down the alley till they arrived at a side road crowded with junk. He glanced at the buildings and cabins along the street. "This should make a fine shortcut," he said, and led Duck onto the cluttered road.

"I hate leaving Nat alone," Duck whispered. "I hope you know what you're doing."

"I hope so, too."

Soon they arrived at the same stable house and pigpen they had discovered earlier with Nat. The pair crouched low, and Keech studied the lodging of the skinny cowpoke who had the Devil's mark. A small light burned inside, but the door was cracked open, the wind pushing snow over the threshold, as if the owner had left in a hurry. Probably to join all the ruckus on Main Street, if Keech had to guess. He gestured to Duck. "It's clear."

As they sprinted toward the stable-house door, a monstrous snort sounded from the pigpen. Henrietta the boar slammed his head into the wooden slats of the fence, making Keech jump.

"That beast truly hates you," Duck said.

"That's what I'm counting on. C'mon. Help me round up some tack."

They slipped into the stable and found the horse equipment. There was only one saddle perched on a post, so Keech figured it had to belong to the white horse, Hector. Keech hauled the saddle to the back stall, where Hector stood in the shadows, unmoving. Duck arrived a second later with a bridle and blanket.

Keech slid one hand through the gate and fluttered his fingers. "Hey, big fella, remember me? I told you I'd come back." The cremello steed woke up from his slumber and strolled over to the gate. Keech unlatched the stall, swung the door wide, and stepped in. He scratched Hector's muzzle; the horse nudged him back. "Time to get you out of here."

Duck helped him saddle the horse and secure the harness. All the tack was a perfect fit on Hector, and the stallion seemed to relish the feel of the old range saddle on his spiny back. As they worked, Keech noticed a set of initials burned into the leather of the saddle horn: **MH**.

"Holy smoke, look at this," said Keech, running a finger over the initials.

When Duck read them, her eyes widened. "Do you think this horse belonged to Milos Horner?"

"I reckon so." Keech teared up at the notion. They hadn't been able to save the Enforcer, but they could still save his horse.

They moved together out of the stable and back into the cold yard. In the shadows, Hector looked like part of the snow.

A strident whistle in the distance pierced the night, surprising both of them. Seconds later, a series of raging explosions thundered across Wisdom. Back toward the town center, a pair of roiling fireballs rose into the sky. Hector jerked back a little.

"Looks like Quinn and Cutter found the whistle-bomb stash," Keech said.

"Let's hurry back to Nat," Duck said. "He's probably looking for us."

Suddenly, the door of the cabin pitched wide open, and the shack's scrawny owner stepped out, holding his lantern in one hand, a fan of poker cards in the other. Three uniformed thralls appeared behind him, muttering.

"What in the name of Sam Hill was that racket?" the cowpoke asked.

Keech and Duck froze, but there could be no hiding. They stood in the open with Keech holding the reins of a giant white horse.

The skinny man raised his lantern to the yard. "Hey now," he sputtered. The poker cards tumbled from his hand and landed in the snow. "They're stealin' my horse!"

The thrall soldiers gathered around him at the door to have a peek. "Interlopers!" one hollered. "Get the muskets!"

The lanky man dropped his lantern and swiveled back to run into his cabin, only to tangle up with the three dead men in his path. The four of them blundered into one another, elbows smashing guts, heads butting shoulders.

Keech seized the chaotic moment to mount up on Hector. Duck dived back into the stable house.

The lanky man appeared back at the door with his pistol. "Teach you to rustle my horse!"

Keech shifted sideways on the saddle the very moment the man squeezed off. The gunshot roared like a bear. The lead ball slammed into the stable wall behind Keech, tearing off a chunk of wood.

"He's not your horse," Keech said, straightening on the saddle. "He's the horse of an Enforcer, and you're gonna pay for what you've done."

The soldiers stumbled around the man, this time grasping musket rifles. One of them took a knee and prepared to fire.

"Keech, get us out of here!" Duck called, pinned down in the stable.

"Hang on!" He kicked his boot heels into Hector's sides. The steed burst forward as if a cannon had fired him and charged straight for the gunmen. Surprise washed over their ugly faces. Keech yanked the reins to the left, and Hector responded in kind, swiveling his heavy body and barreling his rump straight into the fiends, who crashed backward into the cabin's wall.

Keech wheeled Hector toward the pigpen, where Henrietta squealed and grunted with furious passion. Reaching with the toe of his boot, Keech kicked the metal hook securing the pen's gate. The latch fell free, and a second kick swung the gate wide open. The mad boar glanced at the opening, then shrieked.

Keech glanced at Duck, who had jumped to her feet. "Get on!"

Duck bolted from the stable just as Henrietta exploded from the pen. Instead of chasing her, the beast caught sight of its owner and the soldiers trying to gain their feet and charged toward them at full force.

"Get them, Henrietta!" Keech said, then turned back to Duck. "We best skedaddle."

The girl vaulted off a nearby tree stump with one foot, leaped through the air, and landed nimbly on the back of Hector's saddle. "Go!"

Hector galloped out of the yard as the skinny man and the thralls fled Henrietta. The boar, however, didn't appear to be satisfied with his prey. Spinning back around, he looked straight at Keech, as if marking him.

"That's right, I'm over here. Come get me, you disgusting pig!" Keech whipped the reins with a loud "Hyah!" and Hector shot down the muddy road. Henrietta trundled behind them, setting a furious pace behind the horse.

"That hog will tear us apart," Duck said. "Hurry!"

After a few twists and turns, Main Street and the Big Snake Saloon materialized back into view. Burning buildings along the road illuminated thrall bodies that had been dispatched by whistle bombs. Farther ahead, fierce twisters continued to howl, and Keech caught a glimpse of Doyle and Big Ben on the avenue's south end, squaring off in a swirl of smoke. A dozen more thralls had crowded the street, some armed with muskets, others with clubs. They struggled against the winds, advancing little by little toward the battle.

Through a flurry of rain and sleet, Keech pushed Hector onto

Main and bolted up the center of the roadway. The focal point of the battle had shifted to the front of the blacksmith shop and the mercantile store.

Duck clenched his arms. "You're gonna charge into the middle of that?"

"Pa Abner used to say, 'When you have to attack, aim your arrow straight for the heart.'"

Somewhere to his right, Henrietta loosed another diabolical squeal. Keech glanced back. The boar careened onto the sidewalk and rammed headlong into a skinny wooden post, causing the entire overhang of a building to collapse into the street. Screeching, Henrietta rattled back onto the avenue and continued his pursuit.

"I ain't never seen an animal with such hatred." Duck laughed.

Five rotting soldiers suddenly emerged from an alleyway up ahead, blocking their path and raising muskets. "Take your aim!" one of the thralls ordered—but further commands were drowned out by a familiar, high-pitched trill that was louder than the roar of the winds. A screaming black orb soared from the shadows of the east-facing storefront and into the midst of the soldiers. Keech shifted his attention to a lamplit alleyway, where he saw Cutter and Quinn standing side by side at the mouth of the passage, waving him and Duck onward.

The whistler exploded in the center of Main, demolishing the pack of thralls and blackening the snow. The heat from the blast washed over Keech's face. He leaned in the saddle, veering Hector out of the path of the carnage.

"Thanks!" Duck shouted to the boys as they rode past.

Keech looked around, searching for the boar. Henrietta was still behind them, his fur singed and smoking, his savage tusks slashing the air mere feet away. The explosion appeared to have angered the foul critter even more.

The supernatural winds picked up as they drove into the heart of the battle. Galloping into the tornadic wall, Keech couldn't see a thing at first—he could feel needles of ice and rain pummeling his face, and somewhere in the commotion he felt his hat fly off his head—but then his vision cleared, and he saw Nat just up ahead, punching a thrall with Duck's glowing amulet shard.

"Nathaniel!" Duck hollered.

The rancher turned to regard them, but only for a second. Another dead man scuttled toward the boy with a farmer's billhook. Nat arched his back and dropped, letting the blade swoop over his face. He sprang back to his feet and slapped the amulet against the creature's throat. The thrall staggered and collapsed.

As they galloped past, Keech heard Duck shout back to her brother, "Get out of the way, Nat!" The boy yelled a surprised curse as Henrietta sprang into view. Keech glanced back to see the rancher hurdle over a hitching post.

Just ahead, two figures wrestled at the sharp left turn of Main Street, locked in a tight grapple. They looked like brothers embracing after a long-awaited reunion.

Hector sped straight for them.

Duck yelled, "Ranger Doyle! Heads up!"

The Enforcer reared up to look, exposing a bloodied lesion on his right thigh. His buckskin trousers had been split, and Big Ben Loving hammered his fist into the wound.

Keech swerved past the tangled men, then hauled the stallion around.

Suddenly, Henrietta burst out of the swirling wall of rain. The boar lowered his tusks. Doyle leaped aside just as the rampaging critter charged into Big Ben's back. The outlaw plunged headfirst into Main Street's muck.

In a flash, Big Ben hopped back to his feet. Henrietta smashed into his legs with a loud snort. This time the outlaw didn't budge, and the beast crumpled in the mud, as though he'd walloped a stone wall. Big Ben made a fist and slammed his knuckles down on Henrietta. The boar shuddered a bit, then lay still.

Grimacing, Doyle took advantage of the distraction. He lifted his arms and flicked his fingers in a looping pattern. A new gust of wind surged to life, sweeping ice and mud up from the road, and blasted into Big Ben.

The outlaw tried to resist the gust, but like a sling pitching a pebble, the wind scooped him up, tossed him thirty feet into the air, and whipped him down the street. The twister pounded the fiend against a stone building, and a bone-crunching crack sounded above the gale. Keech watched as the brute's limp body smashed against storefronts and bounced off rooftops down the street and beyond, till he disappeared from sight.

CHAPTER 22

THE WHISTLE BOMB

The tornado winds quieted; the whipping rains relaxed to a cold drizzle. As Keech gazed around the battle-torn settlement, he searched for impending danger, but no more thrall soldiers appeared on Main Street. He spotted the Reverend's crows, flying just above Wisdom's highest buildings—at least a dozen of them, circling the torchlit sky—but they didn't swoop lower or try to attack.

Doyle muttered to himself, "You let your guard down, Ben, and now you're finished." The man wiped at the blood trickling from his nose. "Messing with a pig when you should've maintained your defenses against the real threat. Careless."

Despite being thrilled at Big Ben's defeat, Keech knew they weren't safe. Not yet. Somewhere in the town lurked Coward and Friendly.

As Keech and Duck dismounted Hector, the Ranger reached into his coat and pulled loose a leather strap. He wrapped it around his shredded thigh, dark crimson instantly soaking the tie. His teeth clenched as he yanked the belt tight. Once he'd composed himself, he turned to Keech and Duck. "That was a mighty big hog."

"We thought you could use another hand," Keech said, caressing Hector's neck as he and Duck shuffled closer. The explosions on Main Street had speckled the poor stallion's white hair with grime and soot.

When Doyle noticed the horse, his battle-weary eyes lit up. "Say, that's a face from the past! Hello, Hector. Long time no see." With a shaking hand, he stroked the stallion's muzzle. "Your master fell tonight, *amigo*. I'm sorry."

Hector returned a small grunting sound.

Duck bent to inspect Doyle's wound. "Ranger, this wound looks bad."

Doyle's face was turning pale from blood loss. Still, he smiled. "Big Ben pulled a conjure pouch and threw a cutting spell I'd never seen. He would've finished me off had you not interfered."

Nat came limping down the middle of the street. Duck's amulet shard was still tied to his other hand, and it no longer gleamed its golden light. Duck dashed to her brother and embraced him.

"I'm glad you're okay," Nat said.

"I'm sorry we left you," Duck said. "We figured Doyle might need more help."

"You did the right thing." Nat untied the shard and handed it back to her. "Let's just get out of this rotten town. We got a bending tree to find."

Doyle staggered closer. "You've learned the next step to Bonfire?"

"We ain't saying a word till you've answered some questions," Nat said. "Once you've explained a few more things, then we'll talk about what *we* know."

"Fair enough. You've earned the right to be suspicious." Doyle shifted his gaze to the front porch of the Big Snake Saloon, where his old trailmate's body lay sprawled in the mud. He hobbled over to Horner and bent down, a pained groan escaping him. Keech felt a tug and realized Hector was trying to follow the man. He released the stallion's harness, and Hector joined Doyle beside the fallen Enforcer.

Doyle's quivering hand moved to the dead man's face and smoothed back a strand of dark hair. "I'm sorry I couldn't save you, Milos. *Amicus fidelis protectio fortis.*"

Keech recognized the strange words as Latin. He turned to Duck, thinking she might know the meaning from her studies, but Doyle beat her to the translation. "It means, 'A faithful friend is a sturdy shelter.' The Enforcers used to speak this phrase to one another, before the dark days of Rose arrived and blackened our hearts." Doyle paused on the bleak words.

There was movement down the street. Cutter and Quinn were shuffling toward them, weaving around fallen thralls and rubble. The boys were filthy, their faces and clothes covered in soot and mud, but they appeared unharmed. When they saw Horner on the ground and Doyle stooped next to the body, they stopped and stared in silence for a second.

"Who was he?" asked Cutter.

"He was Doyle's partner, Lynch," Keech said. "But his real name was Milos Horner. He was an Enforcer and a good man."

Cutter and Quinn pulled off their hats.

After a silent moment, Keech said, "Much obliged for the help back there."

"*De nada,*" Cutter said, his eyes still on Horner.

Quinn held out Keech's bowler hat. "We found this back yonder on the street."

"Thanks." Keech wiped dirt off the hat's brim and slipped it back on.

"Where'd you get the *caballo*?" Cutter asked, stepping over to Hector and putting a hand on the animal's mane. "He's a beast."

"Long story," Keech said. He took Hector's harness and led the horse away from Horner. The stallion tugged back for a second, as though not wanting to leave his old master's side, but eventually he submitted and strolled slowly away.

Doyle staggered a bit on the street, looking mere seconds away from falling over. Quinn moved quickly to steady the man. "Ranger, you look awful! What happened?"

"He didn't mind Big Ben's warning," a terrible voice said. "That's what happened."

Everyone spun around.

The amber lamplight inside the Big Snake Saloon cast shadows over the small figure at the batwing entry. It was Coward. He was too short to be seen over the top of the doors, so he held one side of the portal open with one hand.

At the sight of the fellow, Cutter wheeled backward. Tripping over a chunk of wood in the street, he fell onto his rump.

Coward looked delighted at the sight of battle-torn Main Street, as if the destruction of the Reverend's thrall army and the violent dispatch of Big Ben were all part of a grand performance. He pointed to Horner's corpse. "He made a fine piece of bait."

Doyle's blanched face took on new colors of fury. "You mangy cur." Slipping Quinn's grip, he limped toward the saloon, but Coward held up a chiding hand.

"We both know I'm no match for you, so why would I come out of hiding and stand here like I ain't got a worry in the world?"

Keech immediately knew the answer. They had walked into a trap. He looked around for some sign of the danger—a sniper in the shadows, a clutch of thralls lurking in ambush—but the town was stagnant.

"Leverage." Doyle sneered.

"Clever, as always."

The Ranger snarled. "You think you've got something on me?"

Coward grinned. "I've got *him*, Red. We found your son." Striped shadows from the batwing doors lined the small man's face. "I can smell your uncertainty. No need to doubt. He's in here with a gun to his back." Coward stepped back into the saloon and disappeared from view.

Doyle turned back to the young riders, his face a mask of confusion and pain. "I don't know what he's playing at, but keep away. He only wants me. No one else needs to get hurt."

The Ranger lumbered toward the entrance, favoring his wounded right leg. He stopped just before going in, then glanced back, his face crestfallen, and muttered, "Please. Take my partner off the street. He deserves better." Then he pressed on. The lights inside the hotel darkened the moment he stepped over the threshold, as if the building itself had been waiting to swallow the man alive.

Quinn called after him. "Ranger Doyle, wait!" But the Enforcer ignored the words.

Nat turned to Cutter, who had stopped retreating only when Coward disappeared from the entrance. "Do you have any whistle bombs left?"

"N-no," Cutter stammered.

"What about you, Revels?"

"I used my last one to clear the way when Keech and Duck rode in."

"All right. Then listen up, everyone. Plans have changed. Doyle fought hard to save his partner, but now he's wounded and can barely stand. We're gonna back him up one last time. Cut, I need you to guard the front. You don't have to get near Coward, but keep your knife ready. Revels, you head around the back. If you see anybody retreat, don't engage without a weapon. Just mark the way they ran."

"Got it." Quinn made to hurry off, then paused. "If y'all see that no-good Friendly Williams, punch him in the gut for Quinn Revels." Then he disappeared around the corner of the hotel.

Keech handed Hector's reins over to Cutter. "Stand tall, Cut," he said, then followed Nat and Duck to the entrance of the Big Snake Saloon.

They stopped shy of entering and hunkered against the outside wall. Keech wrinkled his nose at the heavy smells of liquor and old cigar smoke that piped out of the establishment. He dared a glance beneath the doors and saw Doyle standing in the center of the big room, surrounded by a disorder of chairs, dining tables, and brass spittoons.

"What's he doing?" Nat whispered.

"Not sure."

Nat motioned for them to slip over the threshold.

Inside, Doyle stood rigid, poised to attack, his left fist held high over his head. A strange, afflictive kind of pressure pushed against Keech's skin, like the air just before a thunderstorm. Doyle didn't turn his head or body, but upon the trio's entrance, he said, "I told y'all to stay put."

On the opposite side of the smoke-hazy room, Coward stood on top of the saloon's long wooden bar, one hand resting on his hip. Pa Abner's amulet shard still dangled over the knuckle guard of his sword. Upon seeing Keech and the siblings enter, the small man held up a warning hand. "Stand down, children! Don't make things worse." He pointed.

Keech followed the gesture.

Friendly Williams stood halfway down the hotel's staircase, holding his pistol to the back of a disheveled, heavyset lad. Keech couldn't believe his eyes when the boy lifted his head, revealing the battered face of John Wesley.

"John!" Duck shouted.

"You're *alive*," Nat gasped.

John Wesley didn't speak—it looked as if he couldn't. A spattering of purple bruises covered his skin, and the wound inflicted on his right hip by the Chamelia had stained his trousers black. His breath wheezed out from split lips, and his swollen eyes were downcast, as if he were unaware that anyone else was in the room.

"*John Wesley*," Doyle said.

John's eyes struggled upward. "Papa?"

Dumbfounded, Keech couldn't help wondering if all this was part of some strange dream. The idea that Edgar Doyle—once an Enforcer named Red Jeffreys—was the father of John Wesley seemed preposterous, yet there the boy stood, apparently a trap to snare the Ranger. Once again, fate was at play with the lives of the Lost Causes.

Doyle's fist wavered in the air. "I'm here, my boy. Papa's *here*."

"Touching," Coward said, strolling across the bar.

But Doyle simply stared at John Wesley. "What have they done to you?"

Friendly responded for John. "He'll be fine so long as you do what you're told. Same with your posse of young'ins. But stir up a ruckus, and I'll plug this kid right in the heart."

The Ranger ignored Friendly's taunts, turning instead to Coward. "What have you done to him, you devil?" His fist stirred above his head, and that oppressive tension in the air nearly sucked the wind out of Keech's lungs.

"I received the boy as Big Ben delivered him," Coward said. "In fact, he looks better than he did this morning. You should thank us!"

Doyle's frame shook. "I suppose your rotten nose sniffed him out?"

Coward's eyes flickered with a kind of zeal, as if he'd been waiting all day to answer such a question. "Not *my* nose." He tugged a piece of brown cloth from his pocket and wagged it at Doyle. "Recognize this?"

Suspicion shadowed Doyle's face.

"You dropped this rag during the Blackwood shoot-out back in '45. Remember? You shouldn't abandon your personal belongings. You never know when someone might pick them up and use them for ill."

The Ranger exhaled slowly—a forlorn sigh. "Big Ben gave the cloth to his Chamelia, didn't he? It found John Wesley through my own scent."

"You're not as dull as you look," Coward said.

Keech squirmed in place, wanting to launch an attack, but Nat rested a hand on his shoulder, a wise warning to be patient.

Doyle's voice cracked. "Release my son. Please. He's just an innocent boy."

Coward snickered. "First, open that fist. I know you've got some spell ready to release at the twitch of your wrist. Relax your hex, or Friendly kills him."

John Wesley's shoulders slumped even lower than before. He looked as if he might collapse down the rest of the stairs. Friendly gripped one arm to steady him.

"Just don't hurt him." Doyle loosened his fist.

As the hand lowered, the heaviness in the air softened, and Keech drew in a breath.

"I have no desire to hurt your boy," Coward said. "I only want the Char Stone and the where'bouts of the Crossing. Once I have those in hand, I'll leave you to your lives."

"I don't know the Crossing's location, and do you think me so daft as to bring the Stone here?"

Coward walked the length of the bar, sniffing. His boots knocked glasses and bottles to the floor, where they shattered. "I know it's close, Enforcer. You *stink* of it. As a matter of fact—" An impish grin spread across his face as he inhaled deeply again. He hopped backward, landing behind the bar. Keech heard Pa's amulet shard jangle against the man's scabbard. Coward peeked over the counter's edge. "I'll be stepping out the back for a moment, Friendly. Keep vigilant till I return."

"What?" Friendly said, his eyes widening.

The small man flung open the saloon's back door and scuttled away into the night.

Friendly's face screwed up with confusion. "But this wasn't the plan!" he shouted to the open back door. Suddenly recognizing he was surrounded, fear washed across his face. "Don't none of you move, or I'll shoot the kid, I swear!"

"You'll do no such thing." Doyle flicked his index finger toward the stairs. An ominous wind kicked up and whistled over the stairwell, blowing Friendly's white hair.

"Put that finger down! I mean it!"

Duck began to chuckle.

Friendly's free hand scratched at the Devil's mark on his neck. "What are *you* laughing at, brat?"

"I'm just remembering what Keech told you down in the dungeon." She looked at Keech and grinned, though he could tell she was terrified. "How the Big Snake would dispose of you when you served their purpose. Sure enough, your boss just abandoned you."

Friendly's eyes twitched toward the back exit. "No, he's comin' back."

A low moan emerged from John Wesley's throat, a rumble like that of a mewling cougar. The sound took Friendly by surprise. He stepped up a stair away from the boy. "What's wrong with you, kid?"

John Wesley lurched backward, knocking Friendly into the stairwell wall, and then spun to face him. A pistol shot crackled, and blue gun smoke rose up between Friendly and John. The boy stiffened and gave a small cry. The pair rolled down the final few stairs together, their arms and legs tangling, till they crashed against the tall piano sitting by the staircase.

"No!" Doyle rushed over and landed on his knees beside John Wesley.

"He just shot John," Duck said, her words flat with shock.

But then John Wesley sat upright. The boy glanced down at

himself. There was a tiny black hole in the chest of his coat where Friendly's bullet had struck, but when he pushed a finger into the space, the tip returned clean. He glanced over at the young riders.

"Hey, y'all," he said. "What happened? This don't look like Mercy Mission."

"John!" Nat said.

Convulsions suddenly racked John Wesley's body, accompanied by a petrifying scream. His fingers reached for his coat and ripped it up the middle. Buttons flew across the room. Tossing his head back, he opened his mouth—his jaw unhinging too wide for a regular person—and rows of nettle-thin fangs sprouted from his gums.

"Kid, what're you playin' at?" Friendly said, his face contorting with fear. He tried to back away but smacked against the piano.

John Wesley's hands and neck and face *rippled*. Bumps appeared all over his features, singeing his flesh in places as though fire had charred him. Keech rubbed his eyes with a knuckle, hoping the pressure and smoke in the room were deceiving his sight, but this was no trick of the eye.

"What's happening to him?" Duck shouted.

Disregarding his startled captor, John Wesley turned a pair of eyes as red as fiery coals on Doyle. "*You*," the boy growled, his voice suddenly much deeper. "You murdered my ma!"

Doyle started to mumble something but was cut off when Friendly fired his pistol twice into John Wesley's back. This time, the lead slugs bounced off John's hide and landed on the floor beside the piano. He howled, but the sound was more fury than pain. He spun to face Friendly, and the man's features turned whiter than his fluffy shirt.

John Wesley grabbed the fellow by the neck and tossed him across the saloon. Friendly crashed into a bar stool, groaned a little, then slumped unconscious on the floor.

John's gleaming red eyes locked again on Doyle. "*I'll kill you.*"

If they didn't do something, John Wesley would tear Edgar Doyle apart. Nat and Duck must have understood this, too, for they all scrambled toward Doyle at the same time and grabbed him by the arms to drag him away.

"Ranger, you better go!" Nat said as the trio struggled to pull the man onto his feet.

"Turn me loose!" Doyle roared, his voice cracking with anguish.

Suddenly, one of the saloon's large front windows shattered, spraying glass into the chamber. Keech spun around to see Big Ben dive through the window, very much alive. The brute crossed the room in a flash and slammed into Keech, knocking him into Nat and Duck. Keech tumbled headlong into the stairwell, feeling elbows and knees knock the wind out of his gut.

Big Ben shoved the snarling John Wesley back into the piano, then drove a fist into Doyle's chest. Doyle doubled over and collapsed. The outlaw stepped on the Ranger's wounded thigh, pinning him to the floor. Doyle screamed.

Big Ben bellowed laughter. "You've lost your son, Red. Look at him. He's tainted."

Nat and Duck dog-piled the brute, driving their fists into his bearded face. "You killed our parents!" Duck cried. But their blows did nothing but aggravate the man.

"Help us!" Nat yelled to Keech.

But Keech was already diving from the stairwell. As he came down, his chest smacked against what felt like a tree trunk. He realized he'd landed on Big Ben's arm in midswing. He tugged against the arm, but he might as well have been pulling at a house. "Enough!" the outlaw roared, and twisted his mountainous body. Keech and Nat and Duck went flying across the room. Keech tumbled into a table, and the side of his head smacked wood. Playing cards cascaded around him.

Dazed, Keech glanced up and saw a grotesque version of John Wesley bare his new fangs. The boy seized Big Ben by the shoulders and shoved his lower back into the newel post. Big Ben's face wrenched in pain.

"He's *mine*!" John screamed, then lunged at his father. Keech expected Doyle to be ripped apart, but instead John Wesley hoisted the wounded man over his shoulder. Releasing a loud roar, the boy wheeled in the direction of the broken front window and leaped across the room carrying Doyle. John Wesley's boots landed squarely on the windowsill, crunching the shattered glass that remained in the wood. He glanced back at Keech and the siblings, who were trying to pick themselves up from the dingy floor, and scrunched a brow that had sprouted dozens of thorns. To Keech, the look was one of both rage and bewilderment.

"John!" Duck called, but the boy didn't answer.

Movement at the stairwell made Keech pivot.

Big Ben reached into his riding coat and drew out something black and shiny. Keech recognized it as the whistle bomb he'd been carrying when Big Ben had ambushed them. "You won't get away, Red Jeffreys," the outlaw murmured, and squeezed the orb. The whistler began to whine its mad song. Big Ben reared back the hand gripping the ball.

John Wesley vaulted from the window with Doyle in tow.

From across the room, Nat screamed, "Don't let him throw it!"

Keech bounded onto a table and leaped at Big Ben. Hitting the large man was like running into a solid wall. Yet despite the jarring impact, he managed to wrap one arm around Big Ben's neck.

Nat appeared a blink later and seized the man's shoulder. Duck followed close behind, clutching the outlaw's leg. Big Ben kicked out. There was a loud cry as Duck went flying halfway across the room. Then his free hand reached up and grabbed Keech by the scruff of his coat.

Keech hooked his hand around his other arm and squeezed, hoping to cut off the man's wind. Instead, Big Ben hurled him away.

The violent trill of the whistler grew in pitch. As Keech tried to scramble back to his feet, he saw Nat latch his strong rancher hands around Big Ben's arm. The boy locked eyes with Keech and Duck. He regarded them the way Pa Abner had once regarded the orphans—with a desperate tenderness.

"Go," Nat said to them, almost peacefully. "Get out."

Confusion twisted Duck's face. "What are you doing?"

Nat hunkered low, laboring to restrain Big Ben's titanic arm. Through clenched teeth, he said to Keech and Duck, "I've got him. *Go.* Keep each other safe and never stop fighting."

"Nat, *c'mon*," said Duck.

Lifting his head to the ceiling, Nat bellowed to his sister, "I love you, Duck!"

Understanding melted Keech's paralysis. Time snapped back, and the world became a lightning blur.

Keech scooped up Duck and hugged her to his chest.

He ran for the front door.

"No!" screamed Duck, kicking in his grip. "Let me go, Keech! Let me go!"

Racing as fast as he had ever run in his life, Keech rushed out of the Big Snake. Down the street he saw Cutter running toward the hotel with Hector's reins in one hand. He waved the boy back.

Struggling in Keech's arms, Duck cried, "Nathaniel!"

Keech heard Nat thunder four words—*"Ride, Lost Causes! Ride!"*—then the whistle bomb exploded.

CHAPTER 23
CLEMENTINE

Heat like the sun pressed against Keech's back, and silence clapped over his ears. An invisible hand snatched him up and threw him and Duck violently forward. As he plunged, Keech became distantly aware of jagged pellets of wood and glass flying around him like a swarm of hornets.

Crashing sideways against the ground of Main Street, Keech caught a fleeting glimpse of the explosion. Big Ben's whistle bomb tore away the entire front of the Big Snake Saloon, then a second and third blast followed. The building's walls bulged, then burst; the second-floor balcony ripped apart. Great curtains of fire cleaved the hotel up the middle and climbed high into the air.

Keech's ears buzzed with a distant moan. The sound was far away at first but mounted slowly, and he realized that the power of the explosion had stunned his hearing. As his ears recovered, the moaning grew louder.

He lifted his head. Duck was sitting in the icy mud beside him, her arms hanging useless by her sides. She was looking at the devastated hotel, her mouth twisted in disbelief, and Keech finally understood that the sound was her howling.

He struggled to his feet, slipped in the dirty snow, and felt someone seize his arm at the elbow.

It was Cutter. Horner's white stallion stood behind him, and both the boy and the horse were covered in thick grime. "What happened, Blackwood?" He seemed oblivious to everything that had taken place, even John Wesley's leaping out the front window with the Ranger over his shoulder. Then Keech realized that Cutter had moved Milos Horner's body off the street. He had most likely not seen the confrontation directly.

Cutter shouted something into Keech's ear, but most of the words weren't striking home. Keech blinked stinging grit from his eyes and said, "What?"

"I said, *Where's Nat?*"

Keech looked again at the obliterated saloon, hoping beyond hope to see Nat emerge from the maelstrom, dust off his hat, and smile. But, of course, there was nothing to see but flame and smoke rising into the night sky.

Overwhelming heat rolled off the hotel and baked Keech's face. The world wanted to twist and blur, but he hammered the feeling back. His breath rasped out of him. "Cut, I need you to find Quinn. He went around back to stand watch, but Coward slipped out, and I'm afraid he got hurt. Go fetch him. Please."

Cutter gazed around, stunned, clearly still searching for Nat. "What're *you* gonna do?"

Keech glanced over at Duck, who was still wailing at the sight of the scorched wreckage. "Meet us back at the ravine. Take Hector in case Quinn's hurt. You'll need a fast way out. I'm gonna carry Duck out of here."

"Keech, tell me. Where is Nat?"

"Gone." It was all he could say, and it came out like a cough.

Cutter's face paled. "Okay. I'll find Revels. We'll see you back at the ravine." Then he spun and mounted up on Hector. "*Vámonos,*" he yelled, and the Enforcer's stallion trotted away.

Keech hobbled toward Duck. She didn't look at him, even when he called her name. "I'm gonna get you out of here," he said, and bent to scoop her up.

The girl shoved his hands away. "Leave me alone!"

"We're not safe, Duck. There could be more thralls. We have to get off the street."

When she refused again, Keech dropped to his knees in front of her. He looked her straight in the eye. Though the hotel's fiery tumult scorched every inch of him, he forced a gentle smile. "My little brother Patrick was four. Did you know that? He used to climb up the side of the stairs. Sometimes when I walked by, he would jump onto my back and pretend to be a squirrel. I'd tell him to hang on, and we'd run around the house, then head out the back door and race all the way around the property. Patrick loved those piggyback rides."

Duck glanced up at him, her stark blue eyes disoriented. They reflected the cinders of the nearby chaos and burned like small brands.

"Let me give you a piggyback ride," he pleaded. "I can carry you all the way."

"All right," she said, trembling.

Keech scooped her up, then shifted her weight so that she was resting on his back and holding on to his neck. She felt light for now, but the journey back to the ravine would be long. She clung to him like squirrel Patrick, and by accident, she shoved his bowler hat over his eyes. Keech reached up and pushed it back straight.

They walked down the street, away from the burning hotel and toward the log wall north of town. "Don't look back," he said. He could hear the girl moaning in his ear, a devastating sound he knew he would never forget.

Wisdom's shabby wall appeared just ahead. Keech grimaced when he saw that the gate was closed. "Duck, I'm gonna have to put you down. Okay?"

"All right," she said again.

He set her down, and she returned to her knees in the mud. He hefted the wooden crossbar that secured the passage. When he pushed open the gate, two thralls appeared before him, clutching long torches. They wore army uniforms, like all the rest in town, and when they saw him, they shirked back toward the shallow moat that stretched in front of the wall. One of the rotten soldiers tumbled over, landing in a patch of ice, while the other backed away from Keech on rattletrap legs. "Have mercy, Enforcer!" the creature hissed.

In the darkness, the monsters must have thought he was Doyle. "Duck, can I borrow your shard?" he asked.

The answer returned in a small but grim voice. "No."

Duck rose from her knees, her boots squelching in the mud, and fished the glowing shard from her coat. Her expression was utterly blank, as if nothing would ever again frighten or delight her. She approached the terror-stricken thralls, and they shrank back, dropping their torches at the sight of her.

Duck leaped at them. Before Keech knew what had happened, both monsters were squawking on the ground, their false life rupturing from their black veins. When she returned to Keech's side, her eyes looked like dazzling jewels in the torchlight of the nearby watchtowers. "Nobody else gets this shard," she said. "Not ever again."

"Okay."

Keech allowed himself one more glance back at the ravaged ribbon of Main Street. A few blocks away, the night glowed a pale yellow from the fires burning the town. The whistle bombs that had gutted the old hotel and flattened so many surrounding buildings had scored the earth, making the town center collapse inward like a giant wrinkled mouth. Above this devastation, the Reverend's crows drifted like shadows in the blighted sky, the flames etching red and orange light onto their distorted bodies. The crows had kept their distance during the battle—just as they had at Bone Ridge.

Keech turned back to Duck. The amulet shard dangling from her hand, she had grabbed one of the thralls' torches and was peering out into the black forest. A steep embankment stood like a bulwark before the town, the same hillside the young riders had climbed down earlier, before entering the burg.

Duck leaped over the worthless moat and started slogging up the rise—but then she stopped, and the torch dropped to her side.

Hopping over the moat, Keech stood beside her and again prompted the girl onto his back. "Come on, let's keep going. Just a little farther." She passed Keech the torch, then climbed on again, her breath hitching.

Keech resumed the hike. Moments passed, but he didn't care to count them. All he could see in his mind was the first time he'd laid eyes on Nat Embry. The tall rancher had walked out from behind Copperhead Rock on Big Timber Road, so strong and confident, appearing like another version of Pa Abner in Keech's life. *You have my word no harm will come to you*, Nat had said. Then they had shaken hands.

As Keech and Duck skirted through the cottonwood trees, the cursed darkness began to peel away, like curtains of black cloth ripping back, layer by layer. Keech had assumed they would walk into the sunlight of a new morning—their excursion into Wisdom had felt like an entire night—but when the last gauze of darkness tore free from the natural world, he walked in normal night, illuminated by the gentle glow of a waning crescent moon.

Duck's voice came to him like a breath to his ear. "What time is it?"

Keech gazed up at the sky. Snow clouds drifted over the pale moonlight, but the moon's position told him enough. "It's about ten."

"Put me down."

"We should keep going. We're close to the ravine. We'll be safer there."

She didn't ask again but squirmed off his back and dropped to the ground. Keech propped the torch against a rock and sat beside her. The night was freezing, but it was a normal, rational cold, free from curses and blights.

For a time, there was only silence, then Duck said, "He ain't coming back, Keech."

"I know."

"Nathaniel's gone. He promised we'd meet back in the ravine."

"He meant to." Feeling tears well up in his eyes, Keech placed a hand on her arm. She didn't fight him, but she offered no indication that she felt the touch. He went on. "Let's just rest here for a spell. Cutter and Quinn will be back soon, and we can fetch the horses and go make a camp."

Duck's voice trembled with a new kind of fear. "I got no family left."

Keech lifted his hand up to her neck and drew her close. "You've got me." When her small body began to quake against him, he remembered the wooden doll in his pocket. Though it felt somewhat silly, he tugged it out and laid the figurine on her lap. At the Moss house, Duck had told him she used to have a doll much like this, only with yellow britches and a blue hat. *I called her Clementine*, she'd said. *She was a present from Nat. I played with her in the mud holes out behind the house.*

Duck peered down at the doll taken from Erin Blackwood's grave and brought it up to her neck. She held it close to her throat and squeezed her eyes shut, as if making a wish upon the doll's head. "I don't even like this thing," she said. "But thanks."

Keech didn't know how to fix Duck's broken heart, so instead he did the only thing that made sense. He hugged her close, and together they wept.

PART 3

BONFIRE CROSSING

Big Ben in the Rubble

A shape moved in the heart of the Big Snake Saloon wreckage. A crack of snapping wood sounded inside the smoldering ruins, and wooden beams creaked as if under pressure from an intense weight. Scraping metal knocked, then rattled as a pile of slag shifted.

Big Ben Loving rose, his steaming body covered with ash. Char and cinder had smeared his skin, and his long red beard had been singed. He surfaced with slow agony as each joint in his body creaked. Gashes crisscrossed his arms and face, and his riding coat and shirt were in tatters, exposing his shoulders and chest to the frozen rain.

The fires at the center of Wisdom were burning out, and thick smoke ascended into the cursed sky. The Reverend's crows circled above, watching in silence, and a few perched on the rooftops of leftover buildings that looked down on the devastation.

Wisdom's remaining troops, a pathetic smattering of thralls, had gathered on Main Street. They didn't speak as Big Ben shook himself free of the rubble and stepped onto the avenue. Many of them scurried back as if hoping to hide from his frightful gaze.

He had survived flame and destruction, but now the Prime inside him was weak, and he was cold. He gestured to a nearby thrall. "Give me your coat."

The dead man obeyed, fumbling out of his jacket with haste. Like all the other thralls in town, this rotten creature was a product of Ignatio's necromancy, under orders to obey Big Ben.

One of the circling crows descended to street level, resting on a crooked hitching post. It screamed a wicked *Ack!* and turned a red oily eye to Big Ben.

Always devout in the Reverend's presence, Big Ben bowed his head.

"You've done well, Ben." The crow spoke aloud so that all present heard the Reverend. *"You cornered the traitor Jeffreys, and now Coward has recovered my Stone. But your work in this territory is not complete."*

"The Fang of Barachiel," Big Ben answered.

"Yes. Retrieve the Fang and destroy Bonfire Crossing. It can no longer serve as a sanctuary to Enforcers."

Spasms of pain coursed through Big Ben's body, and he felt he might collapse. "Master, I spent the last of your Prime mending my bones and resisting the bomb. I'm worthless till I've taken time to rest and heal."

"No." The crow flapped its wings, a gesture of irritation. *"We must push our advantage."*

"But what can I do like this? I'm empty."

The crow regarded the small company of thralls that had gathered around Big Ben. The creature's red eyes glowed with a fierce inner light. With a deafening screech, the bird took to the air. It flapped in small, vicious circles, then the Reverend's terrible voice thundered down upon the dazed dead men.

"*You all cowered during the battle, watching from safe corners as your brethren fell. You betrayed the Prime that your master, Ignatio, granted you.*"

Trembling, the pack of thralls screamed denials. Some begged for another chance, and others turned in panic and stumbled over themselves to get away from the crow.

A freezing wind kicked up around the scrambling congregation, blowing the reek of decay into Big Ben's face. The thralls began to shake. Black veins coursed over their flesh, turning the sight of them even more monstrous. Unearthly wails arose from the pack.

Thick wisps of black smoke poured off the soldiers. The dark tendrils floated out over Main Street, wrapped together to form a single pillar, then curled back down to cover Big Ben like a blanket. The fog seeped into his nostrils, his open mouth. Waves of vigor charged his once agonized muscles. The hot ache in his joints eased, his back straightened. Fury and purpose filled every corner of his mind.

Every last thrall tumbled to the ground, their bodies empty husks, their Prime withdrawn.

Big Ben lifted his head and shouted to the crows in the sky. "Thank you, Master!"

The birds released a collective cackle.

A moment later, the Reverend's voice grated directly into his mind. "*Summon your Man Slayer. Send it to track the Enforcer children from a distance, but they are not to be killed. Not till they find the door to the Crossing. Once they yield the location, the Man Slayer may finish them.*"

"Yes, Reverend."

"Red Jeffreys must not be allowed to retrieve the Fang."

Big Ben shook with newfound power and rage. "There will be no quarter given."

"Once you secure the relic, you will join Ignatio and Black Charlie in the mountains to search for Enoch's Key. They will be waiting for you. Lost Tucker will be holding her position farther north."

"Your will be done, Master." Big Ben closed his eyes and bowed his head.

"Go now. I will be watching."

CHAPTER 24
RENDEZVOUS

Keech and Duck traveled back to Edgar Doyle's rally point in silence. The moment the torchlight revealed the group's ponies in the ravine, Keech felt another hefty wallop of sadness. Nat's horse, Sally, stood beside her brother Irving, waiting for Nat to reappear. When Duck saw the Fox Trotter, she dropped the sputtering torch to the ground and began to whimper anew.

Scooping up the light, Keech pointed to a smooth dip beneath a tree. "There's a nice spot you can rest up," he said gently. "As soon as Quinn and Cut get back, we'll head to a safer place to camp, all right?"

Duck sat in the hollow, her face glimmering with fresh tears.

Keech carried the torchlight over to the ponies, checking to make sure they were still healthy. Four animals stood at the rally spot—Irving, Sally, Lightnin', and Chantico—and Doyle's bloodroot barrier still circled them.

But Saint Peter was no longer tied off to his tree.

"Oh no." Keech swung the torch and noticed the bulging dark shape of the Kelpie lying a few feet from the other ponies. The creature had toppled onto his side. Doyle's saddlebags had been torn open, and supplies were scattered across the clearing.

Keech dropped to his knees beside the horse. The Kelpie was still alive but appeared to be in a deep slumber, his bulky sides rising and falling to a peaceful-looking rhythm. Keech pushed against the beast and tried to lift his heavy head, but he couldn't wake the stallion.

He spotted Doyle's knapsack on the ground. The ropes that had tethered the bag to Saint Peter had been cut, and the satchel's buckles had been unfastened. Small boot prints in the snow jogged away from it, plunging west into the woodland. It didn't take a brilliant tracker to identify the owner of the prints.

Coward.

Keech pulled Doyle's knapsack closer, dreading to look inside. Or rather, dreading what he *wouldn't* find. An object rolled from the mouth of the bag and came to rest against his knee. Keech wheeled backward in horror.

He was staring at a human skull.

The thing looked small and delicate, as though it had belonged to a child. The dark caverns of its eyes peered up at Keech with somber curiosity. Shivering, he stepped back from the skull resting in the snow.

"Doyle, what were you up to?" he mumbled. Returning his attention to the satchel, Keech peered deeper inside and discovered more bones bundled together by small ropes. Like the skull, they looked small. "You're carrying the remains of a *kid*." He glanced back at Duck, wondering if she'd noticed Doyle's dreadful cargo, but the girl sat in her frozen hollow, head hung low, the doll wedged in her lap, her arms wrapped around her torso.

Keech dared one more glimpse inside the knapsack, turning the bag over a little to let the bones knock any other items loose, but there appeared to be no sign of the Char Stone. He sighed bitterly and dropped the satchel. The bones clanked within.

There was nothing for it then. Coward had stolen his amulet shard and now he had claimed the Stone—the *one thing* that Pa Abner had warned Keech never to let happen. With the Stone reclaimed, the Reverend Rose would no doubt turn his sights on Bonfire Crossing and the mysterious Fang next.

Keech remembered the times when he had praised the work of fate in their lives. But it was all nonsense. If fate had truly been guiding the Lost Causes to victory, they would never have lost the Stone, and Nat Embry would still be alive.

He reached to fetch the skull. He didn't want to touch the foul thing, but he knew he couldn't leave it lying on the ground. Before he grabbed it, the sound of an approaching horse made him pause. A torchlight bobbed across the ravine, and a second later, a large patch of white appeared, galloping toward the rally point.

"It's Quinn and Cut," Keech said.

The boys rode up with Cutter at the reins. A glazed look darkened Quinn's face. Though he was holding the torch, the kid looked dazed, as if someone had knocked him for a loop. "Hey, Blackwood," Cutter said with a hectic voice. "We've got to light out again. It ain't safe here."

"What happened?"

Leaping down from Hector, Cutter helped Quinn slide off the cantle and onto the ground where Duck sat. "It was Coward." Cutter scowled as he uttered the name. "The way Revels tells it, the man knocked him out with some kind of *cough*."

"A cough?"

"Maybe not, but it sounded like one," Quinn answered. "It was something darker, like he choked up some kind of curse on me." The boy peeled off his forage cap and shook his head as though trying to stir from a nap. "I was over in the back alley behind the saloon, keeping watch, when that fella ran out. He jumped when he saw me, then coughed a weird noise like a sick cat, and suddenly I felt all bone weary, like I hadn't slept in a year. I fell right over and sacked out."

"I found him behind a crate," Cutter explained, then looked at Quinn. "Whatever Coward did to you, *amigo*, I reckon it saved your life, since you dropped behind cover before the bomb went off."

"Guess I'm lucky." Quinn stood, but his knees were shaky.

"Maybe Coward's cough explains this." Keech swiveled his torch toward the sleeping mound of Saint Peter and the scattered mess from Doyle's saddlebags. "Coward got here first and stole the Char Stone."

"Perfect," Cutter spat. He walked around Doyle's belongings till he reached the skull on the ground and jerked back at the sight. "Is that what I think it is?"

"There's a heap of bones inside the satchel. I don't know what Doyle's been playing at, but it's nothing good," Keech said.

Cutter backed away from the skull, then glanced at the distant darkness hanging over Wisdom. "I took Horner's body off the street, like Doyle wanted, but then everything happened so fast, I only saw the explosion. How did the fight go down?"

Keech rehashed the deadly encounter quickly, not wishing to linger on the details of Nat's death for fear that he would lose control of his emotions. When he finally got to the part about John Wesley, the boy's name slipped out so rapidly that Keech didn't have time to stop himself.

Cutter reeled as if Keech had just delivered a shocking blow. "What did you just say?"

"John Wesley is alive, Cut. I didn't mean to break it to you like that."

"That's impossible! We saw him die."

"No," Keech said. "He survived."

"But how?"

Keech paused, not exactly sure how to continue. "Because he's different."

"What do ya mean, *different*?" Cutter's eyes burned with intensity.

"John Wesley's changed, Cut. He started *shifting* in the saloon, then ran off carrying Doyle. Turns out, the Ranger's his pa."

Cutter's face twisted in confusion. "What do you mean?"

"I mean Edgar Doyle is John Wesley's father."

"No, the other thing. You said he *shifted*?"

"He's been infected, Cut. He's turning into a Chamelia."

Cutter fell deathly silent for a moment, then said, "My *compadre* is a Shifter?"

"Yeah. I'm afraid so."

Quinn had been listening to the exchange with patience, but now he swung the torchlight about. "We should finish talking on the trail. Right now we need to move. It ain't safe in this ravine no more."

Keech didn't like the look on Quinn's face. "What is it?"

Quinn shuddered. "Just before me and Cut left the town, we turned back to get one more look at the place. We saw a pack of thralls shimmy over to the hotel wreckage, and Big Ben climbed right out of the rubble."

Duck's head shot up. "What?"

"He wasn't dead. I don't know how, but the bomb didn't get him."

Keech couldn't tell if the sound that Duck made was sobbing or shocked laughter. She clutched the doll, but now she held it with clear malice.

"Then we're *finished*," she said, driving the last word like a nail. "Nathaniel died for nothing. We've lost."

"No, we haven't," Keech said, but seeing Duck's broken stare and the weariness on the boys' faces, he wondered if there was anything he could say to hold this team together.

"I reckon she's right," Quinn said. "We have to scatter, else we're done."

"No! We've still got a mission," Keech implored. "We can't give up."

Quinn's head tilted. "Give up? No, sir. I'm heading out west to track down Auntie Ruth. I'll never give up on her."

Keech glanced at Cutter. "You'll still ride, won't you, Cut? We got a bending tree to find. Mr. Horner gave us clues."

Cutter peered off into the dark woodland. "I'm afraid you're on your own, *amigo*. All I aim to do now is find John. If he's turning Shifter, like you claim, I have to find a way to help him."

Keech turned back to Duck. "You have to stick with me. We've come so far."

"No, Keech." Her voice sounded paper-thin. "I'm gonna head back home to Sainte Genevieve. Folks there know the Embry name. They'll help me rebuild some kind of life."

"Face it, Blackwood," said Cutter. "We're done. *This* is done."

Keech glanced at them all desperately. "No, it's not! We just have to believe we can get to Bonfire Crossing and finish what we started."

"What have we started?" Duck said. "A war with the Reverend Rose we can't hope to win?"

"But I feel like we're one step away. We're close to finding what we're supposed to."

Cutter pointed a finger at Keech's face. "I'm tired of riding on your gut feelings, Lost Cause. That's gonna get us killed some day, just like—" He stopped himself and suddenly veered his eyes away from Duck.

"Go ahead, say it," Duck growled. "Like Nathaniel, you mean."

Guilt and sadness overcame Cutter's face. "I'm sorry, *chica*."

Duck's own face turned a seething red. "What do you know, *Miguel*. You're just a liar. You've been hiding secrets ever since you and John took up with me and Nat."

Cutter dropped his head.

The team was dissolving before Keech's eyes. They only knew anger and loss now, and they aimed to travel their own directions. Even Quinn wanted no part of them. The thought of their wandering off on their own filled Keech with such frustration that he wanted to pummel the earth with his fists.

A memory stopped him.

He was standing over the charred ruins of the Home for Lost Causes, a mountain of black timbers, little Patrick's wooden stick-and-ball toy in his hands. He made an oath to his family: *Vengeance will come. I swear it on my life.* The promise to his Pa Abner, his Granny Nell, his fallen siblings that he would never surrender. *I have to go hunting now*, he had told his lost family. *I have to finish this.*

Keech opened his mouth to plead his case—there was but one final chance to save the group—but suddenly a deep growl sounded at the western edge of the gorge.

Everyone spun to mark the source of the rumble.

"The Shifter!" Cutter said, reaching for his knife.

But when Keech and Quinn brandished their torches, they didn't see the Chamelia that had besieged Mercy Mission.

They saw John Wesley, dragging a senseless Edgar Doyle through snow and mud.

The boy lumbered toward the firelight, shoving away branches in his path. His haggard boots stopped at the lip of the ravine. He looked decidedly more John than monster, even though black scales now covered his arms and neck. Narrow, sharp barbs encircled his face and jutted from the backs of his hands. His eyes no longer beamed red fury, as they had at the Big Snake Saloon, but were dark and slitted yellow. Cakes of mud matted his curly reddish hair, and his clothes were in such tatters that Keech could see his dirty knees and elbows.

As for the body in his grip, Doyle was still alive, but he looked to be on the verge of death.

John Wesley stood in grim silence, his barrel stomach rising and falling. Then he tossed the Ranger down into the ravine.

A small moan escaped the man.

"*John?*" Cutter mumbled.

The sound of the boy's voice must have jarred John Wesley, for his head wiggled back and forth a bit, as if he were trying to shake water out of his ear. He glanced at Cutter with fretful eyes. "Hey, Cut."

Cutter's face leaped from shock to confusion to excitement within the span of a blink. "Hey, *amigo*! Glad to see you're still kickin'!"

"Yep, still kickin'." John Wesley smiled, but the parting of his lips revealed ugly rows of dark fangs. "I died for a spell, I think. But I feel better. A little turned around, I suppose." He then gazed down at Doyle. "I couldn't do it. I *wanted* to kill him, but I just couldn't."

Keech dared a step closer to the boy, moving with care so as not to trigger John Wesley into some kind of Chamelia rage. "It's because you're no killer, John, and he's your pa. You're decent and brave, not a monster."

"You're wrong, Keech." John Wesley's eyes flashed, and Keech thought he saw the red flare up again like tiny candles. "Look at me. I ain't exactly *civilized* no more." He regarded the strange, prickly plumage around his knuckles. "What are these things, anyhow?"

Duck had risen to her feet and moved toward him, one arm outstretched. "Come down, John. Stand with us. Let's figure this out."

John Wesley sniffed the air. "I know what happened to Nat. I can *smell* the grief on ya. I'm awful sorry, Duck."

Quinn said, "I bet there's a cure for what's happening to you. Maybe we can find it."

Peering at his quilled hands again, John Wesley said, "I reckon this ain't your run-of-the-mill cold, Quinn. Ain't no cure for this."

"C'mon, *hermano*. Just step on down," Cutter said. "Shifter or no, you're my partner. We'll lick this sickness together."

But John Wesley was already turning back toward the forest. "Y'all just leave me alone. Don't follow, and don't come looking. Go find Bonfire Crossing, and kick that Reverend Rose in the tailbone. Got it?"

"No, *amigo*. Stay with *me*." Cutter reached into his coat and pulled out John Wesley's bullet-torn straw hat. "I've still got your hat, see? Come take it."

John Wesley's eyes sparked fiery red. "Leave me alone, Cut! Stay with the others."

The boy scrambled back into the woodland, leaving his father in the snow.

For several moments, no one spoke. Keech knew they should be riding farther away from Wisdom, especially if Big Ben was still out there, but no one moved. Keech couldn't imagine going on without the posse. He needed to rally them, no matter what.

"Y'all heard John Wesley. We should stay a team. I know y'all want to go your separate ways, and I can't blame you, and I certainly can't stop you. But here's what I can do: I can be your friend. When my folks died, Pa Abner took me in and gave me hope that I'd never be alone again. That's what I can offer you now: *hope*. We can ride on west, Quinn, and find your aunt Ruth, and Cut, maybe we can find a cure for John. But first we need to finish our mission and get to Bonfire Crossing."

Keech paused his speech to look at Duck. Her eyes were brimming with fresh tears. "Nat's last words to us were to keep one another safe and never stop fighting. He told us to ride on. He wanted us to stand together."

"But we've got *nothing*," Duck said. "No weapons, except for my shard and Cutter's knife. We're just a bunch of kids."

"This bunch of kids beat Bad Whiskey. And blew Wisdom to

the sky." Keech smiled, hoping a show of confidence would give them that touch of hope. "We'll practice Doyle's magic. We'll find our focus. And if things turn sour, we'll use our training. We know better than most how to fight. Quinn, your aunt Ruth taught you a thousand ways to survive. We can do this."

Cutter said, "We don't even know where we're going. We got nothing to go by."

"Mr. Horner gave us plenty. He gave us the riddle that'll lead us to Bonfire Crossing." Then Keech spoke the poem that the Enforcer had taught them:

> *"Follow the rivers and bending trees*
> *to the den of the moon stalker.*
> *Gather the pack and speak his name*
> *before the noontide shift."*

Cutter shook his head. "C'mon, Blackwood, that don't sound like anything."

"Back in Missouri, we solved the Bible verses and found the path to Bone Ridge," Keech said. "We can figure this out, too. I know it."

"What about Ranger Doyle?" asked Quinn. "We can't just leave him to die."

"We'll take him with us and find some help. He may have lied to us about the Char Stone, but he stood tall with us in Wisdom. We won't abandon him. And when all's said and done with Reverend Rose, we'll track down your auntie, Quinn."

Behind them, something stirred on the ground. Saint Peter

was waking. The Kelpie staggered up to his legs, then shook mud and snow off his body. The creature released a heavy bluster, as if telling them he was ready to forge on.

Keech grinned at the horse. "Who's with me? Who's gonna ride to Bonfire Crossing?"

Quinn slapped his forage cap back on. "Count me in, I suppose. Sooner we can find this Crossing, the sooner I can find Auntie Ruth. How 'bout it, Cut? We make a pretty good team."

His face still full of doubt, Cutter shrugged. "All right, I'll go. But we keep an eye out for John Wesley. If I have to ride off to help him, I'll go and won't look back."

"Deal," Keech said, then looked at Duck. "We need you, too. *I* need you. Remember what Doyle said to Horner?"

"*Amicus fidelis protectio fortis,*" she replied.

"Exactly so. 'A faithful friend is a sturdy shelter.'"

Glancing back toward Wisdom, where Nat Embry had given his life, Duck whispered something under her breath—perhaps a prayer or a gentle farewell. Then she stuffed the threadbare doll into her coat pocket and wiped her eyes.

"For Nathaniel," she said. "Let's ride."

CHAPTER 25
THE ENFORCER'S TALE

They decided to travel as far as possible through the night.

Before they lit out, Keech dug through the unconscious Ranger's coat and retrieved the man's amulet shard. The charm was triangular, with one side rounded and the other two ridged. He was sure he could have fit Pa Abner's shard to this one, if only Coward had not absconded with it. Like the others, this charm was secured with a leather cord, which Keech slipped around his neck.

Borrowing Cutter's knife, Quinn ripped a few strips of wool from a blanket and applied a bandage to Doyle's leg. Plum-colored veins had webbed the flesh around the laceration, and when they all looked closer, they saw that purplish welts had also stolen up his neck, like tiny fingers intending to strangle the man. Whatever a *cutting spell* was, as Doyle had called it, it was surely something to avoid.

There had been a quick debate about how to travel with the unconscious Ranger. The only solution was to tether the man to Saint Peter. They had to work together—Keech and Duck at the legs,

Cutter and Quinn at the shoulders—to lift Doyle's limp body into the saddle and tie him off with ropes.

After bundling up to the cold, the young riders set out, Quinn once again mounting Lightnin'. Duck hauled Nat's horse by a lead rope, while Keech took the burden of guiding Saint Peter using one of Doyle's backup lariats. Hector glanced back at the Kelpie as they rode, and Keech wondered if the two horses had once shared adventures together, hauling the Enforcers across the Territories. They certainly seemed at ease with each other.

Back on the prairie, Keech studied the vague endpoints of the crescent moon—a navigational technique that Pa Abner had once taught him and Sam. "From here we head southwest," he said. "Mr. Horner told us we'll find the next bending tree about twenty miles away, near a clutch of round boulders."

Quinn whistled. "Twenty miles in the dark?"

"Snow cover means ground we can't see," Duck said. "That'll be dangerous for the ponies. We should keep in single file."

Keech pulled his scarf up over his nose. "We can camp after ten miles or so. With any luck, the weather will hold, and we'll spot the rocks tomorrow before dark."

Cutter pointed to the Ranger's knapsack, which Quinn had lashed back onto Saint Peter's croup. "I don't fancy riding with a bunch of bones. It feels like a bad omen."

"Doyle must find them important," Keech said. "If he wakes up to find them gone, I worry he won't help us."

For several freezing hours, the horses crept over snowy flatland. They plodded under the sliver of moon, especially when clouds lingered over the crescent, but they held their course.

Sometime in the deep of night, Keech heard Quinn's lilting voice start up his *Odyssey* song again. "*That ol' Minerva . . . she hid them away in darkness . . . and led the boys out of town . . .*" the boy crooned.

Keech smiled.

Long hours passed before the horizon began to glow a steady rose color. Heavy flakes wafted down onto Keech's hat as the young riders stepped into a valley cut by a winding brook. He called for a break, and the troop watered the ponies and snacked on pecans and jerky.

Doyle awoke for a moment as the group rested. He raised his head. The purplish veins on his neck had crept up to his jawline, and his breathing sounded thin. "Son?" the Ranger muttered, then collapsed again over the Kelpie's saddle horn.

Cutter walked over to check on him. "Our lawdog—if he even really is one—ain't doing too good. We best not let him kick the bucket. I'd hate to rattle John now that he's grown fangs."

"He needs medicine, or he *will* kick the bucket," Quinn said.

Keech scoured the valley for something that could help Doyle's wound—though he doubted anything would help a wound magically inflicted. The early snowfall had deadened most of the prairie grasses, but he found a small patch of yarrow beneath the snow near the creek. He pulled up a handful of the wet wildflowers, took them to Doyle, and pressed a smooth bundle of them over the leg wound.

"What's that stuff?" asked Cutter.

"I call it Old Man's Pepper," Keech said. "It'll help slow the blood loss, at least till we can find the Ranger proper help."

The troop rode on for the rest of the morning. Occasionally they passed through clusters of cottonwood trees, where they would pause to gather branches and place kindling inside their saddlebags for drying. Keech kept his eyes peeled for crows but spotted only a pair of hawks probing the plains for mice.

At one point, as the sun reached the peak of the sky, Cutter gestured to several dark shapes meandering over a low ridge. "Look! Buffalo."

The sight of the herd reminded Keech of the bending tree near the Moss farm, the way the sugar maple's shadow had fashioned itself into a buffalo head. The memory took him back a few hours more, to the moment they saw the small Osage band traveling toward the tree. He recalled how they had disappeared without a trace in the snow-covered field. He thought about the young girl riding with them and wondered if perhaps she'd been riding with her father, maybe to a buffalo-hunting camp.

Sometime later, Keech spotted a snow-capped ridge in the distance. "Let's camp there for the afternoon. The bulge over that slope will hide the ponies and block the wind so we can build a fire."

Gathering in the cold hollow, the young riders hauled Doyle down from Saint Peter and leaned his body against the limestone. The gang laid out the kindling from their bags, and Quinn volunteered to build a Dakota fire pit. Soon a well-hidden campfire flickered to life. They huddled close to the flames, listening to Quinn's dream-like singing. Keech grabbed a few cold corn dodgers from Doyle's ration bag.

He was handing out the cakes when a dreadful squawk made them all glance out across the prairie.

A dark bird circled overhead, flying low over the ridge. The kids shrank back against the limestone wall. Quinn's *Odyssey* song died away, but he kept murmuring under his breath, as if trying to pray the creature out of the sky. Duck put a finger to her lips, but Quinn shook his head.

The bird maneuvered east to west, appearing unaware of the group. It lingered below the clouds, swiveled slightly north, then, with another loud screech, soared away.

"That was awful close," Quinn said.

"Do you think the noon sun blinded it?" Cutter asked.

Keech pondered, then smiled. "Maybe Quinn's song hid us like Doyle's humming."

Quinn looked happy at the notion. "Maybe I'm finding my focus!"

"Or sometimes a crow is just a crow," said Duck.

After finishing their corn dodgers, the Lost Causes curled up in their blankets and tried to find sleep. Keech dozed off quickly, but not long after, a muttering sound made him stir. It was Duck, crying out—most likely another bad dream. He put a hand on the ankle of her boot, wishing he could invade the dream so she wouldn't be lonesome inside it. Just one afternoon before, they had shared the dream of a terrible cavern filled with light, and Duck had been more hopeful after discovering she hadn't walked there alone.

Duck woke with a start, her wild eyes roving. She had retrieved the scruffy doll from her pocket and now lifted it close.

"That was my daughter's."

The gruff voice gave Keech's heart a jolt. He turned to see Edgar Doyle staring at the figurine in Duck's hand.

"She called her Turnip."

Propped up under his blanket, Doyle looked like a ghost, his eyes sunken and wet. He glanced around the campsite. When he spoke again, his words were cracked and full of desperation. "Where is Eliza?"

Keech frowned, confused. "Who?"

"My daughter." Doyle's voice hitched, and he coughed. "I assume you've dug through my gear. Please tell me you didn't leave her behind."

"The bones are safe," Keech said. "We left them in your satchel. Maybe you ought to tell us why you're hauling a skeleton around Kansas."

Doyle said nothing for a moment. Then he sighed. "Eliza was John Wesley's younger sister. The joy of my life—*all* our lives. She used to run around the yard with her puppy. Sometimes I'd find her playing with her dolls at the top of a tree or wrestling with our shoats in the pen. Her dresses were always covered in muck." The Ranger chortled, then coughed.

Rustling around the campfire drew Keech's attention. He saw that the others were sitting up, listening.

"She drowned in the Erinyes River earlier this year, just before the turn of spring," Doyle continued, his voice fragile. "She could swim as well as I, but the Erinyes could be a rager in the rainy season, and we worried every time she played near the banks. We should've been watching her that day."

Keech dropped his head at the news.

"I went out of my mind with grief. My wife, Gerty, and John Wesley wanted to mourn and move on. I couldn't."

"What did you do?" Cutter asked.

"I took Eliza's body from the ground and rode west. I had a plan." He lifted his bruised face, and copper flame reflected in his eyes.

Keech recalled the words Bad Whiskey had spoken at Bone

Ridge—*The Char Stone is life. It'll restore me. I'll finally be whole again*—and he suddenly understood Doyle's scheme. "You believe you can bring her back, don't you? *That's* why you broke into my mother's grave and stole the Char Stone."

Doyle grunted. "As I said, I went out of my mind."

"The Stone is gone," Duck said. "Coward ran off with it."

More violent coughs racked the man's lungs. Quinn moved to help him, but Doyle pushed him gently back, showing a hand covered with purple veins. "I'm all right."

Keech knelt closer to the campfire. "Ranger, before my pa died, he said the Enforcers met up in Missouri in 1845 and formed a plan to hide the Stone from Rose. He said you all took the Oath of Memory to cloud your recollections. So how did you find your way back to it? How did you get the Stone?"

"After the skirmish at the Blackwood place in the spring of '45—" Doyle interrupted himself and smiled feebly at Keech. "After what happened at *your* old home, Rose's men went back into hiding. Isaiah insisted they would come back. He said the Stone was too dangerous and the Fang too tempting. So we set out to lose the artifacts, put them back into hiding like the Key."

"The Key?" Duck glanced at Keech, but he could only shrug. Pa Abner had never mentioned any sort of special key.

Doyle ignored Duck's question. "We buried the Stone in Erin Blackwood's grave, then took the Fang to the Osage elders—two beloved friends who had assisted the Enforcers in the past. We begged them to help us conceal it."

"In Bonfire Crossing," Keech said.

"Yes. Our friends agreed to help, but insisted we all take the Oath to ensure we wouldn't be tempted to reclaim the relics."

Cutter spat into the fire. "But you found a way to break it."

On this, Doyle's face darkened, and his voice dropped to a murmur. "The loss of Eliza drove me to tap a dark energy—the only one I knew that could sever the binding on my mind and recover my memories. The energy is known as the Prime."

A recollection of Pa Abner scolding Bad Whiskey at the Home struck Keech: *You've borrowed the Prime. Your soul's sunk deeper into rot than ever. . . .*

Doyle went on. "I conducted an ancient ritual, recited what's called the Black Verse. This made contact with the dark power. It shattered the Oath's wall around my mind, but not before it turned my daughter's body to bones. For a trade, you see. With dark magic, there's always a terrible trade." He took a quick, shuddering breath. "You would all do well to remember that."

"What'd you do then?" asked Quinn.

"I traveled back to the Osage and sought the Protectors, the group designated to watch over Bonfire Crossing. I told them I wanted back in, but they refused, wouldn't even allow me passage to speak to the elders."

Duck's face tilted with curiosity. "We *saw* the Protectors, didn't we? They were the horsemen that were traveling just past the Kansas River. You told us you'd seen them before, on the prairie."

Doyle chuckled. "Nothing gets by you, Duck Embry."

Keech's mind toiled quickly at other pieces of the puzzle. "Pa Abner said the Crossing moves location. That's why you haven't been able get back in, right? Even when your memories of the Crossing returned, the Osage were able to hide the way. They *knew* you would try to recover the Fang."

Doyle tried to appear unruffled by Keech's accusatory tone, but the sudden quiver in his face betrayed his desperation.

When he didn't speak, Keech pressed him. "What happened after the Protectors turned you away?"

"I headed to Missouri to fetch the Char Stone."

"And you went through Floodwood," Keech said.

"I did. There was no way around that infernal wood."

"Which means you traveled to the cave," Duck said.

The Ranger simply nodded.

"We found an Osage man with a longbow in that cave," she went on. "He'd been torn up by a monster bear. He left a warning in blood on the wall."

Doyle's head tilted downward.

"Don't tell me. You *knew* him," Keech guessed.

Doyle's face glistened with sweat. "His name was Wandering Star. He was a nice young man, smart and funny. He'd spent much of his youth training with his uncle to be a Protector of the Crossing. When the Protectors turned me away, he followed after me at a distance. When I confronted him on the trail, he said he was curious about my intentions, but I later learned he wanted to report my actions back to his uncle, as a means to prove himself to his troop."

"Did you tell him what you were up to?" Keech asked.

Doyle's expression was one of weary resignation. "I figured he could be a great help to my mission, so I told him only what I thought he should know. That I was tracking a dangerous object, to keep it safe. The two of us struck out for Missouri, located Floodwood, and were trapped for several days in the tormenting loops. That is, till my young companion found a strange door on the side of a red mountain. My amulet shard opened the door's lock." As he said this, Doyle patted his chest, apparently searching for the shard, and made a sour face when he turned up nothing.

Keech lifted the Enforcer's charm out of his coat to show he'd taken it. "I'm holding this for safekeeping," he said, then tucked it back down. "That was my Pa Abner's door, by the way. He built it to hide the path into the cave."

"I know. The second I touched it, I remembered helping Isaiah cut the planks." Doyle smiled a little, then pushed on. "After we entered the cave, we ran into the great bear. We tried to stand against the beast, but it killed Wandering Star, and I was forced to run."

"You abandoned him?" Duck said, her tone severe.

"No. I stood by his side. But once I saw he was finished, I knew I had no other option but to flee to the river. I never meant for the boy to fall."

"Did you ever tell his family what happened? That he chased after you to seek the truth?" Duck asked.

"I suppose I don't have the courage yet to show my face to his loved ones."

Keech sighed darkly. He could still see Wandering Star's corpse slumped against the cave wall, his bony finger pointing to his final message of doom. "So you walked to Bone Ridge and dug up my mother's grave and left that doll in place of the Stone." He pointed at the figurine clutched in Duck's hand. "Did you intend to send Rose a message?"

"No," Doyle said. "I left Eliza's doll to explain why I had to reclaim the Char Stone. I hoped if any of my fellow Enforcers ever came looking for it, they'd understand I had to take the Stone to save my little girl."

"You must know you can't save her," Keech said. "The Char Stone is cursed. And whatever this Fang of Barachiel can do, it won't bring her back. At least not the Eliza you love and remember. Nothing cursed brings anything good."

Doyle gazed deeply into the fire, his bruised face shiny with tears. "I need rest."

The young riders asked him a few more questions, but the Ranger didn't respond. Keech stepped over and touched his shoulder. The man didn't stir. Were it not for the shallow rising of his chest, Doyle could have been mistaken for a corpse. "He's passed out again," Keech said.

After tending to Doyle's wound, they spoke for a while longer, mulling over the many things Doyle had shared. Keech wondered why John Wesley had claimed the man had killed his mother, when according to the Ranger's story, she had been alive when Doyle fled with Eliza's body.

"Maybe John's grief made him lose his mind, too," Quinn said.

"John's mind is fine," Cutter returned. "I'm sure he's got his reasons."

"Let's get some more sleep," Duck said, but before tucking back into her blanket, she gave the ragged doll a curious look, then placed it in Edgar Doyle's hand. "He needs it more than I do," she said.

Keech's thoughts rattled with questions and theories. To calm himself, he wandered the camp's perimeter, allowing his eyes to read the area.

A minuscule line of pockmarks in the snow told Keech that a field mouse had scurried past the camp recently. He listened to the steady moan of the wind curling across the plain. Plump clouds piled upon one another, obscuring the sun like a candle flame behind stained glass. He closed his eyes and imagined the journey of the buffalo they'd seen on the prairie, the weight of their hooves against the ground, the sounds of their breathing in the herd.

Energies exist inside everything you can see and smell, taste and touch, Doyle had said not long ago.

Something pulsed deep inside Keech, a vibration across his gut. Then another quiver caught him, as if a taut string within his heart had been plucked. He felt as if something were tugging at him from the direction of the distant woods.

The first step to connecting with these buried energies is to clear your mind of distractions.

A stand of snow-coated trees stood alone on the curving horizon. Keech narrowed his eyes, searching for movement within the wooded cluster. He saw nothing. The hair on his arms stood up and, somehow, he knew the camp was being watched.

CHAPTER 26
SHADOW OF THE ELK

The young riders reached the round boulders just as dusk rolled over the prairie.

When Keech spotted them—a cluster of large sandstone masses that stood on the crest of a broad white promontory—he thought of giant cannonballs left to rust in the Kansas weather. There were at least two dozen of them, each capped by a layer of snow, and they formed a natural rampart of sorts on the flat top of the knoll.

Keech drew rein below the strange formations. "This must be the place. Mr. Horner said the bending tree would be down the hill. Let's head to the other side."

Cutter and Quinn trudged over the snow-painted mound first, their ponies looking more weary than the boys who rode them. Duck pushed Irving over the incline and into the boulder patch. She had wound Sally's lead rope several times around her forearm so that her brother's Fox Trotter wouldn't trail too far.

While Duck wove through the boulders, Keech guided a grunting Hector up the hill, talking gently to the horse as they ascended. He led Saint Peter, occasionally glancing back at the wounded Ranger who sat in the saddle, moaning in a grave delirium.

Keech followed Duck's twisting path through the boulders. When he looked down the opposite side of the hill, he saw a bending tree standing at the bottom of the slope, just as Milos Horner had promised. Grinning, he looked back over his shoulder for any sign of pursuers but saw no movement. Whatever was out there was keeping its distance. He returned his attention to the path.

The tree below the hill was a black walnut, its divided trunk favoring a sideways L. The longest of the two boughs pointed north; the shortest steered travelers south. Thick drifts of snow garnished each limb, and tangles of barren branches on both arms reached up to the gray sky.

"Looks like we found it," Cutter said. "What now?"

Keech shrugged. "Let's go listen to a shadow, shall we?"

Snow had fallen more generously in this area, so Keech couldn't see whether four circular stones had been placed around the tree's base or not. Dismounting Hector, he led Saint Peter to a flat spot and said to the groaning Doyle, "Wait here, Ranger. We'll get you help soon."

Never opening his eyes, Doyle muttered something incoherent.

Keech shuffled closer to the black walnut, began kicking snow away from the roots, and saw a perfectly round white stone embedded in the earth. "Moss opal," he muttered.

"Can we hurry this up?" Cutter said. "I'm freezing."

After dusting away more powder, Keech found all four stones.

Duck slid off Irving and walked over, then smoothed the toe of one boot over the south-facing stone. "Just like the others."

Quinn and Cutter dismounted and huddled around the stones.

"I'm stumped," Quinn said. "What's moss opal?"

"It's a precious stone that holds supernatural power," Keech said, recalling Duck's lesson on the Middle Ages. "Apparently, it lets you talk to nature spirits and walk around invisible."

"At least, some folks used to think so," Duck added.

"I'd say that sounds right silly, but these days, I guess I ain't so sure," Quinn said. "So how do we get this nature spirit to talk to us?"

Keech shrugged. "Back at the tree near the Moss farm, Duck and I investigated the stones. We couldn't figure them out, but we did see something mighty strange."

"The shadow of the tree *moved*," Duck finished. "It turned into a buffalo head, then disappeared."

"A buffalo head?" Cutter laughed. "Why not? But you never spoke about this before."

"We didn't want to say anything in front of Doyle, not before we learned more about his intentions," Keech said.

Quinn glanced back at the wounded Enforcer. "I wish he was better. He could help us sort all this weird business out."

"Doyle tried, remember?" Duck said. "He couldn't find the path back to the Crossing. The Osage refused to give him a single clue."

Keech pinched his bottom lip as he considered the marker trees, the bending of the trunks, the moss opal stones, the moving shadow. This time, however, they had Horner's riddle—something Doyle never had. Keech recited it so everyone could hear it once more:

> *"Follow the rivers and bending trees*
> *to the den of the moon stalker.*
> *Gather the pack and speak his name*
> *before the noontide shift."*

"What's the moon stalker?" Cutter asked.

"Maybe the Chamelia?" Duck said. "That monster looks like a moon stalker to me."

"Well, if y'all got plans to find that thing's den, count me out." Quinn moved around the tree, inspecting the warped boughs. He dropped to his haunches to scrutinize one of the moss opal stones.

Keech thought of the shadows again—the phantom buffalo, the slithering stick of darkness he'd seen fleetingly at the tree near Mercy Mission. "Let's look at this thing's shadow. Maybe we'll see something."

"We best hurry," Cutter said. "Daylight's dying fast."

Though dusk was descending over the land, there was enough light in the sky to give them a feeble glimpse of shade. Quinn examined the stones while Cutter and Duck joined Keech at the side of the bent walnut. They watched the L-shaped shadow on the ground. It showed them nothing—no squiggling movement, no phantom buffalo head.

"C'mon, tree, show us something." Keech peered up at the sky, praying for enough break in the clouds to give them a few more decent moments of light.

Cutter snapped his fingers. "The riddle said a *den*. You don't think the Osage would've hid Bonfire Crossing inside the giant bear's den, do you?"

"I can't imagine the Enforcers and Osage would've hidden the Fang and the Char Stone so close together," Keech said. "Mr. Horner said the artifacts would bring about terrible evil if they got too close to one another."

"Maybe we should just head south and talk to the Osage ourselves," Duck suggested.

"That's a good plan," Cutter said.

Quinn had been ignoring their banter, his eyes trained intensely on the ground around the tree. Taking a few steps back, he asked, "What did the riddle say again about a pack?"

"'Gather the pack and speak his name,'" Keech quoted.

Quinn pointed down. "And how many stones are sitting around that tree?"

"*Four*," Keech and Duck said in unison.

"I'd say four is enough for a pack," Quinn said.

Duck's melancholy face brightened. "We were *standing on the stones* when we saw the buffalo move, right, Keech?"

"Yes, we were." Keech hopped over to the walnut. "Everyone, gather around the tree and stand on a stone."

Each young rider hurried over to a moss opal stone. As soon as their boots landed on the circles, the tree's blurred shadow began to tremble. The dark shape vibrated on the snow as if rattled by a heavy wind.

"Whoa! Do you see that, too?" Cutter asked.

"This is what the shadow did at the maple," Keech said.

The shadow began to melt together, reshaping, folding inward. The image was both haunting and beautiful.

Keech dared not move his eyes away, fearing the shadow would disappear as before. As the final fragments of pale sun died away on the horizon, the shadow found its own interior light, turning shades of luminous greens and yellows on the snow.

"*Dios mío*, it's glowing," Cutter said.

The shadow's gleam sparked with brilliant textures of emerald. The spectral light reminded Keech of a story Pa Abner once told about spook lights, ghostly illuminations that would sometimes appear over marshes. *Some folks call them will-o'-the-wisps, but I've always called them treasure lights*, Pa said. *They guide the way to buried treasure.*

Keech doubted he was seeing a spook light—they were nowhere near a marsh—but maybe this was the bending tree's version of showing them buried treasure. Bonfire Crossing, if they were lucky.

The kaleidoscope shadow had been a quivering jumble on the snow, but now it began to rebuild itself into the image of an animal. The distinct visage of an elk materialized before Keech's eyes. A great rack of antlers took shape, then the animal's snout, then a thick, bulging neck. Before long, the entire body lay on the eastern side of the walnut, its knobby legs tugging at the surface, as if trying to emerge from the very ground.

"That's a stag!" said Quinn.

Suddenly, the phantom elk peeled away from its prison of snow. The glimmering green body took on impossible dimension, scattering white powder and dirt as it struggled up into the real world, landed on emerald hooves, and shook the moisture off its glowing pelt.

"This ain't happenin'," Cutter said, rubbing his eyes. "I'm asleep and dreaming."

"It's happening, all right," Keech said.

"Do you reckon this is the moon stalker?" Duck's voice was a mere whisper.

"I don't know."

Keech wanted to say more, but the phantom elk surprised him by turning its luminous head toward the east. The creature's snout lifted and appeared to sniff the prairie. Then a loud blustering noise, like Little Eugena's bugle, issued from its long throat.

"What's it doing?" Quinn asked.

The ghost elk trumpeted twice more over the territory, as though calling to a distant companion, then suddenly the ghostly beast sprang forward and galloped east across the snowy plain, leaving radiant green hoof tracks in its wake.

"Wait, come back!" Duck exclaimed.

"What do we do now, speak his name?" asked Quinn.

The emerald specter continued several more yards till it reached the fringe of a nearby forest and stopped. The elk tarried by the woods and paced over the snow, as if it were waiting for them to follow. Another rowdy honk echoed over the terrain.

"I think it's calling to us," Quinn said.

"'When the shadows speak, listen,'" Keech said, recalling the words that Sheriff Strahan had told Horner. "I think we're supposed to follow east." Stepping off his stone, he raced back to Hector and swung over the saddle. He leaned toward Saint Peter and snatched up the reins. "C'mon!"

Yet as they galloped toward the dark forest, Keech felt a terrible, foreboding twist in his stomach. Maybe it was that old sensation that they were being watched that he'd felt at their camp, or maybe he was just second-guessing his choice.

Lowering his head to the wind, he tucked away the fear so no one else could see it.

CHAPTER 27

DEN OF THE MOON STALKER

Beneath the crescent moon, the young riders followed the winding ghost tracks of the elk. On occasion, the creature's emerald path would veer north or south, guiding the gang around babbling creeks or over switchbacks. Sometimes it would steer them out of the woods entirely and back onto long stretches of prairie. But always their travels resumed toward the east.

To Keech, the group's nighttime pursuit of the living shadow felt like an unending path of misery and cold, and as Hector trotted across the untold territory, his mind kept circling back to the images of his family's demise—the smoldering timbers, Patrick's cries from the second floor, Sam waving Keech away in the midst of the flames. *You're no leader,* a dark thought whispered in Keech's ear. *You drive people to their doom.*

Sometime after midnight, the young riders stopped to rest the horses, check on Doyle, and debate the merits of setting another camp.

"We have to push on," Keech said. "The elk will show us the way."

"Hang the elk!" Cutter said. "If we don't camp, the Ranger will die on the trail."

"We're so close," Keech insisted. "I know it. We have to keep riding."

"All I know is I ain't crossing back into Missouri," Quinn said, his teeth chattering so hard from the cold that Keech could hear them. "Dangerous enough for me to be out here in Kansas Territory. I won't trot back into a slave state."

They decided to forge on, following the ghost tracks over empty fields of dead winter grass. As the night turned even colder, Keech mumbled appreciation to Horner's stallion, though deep down he felt like a true villain for saving Hector from Wisdom only to place him into more discomfort.

After dozing a few times in the saddle, Keech gazed across the open plain and saw the horizon at last begin to blush a salmon color. Dawn was approaching. He couldn't remember ever feeling so relieved to see daybreak.

He remembered the final line of the riddle—*before the noontide shift*—and wondered if it was a warning. "Everyone, get your second wind," he told the group. "I think we need to catch up to that elk before noon."

The gang groaned but picked up the pace.

As the morning sun pushed up into the clouds, the prairie dipped a smidge and turned into another forest. At the wood's edge, the glowing elk tracks vanished.

The young riders lined up along the lip of the timber, searching for the creature's path.

"Well, that's it, the elk's gone," Cutter grumbled. "We rode for nothing."

"Let's head into the woods and have a look," Keech suggested.

They didn't get five paces into the forest before Duck pointed. "Look!"

Standing a few yards away, tucked inside a girdle of wild gooseberry shrubs, was a bending tree. A hefty basswood with twin trunks, cleft at the base, only this one opened up like a giant U.

They approached the bending tree and stopped the ponies inside the gooseberry. Keech swung off Hector and gave a quick pass over Saint Peter and Doyle, who still lay unconscious on the saddle.

Quinn looked around the forest, clearly puzzled. "I thought we was traveling to Bonfire Crossing, not another bending tree."

"Maybe this one's another step along the trail," Duck said, dismounting. She inspected her brother's Fox Trotter, who stood patiently behind Irving on the lead rope.

"How many of these dumb trees do we have to visit?" Cutter asked.

"Only one way to find out," Duck replied. "We have to stand on the stones."

The group worked quickly to untether Doyle and stretch him out on the ground. Afterward, the young riders scattered around the basswood and kicked away the snow that covered the roots. Keech grinned at Duck when four white moss opal stones winked at them in the morning sun.

"Four circles every time," Quinn noted. "No wonder Ranger Doyle could never solve the riddle. A lone traveler can't bring the stones to life."

"Good thing we decided to stick together," Keech said, then glanced back at the bending tree. "Okay, let's hear what this shadow has to tell us."

They stepped onto the moss opal stones and turned their attention to the shadow of the basswood. Keech held his breath, not knowing what to expect. He quietly mumbled portions of the riddle that Sheriff Strahan had passed along to Horner:

"Follow the rivers and bending trees . . . to the den of the moon stalker."

"Something's happening," Quinn said, pointing.

"Gather the pack and speak his name . . . before the noontide shift."

The long shadow of the bending tree fluttered across the snow, just as before, then flowed together into a thick silhouette.

"What is it?" asked Cutter.

The shape of two sharp ears and a long snout began to form. Then a lean, graceful-looking torso, followed by four slender legs and paws. A thick shaggy tail wagged at the transforming shadow's rear end. Keech gasped when he recognized the profile.

"Of course, a wolf!" he exclaimed. "The wolf stalks the moon!"

Like the birth of the ghost elk miles away, vibrant greens and yellows shot through the phantom creature's form, turning the shadow into life itself. When the spectral colors filled the figure from snout to paw, it began to writhe on the ground, laboring like the elk to rise into the natural world. The glowing beast lifted its body from the snow, shook the powder free from its head and tail, then raised its ephemeral snout to the sky. No sound issued from the gaping mouth, but Keech knew what it was doing.

"It's *howling*," Duck said, her voice full of wonder.

"This one ain't running away like the elk did," Quinn pointed out. "It's just baying."

"I don't understand. We found the den of the moon stalker," said

Cutter. "And we got here before noon broke. What are we supposed to do now?"

Behind them, the ponies nickered and shuffled back and forth as a brisk wind whipped across the woodland, rustling the bare branches of the gooseberry shrubs.

Quinn repeated the third line of Horner's riddle: " 'Gather the pack and speak his name.' "

The answer struck Keech. To find Bonfire Crossing, they had to speak the moon stalker's name to the bending tree. Leaning closer to the U of the basswood, he boldly declared the answer: "Wolf!"

Nothing happened.

Keech flushed with disappointment. "Wolf!" he called again, but the tree offered no response. Neither did the creature silently howling at its unseen moon. Keech glanced around in desperation, but the others only shrugged.

"I'm gonna fetch some wood and build a fire before we freeze," Cutter said. He shifted on his stone to leave.

"No, wait!" Duck said, throwing her hands up. "Don't step away!"

Cutter froze on his white circle. "Why?"

Duck turned her attention to Keech. "Ranger Doyle told us that the Enforcers gave the Fang to the Osage elders to hide, right?"

"Right," Keech said.

"We also know that the Osage worked with the Enforcers to build the protection around Bone Ridge. They created the Floodwood blight and turned a bear into a monster to protect the path. You called the bear by its Osage name when you first saw Wandering Star's warning in blood, remember?"

"Of course. *Wah-sah-peh*." And even as he agreed, Keech knew what Duck was driving at.

For as long as Keech could remember, Pa Abner had called him the Wolf and Sam the Rabbit. When leading the family in lessons on their Native neighbors, Pa had always been eager to share the words and expressions he had learned from the Osage language. *My elder friends taught me these words*, he would say as he recited the names of all the animals of the forest, including *wah-sah-peh* for bear and *mah-shchee^n-kah* for Sam's rabbit. But the very first Osage word Keech remembered learning was the one for wolf.

Feeling tears well up in his eyes and gooseflesh bristle on his arms, he spoke the Osage word for his nickname aloud.

"*Shoh^n-geh!*"

The glowing wolf that stood before them twisted toward the bending tree, as if Keech's call had spooked it. The ghostly ears pinned back, then the creature vaulted straight up from the ground. The beast flew between the two trunks, where it stopped in midair and hovered, as though snared by an invisible mesh.

A current of warm wind blasted over Keech, a gust that carried a brackish scent like salted fish. The wind bellowed past him with enough strength to knock the hat off his head. The basswood shuddered, though the ground beneath them didn't move an inch.

"What's happening?" Duck cried.

Brilliant light flashed in the center of the bending tree, where the wolf hovered. It sparked so violently that Keech had to shield his eyes. Peeking through his fingers, he saw the creature shimmer and expand into a flat sheet of light, as if a golden sailcloth had been stretched between the two trunks. A rhythmic hum and a faint breath of briny warmth rolled off the radiant curtain.

Keech looked to the heavens. "You *knew*, didn't you, Pa? All those years, you knew how to get us here. Thank you."

The vibrations surging from the barrier shook the air and reached deep into Keech's guts. He took a step back from the moss opal stone, worrying as he moved that the energy before them might diminish, but the veil of light continued to shine between the boughs.

The others had also abandoned their stones and were walking around the tree, their faces dazed. The ponies grunted and whinnied at the impossible sight.

"It looks the same on the other side," Duck said. "A shimmery gold sheet."

Keech stepped toward the gleaming barrier. "Somebody ought to touch it."

"Sounds like you're volunteering," Cutter said.

Reluctantly, Keech lifted a hand. "Okay. Here goes." He took another step toward the light.

"Wait!" Quinn kicked at the snowy ground, loosened a small stone, and tossed it to Keech. "Test the water before diving in."

"Happy *one* of us is thinking straight," Keech said. He cranked his arm back and tossed the stone. The rock disappeared into the pulsating glow.

"Did it come out the other side?" Cutter asked.

"Nothing came out!" Duck reported.

Keech dug his hand into the snow to find another stone. As he burrowed, something itched at the back of his attention. He hesitated, listened. Except for the curious hum emanating from the veil of light, everything around him was silent. He glanced at the others. "Something ain't right."

The savage howl of a large animal pealed across the forest. Everyone swiveled to look in the direction of the horrible noise.

John Wesley emerged from behind the gooseberry thicket.

He had changed in several ways since dropping off Doyle at the ravine. The motley hide of black scales that dotted his flesh had spread, and his once-round cheeks were sunken and gaunt. His jawline jutted, hinting at the gradual formation of a snout. The strawberry-blond curls that had once framed John's face had fallen out, leaving his head strangely bald and covered in prickled mounds. But despite the beastly changes, he was still very much John Wesley, his eyes brimming with sorrow and innocence.

"John!" Cutter exclaimed.

The boy crept closer, his shoulders hunched. He gave the magical light a cursory, almost nonchalant look, then turned his gaze to Cutter. "Hey."

"You've been following us."

"I didn't want y'all to go off alone. I've been keeping to the shadows. But curiosity got the better of me when I saw the ghost wolf."

"You could've just joined us," Cutter said.

"No. I feel different inside, Cut, like I can't trust myself no more. Sometimes I get angry and can't see, like there's a monster inside trying to take over." He glanced over at Doyle and pointed a clawed finger. "Is Papa still alive?"

Duck stepped over and squatted beside the Ranger. She placed a hand on his chest. The man didn't stir to the touch. "He's still breathing, but I ain't sure how."

John Wesley's distorted face dropped. "I thought I wanted him to die, but now I'm scared I'll never get to talk to him again."

"You told us he killed your ma," Keech said.

As if he couldn't help it, a barbaric growl rolled from John Wesley's throat, but it sounded more woeful than angry. He spoke, and the words sputtered through clenched fangs.

"After Papa left with Eliza, Mama lost all hope. She stopped talking. She took to standing outside the house and staring up and down the trail, like she was waiting for Papa to come back with Eliza. I did my best to care for the 'stead, but I lost hope. Then one day Mama disappeared, and I hunted all over the valley for her. I found her body on the banks of the Erinyes. She had just decided to quit, I reckon. I buried her beside Eliza's dug-up grave and set out in search of Papa. He may not have killed her by his own hand, but leaving us like he did snuffed out Mama's will to live."

Cutter reached a trembling hand toward his friend, but John Wesley skittered back. "I told you, don't come near, Cut! I can't promise I won't hurt you."

"You'd never hurt me," Cutter said, his voice gentle. "We're partners. You helped me chase down *El Ojo*, remember?"

"I wish I could trust myself, but I feel so strange now."

Cutter didn't waver. "C'mon, *hermano*."

As the boys spoke, the strange vibration from the blazing tree surged against Keech's body, like a wall of warm rain cascading over him. He felt the hair on the back of his neck stand on end.

"Take my hand," Cutter said to John.

"I don't want to hurt nobody," John Wesley said, but he took a step forward anyway and reached for Cutter's hand.

The vibration emanating from the tree intensified. Keech turned to face the basswood, noticing that Duck and Quinn were doing the same. Suddenly, a high-pitched cry erupted from the tree, and a young girl on a brown pony charged out of the golden light, as though leaping down from the very sky.

CHAPTER 28
THE PROTECTORS

She looked like the same Osage girl that Keech had seen riding with the six horsemen farther north. A long black braid of hair whipped around her face as the pony landed on the ground before the tree. The girl's thick buffalo robe billowed around her.

Keech wheeled backward, barely keeping his feet. Quinn and Duck yelled in surprise as they flopped into the snow.

The girl gave them all a baffled look, then shifted her gaze to John Wesley. She galloped straight for the cringing boy, raising a wadding of black ropes as she rode.

Cutter shouted, waving his arms, but the girl offered no indication that she heard him. Instead, she loosed a piercing cry, drove her pony right past him, and flung the dark bundle from both hands. A broad, thick net landed on top of John Wesley.

John careened against a maple tree and struggled in the mesh. He screamed, perhaps trying to form words, but any meaning was lost in a series of haggard barks.

Despite the pure surprise of seeing a person materialize from thin air, Keech possessed enough awareness to realize the rider was attacking John Wesley because of his monstrous form. "Wait!" he shouted. "He's just a kid!"

Quinn and Duck joined in his pleas, but the girl ignored them. Her pony hurdled past the maple tree, yanking the net, and John Wesley tumbled off his feet, striking his head on a thick limb as he went down. The rider stopped a few feet away and spun her pony back toward him.

A volley of arrows whizzed into the forest, flying out of the light between the bending tree boughs. One of the arrows caught the netting and pinned it against the maple tree just over John Wesley's head.

A squad of horses leaped out of the glowing rift, and six Osage riders charged into the forest. Keech knew immediately they were the team that Doyle had spoken of, the troop known as the Protectors. They joined the girl, tossing more of the dark mesh. The netting landed on John Wesley, burying the boy in thick tangles. John shrieked again. The horsemen loosed more arrows that pinned the nets to nearby trees. Ropes connected to each rider's saddle horns secured the snares.

The Protectors pulled the lines taut between their ponies, spreading John Wesley's limbs apart. The boy thrashed against the maple tree. Long claws erupted from his fingers but poked through the netting to no avail. His jaw gnashed against a few strands, but the trap held firm.

Cutter dashed toward his friend. "No! Turn him loose!"

Four of the Protectors nocked fresh arrows and lifted their longbows toward John Wesley. The bear-claw necklaces on their bare chests looked fierce in the bending trees' golden light. Their buffalo pelts and sawtooth robes draped over the backs of their horses.

Keech tackled Cutter to the ground. "You're gonna get yourself killed."

"Let me go!" Cutter shoved against him.

When Keech glanced back up, he saw that the girl had driven her pony into the center of the Protectors, her hand now grasping a hefty war club. The mounted men waited for her to proceed. The largest of the six men—a heavyset fellow wearing eagle feathers and war ornaments in his dark hair—glanced at the girl with a stern face. As though taking a teacher's cue, she stepped ahead of the group and raised her weapon over John Wesley, who snarled as he thrashed at the ropes.

Cutter broke free from Keech's clutch. Pulling his knife, he stood in the girl's way. Bowstrings urgently stretched behind her, steering toward Cutter this time.

The girl waved a warning hand at him.

"He ain't a monster; he's my friend!"

Cutter's declaration appeared to confuse the girl. The eagle-feathered man spoke a few brisk words to her, but she didn't budge. "*Meenah!*" the man barked.

Again, the girl advanced on John Wesley with the war club.

Keech and Duck and Quinn scrambled over to Cutter, raising their arms to form a blockade between the Protectors and their snarling trailmate.

"He's one of the good guys!" Quinn said.

"His name is John Wesley," Duck added.

The girl gave each of them a long, inquisitive look—then slowly lowered the war club.

"Meenah, *mah-thee" thee-eh!*" the heavyset rider called out.

"*EE^n-dah-tsee-dah^n*, we should listen to them," she said. Keech recognized the Osage word as "uncle."

"You speak English!" Duck exclaimed.

The girl threw a sideways glance at her. "Of course."

Keech moved cautiously toward the girl's uncle, who appeared to be their leader. "Call off your attack. Please. I swear he's our . . ." He shuffled back through his memories and recalled the Osage word for *friend*, which he spoke loudly: "*EE-koh-wah*."

The eagle-feathered man gripped his longbow, its missile ready to fly at the slightest provocation. "We've never seen such a beast. He's a demon."

"No," Keech said. "He's innocent."

Waving away Keech's plea, the man spoke something in Osage to his team, and the other five Protectors tightened the snare on John Wesley. A second Protector wearing a brown otter hat asked a question to his group. The others responded with apprehensive grumbles.

The girl—whom the heavyset rider had referred to as Meenah—pointed her war club at Cutter. "They say your friend looks beyond control. They say you can't save him." Her voice was steady and deep, her English precise. Keech figured her to be roughly his own age, yet the way she spoke for the company made her equal to the horsemen. He couldn't help wondering if the girl held some kind of special duty in her clan, a duty that would allow a young girl to ride and fight with seasoned warriors.

Cutter squatted at John Wesley's side and wrapped a protective arm around him. As soon as the two touched, John's thrashing relaxed, and the red anger drained from his eyes.

"See? We're *hombres*," Cutter said.

The girl raised a thick eyebrow. "If he still has some control, maybe the elders could help him," she said to the large man, the one she had called *EEⁿ-dah-tsee-dahⁿ*.

Frowning, the man appeared to ponder the girl's suggestion.

Raising her hands to show she carried no weapon, Duck took a step closer to the girl. "Your name is Meenah?"

The girl shook her head. "You don't call me that."

When Duck appeared confused, the girl's heavyset uncle spoke up. "'Meenah' is First Daughter of her family. You would not address her that way."

"Oh," Duck said. "I'm sorry. I don't mean disrespect."

Nodding at Duck's apology, the girl pointed back to the pulsing, luminous curtain at the bending tree. "How do you know about Bonfire Crossing?" she asked.

"We've been searching for it. My pa, Abner Carson—" Keech stopped himself. "*Isaiah Raines* sent us to find it."

Mention of Pa Abner's real name silenced all the Protectors.

"Isaiah?" said the girl's uncle, looking fascinated. "He was your father?"

"Well, not my real one," Keech replied. "My real father was called Bill to some. I learned he was half Osage, but I didn't know this till recently. In Osage he was called—"

"*Zhaⁿ Sah-peh*," the man said, his mouth slightly dropping. The Protectors looked at one another knowingly. "I heard many stories about him."

Keech's heart skipped. "You've heard of my father?"

"He was a close friend to the elders in Bonfire," the eagle-feathered man said. "As stories tell it, he left many years ago on a trading campaign to the north, but when he didn't return, the elders felt it was a betrayal. The stories say he left his people to ride with terrible men."

"But he revolted against the man who led him astray," Keech said. "And now I'm here—*we're* here—to finish his fight."

"You didn't answer Meenah," the man said, throwing his niece a cursory glance. "How did you come to this place?"

"We had some help on the trail. Another Enforcer. But now he's wounded." Keech gestured beyond the bending tree to Edgar Doyle, who lay on the ground under Quinn's blanket. During the struggle with John, the Ranger had awakened, but only to grind his teeth in pain.

The sight of Doyle stunned the Protectors, especially the girl, all over again. "I *know* that man," she said. "He came to my encampment once."

"He's hurt real bad," Duck said. "We're hoping you can help."

The Protectors spoke to one another in brisk voices. Some sounded angry. They eventually deferred back to the girl's uncle, *Wah-hu Sah-kee*, or Strong Bones. He shouted for a moment till the others yielded to his argument. The fellow looked at Keech and said many things in Osage, then finally pointed at Doyle.

"Red Jeffreys betrayed his Oath," Strong Bones said, his words full of concern. "He betrayed everything he stood for."

Apprehension seized Keech's stomach. He worried they had ridden so far just to be turned away at the open door. "We know, sir. But he's dying. You're our last hope. Please don't turn us away."

The Protectors conferred one last time, then Strong Bones held up his hand to silence the negotiation. He sighed.

"We'll bring the Enforcer. Just know the elders may not wish to help him."

"*Web-wee-nah*," said Keech. "Thank you."

Strong Bones gestured to two of his allies, then at John Wesley. The horsemen hooked the nets over their saddle horns and pulled John toward the mysterious gateway. "We'll bring the beast as well."

Cutter stepped after John Wesley, reaching for the mesh. "You ain't taking my friend anywhere without me."

"We won't hurt him," the girl said.

"You have nothing to fear," Strong Bones added. "We'll allow you to follow us, as long as you do what we say." He flashed a quick smile at Keech, then turned his mount.

Through the nets, John Wesley looked at Cutter with lost, fearful eyes. "It's okay, Cut. Let me go. Everything'll be fine."

Cutter released his grip on the nets and watched as the horsemen pulled the boy toward the bending tree.

The other Protectors glanced back, apparently waiting for consent, and their leader waved them onward. One by one, they stepped through the gateway, pulling John Wesley along into the golden light, and one by one, they vanished into thin air. Finally, Strong Bones looked to his niece and spoke curtly in Osage. She replied with a quick nod. Without another word, the man walked his horse between the bending tree boughs and disappeared.

The girl turned to the Lost Causes. "My uncle says to load the Enforcer. Once you're done, you're to follow me."

Keech raced over to lift the groaning Doyle back onto Saint Peter. The other young riders joined him, and the gang tied the Ranger down. Doyle murmured in his darkness, occasionally raising a hand and slapping at the air. His breathing sounded so raspy, it astounded Keech that any breath was getting into his lungs at all.

"He's slipping," Keech said. "Everyone mount up."

The group gathered the ponies around the bending tree.

The young riders had seen a great deal of death. Allies had been laid to rest, and Nat Embry had been buried in fire and rubble. Keech prayed that once they reached Bonfire Crossing, they would all find a trifle of peace. Yet his stomach knotted with worry.

Standing before the light, the Osage girl called out in a strong voice to the Lost Causes. "Stay close!" Then she and her pony walked into the glimmer, and they vanished like stones sinking into a sparkling pool.

The other young riders followed, Quinn leading Saint Peter and Doyle. Keech watched them disappear one by one into the shining curtain, then stepped up closer to the tree. Sliding his thumb over Hector's saddle horn—over the initials that said **MH**—he took a deep breath. "Here we go, my friend. On to Bonfire Crossing."

The stallion stepped forward, and Keech moved into the light.

CHAPTER 29

THE TWO ELDERS

For a terrible moment, the white radiance around him grew so bright, Keech thought it would blind him. He feared he would ramble off into an unknown space, sightless, but then a progression of blurred shapes took hold in his vision, and Keech recognized that he was seeing the full group led by the Osage girl.

Hector landed on a soft surface. Keech blinked, his senses befuddled, and realized the stallion had descended onto brown, wet sand. The salty wind that Keech had detected earlier was strong on his face. There was a swelling noise in the air, like the rise and fall of a ceaseless wind.

They stood on a slender golden beach beside a body of water that stretched as far as Keech could see. The dark purple luster of a long horizon extended before him. A gray sky loomed above the churning water, but here and there the light from the dawning sun poked through tiny breaks in the clouds, dappling the shiny sand with vibrant colors. White birds circled the expanse and dived to the water's surface, rising again with fish in their beaks. All along the beach, tall knuckles of black rock poked up from the mud and foam.

"My God," Keech muttered. "It's an *ocean*."

The water's currents swelled in his ears—the steady push and pull of a heavy tide, a majestic sound he'd never heard before. Delicate white shells dotted the ground around Hector's hooves. Keech remembered a picture hanging in Pa Abner's study, the image of a seashell colored in whites and blues and browns, painted over the page of an old newspaper.

Keech's eyes brimmed. "You stood here, didn't you, Pa? You stood on this very sand with the other Enforcers." He reckoned the picture of the seashell was the only ghost of Bonfire Crossing that had haunted Pa Abner after taking the Oath.

Duck's voice jolted Keech from his stupor. "Look!" She pointed at the landscape behind them.

A bowl-shaped border of sharp cliffs menaced over the beach. They were nearly the size of mountains, molded by more of the black rock, and heavy ranks of evergreens stood at their peaks. Both beautiful and terrifying, the cliffs stood severely against the ocean, giving Keech the suffocating impression of gigantic shoulders pushing them off the narrow beach and toward the water.

A few feet from the cliff line stood a bent cedar tree with a crooked L shape. The dazzling curtain of light they had just stepped from hung between the two boughs. Their young chaperone swung her pony around to face it, then spoke the tree's magical latchkey word: "*Shohⁿ-geh!*"

The radiance engulfing the cedar's limbs began to die. As the light shrank, Keech could make out a ribbon of snowy Kansas forest in the heart of the glow, as if he were peeking through a keyhole. He watched the glimmer diminish till it became nothing more than a pinpoint of illumination in the center of the boughs. The wolf had gone to sleep, he reckoned.

"Where in heck did that tree bring us?" Cutter asked the girl.

She pointed to the eastern horizon. "Look at the sun. Tell me what you see."

Quinn said, "Day's about to break, like we're a couple hours earlier. Which means we've traveled *west*."

Duck looked excitedly at Keech. "Just like your pa told us, go west!"

"No matter where the door moves back east, you always come to this place," the girl explained. "My uncle calls it the Oregon Coast."

Strahan's riddle spoke again in Keech's mind—the den of the moon stalker, the noontide cutoff—as well as Pa Abner's final admonition that the Crossing moved. "Does the door disappear when the noon hour strikes?"

"Each day, the wolf runs to another tree," the girl said.

"And the other shadows we saw? The ghost animals?"

"They lead the way to each day's new wolf tree. Some travelers have seen the shadows move, but none have followed the path to find the wolf as you did."

Keech's head whirled at the idea. "Did the Osage create the door?"

"This *place* created the door." She fluttered her hand and said, "Never mind the door. *That's* what you've come to see." She pointed down the long ribbon of sand.

A towering bonfire stood in the distance inside a C-shaped cove. The heavy tide of the ocean washed into the cove's mouth, battering two upright masses of rock, but the foaming waves stopped short of the great blaze. Beyond the opposite edge of the cove, green headlands curled upward, forming treacherous foothills.

"Mercy!" Quinn muttered.

"What is this place?" Keech asked the girl.

"The elders will explain."

The young riders followed her down the beach. Cinched atop Saint Peter, Doyle rode between Cutter and Quinn, the Ranger's face a pale mask of sweat and purple veins. His mystical horse made no tracks in the dappled sand.

The group navigated a maze of black rocks. As they drew closer to the crescent cove, Keech pushed Hector to walk alongside their guide. "Your uncle calls you Meenah."

The girl simply nodded.

"But what should *we* call you?"

The rider glanced into the distance, her eyes softening as though they had just locked onto a beautiful recollection. "Where I come from, I'm known as 'Strong Heart,' a name my brother gave me years ago. This is what you may call me."

"Strong Heart," Keech repeated. He glanced around at the others, who were listening, then turned back to the girl. "And you're a Protector, like the others?"

When Strong Heart turned a critical face toward him, Keech felt his cheeks flush. "I mean, the rest of the men are trained warriors," he said.

A perceptive grin pressed at the girl's lips. "Before my parents died, they told me about the Crossing and that a Protector carries a certain kind of character. 'Be very proud,' they said. 'You are our

Meenah, our First Daughter. You come from a strong line of Osage who hold these virtues.' I was born with the traits of a Protector; it's part of who I am. I hold much honor for it."

"When did you start training?" Keech asked.

"I began when my uncle came to me, not long ago. He said, 'You will fulfill an important role for your family, Meenah. You will take your brother's place.'"

"Your brother was a Protector?"

"He had been training with my uncle, but he disappeared. And so I began."

It occurred to Keech that he and Strong Heart were very much alike in some respects. They had found themselves learning things few other kids would even dream of. And the task had fallen to both of them to guard what they held dear. "You know, we saw you back in Kansas Territory, just south of the river," he said. "Were you protecting the bending tree?"

"We were searching for my brother," she replied.

"Where did he go?" Keech asked, but Strong Heart turned her face away. He waited for her response, but it never came. Clearly, the girl was finished with the conversation.

As the group neared the great bonfire, Keech felt waves of warmth caress his cheek. The inferno was the size of a house, and it crackled with such intensity that the air along the seaboard quivered from its heat. Orange and red embers exploded from the tips of the flames, fluttering up as high as the cliffs before winking out in the gray mist.

At the edge of the cove, the other six Protectors had gathered on horseback in a semicircle around the blaze. Bundles of weapons rested at the foot of the fire—a collection of long spears adorned with feathers, a couple of wooden slings with leather pouches. The backup defenses for the group, Keech reckoned.

Nearby, John Wesley sprawled inside the nets, groaning.

The Protectors watched in silence as the young riders entered the cove and approached the gigantic pyre. Strong Bones gestured for the young riders to dismount. They hopped down onto wet sand and gathered close to one another. After a brief silence, they introduced themselves to the troop, then waited for the Protectors to respond.

Over the pounding of the surf, Keech listened as the Osage horsemen spoke to one another in their language. He tried to assess their words, seize on anything familiar, but the concepts were too difficult to piece together. As he watched them, he couldn't help feeling disconnected from his father's life, and his hatred of the Reverend burned anew. Without Rose's treachery, Keech would have known a very different existence.

The group finally returned its attention to the young riders and the men spoke their names, for which Strong Heart supplied the translation. *EE^n Zhuh-tseh*, or Red Stone, was a thin fellow wearing silver armbands. *Mah-shoh^n Shkah*, or Whipping Feather, wore the brown otter hat. Another man introduced himself as *Leh-dah^n Zee*, meaning Yellow Hawk. *Xake Sha^n*, or Weeping Cloud, was a stocky horseman with a friendly grin. The final man, *Mi Tho^{n}pa Tuh Kah*, or Big Moon, spoke his name with a deep, serious voice.

"Thank you for letting us in." Duck smiled at the company. "Like Keech said earlier, you're our only hope."

Still slumping on Saint Peter, Doyle moaned a single word: "*Eliza.*"

"Papa, I'm right here," John Wesley murmured. He gnashed his fangs and glared at the Protectors with reddish-yellow eyes. "Turn me loose. I won't hurt nobody. I just need to make sure he's okay."

No sooner did John finish muttering than a man and woman draped in long buffalo robes appeared from around the thundering bonfire, walking side by side. They looked very old, possibly older than Granny Nell. The man's face carried heavy wrinkles and looked tired. A tall fan of eagle feathers protruded from behind his head, the same kind of headdress worn by Strong Bones. The woman's features were kinder, and colorful bird feathers circled her ears and hung from her lobes.

"*Hah-weh*," the woman said.

The elder had not addressed the entire gang; she had spoken directly to Keech. He tried to stand a little taller. "*Hah-weh*."

"She is *Tseh Mee*ⁿ, or in your language, Buffalo Woman," Strong Heart said to the young riders.

Raising a rumpled hand, the elder man spoke his own greeting in Osage.

Strong Heart said, "He is *Loh*ⁿ *Noh*ⁿ*-peh Zhee*, or Doesn't Fear Thunder."

"*Hah-weh*," the young riders replied in unison. These were the folks who had assisted Pa Abner with the Floodwood protection, who had given the Enforcers their Oath of Memory.

Strong Bones pointed at John Wesley and Doyle, speaking to the elders with an urgent voice.

After the man fell silent, the elders regarded the grumbling John Wesley, then shifted their attention to Doyle. They talked to each other in muted tones till the elder man, Doesn't Fear Thunder, turned his gaze on Keech and smiled, his toothless mouth wide with mirth. He began to speak again in Osage.

Strong Heart translated. "He says you're the lost son of *Zha^n Sah-peh*. He says they see *Zha^n Sah-peh*'s eyes on your face, eyes they haven't seen in many years."

Keech felt both exhilarated and nervous to be standing in front of individuals who had known and helped his father. He asked Strong Heart, "Can they tell me about him?"

The girl relayed the question. The old man was silent for a spell, then he shook his head and answered back to her.

"He says Black Wood's story is a sad one, because he never returned to his people. Better you turn your eyes to the path ahead."

Keech flinched at the gentle rebuke but said nothing.

Buffalo Woman called out something in Osage to the Protectors. Weeping Cloud and Yellow Hawk moved to unfasten Doyle's bindings and lift him off Saint Peter. Doyle groaned through clenched teeth as they stretched him out on the sand. Buffalo Woman shuffled over and ripped the deerskin cloth away from the ragged wound. She regarded the pressed yarrow flowers on the gash and smiled.

While she inspected the injury, Doesn't Fear Thunder turned his attention back to John Wesley. The old man stooped and examined John through the nets, his weatherworn buffalo pelt dragging in the moist earth. He murmured Osage words to himself. John Wesley growled again, the bonfire's chaotic light throwing jack-o'-lantern shadows across his face. The old man neither flinched nor showed fear.

Quinn leaned toward Strong Heart. "What are they doing?"

"Shh," the girl scolded. "They're considering ways to help them."

The old man suddenly straightened and brushed grit off his hands. He waited for Buffalo Woman to return to his side, then he addressed the young riders in Osage. Again, Strong Heart translated. "Before we speak of your friends, you must first tell us why you've come."

Cutter glanced at Keech. "Go ahead, Lost Cause."

But before Keech could speak, Duck tore off her hat and stepped closer to the elders. "Our fathers were Enforcers," she began, gesturing first to herself, then to Keech. "The Enforcers came to you ten years ago and asked you to help them. And you did." She paused, as though thinking carefully about her next words. "Our fathers have sent us back here to finish what they couldn't. They gave us clues to fetch the Char Stone from Bone Ridge and to find Bonfire Crossing, but along the way the Char Stone got stolen."

Buffalo Woman shook her head with concern, and then she surprised Keech by speaking English. "The one called *Rose* is to blame. He is the Scorpion. A taker of relics and lands, a murderer of innocents."

The elder's word for the Reverend—*Scorpion*—reminded Keech of what Pa Abner had told Bad Whiskey after the one-eyed fiend had found the Home. *You're under the control of a scorpion, Bad Whiskey. One day soon you're bound to get the stinger.*

"*Tseh Mee*", what will happen when Rose's men give him the Char Stone?" Keech asked, though he feared the response.

Buffalo Woman contemplated the question. When she appeared to struggle with the answer, she spoke it in Osage. The kids looked to Strong Heart.

"She says once the man called Rose reunites the artifacts, a terrible ceremony will begin once more in a place some call the Scorpion's Nest."

A glacial shiver ran down Keech's body. "That's the Palace of the Thunders, isn't it? That's where Rose is. The *real* Rose." He tried to block out the horrible memory, but he could still hear the Reverend screaming through Bad Whiskey's mouth in Bone Ridge: *One day, Blackwood, we'll meet, and then you'll know true fear.*

Buffalo Woman spoke in Osage again, and Strong Heart translated. "She says it's more important than ever to guard the Fang, so that it never falls into the Scorpion's hands. He needs the Fang for his ceremony with the Stone."

Keech gazed over the reaches of the western ocean, which sparkled with morning light. He glanced back at the elders. "Is that why you hid the Fang out here, to keep it away from Rose's men back east?"

This time, Strong Heart didn't wait for one of them to answer. "They shelter the Fang at Bonfire Crossing because this shore is one of the few places of ancient power."

"'One of the few places,'" Duck repeated. "There are more beaches like this?"

"Not like this," Strong Heart said. "There's another place deep in the mountains of the West, and yet another to the north, the one you call the Palace."

"Three sites of power," Keech mused. "Bonfire Crossing, a place in the Western mountains, and the Palace of the Thunders."

Strong Heart sighed. "You must realize, these places existed long before any of our families. We don't *want* this place, and we don't want the Fang. Sometimes people must live with dangerous things they never asked for."

"The Fang doesn't belong to the Osage?" asked Cutter.

Strong Heart tossed back her head, as though frustrated. "The Osage understand the powers these objects hold, but the Enforcers' relics are not ours." She frowned at Keech and Duck when she said this. Keech found himself glancing down, ashamed but not fully grasping why. It wasn't his and Duck's fault that the Osage were protecting the Fang, but then again, Keech felt *everything* was his fault. Both of his fathers had been involved, and now he was carrying the torch.

Buffalo Woman raised a finger and spoke again, prompting Strong Heart to continue interpreting.

"She says to understand this place, you must understand its first dwellers. They came to this coast long ago, searching for a new home. They discovered that this ground possessed great virtues, from which they could draw protections."

Hearing that word, *protections*, Keech recalled the endless loops of Floodwood, what Pa Abner had called a *precaution*.

"The first dwellers discovered ways to hide their homes from danger and build pathways to other places for hunting. This place"— she swept her hand around the cove—"became a sacred ground, where the first dwellers learned many secrets."

"This beach opened up the pathway to Kansas," Duck said, her tone full of fascination. "That's what you meant earlier when you said it created the door."

"And no one can enter except by way of the moon stalker," Quinn added.

Strong Heart smiled at both of them. "Not by sea, not by the cliffs. There's concealment all around. The Protectors guard the door to ensure no one comes, and the elders live alone in their lodges beyond the fire. They watch the Fang and pray to *Wah-kah^n-dah* that one day they can return to their families." She regarded the old pair with veneration.

Writhing on the sand, Doyle lifted his head, his eyes teeming with the darkness of death. He grabbed at the wound on his leg. His flesh had turned a deeper, more unsettling purple.

Beneath the nets, John Wesley cried out, "Papa!"

Keech turned to the elders. "Can you help them?"

When Buffalo Woman spoke again, Strong Heart translated with a forlorn face. "She says the Enforcer can be healed, but nothing can be done for the boy John. Your friend has become a new form. There is no remedy, only acceptance. But the Enforcer's wound came from a dark power, so it can be cured with *light*."

"You can't do anything to help John?" Cutter said. "You have to!"

Buffalo Woman lifted a hand to cut him off. When she spoke again, her tone was darker, more urgent.

"She says there's no more time for discussion," Strong Heart said. "If you want to heal the Enforcer, you must retrieve the Fang. Only the *light* can heal the *dark* inside the wound."

"Are you saying the Fang has *healing* powers?" Keech asked, bewildered.

Strong Heart turned to her uncle in surprise. "They didn't know," she said.

Duck pointed to the Ranger's knapsack. "That would explain why Doyle's been so driven to get hold of it. He thinks the Fang will bring Eliza's body back to normal."

Doyle suddenly screamed, "Eliza! John! Papa's here!"

Keech knew there was no more time. He looked back at the elders. "Where do we find it? Somewhere in the hills? I'll go and fetch it."

Buffalo Woman and Doesn't Fear Thunder looked perplexed.

"The Fang of Barachiel is in front of you," Strong Heart said.

Keech glanced around. "I don't understand."

Doesn't Fear Thunder gestured toward the blaze. After speaking in Osage, he glanced at Strong Heart, who said, "The Fang lies inside the fire, the Lair of the Wolf."

Keech must not have heard right. A person couldn't step near the bonfire without roasting alive. "You mean I have to face a difficult trial? Or find a way to put out the fire?"

Strong Heart repeated the old man's words.

"But stepping into the fire would burn you to death!" Duck cried.

The old woman waved a hand at her. "*Peh-tseh, noh*"*-peh zhee-ah-pah.*"

"Do not fear the fire," Strong Heart said.

Before either Keech or Duck could respond, a sharp *crack* rent the salty air—a loud *pop* that sounded like the volley of a rifle. The discharge had come from behind them. Everyone in the cove turned to look in the direction of the disturbance.

Farther up the coastline, a vibrant sparkle of light danced between the boughs of the bending tree. Another thundering crash echoed down the beach, and the flash of light widened with a horrible tearing noise.

Doesn't Fear Thunder stumbled forward, his mouth agape. "*Hah*"*-kah-zhee!*"

In the distance, a hulking man stepped out of the light. It was Big Ben, and he wasn't alone. The massive shape of the Chamelia scurried after him onto the beach, followed by a large black bird that swooped out of the shimmering gate. The Shifter crouched on all fours beside its master as the bird soared high above the ocean waves.

Big Ben held up one arm, then let it drop with a booming command.

"Kill them, Man Slayer! For the Reverend!"

CHAPTER 30
THE CHAMELIA

As soon as the creature tore away from its master's side, Strong Bones shouted orders, and the Protectors galloped out to meet the charging beast, pulling war clubs and lifting longbows.

Strong Heart reined her pony back as the horsemen raced over the rock-strewn beach. "*EE^n-dah-tsee-dah^n!*" she called out to her uncle. But Strong Bones only turned to give her a swift wave onward.

The girl whipped her head back to the young riders, her long braid lashing the air, and the sudden fear that Keech had read on her features turned quickly to resolve. She shrugged off her heavy buffalo robe, letting it fall to the sand, revealing a buckskin dress and knee-length leggings tied around her calves. Beckoning the young riders to follow, Strong Heart kicked her pony's sides and tore out of the cove.

Keech glanced around, realized they were trapped in a dead end, and suddenly recalled a time when he had cornered a field mouse in Pa's woodshed. The critter had disappeared into the clutter of tools and wooden fragments till Keech had turned over a scrap of pine and revealed the poor thing's hiding place. With nowhere else to go, the mouse sprang at his face. Panicked, he froze, allowing the mouse to scrabble over his shoulder, unscathed. Later, Pa Abner laughed at the story. *With nowhere else to go, what did you expect?* Pa said. *Even the smallest animal will fight back when cornered.*

"Lost Causes, we've got nowhere left to run. It's time to fight," Keech called. "Let's stand with the Protectors and save Bonfire Crossing."

"I'm with you," said Quinn, "but how do we fight it?"

Keech snatched up one of the long spears on the ground and tossed it to the boy. Duck followed Keech's lead and grabbed a leather sling from the stockpile. "Better than a candlestick," she said. They dashed over to mount their ponies.

Brandishing his blade, Cutter raised a boot to Chantico's stirrup but stopped. "What about John?"

John Wesley growled, struggling in the nets. "I can help!"

Keech glanced at the two elders, who were standing defiantly in front of Doyle and the bonfire. "Turn our friend loose. Please. He'll fight with us."

Buffalo Woman nodded quickly. "Release him."

Without a moment's hesitation, Cutter's blade flashed. Strands of netting fell away, and John Wesley rolled out of the snare onto his hands and knees. He shook his spiny shoulders and peered down the beach with red glinting eyes. The backs of his arms bristled with quills, and long fangs jutted from his jaw.

Unleashing a heavy roar, John scampered away on all fours out of the cove, kicking up sand with his ragged boots and clawed hands.

"Let's go!" Cutter shouted.

Keech glanced over at Saint Peter. He had almost forgotten their most important weapon of all.

Sprinting to the Kelpie, he fetched Doyle's pouch of bloodroot from the saddlebag. The supply felt light—the Ranger had used most of it to lay the protection down at the Moss house and outside Wisdom—but there might just be enough to get the job done. Tucking it into his coat, Keech sprinted back to Hector.

The young riders charged after John, leaving the two elders to wait with Doyle at the bonfire.

John Wesley glanced back at the group. "Y'all keep going! I'm gonna try to outflank it!" He bolted off to the left and slipped out of view behind a cluster of charcoal rocks.

"Everyone, support the Protectors!" Keech yelled. "Stay behind their bows. If you can get a shot in with your weapons, strike quick, but if the Chamelia charges, circle the rocks. It might confuse its path."

Midway over the beach, the Chamelia pounced on top of a tall boulder. It had taken on a canine form, the bulk of its hide lined with wolfish fur, but its underbelly was still coated with slick black scales.

Ahead of the Lost Causes, Strong Heart joined her companions, and the Protectors fanned out into a horseshoe formation—four on one side, three on the other. The riders bellowed Osage words to one another. Staring down from the rock's brow, the Shifter released a thunderous roar that echoed up the beach.

The Lost Causes had nearly reached the Protectors when the Chamelia barreled down from the boulder and crashed into Yellow Hawk's pony. The horse tumbled with a terrible squeal, and the Protector careened off the saddle. The Chamelia grabbed the pony by its flanks and lifted the poor animal off the ground, then tossed it down the beach, where it splashed into the surf. Yellow Hawk rolled to his side and reached for his war club, but the Chamelia lunged before he could wield it.

"*Leh-dah^n Zee!*" Strong Bones yelled.

Yellow Hawk dropped to his stomach. A nest of arrows flew as the Protectors tried to stop the monster from clawing into their partner. Dogwood shafts jabbed into the creature's back and neck, but it batted them away as if swatting at mosquitoes. The distraction afforded Yellow Hawk a chance to dash away to his horse, which was thrashing in the surf.

The young riders approached the melee as the Chamelia crouched. The beast looked ready to lunge again, this time at Strong Bones.

"*EE^n-dah-tsee-dah^n! EE-Nah-pah!*" Strong Heart flung her war club. The curved wooden head whistled through the air past the ranks of the Protectors and clobbered the Chamelia's snout. A howl erupted from the creature as two or three fangs flew from its mouth.

"Good throw!" Quinn said.

Strong Heart's attack didn't stop the Shifter from targeting her uncle. In fact, the pain only fueled its rage. It bounded across the short distance, its claws reaching for Strong Bones, but then Keech caught a flash of movement to his left.

John Wesley hurtled down from one of the black pillars and landed on the larger beast's back, driving the Shifter into the sand. John ripped at its furry hide. The creature rolled against the boy, but he held firm, like a feisty cat clinging to a ball of yarn.

The Protectors raised their longbows again, a new batch of

arrows ready to fire, but as the young riders rode up into their formation, Cutter yelled, "Stop! You'll hit John!"

Strong Bones held up a fist, pausing the volley.

As John continued to tear at the Shifter, their combined snarls and whimpers grew into a violent cacophony, so piercing that the shouts of the Lost Causes and the Protectors became suffocated muffles in Keech's ears. Beneath the discord, he heard Duck call out to him. She pointed farther down the beach, beyond the skirmish, to the bending tree in the distance.

Big Ben had stepped away from the door of light and was strolling up the beach, his arms held before him like a man in the throes of supplication.

"What's he doing?" Duck said, boosting her voice over John Wesley's attack.

"No idea," Keech returned, "but we'll have to keep away from him for now. We got our hands full."

As if to confirm Keech's words, the Chamelia broke the vicious hold on its back, and John Wesley went flying over the sand. He smashed headfirst against a craggy rock and collapsed.

Cutter cried out to him, but before the boy could ride closer, the Protectors released their second hailstorm of arrows. This time, all seven shafts buried into the Chamelia's chest—a perfect pattern of uniform shots. The beast stumbled backward, and for one moment, Keech thought the barrage would surely work, that the creature would tumble and die.

But like before, the arrows only infuriated it.

Reaching with a gnarled hand, the Chamelia yanked all seven sticks from its flesh and threw them to the ground. A low rumble filled its throat.

And then it shifted.

The canine features melted away, and the visage became that of a towering lizard on two legs. A hideous, serpentine tongue probed the air, and its saffron eyes fixed on the Protectors, as though marking the source of its most recent pain.

Strong Bones issued a command, and the beach became a bedlam of movement as the warriors scrambled around the rocks. At first, the scattering appeared shapeless and chaotic, but Keech soon realized they were breaking in a defensive maneuver, carefully executed. The Chamelia spun about, bewildered, as Strong Heart and the horsemen disappeared behind the boulders. Keech heard a high whistle as two arrows appeared from nowhere, burying into the creature's hide. It tugged them loose, undeterred, and continued to search—till it suddenly pivoted toward Whipping Feather, the horseman in the otter hat, who was racing around a nearby boulder.

The Shifter vaulted toward the movement. The Protector grabbed his war club, but before he could swing it, the beast dived with a fury and tackled him off his horse.

Galloping into the fray, Quinn heaved his long spear. It whizzed through the air like a lightning bolt and struck the Chamelia in the shoulder. The lizard-thing glanced up from its prey, searching for the culprit. Duck rushed in beside Quinn and shot a stone from her sling. The rock battered the creature's ear and made it flinch, but otherwise it had no effect. The beast returned its attention to Whipping Feather.

"Keech, Cutter, a little help!" Duck shouted.

But Keech was already rushing in on one side while Cutter approached the Shifter on the other. They encircled the beast, hooting and whistling, trying to draw it off the fallen warrior, but the Chamelia hunkered on all fours and refused to budge.

Surprising Keech, Cutter sprang off Chantico and onto the thing's spiny, reptilian back. His long blade drove home between the thing's distended shoulder blades. The creature yelped.

"C'mon, *cuchillo*, work your magic," Cutter yelled, clutching the knife's bone handle. The Shifter spun violently, trying to shake the boy like a mustang.

Reaching into his coat, Keech grabbed the bloodroot bag. He tugged open the bag's drawstring mouth, and a sudden whiff of tart, pungent powder struck him. Distant calls from Strong Heart filled his ears, and he glimpsed John Wesley trying to rise from the sand, but Keech drove everything else away. Dipping his hand into the bag, he shouted "Hyah!" and steered Hector closer to the Shifter.

Still trying to loosen Cutter from its back, the Chamelia frothed at the mouth when it saw Keech approach.

"Cut, get clear!" he shouted.

Cutter yanked back, and his blade tore from the thing's back. The moment he lost his hold, he tumbled head over heels across the beach. Keech swung his arm wide, releasing his hand from the pouch, and a red handful of bloodroot flew into the Chamelia's face.

The response was instant. The monster began to twitch as if on fire, its long lizard snout angled up to the sky. Its snake-like tongue flicked in and out.

And then the creature sneezed.

The force of it dropped the Chamelia onto all fours. Claws digging at the sand, it arched its thorny back and lurched, releasing three more thunderous sneezes as it tottered. The discharges shook its entire body—and mounds of grayish-white fur sprouted up and down the Shifter's stomach, replacing the reptilian scales, as if the sneezing had turned its skin inside out to reveal a whole different animal beneath.

Two of the Protectors, Weeping Cloud and Red Stone, seized the distraction and directed their ponies straight at the Shifter. They flung a pair of nets, hooking the ropes around the creature's barbed shoulders. As the mesh caught, the horsemen turned their ponies and dragged the Chamelia toward the sea. A frazzled-looking John Wesley followed the men, snarling just behind the beast and loping on all fours. Led by Strong Heart's uncle, the other Protectors leaped off their saddles and dashed over to Whipping Feather's body. Strong Heart stooped and fetched her war club from the sand, wiping the grimy curved head across her thigh.

The young riders gathered their ponies around Strong Bones and the others. No one appeared to be scratched or bitten by the Shifter other than Whipping Feather, who lay in the sand unmoving. Keech prayed the fellow would collect a breath and stumble to his feet, but nothing happened. The Protectors spoke solemn words over the man as Strong Bones placed a hand on Whipping Feather's head.

Keech shook with rage. The Reverend Rose had taken life yet again. He stripped his hat off.

The other Lost Causes bowed their heads in respect.

"That takes care of the Chamelia," whispered Quinn, not wanting to disturb the warriors' mourning. In the distance, John Wesley and the two Protectors hauled the monster into the wash. "Now to stop its master."

Keech swiveled around. To his dismay, he saw no sign of the

outlaw. He had tried to keep Big Ben in his sights, but the battle with the fiend's pet had been a powerful distraction.

"He's there!" said Duck, pointing.

Big Ben had traveled well past them. He had marched halfway down the beach toward the cove, completely around the skirmish, undetected. Now his hands twirled in formless circles, summoning a cyclone of sand that whipped about his boots. The swirl of wet grit formed a fierce cocoon around his mountainous body.

"He's going for the bonfire," Keech said.

CHAPTER 31

THE HARVESTER
OF DOOM

Four Protectors, including Strong Heart, mounted back up. Strong Bones shouted something in Osage to his niece, then the three men galloped down the beach toward the outlaw. Hanging back with a frown, Strong Heart glanced at the young riders. "Uncle says we need to help the elders. They can't stand alone against the bad man."

"We're with you," Keech said.

The girl kicked her pony back into motion. "Follow quick!" she said.

Keech and the other young riders fell in, riding side by side, galloping just behind her, occasionally parting to steer their ponies around thick boulders.

Strong Bones and his two companions soon surrounded Big Ben. Yellow Hawk and Big Moon released a series of arrows, but the sand tornado swatted the shafts away, scattering them to oblivion. Strong Bones and Yellow Hawk tried to approach on foot, their war clubs held high, but neither man could gain ground.

"They'll never hurt him that way," Quinn said.

"Doyle's the only one powerful enough to stop him," Keech said. "We need to get the Fang and heal him."

"No, we should attack him head-on," Duck said.

"We'll face him soon enough," Strong Heart said. "For now, circle around and head to the bonfire."

Still following the girl, the young riders trotted their ponies toward the steep cliffs, giving Big Ben and his windstorm the widest berth possible. As they passed the scuffle, Big Ben's cyclone whipped Strong Bones off his feet and slammed him into a boulder.

Seeing her uncle fall, Strong Heart cried, *"Hahⁿ-kah-zhee!"*

Keech looked her firm in the eye. "Go help your uncle. We'll stand with the elders."

Clutching her war club, Strong Heart reined her pony and hurried toward the battle.

Suddenly, a nerve-shattering din thundered over the shore.

Keech turned back to look and felt his heart plummet. The Chamelia stood on its hind legs in the distant surf, ripping away the nets that Weeping Cloud and Red Stone had thrown. Both Protectors had tumbled off their horses. One lay unmoving in the shallow water while the other crawled away from the beast. Nearby, John Wesley struggled through the ocean swell, closing in on the Shifter.

"John!" Cutter yelled, then turned back to the others. "He's alone with that thing!"

"Stay on course," Keech warned.

But Cutter swiveled Chantico back toward the ocean. Despite Keech's plea, he kicked his heels and galloped across the narrow beach, zigzagging through the boulders to get back to John Wesley.

"What's he doing?" said Quinn.

"Getting himself killed," Duck answered.

Keech called after him to no avail. He could see that Big Ben blocked the boy's path to the ocean, but at least the Protectors were still surrounding the outlaw, distracting him with a flurry of attacks.

For one moment, Keech thought Cutter might make it past, but as the boy steered Chantico around the battle, a wall of whipping sand blasted him off his saddle, tossing him onto the ground.

Big Ben shouted to the sky in fanatic praise. "*Reverend, thank you for the Prime! Your faithful servant will see your destiny fulfilled! You shall rise again in the Palace!*"

High above, the fiendish crow answered, *Ack!*

Keech clenched his teeth in frustration. "Keep on to the bonfire," he said to Duck and Quinn. "I think there's a little bloodroot left. I'll fetch Cutter, and we'll help John." He tore off toward the place where Cutter lay.

The Protectors once again approached Big Ben, but with a rapid flutter of his hand, the outlaw sent Yellow Hawk and Big Moon tumbling down the shore along with their ponies. "The Reverend wills that the bonfire be destroyed!" the brute thundered. Only Strong Bones remained to block the outlaw's path.

"Change of plans," Keech said to Hector. "We need to take that man down."

As if he understood, Hector lowered his head and picked up his pace.

Passing the dazed Cutter, Keech aimed the horse at Big Ben, hoping to stampede right over him, but as the stallion closed in on the outlaw, heavy tornado winds lifted Keech off the saddle. He grabbed at the horn with both hands, but the gale snatched his grip loose, and the world went topsy-turvy.

Keech crashed down hard in the sand, narrowly avoiding a rock. When he sat up, he spat a mouthful of grit, noticed his hat nearby, and snatched it. His head felt fuzzy, but he struggled up to his knees in time to see Strong Bones slam into Big Ben. Despite the Protector's own size, he bounced off the outlaw as if he had thumped against a tree.

Big Ben reached down, grabbed a discarded war club from the ground, and swung the blade. Strong Bones rolled out of the way, letting the cleaver bite into sand. The Protector jumped to his feet and pulled a short knife from his breechcloth.

"You can't win," Big Ben said.

Strong Bones charged, and his knife struck the center of Big Ben's chest. With a cruel snap, the metal blade broke from the handle. The Protector tossed aside his ruined weapon.

"Surrender!" Big Ben cracked his meaty fist across the side of the man's head.

Strong Bones dropped like a sack full of stones.

Keech caught a flicker of movement. Strong Heart galloped out of nowhere, heading straight for the outlaw. Big Ben swiveled to meet her. With a ferocious cry, the girl drove her pony into his path and brought her war club down on his head. A terrible *crack* echoed across the beach, but the brute didn't flinch.

"Enough of the likes of you." Big Ben snapped a finger as she raced by. A frenzied gust whipped over the beach, and Strong Heart peeled out of her saddle. The outlaw waved his hand toward the ocean, and the mystical wind hoisted the young Protector over the sand. Releasing a scream of raw fury, Big Ben flicked his fingers, and Strong Heart flew far across the water's shimmering reach. She splashed down in the distance and disappeared.

With no more foes in his path, Big Ben resumed his steady walk to the bonfire.

Keech searched for a plan that could save Strong Heart, destroy Big Ben, and rescue John Wesley and the others from the Chamelia, but his mind was a panicked blank. And when Strong Heart's faint voice called out over the crashing tide, shrieking for help, he felt despair clutch his heart.

Then suddenly, a voice from up the beach shouted Strong Heart's name. A midnight-black horse galloped over the cove and toward the ocean.

Quinn Revels rode Saint Peter, dragging one of the Protector's nets behind him. The Kelpie's hooves met the tide but didn't sink.

"Strong Heart, hold on!" Quinn called as Saint Peter charged across the top of the surf and out to sea.

Keech loosed a victorious peal. "Go, Quinn, go!"

Vicious barks yanked his attention back to the nearby shoreline. Keech spun to see John Wesley waist-deep in the surf, entangled with the Chamelia. The larger Shifter slashed with furious claws, but the boy refused to surrender. They snapped and howled and thrashed in the waves.

Keech was surprised to see that a few feet farther up the beach, Cutter was dragging Red Stone away from the brawl. The boy stumbled but refused to slow, tugging the horseman out of the tide and onto dry land.

Back on the beach, Big Ben stepped up his pace to the cove and the bonfire. A short distance away, Duck stood at the cove's mouth, guarding the two elders behind her, ready for a scuffle. She was whipping her sling, ready to loose a stone, her feet set wide in a fighting stance.

A terrible dread washed over Keech as he realized that Duck would never defeat the man alone. He tore off running, desperate to reach the outlaw first. He bellowed a war cry, hoping to catch Big Ben off guard, but the fiend didn't bother to glance around.

There was no way to help her.

Duck released her sling, and a stone shot like a bullet through the unnatural winds, but it never came close to reaching him.

Big Ben laughed and simply waved a hand.

A violent wind pitched Duck sideways. She tumbled over the cove, past Doyle and the elders, and smacked into a boulder standing in the wash.

Keech's legs and lungs burned, but he refused to slow.

Big Ben had reached the cove.

Buffalo Woman waited under the glow of the inferno, holding her ground. Her partner, Doesn't Fear Thunder, stood over Doyle's body. A few yards away, Duck sat up in the shallow tide and clutched her temples in a daze.

Keech heard Big Ben mutter two words: "You've lost." The man snapped his fingers, and heavy gusts ripped at the elders. The old pair held up their hands and pushed against the magical surge, as though trying to keep a stone wall from tumbling on them. For a moment, their effort worked, but then Big Ben wailed in fury, and the winds howled even louder. The elders plummeted off their feet.

"Big Ben, stop!" Keech cried.

Glancing over his shoulder, the outlaw scowled at Keech. The frenzied light of the bonfire turned his face into that of a red monster. "I am your Harvester of doom," he called back. Then he leaped over Doyle's body and dived straight into the inferno.

Keech skidded to a halt at the edge of the fire.

Struggling up from the ground, Buffalo Woman turned frantic eyes on Keech. She shouted in fierce English, "You must go *now*!"

Do not fear the fire, she had said earlier. But Keech hesitated. After all, Big Ben had survived the whistle-bomb explosion in Wisdom, the blast that had killed Nat. Perhaps fire didn't even hurt the fiend but would leave Keech a cooked goose if he followed.

The crackling, red-hot mountain menaced before him. Terrible heat cascaded over his face, conjuring memories of the burning Home for Lost Causes. He remembered Sam inside the flames, waving him away. He heard the cries of his orphan siblings. He yelled out to them, but he realized he was only shrieking at phantoms.

Keech also realized he had made his decision. He would not hide from the fire.

Nearby, Duck clamored, and Buffalo Woman bellowed to him in Osage. But he didn't turn back. Instead, Keech squeezed his eyes shut and hunkered low in the sand and muttered a small supplication to his fallen brother.

"Be with me, Sam."

Then before he could change his mind, before the magnificent flames could rob his body of all courage, Keech vaulted into the inferno.

CHAPTER 32

INSIDE THE FIRE

He felt no burning sensation as he sprang through the wall of flames.

He landed on his hands and knees, not on tormenting coals but on cool, spongy terrain that reflected a deep golden light. He stood and peered under his boots. The ground flowed like melted stone, giving him the impression that he was standing on a lake of embers, but his feet felt no scorch.

Keech inspected his flesh for burns. Tendrils of white smoke rose from his palms, yet his skin was unmarred, not a hair singed. A steady breeze engulfed him, strangely peaceful and slow, like the atmosphere inside a pleasant dream.

From all appearances, he had leaped into a *forest*, a magical space much larger than the bonfire's girth, a deep woodland full of ever-greens. The giant trees burned from base to crown with a vivid green fire, but the wood never split or blackened. When Keech glanced back to mark what he had jumped through, he saw a thick barrier of cypress trees, all engulfed in green flames. He reckoned he must be seeing the boundary of the bonfire.

"Do not fear the fire," he told himself.

Heavy crackles like boot steps on dry straw sounded behind him. He spun immediately, fisting his hands, but saw nothing but the fiery trees. Pa Abner's voice whispered, *Be careful. Learn your surroundings, but don't waste time gazing.*

Taking a few watchful steps deeper into the forest, Keech dared a glance up.

A halo of night sky, mulberry-colored and filled with stars, stretched above the blazing evergreen canopy. A glistening blue sphere hung motionless up there, like a full moon teeming with captured lightning. Keech knew he wasn't seeing the *real* moon, only a replica, because the shimmering orb floated low in the sky, within reach of a long ladder.

" 'The Fang lies inside the fire, the Lair of the Wolf,' " he whispered, repeating the words the elders had used.

"Lair of the Wolf?" a voice thundered. "Is that what the Enforcers call this place?"

Keech wheeled around to see Big Ben step out from behind a massive burning tree. Before he could set a fighting stance, the outlaw lashed out. A fist with the power of a charging bull smashed into Keech's shoulder, throwing him sideways.

Keech's breath tumbled from his lungs as he crashed onto his elbow. Flopping to his stomach, he gasped for air. He tried to get up, but Big Ben's boot cracked into his gut, sending a screaming pain through his ribs.

The killer stepped in front of him, boots squishing in the curious magma. "Righteous little lamb. You hope to slow the Master's plan?"

Keech dragged in a small breath and wheezed, "We'll never give up."

"Don't be foolish. You're already conquered."

"How'd you even get in?" Keech tried to crawl away, but the outlaw moved into his path. "The Osage closed the door."

Big Ben's disheveled red beard split into a mean smile. "My Chamelia followed your scent to the tree. Then all it took was a hard wallop from the Prime." Big Ben's face teemed with a terrible madness, the lunacy of a rabid dog. "Now tell me where to find the Fang. I know the Enforcers hid it somewhere in this holding chamber."

Keech wheezed. "You think you're so powerful, find it yourself."

"Foolishness is bound in the heart of a child," Big Ben said. Seizing Keech by the shoulders, the man wrenched him up to his feet as if hoisting a simple bag of feathers, then jerked him around to face outward. "But the rod of correction shall drive it far from him."

Keech caught a glimpse of the charred Devil's mark on Big Ben's palm as the brute gripped his chin and cranked his head upward. The fiery canopy of trees filled his sight, and that tiny false moon hovered in the dark sky.

"Tell me where it's hid, or I'll snap your neck."

Pa Abner's voice called out. *Size up your adversary. Find his weakest points.*

Keech closed his eyes, recalling his first encounter with Big Ben in Wisdom. He had seen the man flinch in pain while cracking his knuckles and grimace as he stretched a kink out of his back. Though Big Ben was nearly invincible—he'd survived an explosion, after all—he couldn't hide the fact that he suffered from feeble joints.

And all at once Keech knew what to do.

Before he could move, Big Ben threw him aside, sending him sprawling over the molten ground. Keech's face pressed into cool earth.

"I don't need you after all," Big Ben growled, pointing up at the bonfire's mock sky. "They hid the Fang in that foolish orb. Flimsy smoke and mirrors, just like this whole place. Pathetic."

Keech attempted to rise, but Big Ben planted a boot on his thigh, holding him down. The killer's weight against him felt like a slab of solid bedrock. Searing needles of pain coursed through his side, and Keech realized that Big Ben's kick had broken a rib, maybe a couple.

Big Ben dipped his fingers into one of the pouches on his hip. He stirred the contents, muttering strange words, and when he drew his fingers back out, something that looked like pine resin dripped from his hand. The amber fluid dribbled to the ground, and Big Ben moved his fingers in small circles, letting the substance form a loose coil at his feet. He then puffed a quick breath upon the resin, and before Keech's eyes, the material curdled into a lengthy rope. Big Ben fashioned a long loop in the cord, which he tied off with a honda knot. "Watch closely, little lamb. I'll show you things an Enforcer never could."

Rearing back, Big Ben tossed the conjured rope high above his head. Trapped under the outlaw's heavy boot, Keech watched in horror as the lariat whizzed upward, beyond the flaming canopy, the line growing longer as it flew, and captured the sapphire moon. The rope tightened, and Big Ben tugged at the lariat as though he had roped a stubborn mule. The gleaming sphere pulsed against the dark sky as it descended.

Before long, the flashing orb was low enough that Keech could make out details. Though it had seemed bulkier in the sky, the object was no larger than a pumpkin. A waxy-looking rind surrounded the sapphire light, but the husk was thin enough that Keech could see the flaming trees through it. A dim shape hovered within the blue radiance, barely visible, like a fish drifting in murky waters.

"The Fang of Barachiel," Big Ben said, peering closer. The captured ball sputtered, showering the ground with hot indigo sparks. Big Ben continued to yank the turbulent sphere ever closer. A bolt of blue lightning flashed between Big Ben's feet, but the outlaw didn't flinch. "Flimsy smoke and mirrors," he repeated.

Keech squirmed under the man's boot. "Big Ben, you're a fool. You use the power that Rose gives you but ignore the consequences." He then used the words that Pa Abner had spoken to Bad Whiskey. "You're under the control of a scorpion, and one day soon you're bound to get the stinger."

Big Ben raised his hand to the orb. "Maybe, little lamb, but if I ever do get stung, you won't be around to witness." Then he plunged his fingers into the glowing vessel.

A sudden shower of sparks cascaded around the man, and a shrieking noise issued from the orb. More of the blue lightning shot forth, this time striking Big Ben in the center of his chest. The killer grimaced in pain but kept his feet. He shoved his hand deeper into the globe, and more vehement sparks leaped at him. For a second, Keech thought the orb would overcome the man, but Big Ben turned his fist and squeezed. "Die!" he screamed.

The blue light began to fade. The gossamer shell fizzed away, exposing the object within.

Floating before them was a knife carved entirely from bone.

The blade was about as long as the span of Keech's spread

fingers, the edge curved with a sawtooth spine and the carved handle shaped for a firm grip. Keech stared at the spinning object with wonder. He had thought it would be an animal fang. He also didn't understand how a bone knife could heal Ranger Doyle, but apparently it held properties that could reverse the wound caused by Big Ben. *Only the light can heal the dark*, Buffalo Woman had said.

Big Ben snatched the blade out of the air and held it before him, triumphant. He glanced down at Keech, pressing his boot down harder onto his thigh. "Did you know this relic is said to be the dagger that Abraham carried on Mount Moriah to kill his son?"

Keech didn't answer. Instead, he curled his fingers into fists.

"Stories tell that the angel of the Lord descended from heaven to stop the sacrifice and took the weapon from Abraham's hand. That's why they say the dagger heals, because the angel, Barachiel, blessed the knife so that no blood could ever spill by it."

"If it don't spill blood, why would Rose want it?"

"Let's just say the Master requires it to be *whole*." Big Ben smiled. "You've been a worthy fighter, little lamb, but the Reverend can no longer allow the brood of Screamin' Bill to interfere."

"How about the brood of Bennett Coal?" shouted Duck Embry.

The girl leaped out from behind a blazing tree. One of the Protector's nets flew from her hands and landed squarely on Big Ben.

A victorious cry escaped Keech's lungs. He hollered, "The joints, Duck! Go for his joints!"

Duck charged in, driving straight for Big Ben's legs. Keech didn't expect her small body to faze him, but she kicked at his knee-cap and sent the massive man staggering. He pitched over like a tree,

325

his arms tangled in the net. As he crashed to the ground, the Fang skittered out of his hand. The outlaw bellowed, surprise and fury tainting his voice. He pried at the cords, trying to rip them away.

Holding a hand to his ribs, Keech pushed to his feet.

Delicate white smoke wafted off Duck's clothes and hat. Her face was a crimson mask of rage, and her stark blue eyes burned hatred down on the man who had killed her family.

Still twisted in the mesh, Big Ben struggled to his feet, searching the ground for the Fang. Duck fell upon the killer, kicking straight at the center of his spine.

Big Ben howled in pain. Clutching the small of his back, he swiveled to face her, the mouth behind his red beard grimacing like a wounded animal. "You're dead, kid!" He swung a husky arm at her head, but the net stifled his attack, and Duck jumped out of the way.

Big Ben stumbled past Keech to fetch the Fang. But Duck was already pounding a fist into his elbow. The outlaw screamed, flinching back.

As Keech scrambled for the blade, he noticed Big Ben's hand plunge toward one of his medicine pouches, but Duck shifted to the outlaw's other side, dropped low, and battered the reaching hand before it could scoop out a trick.

"This is for my mother!"

Keech heard the crack of bones as her fist broke the man's fingers.

"This is for my father!"

Duck stooped again and kicked a boot heel into the side of the man's ankle. The outlaw tumbled to one knee, his mouth opening for a scream that didn't come.

"And this is for Nathaniel!"

She flung herself at Big Ben's face, and her elbow crunched into his nose. Keech heard a sickening snap, and the brute collapsed backward.

Keech hurried the remaining distance and scooped the dagger off the ground. "Duck, I've got the Fang," he called out.

Her eyes brimming with rage, she shouted, "Take it to Doyle!"

Keech swiveled toward the blazing cypress boundary, but he recalled Nat's face in Wisdom's saloon and stopped. Nat had pleaded for Duck and Keech to keep each other safe. "No," he said, turning back to Duck. "We go together."

"But I have to finish him!"

"I won't leave you alone. Not ever. We're partners."

Lying on the ground, Big Ben gripped his ruined nose. He tried to rise in the net but crumbled back to his stomach.

Duck's eyes brimmed with tears. She turned away from the killer. "All right."

Keech took her hand. Clutching the Fang in his other, he led them to the edge of the burning cypress. The emerald fire gave off no heat, but Keech's heart still hammered at the beautiful, terrible sight of it. He looked at Duck. "Ready?"

"Ready."

Holding hands, they vaulted through the flames.

CHAPTER 33

THE FANG

They landed hard on the wet sand of the cove, the bonfire at their backs.

Struggling up to his knees, Keech felt a torturous pinch in his side. A fog of sweet smoke clouded the cove, forcing tears into his eyes. With his free hand, he rubbed his vision clear.

Beside him, Duck coughed, spitting into the sand. "You have it?"

Keech lifted the Fang. "We need to hurry." He pushed to his feet.

The endless ocean surf clattered over the black rocks, each foamy wave mounting higher than the last. The two elders stood over Doyle's motionless body. Buffalo Woman held out her hand and shouted Osage words to Keech and Duck.

Holding his wounded side, Keech stumbled over—but he stopped when an inhuman roar rumbled across the land. He swiveled toward the noise. A few yards down the beach, perched atop one of the black stone pillars, was the Chamelia. The other young riders hadn't been able to stop it. The barbed spines on the creature's shoulders fluttered like rattling reeds. Then it bounded off the stone and charged on all fours straight for the cove.

Keech sprinted to the dying man, dropped to his knees, and yelled to the elders, "How do I use this thing?"

Doesn't Fear Thunder mimicked a downward stabbing motion.

"You want me to *stab* him?"

The old man repeated the gesture more vigorously.

Tearing his eyes away from the Shifter, Keech steadied the dagger's tip over Doyle's heart. The motion was so easy, a simple thrust.

Yet he couldn't act. He looked once more at the two elders. "What if this kills him?"

Duck cried, "Keech!"

A nightmarish rumble filled his ears, and Keech turned to see fangs flying straight toward his face. He tried to roll out of the way, but the Chamelia moved with unearthly speed, like a bobcat pouncing on a mouse. It smashed into him, driving him back into the sand.

The ferocious impact knocked the wind clean out of him. He tried to suck in a breath as darkness engulfed his vision, but nothing happened. He couldn't move and realized the Chamelia's full weight had fallen on his chest, pinning him on his back. Despite the lack of air, a feral odor—earthy and mammalian—filled his nostrils.

He pushed against the Chamelia's body. At first, he thought his own strength was lifting it, but then he realized the creature was rising. Keech's lungs opened. Warm air flowed in, relaxing his muscles. Then his vision returned, and he saw Duck kicking at the Shifter.

The Chamelia raised up on its hind legs and towered over the girl. At first, Keech thought it was preparing to bite into her, but then he noticed the bone handle of the Fang sticking out of the beast's rib cage. The creature stumbled back a step and wagged its head, as if trying to clear a patch of dizziness. A clawed hand reached up, plucked the dagger out of its side, and dropped the relic onto the sand.

The Reverend's brand evaporated from the Chamelia's forehead, leaving an unmarred hide of black scales. The creature groaned.

"What's happening to it?" Duck asked.

Staggering, the Chamelia shifted before their eyes. Barbed quills shrunk like melting candles across the creature's shoulders. The murky scales faded into pink flesh, and short reddish hair sprouted from its pores. The beast's long claws receded into stubby paws, and its body diminished till it resembled a gaunt wolf. The animal collapsed onto its side.

"Did the Fang kill it?" Duck asked.

"It's still breathing." Keech leaned closer. "And the Devil's mark is gone."

Duck grabbed the bone dagger and gave its markings a curious look.

Movement up the beach caught his eye. John Wesley emerged from a cluster of boulders, looking more grotesque than ever. Cutter rode beside him atop Chantico, while Quinn and Strong Heart marched along on Saint Peter. They looked exhausted as they entered the cove but sprang to attention when they saw the Chamelia on the ground.

"Did that thing finally die?" Cutter asked.

"Not yet," Duck said.

The moment Quinn and Strong Heart dismounted, Saint Peter trotted over to Doyle's side, as if the Kelpie knew the Ranger's last moments were upon him. John Wesley peered at his father from the shadows of the cove, but he kept his distance from the group.

Doyle's bone-white flesh teemed with purple veins, and his chest hardly moved. "I hope we're not too late," Keech said, holding his hand out to Duck.

Before she could hand him the relic, Big Ben Loving stepped out of the bonfire.

Duck spun to face the brute, but the man was already swinging a fist. His knuckles caught her across the chin, and she flew back, the dagger sailing from her hand.

Keech scrambled for the Fang, but Big Ben scooped up the relic.

"Now, where was I?" The outlaw straightened, his shoulders still wrapped in black netting, and waved a finger across the beach.

As Strong Heart and the other boys dashed across the cove, a shrieking wall of sand stopped them in their tracks. The blockade hovered in place, holding the kids back.

The Fang held loosely in his broken hand, Big Ben started marching back toward the bending tree, dragging his leg with each step.

Duck pushed up to one elbow and yelled, "Keech, Saint Peter!"

Keech glanced over at the Kelpie. He saw the Ranger's coil of rope hanging from the horse's saddle and realized what he needed to do. Grunting in pain, he stumbled to the stirrup, mounted Saint Peter, grabbed Doyle's lariat, and tied the rope to the horn. At the other end, he quickly cinched a honda knot and began spinning the lasso. "Let's get him!" he yelled, and Saint Peter started toward the outlaw.

Although the screaming sand barrier held back the others, the magic to sustain it appeared to require Big Ben's full attention. He was not ready for when Keech let the lasso fly. The loop landed around the brute's shoulders, and Keech pulled on the cord.

Big Ben's face twisted with rage. "I'll break you in half."

Keech kicked Saint Peter's sides, and the Kelpie shot like a bullet from the cove, galloping straight for the open water. The rope yanked Big Ben off his feet. A startled curse tumbled from his mouth.

"Enjoy the ride!" Keech called back.

The moment Saint Peter's hooves reached the surf, the animal caught his wind. The Kelpie lowered his head and pinned his ears back. Then they were truly flying. A spirited wind slapped Keech in the face, thumping his hat off his head, and he cried out from pure exhilaration. He had never felt such speed—not on Hector, not even on Felix.

They bolted over the rolling waves, cutting through the sun's rays and surf. Behind them, Big Ben writhed, trying to free himself. He bellowed curses at Keech, bouncing heavily under the water, only to spring back up, like a stunned fish captured by a line.

Once the shoreline had become a distant crease on the horizon, Keech hauled back on the reins. Saint Peter stopped on top of the water, bobbing gently on the white foam. Keech glanced back to search for signs of the outlaw.

The rope was still stretched taut, running down into the depths.

A monstrous *Ack!* echoed like a scream over the water. Keech looked up to see the Reverend's crow hovering high above.

"Big Ben's done for!" Keech called to Rose. "We're coming for you next!"

The crow circled, watching.

Suddenly, Keech remembered the Fang. Big Ben had been holding the dagger when the lasso had caught him. If the outlaw drowned, they would lose the relic. For an instant, Keech considered allowing the Fang to sink, forever lost, but then he remembered Doyle dying on the beach and knew he had to save the man for John Wesley.

"I have to go fetch the Fang," Keech told Saint Peter. "Please don't run off."

The Kelpie blustered as though he understood.

Steeling himself, Keech took a deep breath and dived off the stallion's back.

The moment he struck water, he reached for the rope. Holding on tightly, he moved hand over hand down the cord, pulling himself farther down into the depths. He had figured the ocean would feel like a cold casket, but the water was warm and pleasant on his face, filled with a sunshine that turned his air bubbles into jewels.

Big Ben loomed into his view. Still bound at the end of the lariat, the outlaw floated motionless in the brine, his eyes closed. Dead, at last.

One hand still holding the line, Keech kicked his feet to drive him down into the darker water, away from the sunlight. Each stroke of his arm sent sparks of pain through his body, and holding his breath made his head pound.

Big Ben still gripped the Fang in his hand, but his fingers were busted and loose. Swimming closer, Keech grabbed for the ancient relic.

In the waters' depths, he had misjudged the trajectory, and the bone edge sliced the skin across Keech's palm. He flinched back. He expected to see blood drift in the water, but instead he felt a strange warmth billow through his body. The spike of pain where Big Ben had struck his rib cage disappeared in a blink, and the dull ache surging through his muscles evaporated.

Even more curiously, Keech felt the old injuries from days past— the bruises and cuts endured while fighting the Chamelia, even the scars Bad Whiskey had left behind—dissolve from his body.

He felt *whole*.

Reinvigorated, Keech seized Big Ben's thumb and pulled it back, releasing the dead man's grip on the Fang. The dagger floated free, and he snatched the bone handle. Spinning around, he pushed off the outlaw's lifeless body, aiming for the lariat to pull himself back up.

As he turned, something clutched his boot, and he jerked to a stop.

He looked back and saw that Big Ben's eyes had shot open and that the brute had grabbed hold of his heel. He was still very much alive.

Keech kicked at the reaching arm, but the outlaw's grip held like a vise. He looked up to the surface, his lungs screaming for air. He jerked his foot again but couldn't break free. Panic crashed over his mind as Big Ben's weight began dragging him down. Keech labored for the rope, but when his hand found the lariat, he discovered the line had gone slack. Saint Peter must've ignored Keech's request and returned to his dying master. The waters around Keech darkened further as he sank.

The edges of Keech's vision closed in. He recalled the dream of drowning, hearing Sam's voice in the deep, while he was unconscious in Friendly's prison. *It's okay, Keech*, Sam had said from the darkness. *Remember what Pa taught us about fear.*

Keech wondered if that dream had been a premonition of this moment.

Sam's voice called to him now. *Who are you, my brother?*

I am the Wolf, he wanted to answer.

Suddenly, a warm hand wrapped around his arm. Keech found himself staring into the kind face of a man, his body and eyes the color of deep emerald. Raven-black hair drifted around the fellow's head. The stranger tugged, and Big Ben's grip on his boot slipped free.

Together they ascended, letting Big Ben vanish below them.

The brilliant light of day engulfed Keech's face. He sucked in mouthfuls of air, distantly aware that the man was holding him above water. The fellow didn't speak, only watched as Keech filled his lungs.

Keech lifted his hand, relieved to see he still held the Fang. He slipped the relic into his coat pocket.

When Keech finally found enough breath to speak, he asked, "Who are you?"

The stranger smiled, his emerald eyes sparkling, then slipped back under the waves.

A mound rose beneath Keech's feet, lifting him from the water. He glanced down and found himself seated on Saint Peter.

"That was you, wasn't it?" he said, amazed. "You're a shape-shifter."

The steed simply grunted.

Then he remembered Doyle lying in the cove. Frantic, he said, "Take us back. If we hurry, we can save the Ranger."

Saint Peter nickered and started back to shore. Soon they were galloping at full speed. As they approached the cove, Duck and Quinn ran to the edge of the water.

The moment he reached land, Duck asked, "Big Ben?"

Sliding off the Kelpie, Keech said, "He's gone. Sunk to the bottom of the ocean."

The look of gratitude in Duck's eyes told a lifetime of

tales—stories of her home, her family, her adventures with Nat—and months of fear and isolation drained from her soul.

He put a hand on her shoulder. "It's over."

Quinn held out Keech's bowler hat to him. "Here. You dropped this in the water. If you keep losing it, we may have to nail it down."

"Thanks," Keech said, and put the sea-drenched hat back on.

Nearby, Strong Heart waited beside the elders, who looked shaken but healthy. Strong Bones had returned to the cove and sat in the sand, his arm wrapped in a makeshift sling. Lying on the ground, the creature that had once been the Chamelia looked even smaller than before, more like a shaggy dog. It rested on its side, its limbs drawn together, and John Wesley crouched next to it on wolfish hind legs. Keech was surprised to see him caressing the beast's fur, as if he were touching a docile pet, but John's eyes were fixed on his father. Cutter lingered a few steps away, unwilling to separate from his friend.

Wishing to offer some hope, Keech held the Fang of Barachiel up for all to see.

Cutter said, "You best hurry, Blackwood."

Keech dashed over to Doyle's side. The man looked done for. His skin had drained of all color, and Keech feared he was too late. Taking a deep breath, he plunged the Fang into the Enforcer's chest, then yanked it back out with a small cry.

All was still for a moment—then Doyle's body shuddered. Violent tremors shook his arms and legs. Then the shaking faded to twinges.

"Papa?" John whispered.

Keech stepped away, clearing a path.

The bonfire cast a vermilion light on John Wesley's grotesque face as he crept forward to crouch at Doyle's side. As his hand touched the man's skin, John shifted, the animal snout pulling back into a human nose, the long quills receding into short thorns. Though black scales still dappled his flesh, he looked like John Wesley again.

The boy said nothing; he merely watched his father rest. Keech and the other young riders gathered closer, and Cutter knelt and put a hand on the Ranger's chest.

"His breathing's stronger. I think this old *vaquero*'s gonna make it."

They all looked at the Fang in Keech's hand, their faces filled with a kind of veneration.

Buffalo Woman shuffled toward him, her long, shaggy robe trailing behind her. She reached and took the Fang from Keech and placed it carefully inside her pelt. Then, glancing up at the bonfire, she began to speak in Osage.

Strong Heart translated. "She says the Lair of the Wolf is dying." The girl looked at the elders with concern but continued. "She wants to know what happened inside the fire."

The bonfire was indeed diminishing. The flames were collapsing, little by little, no longer fueled by the power that had given them breath. "Big Ben broke the Fang's protection," Keech said sadly. "He stuck his hand into the ball of light, and it melted away."

He wanted to explain more—wanted to tell them about Saint Peter, and how the Kelpie had transformed in the water—but suddenly Doyle sat straight up, his face shimmering with sweat.

John Wesley staggered over and embraced the man. Keech heard Doyle murmur against John Wesley's face. "My boy. Oh, John, my boy. I'm so sorry for everything."

Across the beach, the other Protectors were gathering all the horses. Two of the men waited beside the body of Whipping Feather, who had fallen to the Chamelia.

"Keech, we're being watched." Quinn pointed at the sky.

The Reverend's crow continued to circle above the cove. Sending back news, no doubt, of Big Ben's defeat. Keech was glad that Rose had seen his disciples fail yet again. Whatever wicked plan their enemy was forging in the Palace of the Thunders, the Lost Causes had once again stood in the way and been victorious.

Keech felt confidence surge through him. The last few days had been impossibly challenging. They had lost friends, allies; worst of all, Duck had lost her brother, and the Protectors had lost their colleague. Yet they had all continued to stand together, never giving up even when all had been hopeless.

As Keech contemplated his admiration for the team, he felt a clarity of thought galvanize his mind. Each breath felt clean, purified by the Fang. At his core, a vibrational warmth bloomed to life. Around him, he could sense the rhythms of the coast, the pulse of the ocean waves. He saw the world as pure.

Except a dark blight glided through these patterns, like a tick dug into his leg, a parasite that corrupted the natural flow. With his eyes closed, Keech lifted his hand and pointed at the vermin. He sensed the crow sliding across the sky and followed it.

Though he couldn't see it with his eyes, Keech knew he was tracking the Reverend's crow without the slightest waver. *Break the crocodile's teeth.* Then he whispered a single word.

"Bang."

The creature exploded in the sky.

CHAPTER 34
WHEN THE DOOR CLOSES

Edgar Doyle stood at the restless brim of the western ocean, his bare feet submerged in the frothy water. He stared out at the steadily climbing sun, hands propped on his hips. When Keech approached and stood beside him, the Ranger doffed his hat. "Hello, Mr. Blackwood."

"How's the leg?"

Doyle peered down at the ragged tear in his trousers. "Right as rain. The Fang is a powerful tool." He smiled. "Too bad it didn't heal my trousers, though."

"The elders told us it wouldn't cure John Wesley."

The Ranger glanced back toward the cove, where John Wesley and Cutter were keeping watch over the small, gangly Shifter. "They're right. John will never be the same. He's not suffering a sickness. What's happened to my boy is a kind of rebirth."

Keech recalled Buffalo Woman's words. *Your friend has become a new form. There is no remedy, only acceptance.* He didn't know whether to feel a profound sadness for John Wesley or a curious excitement for the boy's new abilities.

"One thing I've been wondering," Keech said. "The amulet shards. They never worked on the Chamelia. Why is that?"

"The silver never worked because the Prime didn't create the beast," Doyle said. "Rules of magic can be chaotic, but they are still rules. The shards only work against creatures of the Prime."

Keech scratched his head. "But Big Ben touched the shard at one point and was unhurt. Back in Wisdom. Wasn't he a creature of the Prime?"

"No. Big Ben was only a man, born of natural means. His powers came from the Prime, sure enough, but the Reverend kept him charged, always feeding him energy the way a bird feeds her young."

Keech slowly nodded, realizing that Big Ben had most likely brought about his own undoing by facing the Protectors and burning through his powers when he snuffed out the bonfire.

The Ranger pointed to the blue-gray sky. "I saw what you did to Rose's crow. Impressive. You found your focus."

"I reckon the crocodile has one less tooth," Keech said.

Doyle chuckled. "You know, not even your father, Bill, could do that. Nor Isaiah. You have a true gift for tapping the energies. I expect you *all* do. Bennett's daughter, Mr. Revels, even your friend Cutter, though he doesn't know it. If you draw from one another and listen to the tune of the world, you can conquer whatever lies in your path."

"We'll be okay," Keech said. "What about you? Will you take John Wesley back to your home and rebury Eliza? John needs his family whole again. His ma is gone. He needs to know his pa is with him."

Doyle stared across the glistening sweep of the ocean. After a time, he wiped a tear from his eye. "You're right. He does need his family whole again."

Somewhere farther up the coast, seagulls chirped and squawked at the tide—a melody Keech had never heard before. He wondered at the myriad voices the world contained.

Doyle drew out his pocket watch and looked at the time. "It's past ten in the morning. We should get back to Kansas."

Back at the cove, Buffalo Woman called out to everyone. The elders were summoning the company for a talk. Keech waited for Doyle to slip back into his moccasins, but the Ranger only stood in the water.

"You're not coming?"

"This is *your* discussion, Mr. Blackwood. My fellow Enforcers and I have played our part. We caused a lot of pain in our time. I tried to turn my back on that life when I stopped using the name Red Jeffreys, but I lost their trust when I broke my Oath of Memory. The elders will want to speak only to you. Now go. Learn what you need to learn."

The two elders gathered everyone into a close circle next to the bonfire, whose towering flames were quickly fading. Two of the Protectors, Big Moon and Yellow Hawk, remained apart from the others, standing near the body of their fallen brother, Whipping Feather. The rest stood next to their ponies, nursing small cuts and bruises. John Wesley didn't want to leave the side of the Chamelia, which had withered down to a shivering coyote. Whatever was happening to the creature, it seemed helpless now. The beast couldn't even stand, much less attack.

Holding the Fang of Barachiel on her palm, Buffalo Woman began to speak, occasionally gesturing to the ill-fated blaze behind her. Though Keech couldn't understand most of her words, he could hear a mixture of sadness and consolation in the woman's voice. When Keech looked to Strong Heart for the translation, she explained that when Big Ben seized the Fang, he destroyed the heart of the bonfire, the enchanted core that the Enforcers themselves had created to protect the artifact.

Keech's cheeks flushed with shame. "I'm sorry. I tried to stop him, but I couldn't."

"This ain't your fault," Duck said. "It's *Rose's*."

"Can't somebody just fix it?" Quinn asked. "Throw a few more logs on to stoke the cinders?"

Strong Heart relayed the question, and when Buffalo Woman answered, the girl said to the young riders, "Understand, it was never ours to fix. The elders were only guarding the dagger, just as the Protectors defended the Crossing."

The girl concluded by saying that the elders' long mission to watch over the Fang on this sacred ground was complete. There was no longer any reason to remain on the Oregon Coast. The elders and Protectors would return to their homes and families in the Osage territories.

"What about the Fang?" asked John Wesley. "Will you take it back to Kansas?"

To answer his question, Buffalo Woman offered the Fang to Keech. "You have all proved yourselves," she said, again surprising him by speaking in English. "We want you to accept this. Protect it, as we have."

"No." Keech shook his head. "We can't take that. We're not strong enough." He looked to the Protectors for some kind of backup, but not even Strong Heart or Strong Bones debated.

"You have everything you need to protect the Fang," Buffalo Woman said.

Duck looked at the dagger like someone pondering a difficult puzzle. "We should try. The Osage have been protecting it for so long. They've done their part. Now it's our turn."

"It healed Papa from his curse wound," John Wesley added.

"Yeah, but it can't heal you," Cutter said.

"Maybe Duck's right. Maybe we should try," Quinn said.

"Are we sure?" Keech asked.

They all looked at one another, silent, till Cutter shrugged. "You heard the woman. We've proved ourselves."

Keech's hand quivered when he took the relic from Buffalo Woman. There was undoubtable danger in accepting such an object, but that had never stopped the Lost Causes. Finally, he nodded. "We'll keep it safe."

Buffalo Woman said something else, her face turning toward the mountains, disquiet slipping across her features. When the gang looked to Strong Heart for the interpretation, the girl frowned gravely as she mulled over the elder's words.

"Well?" said Duck. "What'd she say?"

Strong Heart shook her head. "She says that to protect the Fang, you must also travel to a place in the Western mountains."

A cold, snail-like foreboding crawled up Keech's spine when he heard Strong Heart's translation. He remembered their earlier conversation about the three sites of power. *There's another place deep in the mountains of the West, and yet another to the north, the one you call the Palace.*

"Buffalo Woman says you must go to the House of *Mah-shchee"-kah*," the girl continued.

"What's that mean?" asked Cutter.

"It means the House of the Rabbit," Keech said—and recalled Sam's voice again: *I'm the Rabbit, remember? I can run just as fast in bare feet....*

Strong Heart went on with Buffalo Woman's message. "You must go to the House of the Rabbit and look for the Key."

"The Key!" said Quinn. "That's what Doyle mentioned back on the prairie! He said the Enforcers had to hide the other artifacts, *like the Key.*"

"Sounds like we've got another mission," Keech said. He began to wonder if *this* had been Milos Horner's intention when he had asked the Lost Causes to pursue a man named McCarty.

Buffalo Woman spoke in English again. "The bonfire is dying," she said, pointing back to the sputtering blaze. "The House of the Rabbit will be next to fall. You must hurry to find it first and take the Key. *The Scorpion must not find it.*" She spoke the rest in Osage.

Strong Heart concluded for her. "If the Scorpion finds the Key, she says, the land will lose the sun."

The darkest shiver Keech had ever felt cascaded down his spine.

The elders' conversation turned to the gateway, the mysterious door of light that unlocked Bonfire Crossing. They had declared that the door should forever shut so that Rose or any other monsters like him could never infiltrate the powerful coastline again.

"Now we go home," Buffalo Woman said, and the circle dispersed.

The young riders and Doyle gathered their horses. With the Fang of Barachiel tucked in a deerskin sheath that Strong Bones had given him, Keech followed the Protectors and his weary trailmates back over the beach and to the bent cedar tree.

There had been a brief discussion about the Chamelia, whether the feeble creature should accompany them or not, but John Wesley insisted that he wouldn't leave the beast. He scooped the coyote-thing into his arms and walked on foot behind his father and Saint Peter.

The two elders carried no belongings except for the buffalo robes on their backs, and the old pair never looked back at the dwindling bonfire. Once the company reached the bending tree, Strong Bones called out with a clear voice, "*Shoh^n-geh.*"

Brilliant light sparked between the cedar trunks as the door that spanned entire territories opened once more. The shimmering rift revealed a peaceful day on the other side. Through the flickers of impossible light, a snow-covered clearing appeared, illuminated by the bending tree's vibrant glow. A sparrow called from a nearby forest, and cottonwood limbs moaned in the wind.

The Protectors stepped through the door, carrying their fallen companion, Whipping Feather. Doyle and Cutter and Quinn crossed over next, then Duck with her brother's Fox Trotter on the lead rope.

Holding the weakened Chamelia in his arms, John Wesley asked, "You coming, Keech?"

"Right behind you."

As John stepped into the light with the Shifter, Keech gave the vast ocean, the beach, the crescent cove, and the dying bonfire one final look. "Well, Pa, we found the Fang," he said. "Now just guide us to this Key, and maybe we can finish Rose for good."

Only the delicate whistle of the sea breeze answered his plea.

Turning to the cedar tree, Keech let Hector guide him through the door of light. The salty wind faded from his nostrils; the swelling noise of the ocean surf died away. The warmth of Bonfire

Crossing vanished, replaced by the deep chill of a snow-dusted landscape.

The others were waiting for him in the white clearing, their coats pulled up against a frigid afternoon. Bracing against the cold, Keech guided Hector a few more steps and saw that he'd just emerged from a crooked box elder tree, shaped like a leaning V. It was not the basswood tree the young riders had opened to enter Bonfire Crossing. Their passage across the Territories had taken them somewhere new.

"Don't worry, we're still in Kansas," Quinn said. "Strong Heart said we landed about a mile away from a big buffalo run."

Reining her brown pony, Strong Heart smiled. "The Great Osage Trail. It follows the buffalo paths of the *Wah-zha-zhe*." She pointed to the south.

"Otherwise known as the Santa Fe Trail," Doyle said, riding up next to Keech. "Your posse is lucky, Mr. Blackwood. Though you're a great distance from where you first entered the gateway, the tree dropped you off near a major wagon route. You can follow it where you will. East to civilization, or west if you want."

Keech glanced around the Kansas landscape. The forest where the sparrow had been singing began a few yards to the north. The path itself—the Santa Fe Trail—was nowhere to be seen, but Quinn had said the route was only a mile or so from the tree.

"So what happens now?" asked Cutter.

"Now we seal the Crossing and go home," Strong Heart said.

Yellow Hawk and Big Moon helped the two elders down from their horses, and the old pair shuffled over to the moss opal stones planted around the tree. Strong Bones stepped on the third stone, kicking away layers of snow. Buffalo Woman called out, "Red Jeffreys. Come. This task belongs to you."

Doyle joined Strong Bones and the elders on the stones, and before Keech could ask why they needed Doyle, the Ranger began to speak a strange chant, different from the incantation he'd used in Wisdom. The sounds belonged to no language Keech had ever heard, and when Doyle was finished, a sudden wind kicked up, a chill rush that rattled the bending tree's curtain of light. Keech felt a vibration stiffen the cold air, the way a room thickens when all the doors shut at once. Then Strong Bones began to speak the Osage words for various animals, including *tseh* for buffalo, *weh-ts'-ah* for snake, *oh-pxoh^n* for elk, and finally *shoh^n-geh* for wolf.

A thunderous *crack* sounded between the illuminated trunks, and the distinct shape of the shadow wolf appeared inside the light. The animal's muzzle pointed skyward, as if howling to its unseen moon, and then the wolf leaped out of view. The dazzling light blinked out as the animal vanished, and the vibration in the air fell away.

The four attendants stepped off the stones.

"What just happened?" asked Cutter.

Returning to Saint Peter, Doyle said, "The magics of the world hold their own secret language. A long time ago, the Enforcers learned a special form connected to the Prime, and we used it to tap into Bonfire Crossing. But because Rose also knows the secret language, we knew we had to conceal the Fang's hideaway using another means."

"The elders allowed the Enforcers to use certain words as a way to hold the door closed," Strong Heart continued.

"You used words as *locks*," said Quinn, fascinated.

"More like camouflage," added Doyle. "The point is, no one will ever open Bonfire Crossing again, unless the place itself wills it."

Keech pondered the bending tree one last time, then turned to the elders, Buffalo Woman and Doesn't Fear Thunder. Both looked tired, the faces of people who look ready to see their old homes and acquaintances. "Thank you for your help," he said to them. "And thank you for being a friend to my fathers. They took a wrong path together, but in the end, they stood true. I'll do my best to honor them both."

Though the old pair said nothing in response, Keech saw what might have been appreciation on their faces. They raised their hands, palms out, to the young riders. Each of the kids returned the gesture.

Keech finally turned to Strong Bones, who had mounted back up and was swiveling his pony toward the east. *"Wah-hu Sah-kee,"* he said, using the man's Osage name. "I'm sorry we brought you and your friends such trouble. And I'm sorry about Whipping Feather."

Strong Bones returned a small nod. "I will tell his family you stood beside him." With that, he motioned for the company to begin riding, but then Quinn called out to Strong Heart, stopping them. The boy stammered at first, as though he'd forgotten what he wanted to say, but then he cleared his throat and spoke clearly. "I'm glad we met you, Strong Heart. I hope we cross paths again."

"Weh-wee-nah, Quinn Revels. Thank you for saving my life," the girl said.

Quinn peeled off his forage cap. "I hope you find your brother. I know what it feels like to miss somebody."

Strong Heart smiled, her round face framed by pale sunlight. "When I see him again, I'll tell Wandering Star that you fought with the Protectors and helped save the Fang."

Keech's heart tumbled at the words. He prayed he had just heard wrong. "Strong Heart, what name did you say?"

She gave him a puzzled look. "In my language, I call him *Mee-kah-k'-eh Moi^n*. In English, you would say—"

"Wandering Star," Edgar Doyle finished, his mouth hinging open.

Sudden worry twisted Strong Heart's features. "You know my brother?"

The Enforcer's story echoed in Keech's mind: *His name was Wandering Star. He was a nice young man, smart and funny. He'd spent much of his youth training with his uncle to be a Protector of the Crossing.*

The other young riders had fallen into their own silent daze.

"Strong Heart, I'm afraid your brother is gone," Keech said. "He died in a cave in Missouri helping the Enforcer. That's why you know Edgar Doyle. Because he came to your encampment looking for the Fang."

"And my brother rode after him," Strong Heart finished, her face darkening. "But how do you know he's gone?"

"We saw him." Keech hated to speak the words, but there was nothing for it. "We were passing through a cave, and we stumbled upon his body."

Strong Heart asked Doyle, "Is this true?"

Doyle's gaze didn't budge from Saint Peter's reins. "I'm afraid so. I led Wandering Star to his doom. I didn't know he was your brother. If I'd known, I would've told you the moment I saw you. I'm sorry."

Keech could tell the news had drained the girl's remaining strength. A tear plummeted down her cheek, and she slumped heavily on the saddle. "I feared as much."

"I'm sorry, Strong Heart," said Keech. "What will you do now? I mean, now that you know?"

Strong Heart took a slow, measured breath, even as the tears fell. "I will mourn for Wandering Star. I'll ask *Wah-kah"-dah* to guide his spirit and give him peace."

Saying no more, the girl reined her pony to the east. The Protectors opened their ranks, and she slipped in among them. Buffalo Woman murmured something to her, and the Osage troop began to ride.

They didn't reach ten paces before Duck called out, "Strong Heart, wait!"

The group paused, and Strong Heart looked back, wiping her face.

Still gripping the rope that led Nat's mare, Duck shuffled over the snow and reined Irving to a halt. Sally fell behind them, her saddle empty, her reins tied loosely to the horn. Duck was silent at first, her breath fogging around her face, and the hand holding Sally's rope quivered. Finally, she said, "I lost my brother, too. He died saving my life. I never expected I'd have to say goodbye—I thought he'd be with me forever—but that's not the way it turned out."

Strong Heart looked at the girl with a solemn face.

Taking a deep breath, Duck pulled at Sally's lead rope. When the mare stepped next to Irving, Duck put a hand on the horse's neck. She murmured a few quiet words to the Fox Trotter, then held the rope out to Strong Heart.

"Please take her, and give her a good home."

Strong Heart's hand reached for the rope—but then she hesitated and glanced back at her uncle. With a gentle nudge of the reins,

Strong Bones walked his pony closer and took Sally's rope. He looked closely at the Fox Trotter then said to Duck, "This is one of your best horses. When you offer a horse, it is a good gift. *Weh-wee-nah.*"

Tears tumbled from Duck's eyes. She tried to speak, but her breath tangled in her throat and the words faltered. She watched as Strong Bones handed the rope to his niece, who nodded her appreciation and drew Sally into their fold. The mare resisted at first, glancing back at Irving as though confused, but when the Protectors began to move, the Fox Trotter went along.

"Goodbye," Duck said to the pony.

Strong Heart spoke one last thing to the young riders. "*Wah-Shka^n*," she said, then turned and didn't look back again.

"I wonder what that meant," said Quinn.

Keech knew. It was a phrase that Pa Abner had once passed on to the orphans, having learned it from his Osage friends. "It means do your best, never quit, and *be fearless.*"

CHAPTER 35
THE SHIFTER'S FAREWELL

Inside the snowy clearing, Doyle worked on a campfire while Keech and Duck and Quinn unsaddled the ponies. A few yards from the camp, John Wesley waited beside the sleeping Chamelia. Cutter sat close by, using his long blade to engrave words onto a flat piece of oak timber he'd found near the bending tree.

Leaving Duck and Quinn with the horses, Keech approached John Wesley, moving slowly so as not to spook the Shifter. The creature's new appearance surprised him. Before leaving Bonfire Crossing, the Chamelia had shifted down to something like a coyote; here in the clearing, it had changed yet again, this time resembling a slick cougar. It was as if the stab of the Fang had not only severed Big Ben's hold but had also rendered the beast uncertain of its own true form.

Speaking softly, Keech asked, "Hey, John, how are you holding up?"

"Okay, I reckon."

"Are you sure that thing ain't dangerous?"

John Wesley shook his head. "She's sleeping." He stretched out a clawed hand and patted the side of the Shifter. "Don't fret none about her."

"That ain't so easy for me, John. I've seen what that thing can do."

"No, you saw what the Devil's mark can do."

A realization dawned on Keech. If he were going to trust his friend, he would have to allow him to lead the way with the Chamelia. "Fair enough," he said. He turned to head back to the fire, then stopped. "Hey, John?"

"Yeah?"

"It's good to have you back."

John Wesley didn't answer, instead turning his attention back to the creature.

Back at the campfire, Duck, Quinn, and Doyle had placed their saddles on the ground and kicked off their boots. They leaned against the seats, warming the bottoms of their feet. Keech joined them, and they shared a few rounds of tongue twisters to pass the time. After Quinn stumped him with *Three twigs twined tightly*, Keech returned his gaze to John Wesley. It concerned him how John had connected to the beast. He told the others about his conversation and how protective their friend had become of the creature since Bonfire Crossing.

"She?" Quinn grimaced. "That thing's a girl?"

"That's what John Wesley said, but I don't know how he figures that. He's been acting strange since the Fang took away Rose's brand and the Chamelia passed out."

Duck gazed at the fire. "He sits apart from us now."

Holding a bundle of sticks, Doyle walked up to the campfire. "Give my boy time. He's trying to figure out his new place in the world."

After the campfire had grown comfortably warm, the young riders sagged against their saddles, too sleepy for tongue twisters. Not far away, Cutter's knife still scratched on the wooden plank.

Quinn yawned. "I'm so tired I could sleep for days."

"Me too. I just might." Keech put his bowler hat over his eyes.

After a silence, Duck said, "Do y'all think Strong Heart will be okay?"

"She's a strong person. I think she will," Quinn said.

Keech knew that Strong Heart would undergo months of mourning rituals, a full year's worth in most cases. She would partake in the ceremonies that signified the loss and vindication of a loved one. Keech hated that he had given her the bad news about Wandering Star, but she was better off knowing than constantly hunting for him and wondering.

Keech felt his body slipping off to sleep. He closed his eyes thinking about Strong Heart, John Wesley, and the Shifter, and so he didn't quite hear the words that Cutter suddenly shouted.

He bolted upright. "What's going on?"

"It's the Shifter!" Duck said.

Slipping back into his boots, Keech ran over to John Wesley and saw that the boy had backed away from the Chamelia, which was twisting and snarling in the snow. The creature's hide rippled, the fur retracting and a sea of thorns sprouting across its back.

"That *demonio*'s changing again!" Cutter shouted. He circled nearby, lifting his knife by the blade so he could lob it at the beast.

Duck and Quinn dashed over. Doyle ran up with one fist raised over his head, the same way he'd looked in Wisdom when preparing to unleash a cyclone.

John Wesley grumbled at the creature, but Keech thought the noise sounded more dejected than fearful.

Doyle said, "Move back, John."

When John Wesley swiveled to face his father, his eyes turned a vicious red again. The boy's lips pulled back into a sneer. "Don't come any closer!"

"Okay." Keech held up his hands. "We're not gonna hurt it."

The Shifter's eyes darted back and forth as though searching for the best escape. It took a few steps toward the wood line, but then it turned back and locked its yellow reptilian eyes on John Wesley.

John said, "Go!"

The Shifter barked, a sound between a hound's call and a bobcat's roar, and it turned on wide paws and bounded away toward the forest. Within seconds, the creature had disappeared into the brush.

"Is it gone?" Cutter asked.

"No. I can feel her waiting," John Wesley said.

"What do you mean, son?" Concern scratched at Doyle's voice.

"I'm like her now. A beast." John Wesley lifted a hand and regarded the hooked claws at the end of each finger. "I ain't a person no more. Look at me."

"That's fool talk," Cutter said.

"No, Cut, it's true." John Wesley pointed back to the tree line. "Once upon a time, she was a person, too. She wasn't always like that, but she got changed. Same thing that's happened to me. I ain't *me* no more."

"You're still my son," Doyle said.

Sorrow cut across John Wesley's features, but instead of tears, his melancholy intensified the small shifts happening across his body. Quills pushed out from his shoulders, and with a sudden terrible *crack*, his knees popped backward so that he was hunched on canine legs.

"John, calm down," Keech said. "I think your emotions are making you shift."

When John Wesley spoke again, hundreds of needlepoint fangs slurred his words. "I have to go with her. She can teach me how to control this."

Cutter reached out to him. "I can help you, *amigo*. Stay with us. We've been through this, *hermano*. Your place is with us. With *me*. We're partners."

"I can't, Cut." John Wesley looked back at the woods where the Chamelia lurked. "I feel her calling me. I belong with my own kind."

"John, my boy," Doyle said, his voice pleading. "You belong beside your father. Come with me. I'll take you home."

John Wesley's head tilted at the man. "That's just it, Papa. We ain't *got* a home no more. You took that away when you stole Eliza and left." He backed a step away from the camp.

"Wait, son. Don't," the Ranger begged.

Looking frantic, Cutter reached into his coat and pulled out John Wesley's straw hat. Keech had forgotten that the boy was carrying it. "Take this," Cutter said, and tossed the hat to his trailmate. It landed in the snow between John Wesley's feet. A single tear slid down Cutter's cheek. "Remember, no matter where you go, you're one of us. You're a *Lost Cause*."

John Wesley stared at the hat on the ground but didn't pick it up. Turning to peer at the woodland, John Wesley moaned a deep, rattling sigh. Then he glanced back at his father, at Cutter, at all the young riders. "I'm gonna go find the Chamelia now," he said. "Goodbye."

He bolted from the camp toward the forest, leaving his torn hat to sit in the snow.

"John, no!" Cutter bellowed, chasing after him. "Come back!"

John Wesley kept running. A moment later, the woods enveloped him, and he was gone.

Later that afternoon, the young riders warmed themselves by the campfire, nestling deep in their blankets and letting the crackle of firewood be their only conversation. The horses slept in a tight standing circle, their reins tied off to the boughs of the now-defunct bending tree. Doyle had taken out his leatherbound journal and was silently scribbling on a page, while Duck and Quinn leaned against each other, staring into the fire.

For a long while after John Wesley had run away, Cutter had paced the edges of the forest, calling his friend's name. Now he adjusted Chantico's saddle and mounted up, the plank of wood on which he'd been carving tucked under his arm. When Keech asked him where he was headed, Cutter simply said, "The woods. Not far."

"You should stay close," Keech said. "The crows may be about."

"I can't stay at this camp, Blackwood. I need to be alone for a bit."

Keech frowned. "You won't find him, Cut. He's long gone."

"I won't go looking. I just need to think."

Spurring Chantico, Cutter trotted away from camp, out of the clearing and into the forest. Keech watched the boy disappear in the trees.

Before long, Keech drifted once more into sleep. He dreamed of the Missouri wilderness and Pa Abner's training circle. Sam sat next to him by the campfire, and Pa was giving his lecture on trust and wisdom and the rules of alliance. As they listened to his lesson, Pa walked to the woodpile and retrieved a fresh stick for the fire.

Look at this log, boys. . . .

As he dreamed, Keech shifted on his bedroll. From his deep sleep, he thought he heard small noises—the shuffle of feet in snow, the crack of a twig—but the sounds were not threatening, so he continued sleeping and dreaming of Pa.

On the outside the wood appears to be dry enough, like all the others in the pile. And we desire warmth, so we might be tempted to accept any fuel that promises a good heat. But how do we know the truth of the log? We place it in the fire, test its intent. If the log is our friend, the wood burns clean and gives us heat. If the log is our enemy, moisture hidden inside the wood stifles the burning. . . .

CHAPTER 36

AMICO FIDELI

"And fills our eyes with smoke."

Keech sat upright, realizing he'd spoken Pa's words aloud. The campfire in the clearing had burned down to gray dust, with the smallest hints of cinder beneath. Out of habit, Keech reached under his shirt to touch his charm—the *Ranger's* charm, actually, but now his.

The shard was missing.

Startled, he patted down his body and searched through his bedding. As he rummaged, he called out, "Everyone, wake up! It's gone."

"What's gone?" Quinn's tired voice answered.

"Doyle's pendant." Keech glanced around the campsite. He saw Duck sitting up, quickly alert, and Quinn rubbing sleep out of his eyes. The spot on the ground where Doyle had been resting was vacant. All that remained was the man's blanket, neatly folded on the dead grass. At the bending tree, the ponies stood tied off to the boughs, their heads drooped in slumber.

There was no sign of Saint Peter.

"Where's the Ranger?" Duck asked.

"Good question." Keech pulled on his boots. He was careful not to move. He wanted to read the clearing. He looked at the first yellow rays of day breaking over the horizon and realized they had slept for more than twelve hours. A light snow from the night before coated the camp, but there were no horse tracks leading out. Keech did notice the faintest indication of moccasin prints near their bedding, but the fresh snow had filled most of the divots.

"I can't believe we slept so long," Duck said.

"We needed it," Keech replied, but still he wanted to kick himself. After days of hard riding and brutal fighting, they had all been so exhausted that they could have slept through the Siege of Fort Texas and not stirred.

"Where's Cutter?" said Quinn.

Keech peered past the clearing. "Still in the woods, I reckon. He wanted to be alone."

"But it's been twelve hours," Quinn pointed out. "Shouldn't he be back?"

"Fellas, I think we got a problem," Duck said. She had begun patting her own coat, and now panic cascaded across her features. She searched through her blanket. When she looked up, her face was ashen. "My charm's gone, too."

Uneasiness whittled its way into Keech's gut. He reached into his coat pocket and felt for Strong Bones's deerskin sheath. His fingers wrapped around a blade hilt, and for a second, he breathed in relief. Then he realized the hilt's texture was all wrong. He pulled the blade out of his pocket and looked at it. It wasn't the Fang of Barachiel.

It was Doyle's knife.

"No!" Keech yelled.

The trio scoured the campsite for any sign of the two missing shards or the bone dagger. When nothing turned up, Duck threw up her hands. "He stole everything."

"No way," Quinn said. "He wouldn't do that."

Except Keech knew he would. Doyle had made it clear that nothing mattered more to him than his family. *I went out of my mind with grief*, the man had told them while sharing the story of Eliza's death. *My wife, Gerty, and John Wesley wanted to mourn and move on. I couldn't.*

"I'd wager he decided on this plan when John Wesley went off into the woods," Keech said. "He had no more family left to lose. He knew when we went to sleep that we'd be easy pickings."

"But why ditch us?" Quinn asked. "Why not take us with him?"

"Because we'd try to stop him," Duck answered. "He knew we'd never go along with a scheme to resurrect his daughter."

"And since Saint Peter never leaves tracks, I reckon we've got no way of finding him," Keech said.

Stomping over to the spot where Doyle had slept, Duck kicked at the abandoned blanket with a furious shout. A small cloth bag tumbled out of the folds. "What's that?"

Keech snatched up the bag, hearing something jangle. When he opened it, he saw no relics, only a small book and a few coins.

The book was Doyle's leatherbound journal, the one he had scrawled in while investigating the bent sugar maple near the Kansas River. A blue ribbon marker lay tucked inside, along with Doyle's pencil. Keech held the journal up for Duck and Quinn to see, then flipped through the pages. Doyle had scribbled hundreds of entries, each one beginning with the date.

When Keech reached the blue ribbon, he noticed that the Ranger had scrawled a message to the young riders:

Lost Causes,

I am sorry that you're awakening to betrayal. I never intended to double-cross you, nor to put you in harm's way for the sake of my gain. I leave you this journal, my life's record, so that you may learn from it and hopefully understand where I came from. I no longer need its reminders. An Enforcer's past holds too much torment.

Take this money to the nearest town. Buy feed for the horses and proper gear. Then head home. Do not consider hunting me. You will only find more pain.

Be well and live on,

E. D.

Glancing again at the coins inside the bag, Keech was taken aback when he realized he was looking at a handful of silver dollars, the kind of coin he had only heard about in Pa's study.

Duck and Quinn squeezed in to read the message.

"Home?" said Quinn. "We *can't* go home. We ain't *got* homes."

Duck pointed to the journal. "There's something on the next page."

Keech flipped the page over. Scribbled at the bottom was a final note before the rest of the pages in the book fell blank:

My family will be whole again.

Keech looked at the note with a mixture of sorrow and frustration. His oceanside conversation with Doyle at Bonfire Crossing replayed in his mind. *John needs his family whole again*, Keech had said. *His ma is gone. He needs to know his pa is with him.*

You're right, Doyle had answered. *He does need his family whole again.*

Keech slammed the journal shut and tossed it back into the bag. "We better round up Cutter and have a meeting."

Quinn slipped on his forage cap. "I'll fetch him." He scurried off to the forest where Cutter had ridden off alone.

While they waited, Keech and Duck rounded up their gear. They didn't speak, but Duck occasionally touched the place in her coat where her father's pendant once hung. He remembered her words about the charm in Missouri—*It's a family heirloom. Our pa gave it to us a few days before he died*—and he suddenly found himself battling fresh tears. Duck's pony, Irving, and the clothes on her back were the only things she now carried from her old life in Sainte Genevieve. Doyle had stolen the last reminder of her family, all for the sake of some futile attempt to try to make *his* family whole again.

Duck glanced at him with a frown. "You're crying."

"Yeah." Keech wiped his eyes angrily. "But things will get better. They have to."

"I hope so," she said.

Quinn returned a few moments later, his face looking sweaty and frantic. "Y'all better come take a look. I think Cut found some trouble."

They sprinted to the woods, Quinn leading the way. They ran for a good spell through heavy thicket till Quinn stopped and pointed to a tall hickory tree. "Right there."

Keech approached the tree slowly, keeping his eyes peeled to the ground. A stubby log sat on its side at the base of the hickory—the place where Cutter had apparently sat to rest. Dark red stains blotted the snow around it.

"Blood," Duck said.

"Not too fresh, though. A few hours," Quinn added.

"He'd been whittling on a plank of wood he found," Keech pointed out. "Someone sneaked up and attacked him. There."

A chaotic puddle of mud had been churned up beside the tree. Fresh snow had tumbled onto the forest hours ago, but Keech could still see the indentations of boot tracks leading up to the hickory. A jumble of footprints then stepped away to a neighboring tree, where Cutter had apparently tied off Chantico. From there, the mare's hooves replaced boots and trotted off through the wilderness.

"Cutter's been taken?" Quinn asked.

Duck shook her head. "Not a chance he'd get surprised like that."

"I don't think he was surprised at all." Keech pointed to one of the clearer prints. "Look at the size of that boot."

Quinn stooped. "Small. Like a kid."

"It was *Coward*," Keech said, suddenly recalling the small man's fascination with Cutter in Friendly's holding cell. "He sniffed his way to us."

"I thought he was long gone with the Char Stone," Duck said.

"I did, too. But you heard what Coward said back in Wisdom about how they still had 'unfinished business.' I tried to ask Cut about it, but he wouldn't budge. He was scared to death of that fella."

"All this blood." Quinn pointed at the ground. "Looks like Cutter put up a mean fuss."

Keech squinted at the clues. "This doesn't make sense, though. Based on these tracks, it looks like the scuffle started after Coward walked up. That explains the blood and the mud. But here's the strange part." He stepped over to the disturbed snow leading to the place where Chantico had been tied off. "Over here it looks like Cutter and Coward walked *side by side* over to Chantico."

Duck looked confused. "They rode out *together*?"

"If I'm reading the land right, looks that way."

"He likely had a gun to Cutter's head," Quinn said.

"I can't imagine any other reason," Keech replied.

Duck glanced around the forest. "There must be more clues." Her eyes locked on something beyond the hickory. Stepping over, she plucked a small timber of oak from the snow. It was the plank that Cutter had been carving on.

Brushing it off, Duck gave the board a somber look. She displayed it for them. Across the plank, Cutter's knife had scratched out these words:

AMICUS FIDELIS PROTECTIO FORTIS

"'A faithful friend is a sturdy shelter,'" Quinn quoted.

Silence fell over the trio as they looked at one another, letting Cutter's final message permeate the space between them. Finally, Duck propped the plank on the log where Cutter had sat, then muttered, "I shouldn't have called him a liar."

"You didn't do anything wrong," Quinn said.

"He was keeping secrets about my family, but he didn't deserve this. We've got to find him." Her stark blue eyes turned to Keech. "What do you reckon we do?"

Keech didn't know how to respond. He had never wanted to be placed in a position of leadership. The wrong choices could cost them their lives. He dropped his head and closed his eyes, listening to the wind, hoping to hear the voice of Pa Abner in his mind.

To his surprise, the strong voice that called out to him didn't belong to Pa. It was the voice of Nat Embry, speaking the words he had given Keech and Duck just before his death in Wisdom.

Keep each other safe and never stop fighting.

A strange kind of warmth filled Keech to his bones, and he understood at once what they needed to do. He stepped closer to his friends, Duck Embry and Quinn Revels, his small but fierce team.

"The Lost Causes protect their own," he said, pointing to the path left by Chantico's departure. "I ain't about to let the Reverend Rose take another of our band away. Let's head back to the ponies. We got work to do."

The young riders hurried back to the camp and mounted up. Seated high on Hector, Keech led the group away from the clearing, glancing behind him at the bending tree that had brought them back from Bonfire Crossing. The coastline and the ocean and the great fire seemed like trinkets he had taken from a wondrous dream. Like Pa Abner's painting of the seashell, they would forever hang on the wall of Keech's mind, echoing tales of the bright day when he had stood with friends and fought evil.

As the trio steered back onto the white prairie, the clouds parted, and the morning sun warmed them enough so they could unbutton their coats.

Duck scanned the rolling skies. "Without the shards, we can't defend ourselves from crows or thralls or fish monsters. We'll be wide open."

"We *do* have a defense," Quinn said. "Back at Bonfire, Keech destroyed that devil bird with his mind." He glanced at Keech. "You can teach us that, right?"

Keech pondered for a second, nervous at the notion of being a teacher. He said, "Only if you teach us how to hide from the crows."

Quinn chuckled. "I ain't sure I've actually done that."

Keech looked at both of his trailmates. "There's a lot we can do. Doyle said we have a true gift for tapping the energies. I don't know why, but we can do things. All of us. If we stick together and learn from one another, we'll be okay."

"But we don't even know where to go next," Duck said.

Keech gazed over the yawning sweep of prairie. A long wagon path stretched off to the west, twining through heavy grassland, and he knew he was seeing the great Santa Fe Trail. "We *do* know where to go." He recalled the words of a brave Enforcer who had fallen in Wisdom. "It looks like Cutter's taken the Santa Fe. We'll follow him toward a place called Hook's Fort."

"The place Milos Horner wanted us to find," Duck noted.

"Right. Once we get there, we'll find the trapper McCarty, just like Horner said. He wanted us to find this person for a reason, so that's what we're gonna do." Keech's heart quickened at his own words. He ran his thumb over the initials etched into the leather of Hector's saddle horn—**MH**—and felt the stirring of electricity in his veins.

He felt focused.

He turned back to Quinn. "We'll track Cutter and Coward. And when we find them, we'll find your aunt Ruth, too. I'd wager their paths are leading to the very same place. We'll save her, Quinn. I swear it."

Sudden tears brightened Quinn Revels' eyes, then tumbled down his cheeks. "The Lost Causes protect their own."

"That we do," said Keech. "We also collect on the debts we're owed. We mete out justice, and the Reverend's in need of a heaping lot of it. We'll find this House of the Rabbit the Osage elders mentioned and make good on that promise."

"And what about Doyle?" Duck asked.

"Oh, we'll be seeing him again," Keech said. "He won't stop till he gets the Char Stone back from Coward, so it's only a matter of time before our paths reconnect. When we find him again, we'll get the shards back, too. Pa Abner told us to unite the five, and that's what we're gonna do."

"You know we can't fight him," Quinn said, wiping his eyes. "He's too powerful."

"Maybe we can't, but we know his weakness, don't we?"

"*Eliza*," said Duck.

Keech smiled. "Pa used to say even the deadliest beast has soft skin near the heart. 'Jab at the heart, put the beast on his knees.'"

The young riders snapped their reins, and the ponies picked up their pace. Soon Quinn began singing his curious *Odyssey* song, and his smooth voice rolled over the white plains of Kansas Territory like a breath of courage and strength:

> *"Tell me, O muse, of that ingenious hero*
> *Who traveled far and wide*
> *After he sacked the famous town of Troy."*

Settling Hector into a comfortable gait, Keech listened to Quinn's song with a feeling of hope and led the Lost Causes toward the open frontier.

EPILOGUE

The two horsemen saw the billowing gray smoke on the dark horizon and tugged their mounts to a halt. Whipping winds pulled tendrils of fresh snow from the Kansas clouds, and frost sprinkled their hats, but the chill didn't bother the travelers. More than the cold, the horsemen felt a dreadful curiosity to know the source of the distant smoke.

"Where are we?" the first rider asked, stretching his long back.

The second rider reached into his saddlebag and withdrew a map of the Territories. He traced his gloved finger from the Kansas River down to the Neosho. "Here."

Based on their current position, the smoke was smoldering near the town of Wisdom, which stood farther south. The faint tracks they had been following suggested fast movement in that direction.

"He's near," the first horseman muttered. He wiped a flew flecks of snow off his mustache.

"We best hurry then."

The two travelers snapped their horses' reins and pushed on through the Kansas chill.

The riders wouldn't stop till they found Keech Blackwood and put an end to his journey.

THE END

A NOTE FROM THE AUTHORS

The book you hold in your hands—as well as its predecessor, *Legends of the Lost Causes*—is more than the solitary endeavor of two authors. Since 2015, we've been fortunate enough to work closely with the *Wah-Zha-Zhi* Cultural Center and Language Department—two organizations that help comprise the Osage Heritage Center in Pawhuska, Oklahoma.

Back when we started planning the Legends series, we knew right away we wanted to tell a magical Old West story that included a diverse cast of characters, a group of resourceful kids who could join forces to fight the Reverend Rose's evil. For us, this meant examining the cultures of 1855 Missouri and Kansas. Our research led us to the *Wah-Zha-Zhi* Cultural Center, where we met the wonderful directors and specialists who would become readers of our story and close reviewers of our cultural content.

All of the Osage language and names seen in our series have been directly provided by the Cultural Center and its partner, the Language Department. Though we consulted some written sources in early drafts, such as Francis La Flesche's *A Dictionary of the Osage Language*, the final approval of all words, phrases, and names came from these language and cultural experts who so graciously agreed to help us.

The same holds true for all Osage customs or practices found within the books. Though the Protectors and Bonfire Crossing are figments of our imaginations, the customs to which we allude—such as the giving of horses as gifts, the mourning ritual for Osage loved ones, familial naming conventions—came from extensive conversations with our cultural partners. We also learned a great deal about the traditional clothing, weapons, and traits of Osage warriors in 1855. In addition, the Center's consultants worked closely with us on the character of Meenah/Strong Heart, not only providing her name for the story but also guiding her dialogue and interactions. Naturally, any mistakes or inaccuracies in these details are the fault of us, and no one else.

In the end, *Legends of the Lost Causes* and its accompanying stories are meant to be enjoyed as magical fantasies full of adventure. But it is also our hope that this series grants young readers a larger awareness of the remarkable cultures of 1850s America, as well as a deeper recognition of the country's darker histories of slavery, cruelty, and violence. When we understand where we came from, we can steer the course of our lives into better harmony with one another.

Please visit osagenation-nsn.gov/ to learn more about the Osage Nation.

ACKNOWLEDGMENTS

Well, now, looky here! Happy to see we've all survived another rowdy adventure. The trails were long and the dangers were thick, but we made it back into the light for now. We couldn't have made it this far, though, without the helpin' hand of several kind neighbors, good folks like:

Our agent, Brooks Sherman, who knows all the best roads to help two cowboys along. Brooks, we'll always be grateful for your confidence in us, just like we're thankful to the excellent team at Henry Holt Books for Young Readers, starting with:

The brilliant Brian Geffen, our five-star, top-notch editor, who sees what we think before we even write it down. And Morgan Rath, our publicist, who steers us daily in the right direction. And we certainly can't forget the great Christian Trimmer, the fella who makes it all go 'round. And to our other remarkable trailmates—Lauren Festa, Morgan Dubin, Liz Dresner, Mark Podesta—we can't thank y'all enough. That goes double for:

Alexandria Neonakis, our cover and interior art illustrator, who never fails to amaze us with her incredible eye and dazzling imagination. Thank ya, Alex, for mixing all the best colors into our world.

We're also mighty grateful to Ibeawuchi Travis Uzoegwu, who provided a thorough reading of the novel and offered his profound insights into Quinn Revels, as well as other characters and plot points. Ibe, you're a dandy person, and our book shines even more because of your wisdom.

The same can be said of all the exceptional folks at the *Wah-Zha-Zhi* Cultural Center and Language Department, who have kindly opened their doors over the years to a couple of writers. Director Addie Hudgins, Cultural Specialist Jennifer Tiger, Language Director Vann Bighorse, Language Specialist Cherise Lookout, Language Teacher Alaina Maker, Mr. Harrison Hudgins, and anyone else at the Osage Heritage Center who assisted on the book's cultural content—we're so thankful for your help, your patience, your kindness, and, most of all, your friendship.

Brad peers around suspiciously. Say, Louis? We forgettin' anybody?

Louis says: I suspect so, pard. I'd like to offer my thanks to Kimberly and the dogs for making my life so swell. I'd also like to thank my ma and pa, and my brothers and sister, for being so daisy all the time. I'd also like to thank my sprightly nephews and nieces, as well as my dandy in-laws—Cheryl, Brent, Jennifer, and Kevin—for being so supportive. And as always, I thank Lewis-Clark State College and my creative writing colleagues. What about you, Brad? Who else you want to thank before this here book closes?

Brad says: I'd like to give a special "much obliged" to my incredible wife and stepdaughter, Alisha and Chloe, who always give their full permission to let my imagination run amok. I'd also like to thank Roger and Pat Mullins for opening Bliss Books & Bindery in Stillwater, Oklahoma, and for making a debut author feel so welcome on the bookshelves. Friends, I'll never forget your hospitality. Oh, and Clint Clausing, for playing all the best cowboy tunes at my book shindigs. Also, a mighty shout-out to the magnificent "Electric Eighteens" debut group of authors and illustrators, who've become great friends and colleagues and who pull me up by my bootstraps when I can't take another step. I'd also like to thank my ma, Babs, and stepdad, Joe, for believing in my magic, and my pa, Jerry, for watching all the best Western movies with me when I was a boy.

We also extend our love and gratitude to the late Cindy Hulsey, general manager of Magic City Books in Tulsa, and co-founder/ executive director of the Tulsa Literary Coalition. Cindy and her business partner, Jeff Martin, hosted the very first *Legends* book launch, and we're mighty grateful for the experience. Friends, we'll never forget your hospitality. We'll do our very best to spread the light that Cindy carried daily.

Last but not least, we tip our hats to YOU, amazing reader. May your saddle be cozy, your pony strong and well-fed, and your trail free of trouble. We'll see ya soon, when Keech and his Lost Causes ride again.

Their next mission? Stop Reverend Rose and his henchmen from retrieving an ancient, powerful object that would help return him to his full, frightening strength. As the vigilante orphans race to the dangerous depths of Skeleton Peak, they'll have to outmaneuver Rose's most faithful—and menacing—ally: an inhuman creature spawned by darkness and shadow.

KEEP READING FOR AN EXCERPT.

PART ONE

ON THE
SANTA FE TRAIL

FEBRUARY 1856

MIGUEL ON THE MOUNTAIN ROUTE

For eighty-five days, Miguel Herrera rode on Chantico's weary back.

He knew the count well; using his special bone-handled knife, he'd been scoring the days into his saddle since embarking from eastern Kansas. His riding companion let him keep the big knife, provided he be a "good boy."

Miguel wore his hat pulled low and his blue bandana high to keep the swirling frost off his cheeks. He traveled in silence, following the small man through the shallow foothills of western Kansas Territory and into the Rocky Mountains. Bitter winds colder than the worst Missouri winter blew down the canyon passes. Miguel felt as if his fingers would turn to icicles despite his thick gloves.

"These storms will keep curious eyes out of the canyons where we're headed," his companion said. With the heavy snow flurries threatening to bury them, the Mountain Route they were climbing portended avalanches and impassable ice walls.

When he was a little kid, Miguel's mother had told him

frightful bedtime stories about Shifters and *fantasmas*, but she had never told him tales about unnatural weather. Miguel knew the cruelty of a hard winter well, but this was something different, something fiendish and calculating. Perhaps he was seeing what his old Spanish Bible had called *los últimos días*, or the last days. *Pray when you see fearful things*, his mother had once said. *Give the Sign of the Cross, Miguel, and your faith will spare you.*

But Miguel felt no such salvation.

Peering up at the white peaks rising high on each side, Miguel marveled at the size of the Rockies. Having once roamed across the southern rise of the Appalachians in Alabama with his *amigo*, Frank Bishop, he thought he knew mountains, but these peaks towered with such majesty that they seemed to scrape the sky itself.

As their horses lumbered up the snow-choked path, Miguel's callous chaperone pointed. "Let's stop for the night in that clearing."

Reining Chantico to a halt, Miguel dismounted.

The small man hopped off his own pony, a knock-kneed gelding he had rustled from a lonely farmer in December. "Fetch us some supper. We still have a few days before we reach the Peak, and our beans and bacon are mostly gone."

Miguel moved off into the woods to search for small game. He scanned the drift for prints, watching for signs of a passing rabbit. He kept his long blade in hand. In Missouri, Bishop had said it was a magical blade and would someday kill "the Eye."

Not long after, the one-eyed Bad Whiskey Nelson, *El Ojo*, had killed Bishop in an Arkansas prison. Miguel thought he'd discovered the knife's intended target, but when he thrust the knife into

El Ojo's chest at Bone Ridge Cemetery, the blade did nothing. Only the silver charms and the Reverend Rose's devil birds were able to stop the fiend once and for all.

But now Miguel had *new* plans for the knife. Once he found his opportunity, he would rid the world of his vicious traveling partner.

After fetching a jackrabbit for grub, Miguel fed and watered the two ponies. He muttered kind words to his palomino, asking forgiveness for riding her so hard.

"Enough messing around with those nags. Fetch my saddlebag." After brushing away snow to clear a spot, the small man leaned against a fallen cottonwood tree. He peeled off his ragged hat, revealing a mangy tonsure of gray hair. "Then build up a fire. My feet are cold."

The stolen gelding carried a few saddlebags, but Miguel knew his captor desired a special bundle tucked inside a small leather pouch. Miguel unhooked the bag and carried it over. "Here," he muttered, setting the bag in the fellow's hands.

The man pulled the bag close. "Here . . . what?"

Miguel clenched his teeth. "Here, *sir*."

"That's better. Now, since you and I have become old pals, go ahead and speak my name." The man's satisfied grin melted into a malignant frown. "I insist."

Miguel had no desire to speak his captor's name. He preferred to think of his infernal companion as *el diablito*, small in stature but possessed by evil. He had first met the desperado in Arkansas, locked inside a *cárcel* called Barrenpoint, the accursed prison where *El Ojo* had killed Frank Bishop. Even then the small man had forced terrible orders on Miguel. Yet he knew better than to resist a direct command. "*Coward*," Miguel said. "Your name's Coward."

"Good boy, *Cutter*. Now get that fire built." Coward turned his attention to the bag on his lap, shooing Miguel with a dismissive wave.

Snow-frosted firs crowded the surrounding hills, and powdery drift blanketed the ground. Miguel stomped through brittle, knee-high brush, hunting for wood dry enough to serve as tinder. He emptied the firewood into a pile, placed a few stones in a circle inside the clearing, and set about laying their campfire.

As he worked, Miguel scratched at the charred mark on his forehead—the devilish product of Coward's ambush in November, not long after the Lost Causes had returned from Bonfire Crossing. Miguel had wandered into the woods to be alone and failed to notice Coward lurking in the brush. When the man suddenly emerged, Miguel drew his blade. He landed one lucky jab before the desperado knocked him out with his mystical cough, a strange but potent power the man possessed.

Miguel awoke to discover that his flesh had been branded with the Devil's mark, a gruesome scar maiming his forehead. The wound hadn't taken but a few days to heal, but now he couldn't help scratching at the foul thing.

While he stoked the welcome fire, Miguel noticed Coward removing the tied canvas bundle from inside his saddlebag. The man loosed a twine knot on the bundle and opened the wrap, revealing a small silver box. Strange etchings lined every inch of the metal—inscriptions Miguel had seen before on a pair of amulet shards worn by his two friends. One of those shards, the one Keech Blackwood had carried, jutted from the pocket of Coward's frock coat even now. But Coward cared little for the shard; what he desired lay inside the chest.

Resting the silver box on his knees, Coward ran his fingers across the grooves, then lifted the box lid.

From where he stood on the opposite side of the campfire, Miguel felt a whisper of sour air caress his face. Twilight shadows shifted around them, despite the glow of the fire.

The small black rock resting inside the chest seemed to hum, not a sound that could be heard with the ears, but a vibration that pinched the nerves. Eldritch fumes drifted up from the box's corners. Thin tendrils of raven smoke waved in the breeze but never seemed to dissipate. The stone was no larger than a fist, its surface jagged like a rock found in a field. Yet the darkness painting it appeared to *move*, as though thousands of tiny, swarming spiders covered it.

Coward breathed in, sniffing the object in the box. He wielded another curious sort of magic, this *diablito*: His bizarrely powerful nostrils could track a scent from miles away or sniff out the deepest secrets of a person's mind. Yet every night when Coward snorted in the fumes of the ancient relic, he couldn't seem to inhale enough to satisfy his cravings.

Miguel backed away from the Char Stone. The artifact was cursed. And somehow alive. He felt it calling to him. Not with a voice he heard, but with a whittling gnaw deep in his gut. At night, his dreams were haunted by images of writhing things creeping under his skin. More than once, he'd woken from a fretful sleep, a scream dying on his lips. If Miguel had his druthers, he would destroy the Stone and forget it even existed.

But Coward obsessed over it. He saw the Stone as a talisman

he could wield. "It's beautiful," he said. "Pure power. The Prime in material form." He hovered his hand a few inches above its black surface, as if tempted to graze the Stone with the tip of his finger, but he resisted—as he did every night.

The silver box snapped shut.

Miguel said nothing. Long ago he'd learned when Coward spoke about the Char Stone, he was not seeking conversation. He was basking in the promise of powers to come.

Hunkering down in his thick fur and blanket, Miguel pulled his hat over his brow. Though the Devil's mark forbade any hope of escape, he often retreated to secret hollows in his mind where the power of the dark brand couldn't touch him. Where he could envision his best friend, John Wesley, who reminded him so much of Bishop. John was Edgar Doyle's son, a clumsy kid but a fierce fighter. Miguel had lost him to the Chamelia, the creature that had stalked the boy at the command of Big Ben Loving. John Wesley had been scratched, infected, turned into a monster. The last time Miguel saw his friend, John had dashed off into the Kansas woods to join the Chamelia and adapt to life as a Shifter. Miguel's final words to the boy had been, *Remember, no matter where you go, you're one of us. You're a* Lost Cause.

Miguel reached into his coat and touched the brim of John Wesley's wrinkled and warped *sombrero*, a bullet-torn hat made of yellow straw. He had carried the hat since the Chamelia's first attack at Mercy Mission, and though John was gone, Miguel couldn't bring himself to throw it away. Sometimes when Coward slept, Miguel would stroke the hat's ragged brim. No sooner would his fingers graze the straw than he would hear John's whisper in his head, undeniably sharp and clear: *Don't fret, Cutter; I'm exactly where I need to be. Someday, I'll find ya again. Keep your eyes and ears open.*

Miguel always felt better, gripping the hat and hearing John Wesley's voice. But he doubted he would ever see John again, or any of the other Lost Causes. Coward owned his soul now. They were tethered by the Devil's mark that Cutter despised but couldn't escape.

"Soon we'll reach Ignatio," Coward said, his voice yanking Miguel from his buried thoughts. "We'll find the Key and take the Fang back from Red Jeffreys. Once we have the relics, you and I will take them on a final journey."

"To the Palace of the Thunders," Miguel said.

"Yes. And once there, we'll free the Master."

A shiver coursed down Miguel's spine. "What'll happen when we reach him, Coward?"

The small man smiled. "The Reverend will emerge in his full glory, and this world will tremble at the sight."

3 September 1833

The skeleton holds the key.

——R.J.

CHAPTER 1
THE SCARECROW

Keech Blackwood lay flat in the deep snow, watching the hunched figure down in the pasture wobble in the blizzard wind. His trailmates, Duck Embry and Quinn Revels, waited to his left and right, unmoving, buttoned up to the cold. Over the shriek of the winter squall, Quinn steadily sang his peculiar *Odyssey* tune—the melody his aunt Ruth had taught him long ago while fleeing Tennessee. The song worked as an incantation that concealed the group, placing them inside a mystical bubble of sorts that obscured all signs of the young riders, even their horses' hoofprints. It was a trick Quinn had picked up from the man who'd betrayed them, a fellow who went by two names: Edgar Doyle and Red Jeffreys.

"The wind's gonna knock it over," said Duck, her words muffled behind her scarf.

"No, it'll hold." The February freeze pummeled the otter-fur coverings over Keech's ears, so he couldn't hear much except for the wheeze of the Kansas plain. But Quinn's hum still drifted through the blurry noise, filling Keech's bones with comfort.

"I hope you're right," Duck muttered. "I don't want to go down there again."

"It'll hold. Trust me."

"What if they don't show?"

"They're getting antsy." Keech glanced up at the sky. "They'll show."

The trio's position atop the bluff offered the best view of the pasture and the shuddering scarecrow. But what Keech had in mind was not to *scare* crows. Far from it. The makeshift figure perched in the field was intended to lure them out of the sky.

"Something feels wrong," Duck said.

The girl's concerns held plenty of merit, but since losing her brother, Nat, to the explosion in Wisdom, when Big Ben Loving had come to wreak havoc, she'd been second-guessing her own grit. Sometimes loss did that to a person. Keech had struggled with his own doubts after losing his entire family, including his beloved pony, Felix. He wanted to find the right words to reassure her, but all he managed was a cursory nod.

"We're wasting our time up here," she continued. "If this plan don't work, we may never get to save Cutter."

"Or Auntie Ruth," interjected Quinn, interrupting his *Odyssey* tune long enough to speak. Quinn's aunt had been hauled out of Wisdom in November, after the Reverend Rose's devilish brood, the Big Snake, had seized control of the town. All they knew about Ruth's predicament was that she'd been taken somewhere west in a wagon train, along with any surviving townsfolk.

And based on the original trail Keech had found, Cutter and his captor, Coward, were headed in the same direction, likely planning to marshal with Rose's crew.

"Everything's gonna work." Keech gestured to the clouds. "The crows will come."

They had noticed the Reverend's dark birds on their trail the morning of Christmas Eve, the same day Keech turned fourteen. Duck had spotted a large flock circling the prairie north of the Moonlight River, creatures that were searching, on the hunt. Instead of celebrating Keech's birthday, the Lost Causes spent the day hidden away in a snow trench, watching the turbulent skies.

Though Quinn had continued to conceal their movements with his magical song ever since, it seemed it would be only a matter of time before they made a mistake. If Rose caught a glimpse of their horses or a telltale boot track in the snow, he would send his gruesome birds to tear them limb from limb.

Thanks to Edgar Doyle's betrayal after Bonfire Crossing, they had no silver amulet shards to defeat monsters, or the mystical Fang of Barachiel to heal wounds. All they were carrying on their long ride to Hook's Fort, the place they were headed in search of a trapper named McCarty, were bucketfuls of dumb luck.

Sometimes that luck paid off when they crossed friendly paths on the trail. One day, for example, they met a group of Pawnee travelers headed south, pulling flat carts full of pelts behind their horses. The party had spotted the Lost Causes hunkered down in the drifts while Quinn was resting his throat. The horsemen had sent over a pair of scouts to make sure the trio was okay, and the encounter resulted in a pleasant meal of pemmican and dried squash.

But Keech knew such luck couldn't last forever. As Pa Abner

used to tell him and Sam, *You can ride a streak of fortune for days, maybe months, but it will eventually peter out.*

The afternoon's merciless gale picked up, scattering hard snow over the plain and battering the beleaguered scarecrow. "I'm telling you, the wind's gonna blow it over," Duck said.

"It won't. I drove that pole down myself," Keech said, a speck of doubt lodged in his throat.

The scruffy scarecrow wore a brown buffalo pelt hung over a T-shaped post, and the ragged bowler hat on top was almost identical to Keech's. They had discovered the robe and hat, along with a few other useful items, inside a broken-down wagon some unfortunate traveler had abandoned on the trail. The idea of taking things that didn't belong to them hadn't sat well at first, but after watching the deserted wagon a few hours and seeing no one return, the young riders decided to gather up the provisions and chalk up the occasion to more good luck.

As the scarecrow took a beating from the hateful flurry, Keech prayed the Reverend's birds would arrive. He studied the landscape and felt energy gathering in his mind, a buzz tingling his fingertips. He was ready. The plan would work.

"My lips are about to fall off," said Quinn, pausing his incantation again. "Let's find a ditch somewhere and hole up. The animals are tired." The horses waited below the bluff—Duck's pony, Irving; John Wesley's old nag, Lightnin'; and Hector, the cremello stallion. Keech's steed had once belonged to Milos Horner, the Enforcer who died in Wisdom. If Quinn stopped humming for more than a minute, the horses would lose their enchanted shroud and reappear, along with their prints, as if emerging from a dense fog.